PRIVATEER

ALEXIS CAREW #5

J A SUTHERLAND

PRIVATEER
Alexis Carew #5

by J.A. Sutherland

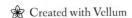 Created with Vellum

Even with no war on, there are always battles to fight.

A cease-fire in the war with Hanover leaves Lieutenant Alexis Carew on half-pay, in-atmosphere, and with her ship laid up in ordinary until called upon once more for the "needs of the Service." She was, at least, lucky enough to be in her home star system when **HMS Nightingale** *paid off, unlike much of her former crew.*

She's left to help manage her family lands, though still with no certainty she'll be allowed to inherit them. It would be a tranquil, peaceful life, if not for the influx of asteroid miners seeking their fortunes, the uncertainties of her inheritance, and the nagging certainty that her current life is not what she really wants.

She'd give anything to command a ship again.

For "Famine"

And those, like him, who've seen the elephant and guard the gate.

"Thank you" is not enough, but it is all we have.

ONE

The building's hatch ...

Door, Alexis reminded herself, as they were planetside. There were so very many things that she'd gotten used to in the four years aboard ship that she'd now have to unlearn.

The building's door was closed, but a discrete sign on the wall beside it and a time-honored red light above the plaque made its purpose clear to the clientele and declared it open for business.

Alexis eyed the half dozen men she had with her. Nabb — her coxswain, if she'd still commanded a ship rather than being in-atmosphere at half-pay — Ruse and Sinkey, also from her former boat crew, as well as Sills and Paskell, former *Nightingales* the lot.

"This the place, sir?" Nabb asked.

He was younger than Alexis, just seventeen to her nineteen, but towered over her at nearly two meters — not that he needed such height to tower over her own bare meter and a half. The others in her group towered also, yet all looked to her for their next move.

It felt odd to be going into action with her lads dressed all in homespun denim and linen, such as she was, instead of ship's jump-suits and her Naval uniform, but she supposed she'd have to get used to that as well. With no war on, neither she nor her ship were needed, and it was only at the request of Dalthus' Crown agent and chandler that her lads were seeing this bit of action.

"It's the address Doakes sent us," she said, sliding her tablet and its directions back into a pocket.

The streets of Dalthus IV's main port town, Port Arthur, were dark and silent in either the early morning or very late night, depending on which direction one arrived at it. Most of the nightlife had ended hours before, with carousing miners and spacers finding a bunk for what remained of the night.

Some few establishments remained open, such as the one they stood before, for the most ardent drinkers or seekers of entertainment.

Or those looking to cause trouble, Alexis thought with a grimace.

"All right, lads," she said, "you know the way of it." She caught each of their eyes in turn and they nodded their readiness. Alexis squared her shoulders and grasped the door's handle. "Let's be about it then."

The door swung open easily. It must have had quite good sound-proofing, as they'd heard none of the raucous babble and shouts from outside. One of Dalthus' founding principles was that one could do as one willed so long as it didn't affect one's neighbors, and that precept followed into the towns as well.

Inside, the scene seemed chaotic at first, but quickly resolved to Alexis' eyes. Music was playing from more than one source, loud and conflicting, though no one seemed to be listening closely enough to care. Men and women sat or stood about the room in various states of undress, and engagement in activities Alexis would truly have rather not seen.

From somewhere in the mass of two or three dozen people, there was a shout, the meaty slap of a hand meeting flesh, and a feminine cry, followed by laughter.

Ruse and Sinkey started forward, hands going to their belt, but Nabb gestured them back. There was a formality to all this that had to play out and they'd been through it before.

A woman made her way through the crowd, shrugging off grasping hands.

"Mistress Auburn?" Alexis asked as the woman came close enough to hear.

"I am, and thank you for coming, Miss Carew." She nodded at the crowd. "It's that same group as what took to the Orchid a month ago. Tab's run up and their credit's dry — leave aside they treat the girls something awful. Will you help?"

"It's why we're here, Mistress Auburn," Alexis said, though she could wish it otherwise.

Lord knows I'd rather be aboard ship, sailing the Dark and running out the guns against some enemy ... that, surely, rather than this.

She grimaced. Distasteful as it was, there was still no doubt that it was needful — and some might argue Mistress Auburn's current troubles were, in part, Alexis' fault to begin with. Or, at least, the Navy's — and as senior officer in-system, even on half-pay, she did feel responsible.

"Sound it, Nabb."

Nabb nodded and raised his tablet. In a moment, a shrieking, ear-splitting whistle sounded through the room, cutting off all conversation as the inhabitants turned toward the doorway. Auburn touched her own tablet at the same time, cutting off all of the room's speakers and ending the music. When the whistle ended, there was dead silence.

"Mistress Auburn," Alexis asked loudly, "do you wish our assistance in clearing your property of those who do not reside here?"

Another of Dalthus' guiding principles was that a person's property was inviolate. Alexis wanted it clear that she was acting on the property owner's request, to avoid any claims against her and her men for what was about to happen.

"I do, miss, and thank you again."

Alexis nodded.

"All right, then," she called out. "You lot've heard her! If you don't live here, clear out!"

"Bugger off, girl! We're not under your lash no more!"

Alexis sighed. That voice had come from the rear of the crowd where she couldn't see, but she should have known it would be him. *Bryant Be-damned Iveson*, she thought. And with him would be Spracklen — a pair of miners she'd pressed aboard *Nightingale* from this very port, and dropped back here when the ship paid off in-place after the cessation of hostilities against Hanover.

And with them, she saw as the two made their way through the crowd, were Chivington and Monks, two hard cases from *Nightingale* who'd stayed on to try their own hands at mining the gallenium deposits in the system's belt.

"No bosun with you no more," Chivington said, twisting his neck from side to side so that the *cracks* sounded clearly through the room. "Just you and yer lackeys, an' yer outnumbered."

Around him the other men were standing, dumping girls from their laps and shoving them away. Alexis recognized two of the others from *Nightingale*, but the rest were miners originally. All were big, rough men, ready to fight.

Monks smiled.

"Is it trouble you want, girl?"

Alexis spared a thought for how she'd spent the last four months since *Nightingale* had paid off. Familiarizing herself again with the workings of her family lands — mines, lumberyards, crops in the fields. All good and necessary work, all to the benefit of her family and the workers who looked to them for their livelihood, all quite worthwhile.

But none of it a ship.

Four months without sailing the Dark between systems, without exercising the guns and hearing her breath rasp in the hot, close environment of a vacsuit helmet as she helped her guncrews carry shot and lay their guns, without the sheer rush of being alive she felt when the boarding tube extended and it was time to cross to an enemy ship, pitting her arm against the enemy and never knowing if the next blow might pierce her suit and end her.

She met Monks' eyes and bared her teeth. A wiser man than Monks would have recognized that she wasn't smiling. Alexis drew a stunstick from her belt.

"Oh, yes."

ALEXIS LEAPT FORWARD. She felt Nabb and the others move with her, but she was at the fore.

Monks' eyes widened at first, then he grasped a bottle from a nearby table and hefted it.

The other miners in the room reacted as well, rushing to meet Alexis and her men. The room was soon filled with sound again, this time with crashes and grunts of battle.

True, they were outnumbered, but Alexis and her lads fought as a unit — perhaps not so much as the army or even marines, but, as in a boarding, every man had an eye on those beside him, and was ready to lend a hand if a mate found himself in trouble.

The miners fought alone, each one thinking only of himself, and that quickly doomed them, as the rabble they were.

That and the ladies they'd forgotten about. Ladies who, while of negotiable virtue, were less forgiving when only one side of the negotiations made good. In addition, the house's own security appeared — just two men, enough to keep order on an ordinary night, but not enough to control a dozen miners intent on causing trouble.

Alexis dodged a swing of Monks' bottle and swung her stunstick in return. Monks blocked that blow, then winced and staggered as a chair broke across his back. Alexis took the opportunity to jab the stunstick into his midsection and by the time she'd assured herself that he was truly down, the scuffle was almost complete.

Nabb drew back his arm to hurl his stunstick at one last miner who'd turned to menace a girl who'd broken a bottle over his head.

Before he could let loose, though, a second girl leapt onto the miner's back, clawing at his eyes, and the first landed a solid kick into his fork.

Alexis winced as the miner collapsed, groaning. He'd likely have preferred the stunstick, whose effects would wear off in less than an hour, to what he'd just received.

The house's owner caught Alexis' eye and nodded thanks.

"I'm sorry for the damage, Mistress Auburn," Alexis said, "I trust you'll forward a bill to Mister Doakes so it can be added to their port fees?"

"I will, but two chairs and a few bottles is cheap carriage to be done with them."

Her lads had things well in hand, slapping restraints on the stunned and otherwise incapacitated miners. Alexis eyed Monks with distaste.

"*Afters!*"

Alexis' head came up at the shout, catching sight of a figure hunched in the room's corner, two of the house's girls nearly blocking her view of him.

"That one's no trouble, usually," Auburn said. "Though he does get a bit loud if the girls taunt him too much." She shrugged. "Never seen a man afraid of drink before."

"Indeed," Alexis said.

Scarborough, for that was who she knew the hunched figure to be, curled into a ball, whimpering. The two girls left off their fun and placed the bottles they'd been tormenting him with on the bar. He'd been the worst of this lot at one time, until *Nightingale's* crew came together and locked him in a vat late one night's watch. A vat filled all but centimeters full of something Alexis rather preferred not to think about.

"He had a bit of a rough time aboard his last ship," Alexis said. "It left him quite unlike himself."

"Well, he, at least, the girls can keep in hand." Auburn ground a long, sharp heel into Monks' thigh, making the unconscious man twitch. "These others ..."

"Why let them in?" Alexis asked. "If you know what the outcome will be?"

Auburn scowled. "Alone they're not so bad — rough, but I've girls for that trade when the price is right. It's when men like this band together that things get out of hand — and out of pocket, when they've run their coin dry as well."

All of the restraints were tightly on and checked.

"Doakes will see their bill set against their mining ships and any cargo," Alexis said. The chandler and Crown agent had the authority to ground those ships or enter liens against future loads of ore the men brought in from the belt, at least — though he didn't have the authority or men to keep order in the town itself.

"Thank you again, Miss Alexis."

"Come along, then, lads," she called. "Back to the boat and home."

"But —"

Nabb broke off, flushing as Alexis glanced from him to the girl pressed against him in far more tangible thanks than Mistress Auburn's. In fact, all of her lads seemed to be fielding similar expressions of gratitude. She wouldn't begrudge them that bit of thanks, truly — at least not those who had no one back on her family homestead who might be looking for them — but they'd have to make their own way back to Port Arthur to collect.

"Shall I tell your mum you'll be delayed, Nabb?" she called over her shoulder as she headed for the door. "And Miss Eliza down to the village, Sinkey?"

Before she could recite a third name, there was the sound of hasty goodbyes, a promise or two to return that she'd pretend not to hear, and her little troop was with her on the street.

TWO

She met Doakes on the way back to the landing field and their boat — well, *Nightingale's* boat and not properly hers any more than the ship itself was after being laid up in-ordinary at the end of the war.

But the warrants still living aboard, bosun Ousley now the senior, hadn't objected to her request of its use. She was, after all, the senior Naval officer in Dalthus System, much as she was on half-pay and in-ordinary herself.

After a moment's grousing that he had no proper constabulary to keep order, and his thanks to her and her men for taking on that task when asked, Doakes set about collecting the unconscious miscreants and Alexis was able to make her way to the landing field.

There were more than a dozen ships' boats on the field — some from merchantmen, but most from the gallenium miners still pouring into the system. One or two would belong to those she'd just left behind in Doakes' custody. A part of her wondered, looking across the crowded field, if Dalthus as a whole hadn't been better off before the presence of gallenium in the Belt had been widely known — even when it was just a few families mining it in secret.

Alexis sighed as the boat's hatch sealed and she settled into her seat.

The trip from Port Arthur to the Carew holding took less than an hour all-told. It was still a dark, early morning when they landed and unloaded, the men making their way back to the barracks or down to the village, while Alexis made for the farmhouse itself.

The light in the kitchen and smell of tea as she approached the house told her that her trip had not gone unnoticed.

She sighed, braced herself, and opened the door, forcing a cheery smile on her face. Julia, their housekeeper, was at the kitchen counter beginning the breakfast preparations. Her grandfather sat at the table; tablet in hand, catching up, she supposed, on the colony news or the holding's accounts, one.

"Good morning," she said as they looked up at her entrance.

Her grandfather raised an eyebrow, a bit of a curl to his lips.

"An early one, as well," Denholm said.

Alexis flushed.

"I'm sorry if I woke you, but the call from Doakes came quite late."

"Slept through your departure and were awake for the arrival," Denholm said.

"The chickens didn't," Julia added, "though that's no fault of yours, Miss Alexis." She turned a stern look on Denholm. "I told the man that landing field was too close to the house."

"Always with the chickens," Denholm muttered. "No landing field, and it's upsetting the chickens; new field, and it's upsetting the chickens. One would think the whole purpose of these holdings was to coddle the bloody chickens."

Julia set a pot on the stove and held up three eggs. "It'll be scrambled eggs for the four of us this morning, and stretched ... the laying was off for some reason."

Denholm gave Alexis a pained look, making her hide her smile. She'd grown up around the two and knew their sniping hid a deep affection — not for the first time, she wondered at just how deep that affection might be and why it hadn't led to more. Her grandfather had been alone since her grandmother died giving birth to her father, and Julia had been housekeeper here since only a few months after that. The two clearly cared for each other deeply, yet they'd never, so far as she knew, acted on it.

"I'll have a bit extra of the bacon to make up for it," Denholm said, turning back to his tablet, "if the larder's so short on eggs after only one night."

Julia snorted in response. She added butter to the pot, then a large scoop of cut oats. The nutty smell of toasting oatmeal quickly filled the room.

"You'll have two rashers," she said, "*after* your oats, and not a bite more."

"Bloody gruel," Denholm muttered.

"And shall I call Doctor Piercefield to remind you of your last results?"

Denholm flushed and cleared his throat as Julia added water to the toasted oats and put a lid on the pot.

Alexis took the pause as an opportunity to sit, pulling her own tablet from a pocket to catch up on the news. No sooner had she turned it on, than a cup of tea appeared before her.

"Thank you, Julia."

"I hope there wasn't too much trouble last night?"

"Miners and former *Nightingales* tearing up a ... well, the sort of place miners and spacers tend to congregate."

A soft sound from the doorway to the rest of the house made her look up. Marie, the French girl from the Berry March she'd brought home with her after the abortive attempt to free those worlds from Hanover had gone so very wrong, slipped in and sat. They — Alexis, Marie, and Marie's young son — were still sharing Alexis' room — something that had not been so very bad when Alexis commanded *Nightingale* and was only home for visits, but turned out to be quite crowded when done for months on end.

Especially with Ferrau growing day by day.

Marie seemed to have settled in quite nicely with the household, assisting Julia with work around the house and farmyard — though never in the kitchen, Alexis noted, which seemed to be Julia's sole domain.

"*Bonjour, merci,*" Marie said as a cup of tea was set before her. Though her English was quite good and improving daily, the courtesies seemed so ingrained that they came out in her native French. "You rush out in the night, Alexis. Is all well?"

"Yes, I'm sorry if I woke you or Ferrau." Alexis sipped her tea. "There was trouble in Port Arthur and Doakes called for us."

"Again? These troubles grow, it seems."

"And it's you Doakes calls," Denholm added. "I still don't see the why of that, what with your ship decommissioned and you on half-pay. Even if you were in command still, you've no real authority in the port — not as we've not asked the Crown for more of a presence, in any case."

Alexis grimaced. She hated to be at odds with her grandfather, but he, and most of the original settlers of Dalthus, didn't seem to realize just how much things had changed. With the discovery of large deposits of gallenium in the asteroid belt, the rare metal which made travel between stars through *darkspace* possible at all, there'd been a huge influx of miners and others. The changes were coming so rapidly that the first settlers, those who owned the system and made its laws, appeared out of touch with the new realities facing the ports.

"Mister Doakes is the closest thing to a Crown authority Port Arthur has, though he's only the Crown agent, and he has no proper constabulary to call upon." She added a bit more sugar to her tea. "It's a different world now, grandfather. The miners aren't properly Dalthus citizens — they've not signed the Charter and agreed to its terms. The Charter itself doesn't set who has authority to do more with off-worlders — short of the worst of crimes, that is — other than send them on their way. That might have worked when our only visitors were merchant crews who'd leave in a short time anyway, but that's somewhat ineffective with the miners. They simply go to the belt for a bit, then come back."

"There's a measure on the agenda for the Conclave which will let Doakes establish his constabulary," Denholm said.

"If it passes," Alexis reminded him.

"Yes, if. You've convinced me, and no few others, that Port Arthur, and the other freetowns, have need of it. Still, I don't understand why you've taken the task on in the meantime."

"Part of the troubles are the hard cases from *Nightingale's* crew, grandfather. They're my responsibility." Alexis fought the urge to sigh. This was a disagreement between the two of them that felt old, though it had only been a few months.

When the latest war with Hanover ended — well, cease-fire, but it seemed as though the authorities were treating it as a proper ending — *Nightingale's* crew was left at odd ends. Many took places aboard merchantmen — either permanently or simply working their way back toward whatever system they'd come from when they joined the Navy. Others stayed on Dalthus, signing on to the Carew farmstead for a time, or trying their hands at the lucrative mining.

Her grandfather might not understand it, but Alexis felt she owed them all a debt, even the troublemakers, for having been their commander. Perhaps not the same debt to all, but a debt none the less, and a responsibility for any trouble those troublemakers caused, as, if she'd managed to reach them when she held command they might not be causing it. No matter that her former bosun, Ousley, had assured her more than once that Monks and his ilk were trouble to the bone, she still thought there might have been something more she could have done.

"After the ship's decommissioned these four months past?"

"*Nightingale's* not decommissioned, she's in ordinary. Merely idle and waiting to be called to service again. As am I."

"Half-pay and wait upon their pleasure?" Julia scoffed. "Seems poor payment, indeed, for all you've done."

"I'm quite a junior lieutenant and they've kept only the most senior ships and captains employed. With the war over, there are frigates such as *Ulysses* available and far better able to patrol this sector than *Nightingale* alone was."

Julia sniffed. "Captains like Gammill. Senior, maybe, but he rubs all folk the wrong way."

Alexis had to agree with that. Captain Gammill of *HMS Ulysses*, *Nightingale's* replacement, had visited Dalthus only twice since the war ended, but both times he'd managed to irritate nearly everyone he encountered. Neither had he approved of Alexis' use of *Nightingale's* boat, but she'd managed to avoid a direct order she not make use of it any longer. Whether Gammill *thought* she'd agreed to such might be quite a different matter, but she was entirely comfortable he hadn't *ordered* her not to.

"Well," Denholm said, "the Conclave's next week and we'll have no worries about half-pay or being recalled after. One good thing's come of your rushing off to save Doakes and Port Arthur so often, and it's that fewer are able to argue you're not capable. I have every confidence the vote will go our way and you'll be able to concentrate on learning to run our lands, rather than a ship."

Alexis merely nodded, grateful for the bowls of oatmeal Julia slipped onto the table, for it meant she had an excuse to look down and not meet her grandfather's eye.

Dalthus' inheritance laws were the whole reason she'd joined the Navy in the first place. They'd been changed shortly after the colony's founding from the original first-born inheriting the colony company shares, and corresponding lands, to the first-born *son*. She supposed it had made sense at the time, to colonists shocked and no little frightened by the implications of a new colony world's lack of medical care and the corresponding risk of death in childbirth. It must have seemed, to many, like they'd been thrust back into the dark ages when humanity was bound to a single planet.

In a sense it was, and they'd responded accordingly by bringing back laws, no matter their distaste for laws in general, which had shaped those earlier societies.

Her grandfather, though, had no other heirs, and after more than one disastrous attempt to find a suitor for her — a husband who'd hold the lands instead of her — he'd determined to lobby for a change in those laws, if he could. And she'd taken to the Navy — partly out of a desire to distance herself and the reputation she'd gained for being ... difficult, and partly out of determination to find something useful and productive to spend her life on. She had no taste for the parties and frivolous activities of the female half of Dalthus' grander shareholders.

Now, though, she found herself uncertain. The Navy might have been an impulsive leap for her, but she *had* found a place there. The men she'd commanded and those who'd led her in turn seemed to have filled a void she hadn't really known existed before she left home.

Not all of them, of course. The Navy had its share of scoundrels and dastards as well, but to stand with men like her first captain, Captain Grantham, or others she'd served with, to lead those who'd give their all, even their very lives, for their mates, for the defenseless ... for her, because she asked it of them — well, the thought of giving that up emptied that void and left her hollow.

She couldn't tell her grandfather that, though — not let him know that what he'd fought so hard for, for her to inherit their lands and run them after him, might not be the reward he thought it was.

THREE

Alexis had never attended Dalthus' Conclave before. The gathering consisted of the heads and heirs of the families who'd originally settled the system. Nearly three thousand of them, though only those who held the actual company shares would be voting. It was held in Port Arthur every five years and was where the colony's laws, such as they were, were made.

The original settlers had felt that with thousands of years of human history to draw on, all the good and necessary laws were likely there for the taking at the start and there was little need for a permanent government or legislature.

For the most part Alexis agreed with them, but the devil was in the details, and circumstances did have an annoying tendency to change.

The Conclave was held in Port Arthur's auditorium, a far cry from her grandfather's stories of first settling Dalthus, when the settlers had met under a huge tent erected for just that purpose.

The auditorium was a grand thing, the largest building in the port town, and a bit ostentatious, to Alexis' view. Her grandfather agreed with that, mentioning that the columns were a bit much and he'd argued against them, but it did serve the colony for plays and musical shows between Conclaves — and many of the larger share-holding families did feel a need for ostentation. The Carew family home, with its clapboard construction and small size, was far from the huge, brick mansions many called home. In their defense, she supposed, their families were quite a bit larger than the Carews, as well.

"Bare grass and whatever we chose to bring for sitting, that first year," Denholm said as they settled into their seats.

Around them was all the bustle of a large, filling space before an event. Old friends who might not have met in person for some time calling to each other, small groups forming to discuss the agenda and express their thoughts on some point or the other, and through it all vendors from Port Arthur's citizenry taking advantage of the crowd to hawk their food and drink.

"It's much changed even since when I first left on *Merlin*," Alexis agreed.

"Not all for the better, neither," Denholm said. He handed over coin for a pair of bottles and handed one to Alexis. "Four pence for a bottle of cold tea and lemon? Robbery."

"Prices are up in all the port towns. With so much coin for the gallenium coming in and the miners spending so freely —" She shrugged.

"Wages as well," Denholm agreed.

Someone in the row behind leaned close and whispered loudly in Alexis' ear.

"Of course, the old miser next to you's always been one to pinch a coin."

Denholm's face broke in wide grin as he turned.

"Sewall! Good to see you, man — and it's frugal, mind you."

Alexis smiled as well. The man was older than her grandfather, near eighty, if she remembered correctly, but still strong and wiry. The woman next to him was plump and cheerful — things Elora Mylin had been all Alexis' life.

The Mylins were the Carews' nearest neighbors, holding lands on the other side of a hilly region to the holding's north.

"Frugal's a word for it," Sewall Mylin said. "One." He nodded to Alexis. "Lexi."

"Uncle Sewall, Aunt Elora," she said. The Mylins weren't really related, but visits between the two holdings had been frequent when Alexis was young. More frequent than visits with those who truly were her aunts and uncles, her mother's family the Arundels, one of whom Alexis spotted waving to her from the aisle. "Lauryn Arundel wishes to speak to me, if you'll excuse me?"

"Of course, dear," Elora said. "Will you agree to have dinner with us soon, though?"

Alexis smiled. "I'd love to, if you'll promise to make your yams."

Elora laughed as Denholm grimaced. Alexis would never understand her grandfather's distaste for yams and potatoes — something to do with the colony's first few years, but she dearly loved what Elora could do with the sweet, orange roots — and they were only rarely served at the Carew house due to Denholm's dislike.

Alexis excused herself and made her way to the aisle. A quick hug and peck on the cheek greeted her cousin, who, strictly speaking, wasn't supposed to be in the auditorium.

"I'll clear out once things are closer to starting," Lauryn said by way of explanation, "not being a 'proper' heir and all."

Alexis herself wasn't a proper heir, come to that, and would have been excluded if she hadn't been asked to speak to the inheritance measure.

"Have you given any thought to what I asked?"

Alexis nodded. "I have, and I'm afraid I can't support it."

Lauryn frowned. "Really? After all you've been through yourself, you can't see the right of it?"

"It's not that I disagree in principle, but there are plenty of worlds where everyone's given the franchise. I simply don't think it's the right thing for Dalthus — at least not just yet."

Lauryn pointed to the stage where the Conclave's speakers would make their cases for or against each of the proposed items on the agenda. "So, you'll stand up there and argue to change the inheritance laws, the voting laws, in one way — a way which will benefit yourself — but not so as to benefit others?"

"The proposed change is not so great, and you know it. Merely putting things back to the original Charter." Alexis sighed. They'd had this disagreement more than once. Lauryn and many of the younger set — though none of the heirs, she'd noted — felt it was time to enlarge the franchise beyond the original shareholding families. "Lauryn, I understand the point you and your friends make, I do, but Dalthus is still such a young colony — most of the settlers who first arrived here are still the shareholders. Do you really think they'll support such a drastic change? One that's not even on the agenda and they haven't had a proper time to think on?"

"Amendments may be made in Conclave. I've read the Charter myself, you know."

"As have I. Do you really think two-thirds of those here would ever agree to such a thing?"

"You could try — you've a historic opportunity today, you know? There've been few speakers in Conclave who weren't shareholders or heirs themselves. And you've influence, what with your Naval doings."

"I'm aware." In truth, she wasn't at all comfortable that her "Naval doings" might grant her such influence. It somehow didn't seem right that she should reap that benefit when so much of it had been because of the men serving with her and not any of her doing. "I do plan to mention — *mention*, mind you, and not actually suggest — that 'first-born' may not be the best mode of inheritance, male or female or either. There's some thought that might make a change more palatable to those like the Scudders."

The Scudders' first-born, Lilian, was quite vocally appalled by the proposed changes, stating repeatedly that a household was quite enough for her to run and she had no interest at all in any aspect of mining, farming, lumber, or, usually with a perfumed handkerchief held dramatically near her nose, *good lord can you imagine having to oversee the fisheries?*

For Alexis' part, she thought it just as wrong to force someone into a role they had no desire for as it was to deny the thing to one who did.

All of which had little to do with the thrust of Lauryn's argument, which was to have everyone, first settler, indenture, and freemen alike, each have a single, equal vote in how the colony was run.

"While universal suffrage may be a fine thing on other worlds, back in the Core, perhaps, where they've been settled for centuries, I still don't see it right for us here. The families who settled here gave up everything to purchase the system and run things as they will — and everyone who came after, indenture and freeman alike, knew how the Charter said things were to be run. They didn't have to come — could've moved on to another system more to their liking."

"Could they? Perhaps, but what of those born here after the settlement?" Lauryn waved a hand at the assembled crowd. "Oh, you and I and all those related to this lot are quite well off enough — a say or not in how things are run — but what of those born to the indentures and freemen since coming here? They had no say in what they might be born into, now did they?"

There was some sense to that, though Alexis couldn't completely agree.

"All of our parents and forebears made choices which affect us, Lauryn. I'm sure some of the first generation born here, or on any colony world, might well have wished their parents had stayed behind on some Core world. And it's certainly not as though Dalthus is all so bad in that regard — there are two worlds fringeward of here that I'd certainly not wish to have been born into."

"That there are worse is no reason not to make our own better. Will you not just —"

A chime sounded, announcing the imminent start of the Conclave and that those who weren't shareholders, heirs, or speakers should leave the auditorium while those who were should take their seats. The sound came as a relief, for Alexis didn't care to continue these same old arguments with Lauryn, much as she liked the girl in general.

"I'll think on it, and listen to you," Alexis promised, "but I won't propose it — not today. Change takes time, remember. When our ancestors settled here, their stop at Zariah was in a walled enclave to keep them from 'corrupting' the average Zariahn — now they've a Crown magistrate there and the world is open."

"Five years until the next Conclave, Alexis," Lauryn said. "Long years for some."

"Change comes in steps, not leaps, I think, cousin. Remember, I've just come from a Service where everyone must call me 'sir' so as not to grow confused at the novelty of my presence."

The chime sounded again.

"I must go, I suppose." Lauryn sighed. "Will you have dinner with us here in town after the Conclave?"

"I will, but no politics, please? After I get through speaking today I could wish a month or two talking nothing but lace doilies and the proper calligraphy for place settings with Lilian Scudder, I think."

Lauryn shuddered, but smiled before leaving.

Alexis made her way back to her seat.

"You look pensive," her grandfather noted.

"My cousin and her friends wish more than is achievable, I think." She settled herself into her seat as the lights dimmed and the crowd set their tablets to register their votes on the upcoming agenda. "Perhaps more than is wise."

"Hmph." Denholm's mouth twisted. "I've heard. If people want a world like that, that's what they should pick, not try to change what others have chosen."

Alexis wasn't entirely sure it was that simple, despite her words to that effect with Lauryn. She was saved from further thought on it by the arrival on the stage of Jerel Wilber, who'd got the task of chairing the Conclave. Wilber called the session to order.

The Conclave began with the less contentious issues. Matters of trade, duties, and capital expenditures for the colony as a whole, as well as reports on the status of mining and the two orbital stations being built — one at the planet and one at the primary moon for ore transshipments.

The latter was almost complete and the former well on its way to being so — already in use for some things.

"That should relieve some of the pressure on the ports, don't you think?" Denholm asked her. "If the spacers and miners can take their leave aboard the station, rather than here in town?"

"For the Naval spacers, yes," Alexis agreed, "as their captains won't want the men to run and the marines will keep the them in the Naval ring aboard station." She leaned closer so as to be heard over the current speaker, who was going on about the number of tonnes of gallenium ore transshipped at the lunar station versus in planetary orbit. Why the data had to be read aloud, instead of just provided on everyone's tablet she couldn't fathom. "But the miners and merchant crews prefer to come planetside — they like the novelty of open air after so much time a'space."

"Do they?" Denholm sighed. "Then I suppose we'll have to give Doakes his constabulary —" He smiled. "— so as to allow you to concentrate on the holdings."

"You seem quite certain our measure will carry."

He shrugged. "I've done all the politicking I can, I think."

"As have we," Mylin whispered from behind her, clapping a hand on Alexis' shoulder. Alexis reached up and squeezed it gratefully before he withdrew it.

"And I've confidence in your speaking to it," Denholm said.

"I wish I had the same."

The first of the more contentious issues was up on the agenda now, with Doakes speaking in the affirmative for the levying of increased port fees, the purpose of which would be to establish an official constabulary in the freetowns.

The chandler appeared nervous to be speaking, though he was one of the shareholders himself — just a few shares which had bought the concession on the chandlery and a bit of land in Port Arthur, but a shareholder nonetheless.

"Fees'll be passed on to those receiving the goods," Denholm muttered, "and that strikes at everyone, even those who'll receive little benefit." He turned to Alexis. "You say it's the miners causing the trouble, not the merchant crews?"

Alexis nodded. "For the most part — merchant crews will get their blood up from time to time, but they generally keep in good order. The merchant captains wish to keep the goodwill of the ports they visit, so keep the lads in line. The miners are a rougher lot."

Denholm pursed his lips, then touched his tablet.

"A move to amend, Holder Doakes," Wilber said as Doakes paused for breath. "Will you yield a moment to Holder Carew?"

Doakes wiped his brow and took a sip of water. "Aye, yes, I will."

"Do you desire the stage, Holder Carew?" Wilber asked.

Denholm raised his tablet to his mouth and spoke, voice coming from the hall's speakers.

"No need, I think, merely a proposal for a small amendment." He cleared his throat. "Upon passage of the measure, an additional vote to amend, in that the general port duties be struck in favor of a specific duty on gallenium transshipments." There were some mutters starting in the surrounding crowd. "Not to exceed the expected amount of the general port duties laid out in the original proposal, but to be levied solely on gallenium ore."

The mutters grew louder, but Alexis saw more than one head in the hall nodding in approval.

Denholm raised his voice, or Wilber raised the volume of the speakers, in order to be heard. "It's the belt miners who cause the trouble, is it not, Holder Doakes?"

Doakes nodded, eyes darting about the hall. "It is, sir, for the greater part — we have little trouble with the merchant crews, and their ships' officers are always at the ready to deal with what there is."

"All right, then," Denholm said. "Yes, it'll mean fewer of us paying for this new constabulary, but it's our gallenium that's caused the troubles. Not fair for some freeman running a bakery in Port Arthur to pay his three percent on a new tablet when it's our profits caused the trouble he's paying for, now is it?"

There were more murmurs at that and Alexis heard movement from behind her.

"Yes, Holder Mylin?"

"Seconded," Alexis heard from the row behind her and over the speakers. Mylin leaned forward and clapped Denholm on the shoulder. "Good thinking."

"Moved and seconded," Wilber announced, "the amendment will be added to the agenda for a vote immediately after the primary item."

Denholm leaned back in his seat, a satisfied look on his face.

"Both will pass now, certain."

Alexis frowned. "How can you be so sure?"

"The smaller holders might have voted against it to avoid the cost," Denholm said. "Now they know Sewall and I'll be voting for that amendment, they'll see the value in it and know it'll cost them nothing. With both our shares, plus theirs, the others with gallenium deposits haven't the votes to oppose it."

When the votes came, Alexis saw it was much as he'd predicted, with the opposing votes to both the measure and amendment being from those holders profiting most from the gallenium ore, but even the whole of them having too few shares to prevail against those in favor.

Alexis had mixed feelings about the outcome — happy for Doakes, Port Arthur, and the other freetowns, but disappointed that she and her lads wouldn't be called on for a bit of excitement now and again. Perhaps she could still volunteer to assist as some sort of adjunct to the official constabulary?

Further measures were heard and either passed or voted down, until finally it was time for her to speak.

FOUR

For that, she took to the stage when she was called and found it not nearly so terrifying as she thought she would. True, there were several thousand people watching her, but she could barely see them beyond the lights which illuminated the platform.

Terrifying or not, though, the experience did end in a blur, where she couldn't quite remember if she'd gotten in all the words she'd prepared to. The most she could remember at the end, was what she'd finished with.

"In short, holders, this measure is not so much a change as it is a return to what Dalthus' original settlers, some of you still with us today, planned for the colony from the start. The original Charter laid out that the first-born, regardless of gender, should inherit each holder's shares, and through them the lands. It was only after the shock and truly grievous deaths of so many in those hard, early years — my own grandmother among them — that the Charter was changed to what it is today.

"That change may have been wise at the time, and we are not here today to sit in judgment of it. Today we are merely here to answer whether times have again changed, and should this law change with them?

"Those days, with limited transport and the colony's only doctor a day's ride or more away, when the limited air transport meant help might or might not arrive in time — those days are done here. We've modern medical care in nearly every town of any size now, and the most modern in orbit aboard our new station. We've more antigrav transports than ever, and there's no outpost so remote that it's more than an hour's time from care — most are far less than that, and many of our regions have dedicated transport for medical care.

"The reasons given for this law's enactment have changed, holders, and it's time to give your daughters back their birthrights.

"True, there are some who have neither the interest nor skill to hold your lands — just as there are some first-born sons who lack the one or the other." She paused. Should she risk a bit of a joke? It was hard to tell the audience's reaction. "Or both," she hazarded and felt a flush of relief as she heard some chuckles in return.

"That's a thing to consider whether it's first-born son or daughter, either, but not our decision today." That was as much as she felt she could say about some further change — it was enough to plant the seed, seeing as how the change she was asking for primarily benefited herself.

"If the original terms of the charter were truly the best thinking of Dalthus' original settlers, then surely returning to them cannot be so very controversial." She thought it best to end there, reminding them once more of that fact. "Thank you, holders."

She resisted the urge to hurry as she left the stage and made her way back to her seat. There was some applause — not much, which didn't surprise her. The shareholders of Dalthus were generally a reserved lot and none of the other measures heard that day, no matter how popular, had been greeted by much more enthusiasm than her speech had been.

"In opposition," Wilber was announcing as she reached her row and took her seat again. "Holder Coalson."

Alexis sat, watching Edmon Coalson take the stage.

"Prat," her grandfather muttered.

"Buggering prat," Mylin commented from behind them.

Alexis found herself in the odd, and not entirely comfortable, position of defending the scion of the Coalson family.

"I met with him and his fellows quite often when I was in command of *Nightingale*," she said. "He's not nearly as bad as his father and grandfather, I think."

That those worthies had been either directly or indirectly responsible for the deaths of not only her grandmother but also her parents, and that she'd killed the father, Daviel Coalson, herself when she learned of it, did make "not nearly as bad as" faint praise, she supposed. But the two men, especially her grandfather, knew nothing of that. They only knew the petty feuding that had gone on between Rashae Coalson and Denholm Carew during the colony's early days — that and the general unpleasantness the elder Coalsons had engaged in — such as illicit gallenium mining and outright piracy.

"Faint praise," Denholm said, echoing her thoughts.

"He did seem to have the colony's best interest to heart," she said, "and not only his own during those meetings."

"And he's opposed this measure every step of the way," Denholm reminded her.

She nodded, knowing that. The Coalsons had opposed this change at every turn — some suspected because there were so very many sons in the household and marrying into families who had no son to inherit increased their power and influence. There was no doubt they'd done so, but Edmon, at least — despite the fact that he'd been a youth so callow Alexis had once dumped a full teapot over his head during a courting session — struck her as more mindful of the larger picture.

In aspects other than inheritance, at least.

Denholm sighed. "Well, let's hear what the boy has to say."

"Did you think to bring any produce?" Mylin asked.

"What?"

"Isn't that what they used to do when a fellow on stage was disliked? Have at him with the spoiled crops?"

"Hhm, no, none with me." Denholm took his bottle of tea from the holder in the seat's arm. "Do have some tea, though." He held the bottle out to Alexis. "Care to do the honors, Lexi-girl? You've a decent arm for it, if I remember truly."

"I was *fifteen*," Alexis said, flushing. "And the boy, who *you* invited to court me, I might add, had just suggested a good thrashing might do me no harm."

Both Denholm and the Mylins laughed. Alexis shook her head.

"Shush and listen."

On the stage, Coalson was ready to begin. He walked to the center of the stage — quite confidently, and Alexis wondered if she'd shown nearly that same confidence. She hadn't felt it, far more used to giving orders from a ship's quarterdeck than trying to convince others of something. Coalson did look the part of the first settler, though — trim, youthful. One could quite imagine him riding about his lands, alighting here and there to ensure all was in order.

If only the man didn't have such outrageous taste in clothing. She wasn't at all certain what one would even call the color of his waist-coat — something between red and purple with a name she couldn't remember — and his jacket was likely called umber, or some such, instead of the orange she'd simply name it.

Regardless of what Alexis thought of it, many of the younger set found it quite the thing and looked to Coalson as some sort of fashion trendsetter. She hoped that wouldn't carry over to his opinions on the matter before them.

"Fellow holders," Coalson said, reminding the listeners right from the start that *he* was their peer, the holder of his family's shares in his own right, unlike Alexis. "I am called upon to speak in opposition to this measure — a call made, I imagine, due to my frequent and unflag-ging words to that effect since it was first proposed.

"I have felt, and said, since that first proposal, that there is no cause to change that which has served us well. No cause to return, as Miss Carew put it, to the original Charter's language, if the change made was for good reason by wise men — and women, I will remind you, who were among those original shareholders, some of whom are still with us here today."

A number of boos and catcalls sounded at this — sparse, as there were few of the original settlers left who were women without husbands and their shares in their own names, but some were present nonetheless.

"And not a one of those voted for this at the time, I'll tell you," Mylin muttered.

"I have said this often and at length," Coalson went on, ignoring the sounds from the audience. He paused, frowned, then continued, "What I will say here and now may anger some of you, but I feel I must say it."

He stepped forward, closer to the stage's edge.

"In these more recent times, I have come to know Miss Carew ... Lieutenant Carew, for I came to know her through her command of the ship which sits idle above us even now. In preparation for those meetings with Lieutenant Carew I researched her Naval career ... quite thoroughly, and through sources more directly involved than what's reported in the Naval Gazette."

Alexis flushed, wondering what Coalson was about with this line. Beside her, Denholm frowned.

"Bastard," he muttered.

"What?"

"If he thinks he'll lose the message, he'll attack the messenger."

"What, me?" Alexis flushed further, wondering if her own actions might be the doom of this endeavor. There was certainly enough in her Naval records for Coalson to use if he chose — the charges of mutiny, though found blameless and the records sealed, would be damning enough by themselves.

"Quite thoroughly," Coalson repeated. "And as I said, my words here may anger some, but I feel compelled to speak."

"I'll challenge the little bastard if he does it," Denholm muttered. "Run him straight through."

"With me as your second," Mylin said.

"Grandfather! You'll do no such thing!" Alexis said, not so much because she wished to keep her grandfather safe as that if Edmon Coalson did step a word out of line with the absolute truth, she had every intention of issuing the challenge herself. *And I'll make damned sure I've killed this Coalson properly the first time.*

"Upon review of these records I've obtained, I can reach but one conclusion." Coalson paused, bowed his head for a moment, then looked up, seeming to stare directly at Alexis.

She caught her breath, hand going unconsciously to her waist where her sword would be in dress uniform, and waited to see if the man's next words would doom him.

Coalson's eyes narrowed.

"If such attention to duty, such loyalty, such skill as I have been informed of —" His lips twitched. "— may reside in so slight a package as Lieutenant Alexis Carew, well, then fellow holders, we have done ourselves and our entire world a greater disservice with this law than we shall ever comprehend."

There was silence in the hall for a moment, then muttering rose.

"What?" Denholm asked.

Alexis wasn't entirely certain she'd heard correctly herself, she was still trying to parse what Coalson said when he continued.

"Fellow holders, the Coalson shares will be voted in the *affirmative* on this measure and I urge you to do the same, moreover —" The muttering rose, joined by applause from those in favor and shouts of outrage from those opposed, forcing Coalson to all but shout his next words. "*Moreover*, I will propose the amendment which Lieutenant Carew alluded to but did not voice! That the phrase '*first-born*' be struck from the Charter, as well as 'son', and that a family's shares may be inherited, in their entirety, by the child, regardless of gender or primacy, each holder deems best suited!"

"*Seconded!*" Mylin bellowed, not bothering with his tablet.

FIVE

"Well," Denholm said into the resulting furor. "That was unexpected."

Alexis looked around the hall, trying to take it all in. Several holders had rushed the stage, yelling and waving their arms at Wilber, but the moderator appeared to be shrugging off their concerns. All around them, groups of holders were forming and reforming as the impact of Coalson's declaration and amendment took effect.

"What just happened?" Alexis asked, thoroughly bewildered at the turn of events.

"You're my heir," Denholm said, "as it's all over but the counting now."

"And that young lad's just ruined his political career for it," Mylin added.

"Ruined?" Denholm shook his head and nodded to the stage where Coalson still stood, calm, face impassive in the midst of the hall's chaos. "Do you not realize what he's just done?"

"Betrayed his coalition," Mylin said. "They'll never trust him again."

Denholm snorted. "Those hardliners there," he said, pointing to the group around the stage, "will never trust him. But the lad's cleverer than that — it was the Coalson shares that made them a force in the first place. *They* needed *him*, not the other way around." He surveyed the hall. "He has his shares and the brothers' and uncles' who married into other families. That's a solid block, and now he has the reformers, too. No, what the lad's done is seen which way the world was marching, then got himself out in front and waved them on in the direction they were going anyway. Took them clear across their finish line and on to the next one — made *himself* the leader."

"He's that clever, do you think?"

Another snort. "Either that or he's had a true-blue change of heart on the matter — which will you believe of a Coalson?"

"Clever bugger," Mylin muttered.

Alexis wasn't certain of their evaluation. For all the history between the Carews and the Coalsons, she'd judged him to be sincere in their own meetings. The crowd was settling now, Wilber calling for order and waving those who'd approached the stage back to their seats. Coalson still held the stage, but appeared to be done speaking, which led her to wonder if her grandfather and Sewall Mylin might be just a bit too optimistic in their pronouncements that the measure would pass.

"With Edmon changing sides as he has, won't there be a new speaker in opposition?" she asked. "Someone who might convince the vote against us?"

"Oh, it's Edmon now, is it?" Mylin asked with a grin. "Now he's won the day and all?"

Alexis flushed, unsure why she'd used his given name at all and not liking that she had.

"Not unless *Coalson* yields his time," her grandfather said, with what Alexis thought was an entirely unnecessary emphasis on the name, "which I doubt he'll do. The speakers are set in the agenda and we'll hear from no one else unless the speaker yields — we chose you and the opposition chose Coalson, so that ends it."

"They chose poorly," Mylin said with a chuckle.

Their prediction proved true in just a few moments, as Coalson finally spoke again.

"Mister Wilber," he called out, "I relinquish my remaining time and ask you to call for the vote on this measure."

That raised more shouts from those opposed to the measure, but Wilber merely shrugged and showed open palms to those still at the foot of the stage, as if to indicate his helplessness. He called for the vote, which went much as Denholm and Mylin had predicted, with both the measure and amendment passing — and by a margin which surprised both men.

Wilber called for an adjournment for the day immediately thereafter, and the hall slowly emptied, most of the holders in groups, heads together and whispering about the day's events.

"I believe I'll avoid the parties tonight," Denholm said. "The talk will be all about Coalson, and they'll not want to hear a word against the lad. I'm still suspicious enough of that family to say the wrong thing, I fear."

Mylin nodded. "A quiet dinner and an early night's what I wish after today's excitement."

The two men turned to Alexis. She felt confused and torn by the day's events, for more than one reason, and certainly didn't want to attend any parties or formal dinners — neither did she wish to join the two men in a private dinner, though. A bit of time alone, to gather her thoughts and bring some clarity to the day might be in order.

"I think that I'll take *Nightingale's* boat back home for the night, if you don't object, grandfather."

She said her goodbyes and made her way to the landing field. The Conclave had lasted until after dark, and the area around the field was in full, raucous swing as she passed. Shouts, laughter, and music poured from the pubs and music halls, spacers and miners hurried from place to place, desperate for one last bit of entertainment before heading back to weeks or months in the belt or *darkspace*.

Alexis' boat crew was full of smiles and congratulations when she reached the boat. They'd known what the stakes of the day were for her and news of the result had apparently traveled fast. She tried to accept their words with a smile and look the part of a happy winner, but inside she was wondering at what would come next.

She took her place in the cockpit with the pilot, instead of the passenger compartment, and the boat lifted. It crossed her mind to wonder how many more times she'd have a full ship's boat to command, much less a ship. If all her time was to be spent in managing the family lands, she'd have to resign her commission, and that meant even the tenuous claim she had to *Nightingale's* boat would be lost.

The Carew farmstead did have its own antigrav hauler now — small, not like the massive ones owned by the colony. She could use that to get about on the holding's business, but it wasn't the same at all.

Perhaps she might convince the colony to purchase *Nightingale* out of ordinary and use her for security around the system. They'd need a crew and captain in that case, and she might get some time in *darkspace*. It would mostly be patrols to the belt and back, but she thought there was a case to make it worthwhile — and such an endeavor, if it were kept to only part of the time, wouldn't interfere with her duties to the holding *too* very much.

She'd suggest that — perhaps to her grandfather, but perhaps also to Edmon Coalson. He was quite forward thinking and might see the value in Dalthus having a *darkspace*-capable ship of its own, even one so small as *Nightingale*. In fact, she should probably speak to Edmon in the morning, before the Conclave came to order, and thank him for his support. He'd be busy tonight, but she might also send him a note of thanks — and of congratulations for what was surely a great victory for the young man.

At least a bit of a plan, she thought, settling back into her seat and gazing out at the night sky. Not at the stars themselves, but at the blackness between them.

"There's a boat on the pad," Gutis, the pilot, said, pulling Alexis from her reverie.

At first what he'd said didn't properly register, but then she looked toward the ground as they circled the farmstead and she saw it. Another ship's boat on the farmstead landing pad, which wasn't unusual in itself, merchants frequently landed to deal directly with her grandfather for goods, trading the time and fuel for an extra stop for the savings of cutting out the middlemen in Port Arthur — what was unusual, though, was for a boat to be present after dark. Most merchants would land in daylight, load, and be off — it was only a rare old friend who might be invited to stay the night and dine with the family. Something which would not be the case now, as her grandfather was still in Port Arthur and the Conclave's timing was well known.

Her first, worst, thought was of the tales she'd heard as a girl, of pirate attacks on the remote farmsteads. The holding looked peaceful and ordinary, though, and Dalthus had far more traffic than a pirate might wish to risk — still, they were not the wisest of men, pirates.

"Put us down quickly, Gutis. There's space enough." She rose and slid open the hatch to the main compartment. "Nabb! Arm the lads and be ready! There's no call for a visitor at home and I'd not wish us taken unawares."

"Aye, sir!" Nabb called back, already moving toward the boat's arms locker.

Gutis brought the boat down and Alexis was first off the ramp, the tiny yet effective flechette pistol she typically wore at the small of her back in hand, and Nabb along with the rest of the crew behind her, armed and ready. Spacers they might be, but the Carew farmstead had become their home as well, and she could see the steely determination in their eyes to defend it as they would their ship.

She took note of the strange boat in passing. Smaller than *Nightingale's* and well-kept. The bow bore the name *Elizabeth*, which was not a ship Alexis recognized as captained by one of her grandfather's friends — though having spent the last few years in space, she couldn't know them all. She spared a quick, appraising glance for the farmstead as a whole.

All did seem peaceful and ordinary.

It was early enough that there was still music and voices coming from the indenture barracks — no sounds of fighting or conflict.

As they drew closer to the family house, Alexis noted the lights were on and all seemed well. Then voices from the kitchen as they drew even closer — Julia's and Marie's she recognized, then a man's voice which she didn't and the sound of Marie and Julia laughing.

She relaxed a bit — but only a bit, for there'd been no message to her or her grandfather that there was a visitor, and she could think of no reason for that.

"Stay close, lads," she whispered. "It sounds well, but be wary."

"Aye, sir," Nabb answered. "I'll go through first, shall I?"

Alexis held up a hand. "No, I will, but stay close."

They closed with the house. Alexis dashed the last few steps, heart beating faster and feeling Nabb and the others right at her heels. She took the door in one motion, open, through, and several steps into the room so that there'd be room for the lads.

Julia and Marie sat at the kitchen table, smiles turning to looks of confusion, teacups frozen in place at the surprise of Alexis' sudden entrance. Their eyes took in the flechette gun in Alexis' hand, as well as the laser pistol in Nabb's, and their confusion deepened.

A man sat at the table, back to the door. Slowly and deliberately, as though he knew the newcomers were armed even though he couldn't see them, he turned.

Dark hair growing a bit grey, neatly trimmed goatee, and features one might consider dashing if one hadn't actually met the man and been aware of what chaos and trouble he could bring.

"No," Alexis said, resisting the urge to raise the flechette pistol and fire. "No. Absolutely not."

The man grinned widely and nodded to the pistol in her hand.

"Ah, Ricki," Avrel Dansby said, "is that any way to greet an old friend?"

SIX

"Alexis?" Julia asked, concern in her voice. "Is it all right?"

Alexis kept her eyes on Dansby, the one-time pirate, sometime smuggler, and always rogue, who'd shepherded her into Hanover space. The man's grin widened and he seemed on the verge of outright laughter.

"He said he knew you," Julia said, casting a now suspicious eye on Dansby. "That you were old friends and he'd dropped in to visit." The housekeeper's eyes narrowed and her hand reached out to grasp the teapot as though it were the closest weapon to hand. "Boots seemed to know him, as well."

Alexis' gaze dropped to the floor where Boots, the ill-named mongoose Dansby himself had saddled her with, was curled around one of the man's legs, and casting her, as nearly as Alexis could tell, a rather accusatory glare from its little brown eyes.

"No," Alexis said again. "Whatever it is, the answer's no." She began pointing. "So you may take the creature —" A point at the mongoose. "— yourself —" A point at Dansby. "— back to your bloody boat —" A point toward the doorway, which caused Nabb and the lads to duck, as she realized she was doing all this pointing with the

39

hand holding the flechette pistol. "— and be about your mischief someplace else!"

"Now, Ricki, I'm merely the messenger in all this — no cause for the fuss."

"There's a rather traditional thing done with messengers, Mister Dansby. Shall I enlighten you to it?"

Dansby shrugged. "You'll hear it from me or from the principal, one," he said. "Your choice."

"No," Alexis said again, knowing who Dansby must be referring to. "I want nothing more to do with him. The man's mad — his last scheme had me setting fire to a Hanoverese agent in order to get loose and I'm done with him."

"Alexis?" Julia asked, eyes wide.

Oh, bugger it, she thought. Julia and her grandfather weren't supposed to know about that. Weren't supposed to know most of the things she'd seen and done in the Service, come to that. It would worry them needlessly to know she'd gone into Hanover undercover, been all but captured by one of the enemy's agents, and made a neck-or-nothing run for escape aboard Dansby's ship.

Julia squared her shoulders.

"Have you presented yourself under false pretenses at my door, Mister Dansby?" she asked. "You claimed to be a friend to Alexis, yet she doesn't seem to find you so. I'd not like to think you came to my kitchen, sat at my table, and drank my tea without being honest with me."

Dansby turned to her, opened his mouth to speak, then flushed. If anything, he seemed more cowed by the housekeeper's ire than by Alexis' pistol or the armed spacers still in the doorway.

"Who is this 'principal' you claim to represent and what does he want with my Alexis?" Julia demanded.

Alexis sighed, her initial anger fading along with the adrenaline of having thought there might be trouble. She signaled to Nabb that he and the lads wouldn't be needed, though Nabb stayed behind after ushering the lads out and closing the kitchen door, his gaze on

Dansby and his fingers still near the stunstick at his belt. He'd holstered the laser pistol, at least, and Alexis did the same with her flechette.

"I'm afraid I can't say," Dansby said at last.

"Malcome Bloody Eades," Alexis supplied, "of the ever-conspiring Foreign Office."

Dansby winced. "He really doesn't care to have his name bandied about, you know."

"Then he oughtn't hand it out to those who'd not give a bugger's sheath for what he wants!"

"Alexis!"

She winced at Julia's tone, flushing, as she had to admit that particular curse wasn't at all proper in the family kitchen.

"I'm sorry, Julia, too much time around bosuns, I'm afraid — and no care at all for what Mister Eades might want."

"Well," Julia said firmly, "as it's clear you two have a thing or more to speak about — and there's no one in any particularly *immediate* need of killing —" She pointedly placed a large carving knife on the table before her, causing Dansby's brow to raise. Alexis realized the housekeeper's reach for the teapot had been a feint, but where she'd produced the blade from remained a mystery. "— I'll refresh the tea, then leave you alone to your discussions."

She set about doing that and, with a fresh pot of tea on the table along with a full plate of pastry, she ushered Marie from the kitchen.

Nabb opened the door to excuse himself as well.

"I'll be just outside, sir," he said, never taking his eyes from Dansby.

"Thank you, Nabb." Alexis would have liked to tell him to go and return to his home and bed for the night, but she did feel more comfortable with him nearby.

Once they were alone, Alexis seated herself and poured a cup of tea.

"You do surround yourself with the most interesting fellows,"

Dansby said, then grinned. "I count myself chief amongst them, of course."

"Eades' message, Mister Dansby?" Alexis asked. "That I might refuse him with alacrity and we may both be about other business?"

Dansby reached down to the floor and came up with the mongoose. He placed the creature on the table and fed it a bit of pastry. The creature chewed, swallowed, then looked at Alexis and licked its lips, though she couldn't shake the feeling that it was actually sticking its bloody tongue out at her in some sort of taunt.

"'Boots?'" Dansby asked.

"*Nightingale's* crew named it for some ... proclivities. You're welcome to it back."

Dansby fed it another bit of pastry.

"No, Ricki, I think he's quite happy here with you."

"I do wish you'd not call me that."

Dansby's nickname for her, Ricki, had come when they'd first met. Her intense dislike for the man on first seeing him had prompted Eades to remark that it was natural for a Naval officer and pirate to dislike and distrust one another — rather like a mongoose and cobra. Alexis had been quick to name Dansby the serpent, and he'd been quick to name her the "cute, cuddly one," and thereafter "Ricki" after some obscure literary work he insisted she read and she refused on principle.

Dansby shrugged. "Come now, Ricki, our times haven't been all bad, have they?"

Alexis sighed. He did have a point. Her objection to the man was more due to his enterprises than the man himself. She regarded him for a moment ... and he was a charming bastard, come to that.

"Very well, Mister Dansby," she said finally. "Pass along your message."

"More of an invitation, really."

"Invitation? I have no intention of traveling anywhere on Eades' word. In fact, I may be on Dalthus for some time — we've just amended the inheritance laws and I can finally look forward to simply running my family holdings, rather than rushing about the galaxy to Eades' tune."

"Or the Navy's," Dansby said. "Yes, I can see you looking forward to that. A peaceful life in-atmosphere — just the thing for you, I'm certain."

Alexis flushed, wondering if she was truly so transparent or if Dansby had simply made a guess and confirmed it with her reaction.

"In any case," he went on, "you've no need for much traveling at all. Just a quick jaunt up to the station. You may find it worth your while."

Alexis frowned. "The station?" Her eyes narrowed at the implication. "Eades is here?"

Dansby nodded.

That did change things. Malcome Eades here? The orchestrator of the plot to free the Berry March worlds from Hanover — the plot which had ended so very badly. Ended in a rushed evacuation, thousands of civilians, Marie and Ferrau amongst them, displaced as refugees, Alexis' lover, Delaine Theibaud, missing for more than a year now with the fleet haring off into Hanoverese space at the end — moreover, the it was the plot which had resulted in Alexis' ship, *Belial*, being pounded to ruin by a Hanoverese frigate while defending the hundreds of little ships evacuating Giron. Her ship, most of her crew, and the true hero of that action, Midshipman Sterlyn Artley, dead and gone in Malcome Eades' tangled web.

The architect of all that pain and horror here in Dalthus?

Alexis' jaw clenched.

"You're quite correct, Mister Dansby, I find myself quite willing to accept that invitation."

SEVEN

Alexis had Nabb retrieve her boat crew, apologizing for taking them away from their dinners and reveries, but promising some time aboard the station to do as they will. She could have ridden in Dansby's boat, but didn't like being so much in the man's power. Curiously, she noted that Dansby had no boat crew of his own, he'd piloted his own craft down. That was something Alexis thought she might like, but hadn't the opportunity to do in the Navy — officers were passengers, not pilots.

Perhaps she could change that if her suggestion that Dalthus buy *Nightingale* into local service was successful. They'd be establishing their own Service in that case, local and small it might be, and if she were to be the one to first command it, then she could establish any traditions she liked. That might, in fact, be both satisfying and enjoyable — there were things about the Navy she'd change if she could, after all.

Port Arthur and the Carew farmstead might be in night, but orbital stations never were. Construction was still ongoing, and would be for months to come, but three of the main ring's levels were operational, and much of the quay was in use.

Merchant ships, those carrying goods and others with construction materials, were docked around the outer edge, with the inner side of the ring reserved for the smaller boats.

Alexis caught a distant glimpse of *Nightingale* trailing behind the station in orbit. Close enough for supplies to be transferred as needed, but not so close as to interfere with traffic. Her ship — no, not hers now, but she couldn't turn off her feelings of possession for the vessel — looked forlorn and sad to her eye. Masts unstepped, rigging all put away inside — only the barest of navigation lights visible on her hull. She'd sit there, mostly dark and silent, until put to some future use.

She wondered which of the ships was Dansby's *Elizabeth*, but didn't bother to query the console to identify her. Gutis brought the boat alongside the quay and eased it into contact with the docking tube. Dansby was at the tube just ahead of them.

"Lock the hatch," Alexis ordered Nabb as they waited for the docking tube to air and seal against the boat's hatch. "Then you and the lads find some entertainments. I'm not sure how long I'll be, so keep your tablets handy for my call."

"Aye, sir," Nabb said. "Will you want an escort to your meeting?"

"No." She shook her head. "I'll be fine, I'm sure."

In truth, she wasn't so certain as that, but she did know that she wanted none of her lads coming too very close to Malcome Eades.

Nabb looked doubtful, but acknowledged her order.

Dansby met them on the quay and led the way for her. Alexis glanced behind a few times to assure herself that Nabb hadn't taken it into his head to follow her anyway, but saw none of her lads in the corridor. The crowd consisted more of those working on constructing the station than spacers at the moment, but she knew that would change with time. In fact, the corridor itself seemed still unfinished, with men working here and there to install fixtures and trim up final details. It would make a fine addition to Dalthus when it was finished, she thought.

"So ... *Elizabeth* and not *Marylin*?" she asked.

Marylin was the ship of Dansby's she'd last sailed on.

"Anya has *Marylin* on some jaunt to Hissie space," Dansby said without looking at her.

Alexis breathed a bit of a sigh of relief at that. She'd not been looking forward to another meeting with Anya Mynatt, one of Dansby's captains. She'd never got on very well with the woman, and things had gone downhill after Alexis shot Mynatt in the foot during an altercation ... and the knee ... and threatened to do the same to a few other places before the situation settled into an uneasy peace. At least, though, Dansby had made good on his promise to finally give Mynatt the captaincy of *Marylin*.

"Small favors I'll not have to deal with her," Alexis muttered.

Dansby winced.

"What?"

Dansby stopped and faced her. "Well, Ricki, I know you never got on well with Anya, but ..."

He scratched his neck with his left hand and Alexis caught a glint of gold there.

"Is that ..."

"Aye, you're speaking about my wife, now, Ricki, so I'll ask bit of civility."

Alexis stared at him, shocked to her core. Avrel Dansby married was one thing — a shocking thing that might make one question the very order of the universe. Dansby married to Anya Mynatt, when Alexis had seen the two squabble and nearly come to not only blows, but blades and firearms, was simply unfathomable.

"But ... you just said she's off to *Hso-Hsi* ... that's a year's trip at the best of times ..."

Dansby flushed, something she didn't know him to do very often.

"Well, you're young, Ricki. In time you'll learn, perhaps ... there are some marriages as work best do the principles not spend too very much time in each other's company."

DANSBY LED Alexis through the station as though he'd lived there all his life and knew its every turn. Alexis was left to ponder the novel idea of anyone catching Avrel Dansby into marriage paired with the equally unlikely idea of anyone being willing to marry Anya Mynatt at all — that the two things should come together as one pairing bewildered her.

"So, really, you and Mynatt?"

"Enough, Ricki."

"I mean, I know you used the promise of a ship to bed her, but marriage?"

Dansby winced. "It wasn't like that."

"I'm fairly certain she said it was. I remember her wanting to shoot you over it — that should stick in a man's memory, I think."

"Can we not do this?"

"I'm only asking."

"Well, don't." He stopped at a nondescript pub, doing quite good business despite the lack of installed signage in the corridor. "We're here."

Alexis braced herself and followed Dansby in. They entered, ignored by patrons and staff both, who were intent on the serious businesses of drinking and facilitating, and then up a set of stairs to the upper level. There were a series of hatches off a corridor which Alexis presumed to be private meeting rooms — something Eades had a penchant for finding.

Dansby keyed a hatch and motioned Alexis to proceed him, which she did, then froze in place two steps into the room as she saw him.

Malcome Bloody *Eades*, she thought.

The man stood to greet her and Alexis was in motion, crossing the space between them, hand raised to strike.

Even as she swung her arm, though, she knew it wouldn't connect — that she had made a horrible mistake, in fact, for Eades' bland smile of welcome, his whole demeanor, changed in an instant. No longer the plain, nondescript functionary no one would give a second glance, his eyes hardened, his face set, and his posture changed from one of bureaucratic indifference to the lithe grace of a cat.

His own arm came up to block hers so quickly that she could swear she hadn't seen it move.

Then, just as suddenly, Eades' arm lowered and her own swept through the suddenly open space, her palm connecting with the man's face in a loud *crack* that filled the compartment.

Alexis glared at Eades, caught between her anger and her astonishment at how quickly Eades had moved — he'd readied himself to block her, apparently decided not to, and lowered his arm again all as she swung her own She was quite certain that she would never, no matter how much she trained with her shipboard marines, quite match the man's speed.

"I shall allow you that one blow, Miss Carew," Eades said, "out of respect for your pain and loss." He gestured to the table and accompanying chairs. "Will you sit and listen now?"

Alexis sat. Dansby set a glass before her and poured. She raised and gulped, letting the fire of the liquor settle in her belly. She took a deep breath and relaxed her shoulders, finding that the blow, symbolic as it might be, had released a great deal of her anger as well. She felt ready now to, perhaps, hear Eades out, though she didn't know what he might say to excuse his role in the debacle of Giron.

Dansby set the bottle next to her glass and she noted that it was a fine Scotch — which Eades must have felt truly guilty, or need her help very badly, to have provided. True Scotch was hard to come by and dear, especially as far fringeward as Dalthus.

She refilled her glass, happy to swill the man's guineas given the opportunity.

Dansby sat and took a glass of his own — wine, she noted. As did Eades himself.

Alexis pointedly set her own glass down again, wanting her wits about her for this meeting.

Though I'll leave here with that bottle in hand, she vowed.

"I suppose I must start with an explanation," Eades said.

"Please do," Alexis said. "Should you have one, at all."

"I assure you, Miss Carew, that I am as ..." He paused and pursed his lips as though tasting something unpleasant. "No. No, I won't make that claim — your own involvement was far more personal than my own.

"The plan for Giron and the Berry March was sound," Eades said. "I still believe so, even after what happened. What it lacked was proper execution. In that I relied on the expertise of others — military others who, apparently, fatally underestimated the forces necessary to carry out that plan."

"So you'll blame others for it," Alexis said. "I might have known."

"There's enough blame to fall in many laps, Miss Carew. My own included, I'll admit. I should have asked others and not rely solely on those I did. They should have seen the need for more forces than they recommended."

"General Malicoat told you there were not enough. He wanted more of his own forces, and not uniforms for French you hoped would rise to join us. In the planning sessions — I was there."

Eades nodded. "By that time the execution of the plan had been turned over to the forces involved — I could not have influenced things then to any great degree." He sighed. "In the end, it might not have mattered if those voices had been heeded — might, even, have made things far worse."

"How could it possibly have been worse?"

"Have you ever wondered, Miss Carew, how the Hanoverese were able to bring to bear the forces to outnumber General Malicoat as they did? They might just have easily shown up with far too few, you know, but they arrived with enough right at the first. And why, have you ever questioned, were they so very harsh with the civilians of that world? Leaving aside those who openly rebelled and joined with our forces, the Hanoverese reprisals against Giron's towns and villages was brutal even for a people known for their harshness."

Alexis frowned, wondering at what Eades was getting at.

"We were betrayed, Miss Carew, from the very start. The

Hanoverese were told our plan and the composition of our forces — they knew where we would strike and with how many troops. Oh, not Commodore Balestra's fleet — I think that came as quite a surprise to them — but Giron itself." He sipped his wine. "They allowed us to land, allowed the people to rebel, and then came in with the force necessary to wipe out General Malicoat's forces and that entire world.

"It was only through the miracle of that ragtag fleet you put together that our forces escaped, and even so Giron is now an example rivaling Abentheren in the litany of reasons not to resist Hanover. It will be generations before the other worlds in the Berry March think of freedom without shuddering at Giron's fate."

Eades rose and began pacing.

"This peace with Hanover will not last, Miss Carew — it never does — but while it lasts, there are other issues, other enemies of the Crown, which bear addressing."

"I'm no longer an active Naval officer, Mister Eades," Alexis reminded him. "I'm a half-pay lieutenant, in-atmosphere, and soon to be quite occupied with other endeavors. I fear you must look elsewhere to address your schemes."

Eades smiled.

"Your recent political victory notwithstanding, Miss Carew, will you not at least hear me out? Will that fine bottle of Scotch, and the second I have to gift you on your departure from this room, not buy me that, at least?"

Alexis grunted. Two bottles of Scotch, and this was a fine label, indeed, were dear at any time, but more so on half-pay. True, as her grandfather's heir now, she could draw on the family funds, but she'd never think to do so for something so frivolous. She had a healthy cache of prize money, still, but even with that it was an extravagance she couldn't feel comfortable with — taking it off Eades, though, would be a pleasure, even at the cost of listening to his schemes.

She nodded and settled back into her chair.

"Are you at all familiar with the Barbary?" Eades asked.

"Some space between New London and *Hso-Hsi*, isn't it? I've heard a spacer or two curse the dangers of transiting it."

"The dangers," Dansby said, "and the nature of the ports. They're lawless worlds, and the areas around their ports even more so. Full of graft, corruption, and wickedness."

"So the sort of place you're quite at home?" Alexis asked.

Dansby grinned. "Upon a time, quite."

Eades nodded. "Named by spacers for that very reason, and for the sorts of spacers' haunts in-system where a man will find a blade in his belly as easily as a pint of ale. The Barbary teems with such, with the natives being quick to separate crews from their purse — or life, barring that. I believe many of the inhabitants may trace their ancestry back to some ancient shore of the same name, but it's spacers' slang which stuck."

"The Barbary transects Hanover, stretching from a portion of New London territory, across Hanover, to *Hso-Hsi*. It is a barren, desolate patch of the galaxy, with few systems and fewer habitable ones. That desolation has two effects. First, that there are few colonized worlds in the Barbary, and of those none that any sane man would wish to live on, and, second, that it is the fastest route between New London and *Hso-Hsi*."

Alexis nodded. The lower number of systems meant less normal-space mass. Since a ship in *darkspace* tended to move farther, relative to normal-space, the farther it was from any corresponding normal-space mass, a route which came close to fewer star systems would be faster than one which kept close to many, regardless of the normal-space distance traveled.

It was as though *darkspace* itself grew larger in response to normal-space masses and shrank in their absence. Or, perhaps, the ships themselves traveled relatively faster — it was nearly impossible to tell which, as the only way to truly know where one's position in *darkspace* correlated to in normal-space was at a transition point, the Lagrangian points associated with orbital bodies.

"The Barbary worlds are a constant source of trouble for all civi-

lized star nations. More than piracy and ransoming crew and passengers, some worlds have regressed to outright slavery," Eades went on.
"We, New London, may tolerate and even encourage the savages at
times, since the region bisects Hanover itself — that they must deal
with the barbarians merely to access their Fringe worlds is a constant
source of amusement. At other times, however, the depredations
against trade become so great that we must act. Act strongly and
show them that a New London flagged vessel is best not trifled with."

Alexis found herself nodding again. Trade was the lifeblood of
the kingdom — something which had been drilled into her head as
gospel not only since she'd joined the Navy, but at her grandfather's
knee. Trade had created the fortunes of many of those who'd settled
her world. Trade in the various luxury goods, bulk grains, and now
gallenium filled the colony's coffers, allowing them to purchase
manufactured goods they still lacked the technological base to make
themselves, and trade filled the Queen's coffers, coffers which then
financed the Royal Navy and their protection of that trade.

"Such a time is now, given that we are not fully in a state of war
with Hanover, and an expedition is planned to show those worlds
that a New London merchantman is best left alone."

"That's all well and good," Alexis said, "but what does it have to
do with the Foreign Office? Won't the Navy be putting together
a fleet?"

Eades shook his head. "Not at this time, not directly. Though we
have a cease-fire with Hanover, that could end at any time. It is
thought this is not the best time to send warships through the
Barbary, seeing as how those ships would then be, for all intents and
purposes, within the boundaries of Hanover itself. A provocation of
that sort would be unwise at this time."

Alexis found herself becoming more and more wary as Eades
spoke. It was beginning to sound like Giron and the Berry March all
over again — "war on the cheap" as Dansby had once called it. And
likely to bring only what value such a thing was worth — failure and
ignominy.

"How do you propose to avoid such a thing?"

"The expedition will be made up of armed, private vessels," Eades said, "with no official involvement by the Navy."

Alexis pondered that for a moment, then shook her head.

"You intend to fight piracy with pirates?"

Eades cleared his throat and Dansby laughed.

"Not pirates, Miss Carew, I assure you."

"Well, what else would you call them, then, if they're not proper Navy?"

"The term is 'privateer'," Dansby offered.

"That even sounds like pirate," Alexis said.

"It is *not* piracy," Eades insisted, almost huffing. "Each ship will receive a Letter of Marque, a document authorizing the vessel and its captain to seek out the Queen's enemies named therein. You would be a fully-authorized agent of the Crown in that regard, not a pirate."

"*I* would?" Alexis repeated. "Is that what you think?"

"It is my intent for you to command one of those ships, Miss Carew."

Alexis was tempted. To walk a quarterdeck just once more, even if not a proper Navy ship, and to command a crew in action — just once more, before taking up the mantle of a proper Dalthus holder. But not in one of Eades' mad schemes, she decided. Not again.

She shook her head.

"I think not, Mister Eades." She stood and grasped the bottle of Scotch. "The second bottle you mentioned? The one for listening? I believe I've fulfilled my part."

Eades nodded and set another bottle of Scotch on the table between them, but kept one finger on its top.

"Not even for a chance to command a ship again, Miss Carew?" he asked, echoing her own thoughts. "One last time, before it's all atmosphere and grubbing in the dirt?"

Alexis' jaw clenched, hating how easily the man could read her. "We may be farmers, Mister Eades, but we do not grub. Thank you for your offer, but no." She took the second bottle from under his finger and turned to the hatch.

"Before you leave, Miss Carew, one last thing?"

Alexis sighed and turned back.

"Knowing your lack of knowledge in some things as I do," Eades said, "do you have the look of the Barbary fixed firmly in your mind? Its borders? Where it is, I mean?"

"Between New London and *Hso-Hsi*, crossing Hanover, it's been made quite clear."

"Has it?" Eades smiled. Not his jovial, nondescript smile, but the one that always made Alexis shiver a bit. The one that made her wonder at the man's thoughts, then push down the imaginings as far more than she might wish to know. "Across Hanover, yes — from New London to *Hso-Hsi*. Between the Core Hanover worlds and their Fringe — well, what's become their Fringe and some of which once belonged to others. Just coreward and a bit above some worlds which once belonged to the French Republic, in fact. The Berry March, that is."

Alexis frowned. What was he driving at and what did this scheme have to do with the Berry March? And why should she care?

"The aftermath of Giron, Miss Carew." Eades sat back down. "Admiral Cammack returned with you and your ragtag fleet of little ships. Quite the story — all of the feel-good elements to it." He shook his head. "Quite overshadowed the losses, that. And the questions."

"Questions?"

"Admiral Chipley, Miss Carew, and his fleet. The Hanoverese he pursued."

Alexis felt a chill.

"No official word from Hanover, of course, as they wish us nothing but ill, still. I've heard things, though."

"What? What have you heard?"

"Stories, Miss Carew. Stories of battle after battle, of fleets leaving a trail of broken, dying ships through *darkspace*. Coreward from Giron, Miss Carew — through the Berry March to the edges of the Barbary and beyond into that vast, unruly realm." Eades frowned. "Weren't there more than just Chipley and the Hannies involved in that last action? What was it ... yes, those Berry March ships under Balestra. You're acquainted with a young lieutenant under her, are you not?"

EIGHT

It was dark, early morning, when Alexis returned planetside, choosing to put down in Port Arthur rather than the farm, since she'd only have to return to the town for the day's Conclave session in any case.

The night had been spent in conference with Eades, picking the man's brain for any bit of information he had on the Berry March fleet or Delaine Theibaud — which was precious little, come to the whole of it. Bits and pieces, rumor and story, but enough to make Alexis believe him that there was a chance the survivors of that brutal, running battle might have made the Barbary — and might be there still, somehow unable to send word or return home.

She left Eades without giving him an answer, though she was certain she'd decided. If there truly was a chance to find Delaine, if he might be in need of her help, then she would go. Still, it wouldn't hurt for Eades to stew a bit over whether his plots and plans would come to fruition.

Likely, Eades knew her answer as well and there'd be no real stewing on his part, despite her efforts.

There would be stewing on her own, though — not over whether she'd go, but how to tell her grandfather.

The second day of the Conclave passed in a blur, with neither the drama nor important questions of the first day. Alexis found herself distracted time and again, having to desperately search her memory for the last thing she'd heard whenever her grandfather asked an opinion of her on the current measure. Her thoughts were scattered, leaping from hope she could find Delaine, fear that she'd find he was no longer alive, and anxiety over telling her grandfather that she was about to sail off again on some mad quest.

ALEXIS CHEWED another forkful of peas. Her thought to tell her grandfather over dinner, at one of the nicer restaurants in Port Arthur, might have been effective in keeping the volume of his objections down, but not the content.

"Are you mad?"

"The last man to ask me that, I threatened to shoot," Alexis muttered, carving a bite off the slab of roast beef on her plate.

"What?"

"Nothing, grandfather, I'm sorry."

Neither was the Mylins' presence having the mitigating effect she'd hoped for, though they did seem to be less inclined to call her mad.

"Now, Denholm ..." Mylin began.

"Don't you 'now, Denholm' me, Sewall, as though it's me being unreasonable. It's a 'now, Alexis' we should be hearing over this nonsense."

"It is *not* nonsense, grandfather, nor am I mad." She stabbed at a pea, sending it skittering off her plate, over the table, and into Sewall Mylin's lap. She flushed and shot him a look of apology, getting an amused grin in return. "I've a duty as an officer to go."

Alexis knew, even as she heard her own words, that it was the wrong tack to take with her grandfather. Not that he was a stranger to duty, but because he had a different opinion of what hers should be.

"Your duty's to the lands and the people on them now, Lexi-girl. Next in line for the holding shouldn't be off to parts unknown on a whim."

"Hardly a whim, grandfather, and I'm no longer your little girl, I'll thank you to remember."

Alexis immediately regretted saying that, as well — even before she saw the hurt in her grandfather's eyes and the reproof in Sewall Mylin's.

"No. No ... Lexi, Alexis, you're not, I suppose. But you *are* my heir now, and I'm getting no younger."

"That is not a good argument," Alexis pointed out, "as we just yesterday argued that we've the very best of medical care on Dalthus now. Argued it before the whole of the Conclave, in fact."

"She has you there, Denholm," Mylin said. "You'll likely double my age now we've proper health facilities and treatments — and I've another forty or more years."

"Accidents happen," Denholm said, with a glare that made one wonder if he were speaking of his own or Mylin's chances.

"Do you plan to tangle with another bear-cat, grandfather?"

"Shite-weas ... look, that's not the point either." Denholm sighed. "You have no idea, Lexi, how glad I was when the news came that your ship was to pay off — how relieved. These last few years, I've picked up the Naval Gazette and feared I'd read your name on the lists of dead."

Alexis closed her eyes. She knew he'd worried, but to hear him voice it too was different.

"The whole point of the Navy was to give you a bit of time away from Dalthus," he went on. "Time to change the laws so you could inherit, and we have that now. Isn't it the perfect time, with your ship paid off and you on half-pay, to resign that commission and come home for good?" Denholm took a deep breath. "This isn't even the

Then, though, she thought of Julia. There was affection between the two, she knew, but suspected Julia, at least, felt more. Stolen glances around the kitchen, a hand on laid lightly on his forearm or shoulder, even the good-natured teasing that passed between them.

Alexis pursed her lips.

Yes, the signs were there, if one could read them — or weren't blind to them from being dense as stone. Perhaps there was some way she might penetrate that stone and make her grandfather see what was right before him —

"So you love him?" Denholm asked suddenly.

Alexis started, not expecting that question — she'd already answered it, hadn't she? She felt her face grow hot, not really wishing to discuss Delaine with her grandfather. It was her love life, after all, and no part of his —

She broke off, realizing what she'd been musing on even as he'd asked.

Bother.

"I believe I said as much," she said.

Denholm chuckled.

"Said 'enough.' That's an answer to a different question entirely, I think."

"I —" Alexis paused. She *did* love Delaine, but she knew the question Denholm was asking. Was Delaine to her what Lynelle had been — was — to him?

She caught her lip between her teeth and chewed. She'd thought of this more than once, and her thoughts disturbed her. She thought of Delaine and building a life together, but there was no clear vision of what that life would be. Too many other things crowded in from the edges — her ship, though she had none at the moment, her crew, both as some sort of faceless mob gathered around her and all clamoring for a bit of her time and needing to be watched over, and a few more distinct.

Isom needed her, obviously, for she'd have to find some way to get him back to his former career as a legal clerk, no matter how he might claim he was content to serve her. Nabb, obviously, for he was so young — she shrugged off the annoying fact that he was not so very much younger than she herself was — and setting him up in some situation of his own if they weren't called back into the Service soon. All of the *Nightingales* who'd been stranded on Dalthus when the ship paid off needed looking after — even bloody Creasy, who'd somehow managed to convince even some of the Carew farmhands that the vile creature was a sort of spiritual being.

The creature itself held no place in her thoughts, despite her having to admit that she *might* find she woke a bit better rested when the thing somehow managed to find its way into the house and past her locked door. Likely the thing simply took advantage of her more peaceful nights to claim a place in her bedding.

Then, if she were to take over the lands, there were all of the men and women who worked the Carew holdings. The farmhands, those in the villages, the miners — and now, even, the gallenium mining in the belt. Independent and rough as they may be, they deserved her attention too — at least to see to it they had as safe a way to do their work as she could manage, and a fair price paid for their goods. There was talk some of the merchants already setting up shop on the stations were running the sorts of scams that seemed to come with every mining boom and —

No, she broke off, there was just *so* much and so many she must be responsible for.

How could she ever devote the effort to Delaine that he deserved when there were so many others she had to care for? Come to that, how had the Mylins managed it for so long? They had nearly as many hands looking to them and seemed as conscientious as —

"Lexi-girl?"

Denholm's words brought her back from her thoughts and made her smile. At least her objection hadn't stopped him from calling her that — she'd have been saddened if it had. There was a comfort to it, even if it came with him questioning her a bit.

"I'm not certain how to explain it."

Denholm smiled. "There's a lot of that comes with love."

"I suppose so." She caught her lip between her teeth, worrying at it, then decided to press on with her own question. "Grandfather, have you ever — since Grandmother passed, I mean — well ..."

Denholm snorted. "Sauce, eh? No. No time for courting, not with the lands to manage." He paused, as though deciding what to tell her, then went on, "To tell the truth — I just can't bear the thought. There'll never be anyone like your grandmother for me again, I think."

"Is it not lonely?"

"Brandon and Mercia come up to the house to pass an evening now and then, and there're the Mylins, of course. See them nearly once a month, I think."

Alexis had meant something more than an evening's talk with the farm's foreman and wife, or the rare dinner with a neighbor. She had the sudden decision that her grandfather had been alone long enough — Julia, as well, if she judged things correctly, for it seemed to Alexis that the woman was waiting on her grandfather to see what was right before his eyes all these years.

"And Julia, of course," Alexis said.

"Aye. Don't know what I'd have done without her. Your father was a handful as a lad, and you got a double portion of it yourself."

"She was, is, like a mother to me — to my father, as well, I imagine."

Denholm nodded. "We're all lucky she made her way here."

Alexis winced as she bit her lip a bit too hard, wondering at her next words.

"Have you ever considered it?"

"Considered what?"

"Well, that you and Julia do get on quite well."

"Near forty years together, we'd have to." Denholm grinned. "She'd have trussed me like one of her chickens long since, else."

"I meant," Alexis said carefully, "that getting on so well, for so long ... perhaps there might be ... something there?"

Denholm stopped walking.

"What 'something'? Are you suggesting —" He frowned at her. "Now don't you go poking around in what's not your business, Lexi-girl. Julia and I've worked out all the 'somethings' we might need over the years without any help from you or anyone else. Besides which, the thought's laughable — I'm nearly twice her age."

"There's only a dozen years between you!"

"Well —" Denholm cleared his throat and resumed walking. "I was nearly twice her age when I bought her indenture, so it's quite the same thing."

NINE

Her second meeting with Eades aboard the station at least started without the drama of a slap, much as she might have liked to repeat that. Despite his explanations, she still blamed him for Giron, and didn't trust him in the least.

"So how will this work, then?" she asked as the last of the servers left the private room. Eades had, at least, offered dinner for this meeting, and the plate before her was full of good food. "Do you have some writ to take *Nightingale* out of ordinary and put her back into service?"

"*Nightingale*?" Eades asked.

"My ship —"

Eades laughed and Dansby shook his head.

"That thing?" Eades asked. "No, far too small for this undertaking."

"You'll need more than a little cutter for this, Ricki," Dansby said. "The Barbary worlds may not have frigates — they're limited to gunboats and an occasional xebec — but a cutter's not enough."

Alexis frowned. "What will I be commanding, then?"

"*Elizabeth*," Dansby said.

"Your ship? Are you planning to come as well?" She didn't know how she might feel about that. Her last voyage with Dansby had been ... difficult. What with shooting Anya Mynatt and having to hide her status as a Naval officer from the crew. She didn't relish the idea of sailing with any of Dansby's crew again, come to that. They were a hard lot and none too reliable, she thought — at least not in any way she valued.

Dansby's gaze hardened. "Never. I had my fill of the Barbary long ago and I'll never return. Nor will any of my crew."

Alexis raised an eyebrow. What was she getting herself into, that a crew of Dansby's, smugglers and the next thing to pirates themselves, wouldn't go for?

"You're giving me one of your ships?" Alexis took a moment to let that sink in. She'd been expecting all along that Eades had *Nightingale* in mind — it hadn't occurred to her that she'd be commanding a different ship entirely, much less one of Dansby's.

"*Loaning,* Rikki, I expect her back." Dansby's eyes were flint. "Back and whole, I'll hold you to that."

Alexis nodded. She knew how Dansby felt about his ships.

He grinned suddenly. "Back, whole, and with my share of the profits, mind you."

"Your share?"

"As ship-owner, yes — sponsoring your enterprise, as it were."

"Of course, there'd be some profit for you in this."

Dansby shrugged. "Profit for all, if you do it right."

Alexis frowned. She took the moment to eat a bite of food, realizing that she really had no clear idea of what she was about to embark upon.

"What ... No, pardon me, *how* exactly does one profit in this endeavor? If I'm not under a Naval commission, that is."

"Mightily," Dansby said, taking a grin.

"If done properly," Eades added. He slid fingers over his tablet and Alexis' *pinged* in response. "Here is your Letter of Marque and Reprisal, authorizing you, Alexis Arleen Carew, as a private person, to equip, command, and sail a private vessel in furtherance of the Crown's campaign against certain enemies. Very specific enemies, in this case — any and all ships, private or of local government charter, of the worlds of the Barbary, which you may reasonably believe to have engaged in the acts of piracy or in the slave trade."

"Slavery?"

"Oh, yes," Dansby said.

"The worlds of the Barbary are remote," Eades said, "some very much so, and sparsely settled, with little to entice new settlers or merchants. As such, the pirates there, attacking the ships enroute to *Hso-hsi* and back, found an easy outlet for some of the merchant crews."

"Black-hearted devils, the lot of them," Dansby added.

"As may be. Slavery is not uncommon there."

Alexis took a moment to read the document.

"This bit — 'Any allied Court of Prize, foreign or domestic'? What does that mean, exactly?"

"Working, as you will be, far from New London space, it would be impractical for you to bring prizes back to New London worlds. This authorizes foreign prize courts to reach a determination on any ships you take, awarding you accordingly."

"I see."

Alexis read through the document. There were bits that bothered her, but she'd looked up the whole concept and it was legal ... just. The Crown, at least, endorsed it.

"What is *Elizabeth*, then?" she asked, wanting to know more about the ship she was to command.

"Topsail schooner," Dansby said. "Fast enough in a following wind, with fore-and-aft rigs to sail close. Pierced for twenty-four guns — more than her size warrants, but —" Dansby shrugged. "She's had a checkered past, our *Elizabeth*." He took a deep breath. "You'll want to rechristen her something, though — the name and ship are known in those worlds."

"I thought you didn't frequent the Barbary?"

"There're some have long memories. So many guns at her size is a thing people mark, so I'll show you how to rechristen her so she'll respond as whatever name you choose — she'll not mind. She's used to wearing a disguise or two. Best not to mention my name in those worlds, either — save to one or two contacts I'll leave you."

Alexis raised her brows at that. "It sounds as though there's a tale there."

Dansby shrugged. "Some things were done to me and there were things done in return." His eyes gained that hard look again. "There's no need to dredge up the past, though. *Elizabeth's* a fine ship, the best for these purposes in that region. Better by far than a frigate, getting caught up in shoals there — you'll want to review your sailing notes, by the way, for they've some tricky systems. More heavy stars than you'd expect — far apart, so the dark matter collects more readily about them. That makes for difficult sailing. The shoals will be more fully-formed there, you'll find, and quite a bit shallower than you're used to — Elizabeth spreads her mass out well-enough, but you'll still find trouble if you look for it. More than one system in the Barbary has a full halo, and you'll only be able to approach at all along the ecliptic."

Alexis nodded, still curious about Dansby's history with the region, but feeling this wasn't the time to ask more. His words about the shoals bothered her more. There was a reason the Navy's lieutenants' examinations went on about shoals to leeward so very much.

In *darkspace*, the dark matter tended to collect around normal-space masses, forming shoals that interacted with ships in distressing ways — miring them in place and crushing hulls if the collection of dark matter were great enough. Since normal-space masses generally meant stars and planets, the shoals formed mostly in systems — to a greater or lesser degree, depending on how many other systems were nearby. Since the dark energy winds tended to blow toward normal-space systems, the shoals were nearly always to leeward of an approaching ship.

"*Elizabeth's* not massy — she's a shallow enough draft to get you through most, though you'll have to find channels."

Alexis nodded. She'd have to take his word for now, at least.

"And a crew," she asked, "if yours won't go?"

"That," Eades said, "is for you to arrange."

"What?" Alexis was liking this less and less. "I've less than three dozen former *Nightingales* on Dalthus — barely enough to make sail on a schooner, let alone fight her."

Eades gave her an odd look. "This is not a Naval operation, Miss Carew. You are a private ship and responsible for your own crew — there'll be no levies from the hulks nor impressment service helping you in this. Recruit a crew in various ports as the merchantmen do — there are always men who think prize money is preferable to wages."

"Zariah's flush with men off ships put up in ordinary," Dansby said. "Penduli and Lesser Ichthorpe more so, and they're all much on your way to the Barbary, as well. You're not unknown there."

"Unknown?"

"A reputation, Miss Carew," Eades said. "Men won't want to sail into danger such as privateering with just anyone — they want *some* reason to expect a profitable journey, after all."

"I have a reputation?"

Eades smiled. "In some quarters."

Alexis wasn't at all sure how she felt about that. What quarters and what her reputation was were questions she'd like to ask, but she suspected neither Eades nor Dansby would be able to resist the urge to tweak her with some tale. She'd endeavor to find out some other way.

"Taking ships when we're not at war," she said instead, "selling them at foreign prize courts, recruiting a crew by dint of profit ... this privateering sounds more and more like piracy by the moment."

"You're missing the crucial difference between them, Rikki."

"What's that?"

"There's one of the two what doesn't get you hanged."

DANSBY WALKED her from meeting with Eades to her boat, seeing her off, she supposed.

"When will you leave?" he asked.

"The evening the Conclave ends. I owe it to my grandfather to stay through that, I think."

Dansby nodded. He seemed almost pensive now, not his usual ebullient self.

"Why are you helping Eades in this?" she asked. "I'd thought you were done with him before."

"The man has hooks and lines set everywhere, Rikki. He'll snag you and reel you in, no matter how you try to evade it — just as he did with this tale of your young man."

"Tale? Do you think he's being dishonest about it?"

"No, one thing about Eades is everything he tells you will turn out true — whether it's the entire truth is quite another matter, but it will be true."

"Why is it you won't go back to the Barbary yourself, Mister Dansby?"

Dansby shook his head. "Still a tale for another day, and nothing to do with yours." He paused. "I do have a bit of advice for you, if you'll take it."

"I'll hear it."

Dansby grinned. "That's my Rikki — a skeptical thought'll do you well where you're going." He sobered. "You've never sailed aboard a private ship before, Rikki, so know this. There's no fleets, no admirals, and no Admiralty to this — you're answerable to no one but yourself." He grinned again. "And the ship's owner, which is me, so keep an eye toward profit, will you."

"As much as I may."

"Oh, I know where your priorities lie — with that Frenchie, no doubt. But you'll need to pay your crew and supply your ship — my ship — so profit's needed. Quite a lot of it — none of your crew will be satisfied with the Navy's rates. They'll want prizes and the promise of more."

Alexis nodded. She'd caught that already in the expectant mutters amongst her *Nightingales* — they were loyal to her, she had no doubt of that, but they were also looking forward to a cruise that would fill their purses.

"I'll keep that in mind."

"See that you do. And take care of my ship — she's one of my first, named after my mother, and I'll have her back sound, if you don't mind."

Alexis raised an eyebrow at that.

"Why, Mister Dansby, I'd thought you named all your ships after women you were trying to bed."

Dansby frowned for a moment, then laughed. "No, Rikki, what I told you was that it's remarkable what a girl will do when she *thinks* you've named a ship after her — the actual naming isn't all that necessary."

Alexis shook her head at that, but had to smile. The man was a rogue, no doubt.

"Just be easy with her — I've seen what you do to ships."

"My last ship is right out there, all in one piece, thank you."

"And I note you weren't actually aboard her in her last action, so ..."

TEN

The last day of the Conclave ran later than expected, with several measures becoming unexpectedly contentious. It was after dark when the meetings ended, and Alexis walked with Denholm and the Mylins back to their hotel. Her grandfather would be returning to the farmstead in the morning, but Alexis planned to leave for the station, and thence the Barbary, that very night. She'd already returned to the farmstead to say her goodbyes there the day before, and it was only her new position as her grandfather's heir that kept her at the meetings.

It wouldn't do to rush out of the Conclave when I've just been granted reason to attend, after all.

Isom was waiting in the hotel lobby, an antigrav cart with their belongings beside him. She was disheartened to see the creature's pressure cage atop the pile of her chests and spacebag. Wishful thinking and a hint or two had clearly not been enough to convince Isom to leave the vile thing back at the farm.

"You're set on leaving tonight, then?" Denholm asked on seeing Isom and the baggage.

Alexis nodded. "The boat's on the field now."

The boat and nearly every *Nightingale* who'd stayed behind on the Carew farmstead when the ship paid off. Only two of those were remaining behind, taken with the colonial life more than spacing, once they had a taste of it — and, truth be told, in the process of courting girls in the village, so could hardly be blamed.

On the other hand, there were more than a few waiting at the field precisely because they'd been courting girls in the village — both for the courting becoming a bit more serious than they were entirely comfortable with or, in the case of some, where the girls had found out about each other.

Altogether, she had a core of nearly thirty men from *Nightingale* and another half dozen farmhands who'd signed on — enough to sail *Elizabeth* to Zariah, or anywhere reasonably civilized, but not enough to fight her, should it come to that.

Denholm turned to her, opened his mouth to speak, then closed it and sighed. Alexis laid a hand on his arm, knowing he wanted to ask her once more to stay, and grateful he'd made the effort not to.

She wrapped her arms around him and squeezed. "I'll write often."

Her grandfather sighed again. "Aye, as will I."

HER EXCITEMENT GREW as they made their way toward the landing field. She might have hired a cart to get them there, but it was a pleasant night and her last in-atmosphere for some time. It was odd, she thought, how one could long for an open sky while aboard ship, yet equally long for close bulkheads when planet-bound.

The way to the field led them from the areas of Port Arthur catering to the colonists with finer shops and hotels to the few blocks surrounding the field which held the establishments meant for visiting spacers — and now miners in from the belt.

Oddly, Alexis felt more comfortable away from the finery — not perhaps, in the environs down some of the darker alleyways, but far more comfortable with the spacers' pubs than some place where the host insisted on tossing a napkin in your lap as though you couldn't accomplish such a feat for yourself.

With no warning more than a moving shadow, figures appeared in the alley beside her. Alexis turned, but before she could identify them, a bag of some sort was tossed over her head and cinched tight at her neck. Her fingers made it to the cord too late and could find no purchase.

She heard Isom cry out, and the crash of baggage tumbling from their cart.

Whoever had slipped the bag over her head had a knee or forearm in her back for leverage.

She swung at her attacker — hands, elbows, and even kicked back with her heavy boots, she connected, but not with enough force to drive him off. She raised a foot again, hoping to connect with a shin, but her other leg was knocked from under her and she went to the ground.

Breath driven from her, she was pinned beneath her attacker's weight.

"Careful! Get her feet!" a voice whispered, and a second attacker did, catching her feet and holding them down while wrapping something around them.

Her left arm was stuck under her body, while she groped with her right to find something, anything, to grasp and twist that might drive off the man on her back — or to reach the small flechette pistol tucked at the small of her back. Even that effort was stopped as her hand was grasped and yanked painfully up to her shoulder blades.

"Enough of that, you bloody bitch," a harsh voice whispered.

She heard Isom cry out again, and the meaty sound of blows, then more distant shouting.

Then there was a sharp *crack* of ionizing air from a laser shot, and the hands holding her were suddenly gone. She rolled to her back, clawing at the cord around her throat, finally loosened it enough to pull the bag from her head, and kicked at the cord binding her ankles.

Cool air made her realize how hot and stuffy that bag had become in such a short time.

There were more shouts and footsteps.

Hands grasped her shoulders to pull her up and she almost struck out, before sense told her the attackers were long gone and this was just someone come to help.

"Are you all right, Lieutenant Carew?"

Alexis turned to find it was Edmon Coalson helping her to her feet. He grasped her arms firmly as she swayed. A slight pain twinged her shoulder, where the arm had been pulled behind her, but otherwise she felt uninjured.

"I am, I — damn me, Isom! Is he all right?" She shrugged off Coalson's hands and made her way to Isom's side. There was a bag over his head, as well, which one of Coalson's friends, Warriner, was only now removing.

After she assured herself that Isom was whole, if a bit battered, she looked around the street, which was crowded now, though it had been nearly empty when they'd been attacked. People gathered to watch the aftermath, but those who'd intervened seemed to all be of Coalson's group — him and a trio of friends.

"I heard a shot," Alexis asked. "Did you manage to strike any of them?"

Coalson shook his head.

"No, I fired into the air, not wanting to strike you or your man. The bastards ran off when we got near, but Moring and Kenderdine went after them and may have — ah, here they are now and we'll see."

Two other men were approaching through the crowd, also part of Coalson's set by their clothing and bearing, but Alexis could tell there'd be no joy there. From the look on their faces she was certain the assailants had got away.

"Moring and I were on their heels," Kenderdine said, "but lost them in the alleyways nearer the field — once we broke out onto the field itself ... well, even so late there's a great deal of to and fro from the boats." He shook his head. "Could have been any of them out there."

"Damn," Coalson said. He turned to Alexis. "I'm sorry we couldn't catch them — do you have any idea what they were about?"

Alexis picked up the bag which had been thrown over head from the ground and fingered it. It was the heavy, waxed canvas many of the miners used to contain their tools. Perhaps Doakes and his new constabulary might make some use of them to identify the assailants, but she had her ideas of it already. Monks and his ilk were just the sort to pull such an ambush, she thought, but without proof and with her set to leave the system, there was little she could do about it.

She shook her head. "Nothing above suspicions, I'm afraid."

"World's turned upside down when a lady can be assaulted in the streets," Warriner muttered, helping Isom in setting their cart to rights.

Alexis had to raise an eyebrow at that, for she'd never been on friendly terms with Warriner — the man was usually too smug and superior for her tastes — but they were of a similar class of holder and she assumed he'd like to see no one of the original settlers so treated.

Coalson held out his hand. "I'll turn that over to Doakes, if you like — along with the other. I'd heard you were leaving this evening and I assume you've not the time to do it yourself."

Alexis nodded and handed him the bag. "Thank you. I fear I've nothing to tell him that might be helpful, either — only some muffled curses in voices I couldn't identify." She frowned. "It does seem odd that they treated Isom so much more harshly than me, though." She felt at herself and realized that, aside from the bag's abrasion about her neck, she wasn't very much injured at all. "It was almost as though they made an especial effort to avoid doing so."

Coalson grunted while Warriner said, "Afraid to truly harm their betters, as it should be." He scowled around at surrounding buildings. "We'd crack down on this cesspool if that ever happened."

"Indeed," Coalson echoed, then to Alexis, "Will you accept our escort the remaining way to the field, lieutenant? I doubt these miscreants will try again, but one can never be too careful."

Alexis nodded. She doubted that as well, but it would do no harm. "Thank you, Mister Coalson."

In a trice Coalson's friends had her baggage — vile creature included, it not having been released to Port Arthur's mercies in the ruckus, as any benevolent universe would have seen fit to grant her. Warriner even took the managing of the cart from Isom, patting him on the back and telling him to rest himself.

They reached the edge of the landing field, where Nabb and the other *Nightingales* waited, without incident. Nabb eyed Coalson warily and his jaw clenched as Isom explained what had happened.

"We got her from here," Nabb said, edging Warriner away from the luggage sled with his bulk, two others from her boat crew flanking him.

Warriner gave way with an amused smirk, but Coalson looked around at the field, brow furrowed with concern.

"Most of these boats are owned by some rough folk, lieutenant," he said. "Perhaps we should —"

"Not so polished ourselves," Nabb muttered.

Coalson grinned at him, causing Nabb to clench his jaw. "Indeed."

"Meant we can protect the captain," Nabb said.

"Certainly," Coalson agreed. "My friends and I were only necessary while you were ... elsewhere."

Nabb bristled and squared his shoulders while Sills and Paskell, flanking him, cracked their knuckles.

Alexis sighed. Were they really prepared to argue about who might best escort her across the landing field? Men were such ... boys, at times — as though she needed their escort. Though Coalson's arrival had been timely. She supposed she did if she were taken by surprise, outnumbered, and outweighed by assailants — she'd have to take pains to see that the first didn't happen again.

"Surely you and your friends were on your way somewhere,

Mister Coalson?" she asked. "I've no wish to delay you further — glad as I am for your assistance already." She nodded to Nabb with a smile. "I'm certain two dozen and more burly spacers can see me safely through any roughness we may encounter from here on."

"If you're certain," Coalson said. "May I be of any further service, lieutenant?"

Alexis had to smile, he was being so bloody courteous and such a far cry from their meetings years ago — it seemed he had truly changed and was almost charming now. She supposed she'd changed as well.

He's not nearly so full of himself and I'm not nearly so inclined toward indulging my temper. I suppose we've both matured ...

She realized with the thought, that they'd each had experiences thrusting maturity on them — experiences that their peers, such as Warriner for Coalson and Lauryn Arundel for Alexis, lacked. She had all she'd been through in the Navy and Coalson had faced the loss of his father, the disgrace at his family's involvement in some nefarious doings, and the need to take over running his family holdings at quite a young age.

It may be we've far more in common than we did when I was fifteen, as well.

She gave Coalson a grateful smile and, for the first time between them, she supposed, there was real warmth in it. She held out her hand to him.

"I believe that will be all, Mister Coalson — I have my *Nightingales* about me now. Though you have my true gratitude for coming along as you did. It was the nick of time, as they say."

Coalson smiled as well, surprising her by taking her hand and raising it to his lips. Alexis flushed, as only one other man had ever done that — and the association with Delaine quite confused her when standing next to Edmon Coalson.

"Nothing more than a gentleman must do, lieutenant," Coalson assured her, lowering her hand and releasing it. "I'm only sorry I could not have been there sooner."

ELEVEN

They made their way across the field, winding their way amongst the other landing craft, to Dansby's boat. The field was dark, lit only by the lights of the boats they passed, and those were concentrated at the loading ramps for the most part.

A glance behind showed Coalson and his friends following and Alexis smiled. Obviously they'd not wanted to risk her, despite the group of muscled spacers and farmhands she was walking with.

The other group, Coalson especially, was attempting to look as though they were quite nonchalantly making their own way, and doing a poor job of it, as the field itself led nowhere but to the boats sitting on it.

Her glance back was caught by Nabb pushing the luggage sled, his own bag carried by Sills. She smiled tolerantly as her coxswain looked back as well, caught sight of Coalson's group, and scowled.

"Mister Coalson," Alexis called loudly enough to be sure he heard. "If you're going to insist on tagging along like a lost puppy, then you may as well walk with us the rest of the way."

She heard some muttered words, not clearly enough to make

them out, but saw Coalson give Warriner a shove and the others laugh at it.

Almost sheepishly, Coalson approached — his friends following behind with grins.

"It's only that I wished to see you safely away." He paused, then rushed on, "Not, I mean, that I wish you away — I don't. Damn me, not that I wish you to stay, either ..."

Warriner and the others were nearly laughing out loud and Nabb openly snorted.

Coalson glanced back at his friends and looked quite embarrassed, something Alexis had never noted in him. He took a deep breath. "I'd not see you attacked again is all I'm saying."

Warriner was whispering to the others and grinning openly, which set Alexis' teeth on edge. Of the group, she had to admit she liked Coalson better than Warriner, and saw no need to mock a friend's concern, no matter how poorly phrased. She regretted, now, her choice of words in calling him over — certain Warriner would make use of the puppy label to needle Coalson for some time.

"Come along, then," she said, and making a sudden decision, "Edmon."

She reached for his arm and he extended it automatically, though his eyebrows raised at that and the familiarity of her using his given name.

They resumed walking and a moment later Coalson said quietly, "Thank you ... Alexis."

"For walking with you?"

"For deflecting Warriner a bit," Coalson said, still quiet. "My ... concern for you has given him a bit of a target for his wit."

"It must be a large and rather slow-moving thing for his wit to have a hope of striking true."

"Certainly large," Coalson said, "and growing more so."

Alexis glanced over at him with a raised eyebrow.

"I —" Coalson's step faltered for a moment, then he grinned and shook his head. "You do have a way of flustering a man. I meant to say that my concern for you has grown."

Alexis was suddenly more aware of their closeness as they walked. Her hand on his forearm and her own forearm held tight to his side — tighter, perhaps, than was entirely appropriate. Closer than was appropriate, as well, for his arm brushed against her side with every step.

"I believe it's I who owe you some further thanks," she said, changing the subject.

Coalson's brow furrowed. "For chasing off those fellows? You already did —"

"For your act at the Conclave," Alexis said. "We didn't speak after, and I believe you did carry the day for me."

Coalson snorted. "It was only the right thing to do — time we put away some things from the past. Past time, perhaps."

"Still, you have my thanks."

Coalson laid his free hand over hers on his forearm. He was silent, but Alexis thought there was more of a message there — one she had no time to understand, for they'd arrived at Dansby's boat.

Alexis paused for a moment and stared at the craft, remembering another time, years ago, when she'd left Dalthus from this very field. Then it had been to join the Navy and all that entailed over the last few years. Now it was to something very different — and she was leaving not because she had no future on her home world, but because she'd gained one and wasn't at all certain it was right for her.

One more time — once more on a quarterdeck. I'll find Delaine and bring him and any others home, then I'll settle in to help Grandfather. She turned to regard the growing town of Port Arthur and smiled a bit sadly. *Once more.*

"Come on, then, Rikki!" Dansby called from the boat's ramp. "Before your churlish sot of a chandler levies me another day's landing charges! You, rather, as I'm starting your accounts for this endeavor this very moment!"

Alexis bit her tongue to keep from snapping back at Dansby, not wanting to show her temper with Coalson and his friends about. She'd managed to alleviate some of her previous reputation for having a sharp tongue, after all, and didn't wish to build a new one. She'd have to work with those young men for decades, once she returned to actively working her family lands.

"He's a rather familiar sort," Coalson murmured to her.

"He has his ways," Alexis allowed, then, not at all certain why she felt the sudden need to defend Avrel Dansby, "Not a bad sort, though, once you get to know him."

"He's the look of a rascal about him," Coalson said. "Are you certain he's to be trusted? You'll be safe?"

Alexis almost laughed. She was about to set off in command of a private ship, with only the barest core of a crew from *Nightingale* and a few hands from the family farm, off to hunt pirates in one of the most lawless sections of space this side of the Core's settled planets.

"Avrel Dansby is the least of my worries about this endeavor, I assure you."

Coalson looked skeptical, but said no more.

"Thank you for the escort, Edmon, sirs," she added, nodding to his friends. "And the rescue."

"Of course." Coalson shook his head. "I can't imagine what Port Arthur's come to, when one can be accosted in the street like that."

"I suspect it was some of the miners I've had run-ins with, and not some larger problem."

"Perhaps," Coalson said. "In any case, I wish you good fortune in your endeavor, Miss Carew ... Alexis." He offered his hand, raising Alexis' to his lips again when she took it, and giving her the same sense of uneasiness she'd felt before. "I hope to see you safely home again, soon — perhaps you'd do me the honor of allowing me to host a welcome party when that day comes?"

"I —"

"Merely give it some thought, will you? After all, we younger holders —" He gestured to his friends and Alexis. "— are the future of Dalthus."

"Yes — thank you. All of you, for your help today, again."

Coalson and the others nodded, smiling, and left. Alexis made her way up the ramp, followed by Isom and their baggage cart.

"About time," Dansby said from the ramp's top. He nodded at the departing group. "Who's that fellow?"

"One of the other settlers," Alexis said, deciding to say nothing about the attack on her and Isom. "Seeing us off."

Dansby's eyes narrowed. "I'd watch yourself, Rikki," he said, turning to enter the boat. "Looks the proper rascal, that one."

DANSBY TOOK the pilot's seat for the trip up from Dalthus, Alexis in the cockpit to starboard.

The passenger compartment held a little over thirty men, former *Nightingales* and a half dozen from the farmstead who'd never been into space before, but had stepped forward when it became known Alexis would be setting sail once more. Some of those last were indentures and she didn't know how that would be handled in the farmstead's books. She felt a bit bad about taking men off when her grandfather had made such an investment in their future labor, but he'd shrugged the matter aside.

She couldn't help feeling that she'd taken advantage of him, both in removing hands from the farmstead — he'd come to rely on those *Nightingales* who'd stayed with her, as well — and to be leaving again. Perhaps "taken advantage of" wasn't the proper term, either — perhaps it was that she felt she'd disappointed him in some way, though he'd said nothing of the sort.

"You're unusually pensive, Rikki."

Alexis looked around to find that the boat had already lifted while she was lost in thought. Dansby was talking while piloting the boat, looking from the controls to the viewports and not at her.

"Isn't leaving one's home always a bit pensive?" she asked. Dansby grunted and it occurred to Alexis that she knew very little about the man, despite all they'd been through together during their incursion into Hanoverese space. "Where is your own home, Mister Dansby? I don't believe you've ever said."

"No, I haven't." He nodded to the viewport. "*Elizabeth's* in a low orbit, you should be able to catch sight of her shortly."

That caught Alexis' attention and she was hunched forward, searching the darkening space in front of them for sight of an orbiting ship, before she realized that his words were likely an effort to distract her in just such a way. She sat back with an effort, still keeping her gaze ahead of the boat, but also paying some attention to Dansby. It might bother her that he knew her well enough to choose exactly what would throw her attention elsewhere, but he'd also given a bit of himself away at the same time in avoiding the topic.

"Why is that?" she asked. "Surely your operations have some base, at least?"

"I prefer to be mobile." Dansby nodded toward Alexis' side of the viewport. "There — trailing the station."

Alexis turned, knowing she'd been put off again, but the chance to see a new ship, her new ship, overcame any curiosity about Dansby.

The station was easy enough to pick out now, a large light, details still indistinct, but clearly what it was. There were any number of smaller lights visible around it, though — ranging from merchantmen to ore carriers to the miners' small sleds, barely large enough for a man to live in for weeks at a time.

She kept watching as they drew closer. A topsail schooner, Dansby had said, so she'd have three masts, midway back along the hull instead of radiating around the bow as a ship-rigged vessel would have. She couldn't make out which ship he meant at this distance, but had no doubt Dansby could — and no doubt she'd be able to after sailing in her for a time. A spacer learned to recognize her ship in ways others simply couldn't.

"The last of my crew will leave as we approach," Dansby said.

Alexis noted that his jaw was a bit tight. "Your lads will have to take it from there."

"Why are you doing this?" Alexis asked. There had to be something more to it than had been said, she thought. Dansby would certainly never volunteer to help Eades in one of his schemes, and the turnover of the ship all entire, without even an officer known to Dansby aboard, must irk him.

Dansby gave her the grin she'd become so familiar with while traveling with him. "Money, of course."

Alexis shook her head. Dansby's light tone and grin aside, the rest of his body belied a tension he didn't voice.

"No," she said, "you're worried about something and don't like it. I can't imagine Eades has such a hold over you that it's worth an entire ship."

Dansby sighed. "No. But never underestimate him — his hooks have barbs, and they set themselves deep. Remember that in your dealings with him."

He was silent for a moment, but Alexis let it build. She had a feeling he was working his way toward saying more.

"I can't return to the Barbary," he said at last. "I've too much history there and too many old ... acquaintances. But neither do I like Eades' sending you there — you're too much a babe in the woods for that place."

Alexis raised an eyebrow at that.

"Oh, don't get your hackles up, Rikki, you're, what? Sixteen?"

"Nineteen, thank you. Nearly twenty."

Dansby nodded. "A babe. Oh, you've seen things no babe should, and done things no babe ought, but still a babe."

Alexis thought it a measure of her own gained maturity that she said nothing to this, merely allowing Dansby to go on. She'd learn more from letting him speak than taking offense at his words.

"But, still, I knew when Eades told me of his plan that you'd jump at it, besotted as you are with your young lieutenant. Love turns one's brains to mush, you know, and at your age the thing's not fully baked to begin with."

Yes, I'll let him keep talking — there'll be time to shoot him later.

"I can't go with you and I can't stop you, so the most I can offer is a decent ship. The Dark knows what sort of tub Eades would find for you, left to his own devices."

That left unsaid, of course, the *why* of Dansby's wanting to help her at all.

"And if you should manage to make your way out of this mad journey, I imagine there'll be piles of prize money in it." Dansby grinned again. "Better it fill my purse than another's."

He sobered.

"I've left you some notes in the log. Systems and people it'll be safe for you to talk to ..." He frowned. "Not safe, no, most of them, but a few who owe me and will want to clear their ledgers of it. Some few of them will be willing to take a ship or two off your hands, as well — closer to the action than any of the prize courts Eades will allow." He paused again. "There'll be less red tape involved selling to those, so I'll expect you not to cheat me too much on ship's books."

Oddly, Alexis found that she took more offense to that than to his calling her a "babe" or suggesting her brain wasn't fully set.

"I've never cheated anyone, Mister Dansby, and would not even you."

Dansby shrugged, working the boat's controls and altering their course to pass behind a mining sled which was crossing their path.

"No, you wouldn't, Rikki — and that's much of what you have to learn, I think. There's a universe of people who'll cheat you as their very nature. One has to think a bit like them to recognize that, and I fear you're ill-prepared for them."

Alexis bristled at that. "I've found most people will behave honestly, if that's what they receive in turn."

"Have you really, Rikki?" For the first time since they'd boarded, Dansby took his eyes from the controls and viewport, and met her gaze.

Alexis was surprised at the look in Dansby's eyes, for it was far softer and more serious than she'd expect of him. The surprise gave her pause, and she considered his words. What *had* her real experience been in the wider universe off her farmstead?

Her first thoughts were of the officers and "gentlemen" she'd encountered. They were a mixed lot, no doubt — *Hermione's* a seeping pile of rot she never hoped to encounter again in life, while she still had Captain Grantham and the officers of *Merlin* as a sort of ideal to aspire to.

Dansby seemed to view the world so differently than she did, and the difference made her uncomfortable think on.

DANSBY WAS as good as his word about the ship, at least.

As they approached, another boat undocked and sped toward the station. Dansby brought his into contact and waited at the docking tube while her men went aboard. Alexis waited with him, despite the protocol that officers should be the first off a boat.

"You're not coming aboard?" she asked.

Dansby shook his head. "She's yours now, until you return." With that and a last, "Remember, Rikki, keep an eye to my profits," he fairly shoved her through the tube to the ship and closed the boat's hatch. A moment later he was undocked and making his way to the station.

Alexis' first experience of *Elizabeth* was one of odd, almost eerie, silence. The area near the docking tube was empty except for Isom and Villar, the rest of the crew having scattered to the far points of the ship. First to the berthing deck so as to lay claim to the prime spots and then to explore. Only an occasional shout or laugh echoing from a companionway showed the ship wasn't still deserted.

Elizabeth's deck and bulkheads all showed that she was a Dansby ship, with what Alexis knew to be a carefully applied and maintained layer of grime and wear. The effect, as Dansby'd once explained to her, was that of a hard-working merchantman, more concerned with the next cargo than with the spit and polish of a Naval vessel — all in the hopes that the Revenue man would see only what he was supposed to.

Behind that facade, however, she knew that *Elizabeth's* systems would be well-, almost lovingly-, maintained, especially those concerned with Dansby's primary business.

"Have some of the likelier lads begin a search for hidden compartments, will you?" Alexis asked. "I'd like to know about any illicit cargoes aboard before we're stopped and searched by our own Revenue people."

"Aye, sir," Villar said. "And a steady man with each search party, in case they find something the crew shouldn't get into."

"Indeed."

Elizabeth's plan placed the quarterdeck and master's cabin forward, so they made their way there.

The hatch to the master's cabin slid open at Alexis' touch. Dansby having keyed it to her before leaving the ship, and he'd simply used her biometric data stored when she was aboard *Marylin* with him. It bothered her a bit that he'd kept that so handy as to have it available to him now.

The cabin's deck carried the same worn, patina of artfully applied grime as the rest of the ship, though the furnishings were neat and reasonably clean.

"Mister Villar?"

"Sir?"

"We're a bit under-crewed even for an easy sail and with *Elizabeth's* sail plan," Alexis said. "I'll not want the lads overworked, but I'd admire it did we put a bit of polish on the ship." She nodded at the deck and the corridor walls. "If you take my meaning?"

"I do, sir."

"The 'poor merchant' ruse is well enough for Dansby's business, I suppose, but we'll have no need of it as a private ship. You'll see she's squared away?"

"Aye, sir."

Alexis frowned. Would that do, really? Or would the men balk at Naval standards of cleanliness aboard when they weren't, strictly speaking, a Naval crew?

Well, Naval or not, they were *her* crew, and she'd have her ship at her standards.

Her ship.

More than any other, *Elizabeth* would be hers, with no Admiralty to answer to — no one to answer to, in fact, other than possibly Eades and Dansby, her ostensible "sponsors".

Oh, Eades' involvement might make her more "official" than the typical private ship, but there'd be no admirals or senior captains looking over her shoulder.

Nor looking out for me, come to that.

She'd be nearly entirely on her own bottom out there in the Barbary, with little in the way of support, either.

No matter. It won't be the first time I've had no one to depend on but my lads.

The degree of independence and freedom from Naval traditions, though, might have at least one additional benefit.

"One more thing, Mister Villar?"

"Sir?"

"Yes, that."

Villar frowned, and Alexis grinned at his confusion.

"It's always struck me as a bit of nonsense, that form of address." She could see that Villar wasn't understanding. "That 'sir' business. If we're a private ship, then we're not bound by Naval conventions. The merchants and other navies don't adhere to that, do they?"

"No, sir." Villar paused, then returned her grin. "I suppose not. Ma'am, then?"

Alexis started to nod, then stopped. "Why do I picture the village schoolmarm when you say that?"

"I couldn't say ... ma'am. But it does seem ... unsuited to you."

"Indeed."

Isom poked his head in from her pantry. "Perhaps 'miss'?"

Villar nodded. "I did note that was what the folk on your lands called you."

His calling them *her* lands reminded her once again that they would, indeed, be hers, and that there was a bit of running from it in her taking on *Elizabeth*. She'd have to give a great deal of thought to her feelings about the lands and those responsibilities over the next few months.

"That is what they use," she allowed. "Though it's not quite right — it's what one calls a girl, which might be appropriate to my age, and although they say it with respect, I've always felt there was a tiny bit of ... I don't know, condescension in the word."

Villar nodded. "Perhaps. It does have that sort of flavor to it — rather like when the older hands call a snotty 'sir,' as well."

"Yes, exactly like that. As though one has the position of authority without the experience and we'll just humor him, shall we?"

"I'm not certain what else could be ... 'mistress', perhaps?"

"I think not. I've no intention of marrying anytime soon."

Villar grinned. "Well, they do say a captain's married to their ship, so ..." He sobered and cleared his throat at her glare. "So that's right out, then."

Alexis sighed. Was there really not a term for a woman in authority that carried the same sort of gravity and meaning?

"We'll give it some thought," she said finally. "Not too much, mind you, as there's plenty of real work to do."

"Aye ... sir?"

"It'll do for now, I suppose." In truth, she'd been in the Navy so long that anything else seemed unnatural.

They've trained me to it, I suppose.

Villar left to see the crew settled and Alexis closed the hatch behind him.

She surveyed the master's cabin, her cabin now.

Dansby had cleared out his things, as all his crew had, so the space was bare of personal items.

The mode of address still bothered her for some reason. She supposed she should just go with "ma'am," as the merchants and other navies did — though the exact term used in those navies might carry some other weight, coming from a different language, as it did.

Regardless, there were a hundred other things more pressing in *Elizabeth's* fitting out and sailing that were of more import.

She took a deep breath and closed her eyes, seeming to feel the ship settle about her. She'd give the crew a bell or two to find their places and look about their new home, then take a second tour of the vessel and see them set at their tasks. She could hear Isom rattling about in the pantry, seeing to her supplies and his own items, as that would be his berth and her cabins his domain.

The hatch slid open and she opened her eyes to glance that way, expecting some question or aside from him.

Instead it was the vile creature, darting through into her cabins.

It leapt to her tabletop, rose on its hind legs and chittered at her for a moment, as though laughing at her, then was off in a flash into her sleeping cabin.

She felt her lips twitch, then forced them down into a disapproving frown.

"*Isom!* The creature's loose again! If my bedding's soiled by it, I swear by the Dark I'll see it spaced before we clear the Lagrangian point!"

TWELVE

Alexis chose to bypass Zariah and seek a full crew on Penduli. *Elizabeth* was an easily handed ship for sailing and those men she had could manage it for the trip — sailing straight for Penduli shaved a fortnight or more off the transit time, and she was in a hurry to seek out word of Delaine.

As well, the Prize Court at Zariah, primarily a Mister Bramley, was sending her regular letters about her prize award from years ago on her first cruise. The Prize Court then had muddled the facts and reports so badly that they'd had Alexis and only a few others taking a pirate ship themselves, thus awarding the capture's full value. No one, not even her captain at the time nor the ship's full crew, had begrudged it. Those with her had collected hundreds of pounds for the one ship and she herself had several thousand.

Bramley, however, had taken some dislike to her on her last cruise and set about investigating her past. His letters, demanding the whereabouts of all those crew members — which Alexis certainly didn't know — and the location of everyone's awarded prize money, grew more querulous with every arrival.

Alexis was certain he'd receive some notification of her arrival at

Zariah and track her down, so best to avoid that. Penduli would certainly have enough idle hands to crew *Elizabeth*.

She was also unsure of how locating a crew would actually work, but Penduli was a major Naval station, with dozens of ships laid up in ordinary after the cessation of hostilities with Hanover. Thousands of men would have been paid off and at loose ends, and the merchant traffic couldn't have absorbed them all, no matter how lessened by impressment their crews had been during the war.

With so small a crew and *Elizabeth's* full hold of stores, she could have, in fact, made the trip nonstop, but Alexis did make port calls at some systems for fresh supplies and news, and at each stop there were a few prospects looking for a berth. They reached Penduli System some six hands greater than they'd left Dalthus, but Alexis began to question whether she'd manage to field a full crew at all.

Her worries grew when they finally docked and there was no one at the berth in response to the announcement she'd sent to the station's newsfeeds.

"What did you place, sir, if you don't mind me asking?" Villar asked.

"The same as all the other systems we've stopped in," Alexis said. She brought the station's feed up on her tablet and showed him.

Spacers Wanted
Former Royal Navy Preferred
For action in the Barbary
Standard wages and prize distribution
Apply at the private ship Elizabeth
Penduli Station, Quayside

"I ... see," Villar said.

"Hhmm," Isom added, reading over his shoulder.

"What?" Alexis asked. "Is it not good?"

"It is ... straightforward," Villar said.

Isom pursed his lips. "Lacks a certain ..."

"Something," Villar supplied.

"Aye, a something," Isom said.

"What 'something'?" Alexis asked. "It's perfectly factual."

"Well, yes ... yes, it is." Isom nodded. "Factual is a thing, I suppose."

"Indeed. Entirely factual."

"And there is the ship's name," Isom said.

"You did say she'd be renamed," Villar said.

"Well, yes, but I really haven't thought of anything ... I supposed we'd do that prior to reaching the Barbary."

"Hhm," Isom said.

"What?"

"It's only that, well ..."

"It lacks something, sir," Villar said. "For a private ship, I mean."

Alexis stared at them for a moment.

"I suppose you two think you could do better?"

Villar rose quickly. "Happy to help, sir, we'll just ..." He gestured for the hatch and Isom rushed to open it.

"Yes," Isom said, "don't you worry on it. We'll just ..."

"Give it ..." Villar shared a look with Isom.

"Something."

"Aye, something, sir. Never you worry."

THIRTEEN

SPACERS WANTED!
Men of Heart! Men of Action!
Ship paid off and left you IN-ATMOSPHERE?
Are your fortunes still held HOSTAGE by the Navy's PRIZE
COURT?
Seek your NEW FORTUNE amongst the WORLDS of the Barbary!
Captain Alexis Carew, late of HER MAJESTY'S Royal Navy
HERO of Giron!
SAVIOR of Man's Fall!
Now commanding the Private Ship
MONGOOSE
In action against Vile Pirates and Nefarious Slavers,
The Very SERPENTS of the BARBARY!
Captain Carew's first command saw each Man near
FOUR HUNDRED POUNDS
Prize Money!
Her last saw Salvage of
TWO MILLION GUINEAS!
Only the FINEST shall be ACCEPTED!

Apply berth 32, Ring 7, Quayside

ALEXIS STARED at her screen in disbelief. She looked to Isom and Villar, both of whom were grinning widely, then back to her screen.

"This is your something?"

"Aye, isn't it?" Isom said proudly.

"I do think it's quite good, sir," Villar added. "Strikes the right notes."

"Leaving off this 'hero' and, sweet Dark, 'savior' nonsense," Alexis said, "four hundred pounds prize money?"

"You have told us the story of *Grappel*, sir," Villar said.

"Yes, but there were only two regular crew aboard and I hadn't taken the ship to begin with! It was all a great muddle made by the prize court!"

"Still," Villar said, "the men did receive that sum, did they not?"

"I mean, they did, but ..." Alexis sighed. "Well, this two million guineas bit is right out."

"That was the value of the gallenium salvage *Nightingale* recovered, sir."

"We saw not a farthing of that! It was all the Queen's to begin with! Droits of the Crown, not of Admiralty!"

"Strictly speaking, sir, we did salvage it."

"And I'm captain of the bloody *Mongoose* now, am I? When did that happen?"

Villar nodded toward Alexis' bunk where the vile creature lay curled atop her blankets. "We do have the mascot for it, sir."

"And it goes nicely with this serpents bit right here, sir," Isom added, pointing it out on Alexis' screen. "Sets up a proper good versus evil sort of ..."

Isom trailed off and stepped back as Alexis glared at him.

"No," she said.

"'No', sir?" Villar asked.

"Yes, no. No, we will not be running this ..." She trailed off, unable to find words to describe it. "No."

"I see," Villar said, sharing a look with Isom, then frowning and scratching his neck. "Do you suppose, sir, that we might run this ... just today, perhaps?"

"To see the results, sir," Isom added. "As a sort of test, say?"

Alexis looked from one to the other. Villar looked away and Isom swallowed heavily.

"So it's already on the station's feed, is it?"

Isom nodded.

Alexis sighed.

"Well, we'll pull it off and put mine back up, before there's too much damage to the ship's reputation." She glanced at the advert again and shook her head. "Hero and savior, my arse."

Her tablet *pinged*.

"Yes?" she snapped, keying it.

"Ah ... Nabb here, sir, you set me to guard the docking tube?"

"Yes, Nabb, what is it?"

"Well, sir, it's only that you didn't say what to do with this lot what's showed up, see?"

Alexis closed her eyes and rubbed her forehead. So now there were spacers showing up in response to this rubbish and she'd have to at least give them the courtesy of a hearing, though the chances of finding proper crew from it were ...

"I'll deal with you two after I've seen off the load of rubbish you've turned up." She keyed her tablet. "Send them up to my quarters, Nabb, I'll speak to them."

"Ah, which, sir?"

"Which what?"

"There's the lot which is asking about a berth and then there's the station patrol, sir — which would it be you'd like sent up?"

"Station patrol," Alexis muttered. "Bloody wonderful." She glared at Isom and Villar in turn. "I can only assume this ..." She waved her tablet and their announcement at them. "... has violated any number of Penduli's ordnances against outright, bloody fraud."

"Ah, no, sir," Nabb's voice came from the tablet and Alexis flushed as she realized she'd left the connection open. "I imagine it's about the queue."

"Queue?" Good lord, could so many have been gulled by Isom and Villar's work that there was a bloody queue? "How many are there?"

Nabb paused, then, "Can't rightly say, sir ... the corridor curves out of sight at near a hundred meters, so ..."

Alexis buried her face in her hands, but not before seeing Villar's grin.

FOURTEEN

The line did extend past the curve of the station some hundred or more meters away from *Elizabeth's* berth, and the two station patrol officers at the hatch looked none too pleased about it. They did, at least, show Alexis the kindness of directing her to an empty warehouse nearby — if "Look, you, move your bloody circus to that empty warehouse up the quay or we'll charge you fees for every berth you block," could be called directing.

After Alexis apologized to the masters of other ships berthed nearby, no few of whom had also gathered to express their displeasure at having their loading and unloading blocked by *Elizabeth's* queue, and promised to have things set right instanter, she had Villar and Nabb chivy the queue along behind her while she and Isom set off for the empty warehouse.

That proved to be a bit of a mistake, for when the station patrol had said "empty" they did not mean available for use — not without a fee to the warehouse operator, at least, and that worthy, seeing the crowd behind her, and perhaps let on by the officers, clearly noted her need and named an exorbitant fee.

"For a few hours' time?" Alexis asked, stepping on her outrage.

The warehouse operator shrugged. "Supply and demand," he said.

"What?"

"You've a large supply of men there needing a place to stand about and it's me demanding thirty pounds for the day's use."

"I don't think that means what ..." Alexis sighed. "Twenty," she offered, and at that it was still usury.

"Thirty-five."

She fought down her irritation and sighed. The man did have the right of it — she could likely find meeting rooms in a pub, but not for so many, nor did she relish sending them away — the best of the lot would see that as *Elizabeth's* captain being unprepared, and none but the desperate or uncaring would like to sail on such a ship.

"All right, thirty," she said, then, as she saw the look in the man's eyes and he started to open his mouth, "Thirty-five. For the day — a full station cycle, if I've need of it."

She wouldn't, but damned if she'd let the man collect double rents for time she'd paid for — paid for and again, thrice over or more.

The man grinned and flipped a finger against his tablet, sending Alexis the contract.

"Have your captain sign this, then, and you'll be set."

"I am the captain," Alexis said, as she reviewed the contract to ensure he hadn't slipped any extra bits in on her.

The man grunted. "Thought you were a clerk or cabin girl, straight off the farm dressed like that ..."

He broke off at Alexis' look.

She added her approval to the contract, sent it back to him along with the payment, then frowned.

"Is there a pub nearby with the means to put together something for a large crowd?"

She thought to have some sort of refreshments brought in for those hired on — it would be a long day of interviewing, and she'd like to give those selected, and those spending the day selecting, a bit of a wet and some food.

"Just there." The man nodded toward a place a few compartments down. "Tell them Alfred sent you and they'll do you right."

"Thank you."

The high, wide warehouse hatch was slid open and the man took his leave.

Alexis entered the cavernous space and nodded. Villar had finally got the queue to understand that they were to move forward in order, not rush the warehouse to form a new queue, and was moving them toward her. She noted Nabb had her boat crew off *Elizabeth* and spread out along the queue, putting an end to any squabbles and scuffles over place. He'd be noting the faces of those, she knew, to keep an eye on for trouble if they were brought aboard.

"Isom. Go see to that pub, will you? A weak beer served to those waiting, stronger for those selected —" She eyed the space, thinking of how to organize this — what had the patrol officer called it? Circus, yes, was a proper naming. "We'll put the men selected there at the back until we can organize them aboard ship. Some sandwiches, as well, and a half dozen bottles of wine for Villar and I, as well any officers we might find in this lot."

She glanced after the departed warehouse operator.

"Do not, I think, tell them Alfred sent you."

FIFTEEN

"Name?" Alexis asked. "And position?"

"Wilmer Dockett, ma'am," the man seated across from her said. While the warehouse lacked true seating, there were a number of empty crates they'd employed for that purpose. Though they were a bit large for Alexis' taste, as none were small enough let her feet touch the floor. She found herself interviewing prospective crewmen with her feet dangling several centimeters above the deck. "I hope for bosun, if I may."

Alexis scanned the work records he sent to her tablet. She was already weary a mere hour into the interviews. They'd broken the mass of applicants into three groups. At the far side of the warehouse, Villar had the larger group, interviewing and selecting the common crew — topmen, gunners, and even the unrated spacers whose job was merely to haul on whatever line they were pointed at, all the myriad specialties that would make up the, she hoped, nearly two hundred men she'd take aboard ship.

They'd be berthing cheek to jowl in the ship's berths, but she'd need so many in this endeavor — both to overwhelm an enemy in boarding and to man their prizes without leaving her under-crewed herself.

To the other side, Isom had charge of another, the smallest group — those seeking a place in the hierarchy of servants aboard ship. A cook for both the men and one for herself, as her former cook had chosen to stay on Dalthus, opening a small restaurant in Port Arthur with his prize money from their last cruise aboard *Nightingale*; servants for her quarters and the officers, as well as what full-time assistants the cooks and those servants would require — part time assistance would come from whichever members of the crew might be so inclined; and all the other positions aboard ship which were neither properly crew nor officers.

She'd taken charge of the middle group. Those seeking a place as officers or warrants — or what passed as warrants aboard a civilian ship, at least. The bosun, a gunner, purser, engineer and his mates, and she hoped for two other officers in addition to Villar, there being no place for midshipmen aboard a private ship.

With luck and, she admitted, thanks to Villar and Isom's advertisement, fantastical though it might be, she'd leave Penduli with a full crew for *Elizabeth*.

Mongoose, she reminded herself with a grimace that made the man, Dockett, in front of her slump his shoulders, clearly thinking her expression was meant for him, when really, it was only that she was now stuck with being captain of the bloody *Mongoose*. One couldn't very well advertise such a thing, hire on a full crew, then tell them their ship was named something else.

That Isom, when she'd said with some resignation that she supposed he should look into the details of renaming the ship before they left Penduli, had presented with her with a fully prepared set of documents bearing that name — merely needing her authorization to make it official ... well, he was nothing if not efficient, she supposed.

"Your last ship was HMS *Prosaic*?" she asked, scanning Dockett's history. "Master's mate, but not bosun?"

Dockett nodded. "The frigate *Prosaic*, forty-four guns. Acting bosun, a time, though, you'll see, ma'am," he said. "Thrice on *Prosaic* during the war, as the bosuns were shot down in actions ..."

He trailed off, perhaps at her expression, which this time was meant for him, or at least knowing what she must be thinking.

Aside from the thought that *Prosaic* had been a singularly unlucky ship for bosuns, this Dockett had been raised to acting in that position three times aboard her, but then replaced those three times by someone else. That he'd not managed to secure his own warrant for the position after so many chances didn't speak well for his abilities.

Still, *Prosaic's* captain had thought well enough of him to put him in the acting position three times, so there must be something else to the tale.

She'd not find a Navy bosun to act as bosun aboard *Elizabeth — Mongoose*, bloody *Vile Creature* — as that position held a Naval warrant. Even if the ship were laid up in ordinary during the peace, such men's positions were secure. They'd still live aboard, perhaps bring their families, along with the purser, gunner, and other warrants, still receive their full pay, and still eat, along with those families, off of ship's stores — it was a peaceful, profitable state of affairs and few holding such a position would give it up to sail on a private ship.

A man with experience as a civilian bosun, on the other hand, would have little or no experience with the crew of a warship, which — she sighed, resigning herself to the name — *Mongoose* surely was.

Dockett squared his shoulders and met her eye.

"I've a temper, ma'am," he said, then hurriedly, "Not with the crew. Never them, no, but on station. It's why the three times acting and never a warrant to my name, do you see?" He shrugged. "I know my way about a ship, I assure you — sails, the guns, I've no worries there." He took a deep breath and his shoulders slumped as he let it out. "But I've troubles in ports, ma'am, and I'll not lie to you about that. There's some can't pass glass or girl without giving it a go, ma'am ... well, I've trouble passing a man who'll raise his fists to me." He shrugged. "Your pardon, if I've wasted your time, but I swear to you I'll keep your *Mongoose* taut and the crew in line, do you but give me the chance."

Alexis caught her lower lip between her teeth. She had no desire for idle brawlers aboard, but the man's records did bear out his words. Raised to acting-bosun, then back to master's mate — and sometimes back to able spacer — but always for a fight in port. Never a bit of trouble aboard ship, and all high praise from his officers.

She raised an eyebrow at one note, which read: "Mister Dockett will make an exemplary bosun — on the day which he first resists the urge to stand on bartops whilst shouting, 'Send up your best man!' at passers-by. Were it not for his fine hand at working the ship, a transfer to the marines' berth might be in order."

Dockett's expression warred between hope and despair as she glanced from him to her tablet and back again. She called up the records of all those others seeking the position of bosun and found that none could claim more than Dockett's experience. She met his eyes once more.

"So. Brawling?" Alexis thought for a moment. "Is there anything else, Mister Dockett? And do remember that there are no secrets aboard ship — any other proclivities will be found out, and we're sailing for the Barbary." She hardened her gaze. "Not a place a man wants to be put in-atmosphere for something he didn't disclose as he should."

Alexis knew this was no idle threat. Oh, any decent spacer would be able to get a berth out of those worlds … eventually. It was the fear of weeks, or even months, in-atmosphere while waiting for a merchantman to visit — all on some barren world with little to offer — that she hoped would prompt him to tell her.

Dockett's shoulders slumped. "There was some talk of a book, ma'am."

Alexis raised an eyebrow at that, as she knew he wasn't talking about reading. No, Dockett meant that he'd run a bit of gambling, and more than the lads did only amongst themselves as individuals.

"There was never no trouble, ma'am, so no real complaint, see?" His shoulders slumped more. "It's only that I know the numbers — can see 'em, like — and once a man says, 'Oh, I can do a thing,' and I see the numbers says he can't, well, it's hard not to tell 'im so. And once the numbers is out, well, it's every man's hand for his pockets to put coin on for or against, isn't it? Human nature, like."

"I see."

Alexis had already gone over the long list of Naval ship regulations with Villar, to weed out what *Mongoose's* articles would be. Most would be kept, though the ending bits about how everyone "shall suffer death or such other punishments as the Captain shall deem" were right out. No private ship crew would sign such a thing. No, there'd be no cat in use aboard this ship, and the ultimate punishment would be to be left in-atmosphere — put off the ship on some world with any unpaid shares in prizes forfeit.

Gambling, one of those things forbidden, but mostly overlooked even in the Navy, was an article they'd struck. The lads would gamble amongst themselves, for coin, chores, or sippers and gulpers from the daily rum issue, depending on each man's wealth at a given time, but they would gamble. It passed the time and offered some bit of excitement on longer cruises with no action.

The one thing she wouldn't have was cheating, and they'd left that bit in, though moving it to the article which included theft and the punishment being put off the ship.

"A *clean* book, Mister Dockett?"

Dockett's face firmed. "Always, ma'am, and I've ways to spot a cheat in the hands' games, if I spy 'em."

"Well, so long as it's clean — and I'll have no real debts amongst the crew, either," she added, thinking of the tens of thousands of pounds wagered and lost in dishonest games aboard *Nightingale* when the crew had thought they were to receive shares of millions in salvaged gallenium. "No more than the normal sippers and gulpers owed."

"Coin or kind, ma'am, even in their private gaming, aye," Dockett said, hope in his eyes and clearly already thinking as bosun and how he'd see the ship's Articles kept within the crew.

Alexis nodded. "And certainly no hint that I approve of such a thing, Mister Dockett. Looking the other way, as it won't be in *Eliza* —" She paused, closed her eyes, and took a deep breath. It did appear she was stuck with it. "Gambling won't be forbidden by *Mongoose's* Articles, but I'll certainly not be thought to endorse it, do you understand?"

"Aye, ma'am."

"Do your ... *entertainments* once interfere with my ship, Mister Dockett, I'll set you in-atmosphere instanter, do you understand that, as well?"

Dockett's eyes brightened. "Aye, ma'am!"

Alexis nodded. "We keep to a certain Naval protocol aboard *Mongoose*, as well, so drop that business and use proper address, will you?"

Dockett grinned. "Aye, sir, gladly."

"Have a pint and a bit to eat from the publican's back there —" She nodded toward the serving area set up for the selected crew. "— and see Mister Villar there with the common crew. He's a goodly selection by now and you can begin settling on recommendations for your mates."

SIXTEEN

"Thank you for your time, Mister Dursley. We'll be making a decision sometime this evening and will let you know."

Alexis smiled as best she could, though the man set her teeth on edge. An assistant purser off a laid-up ship of the line — the list of ship's names blurred in her head as badly as the list of applicants — Dursley was a fattish, pigishly-faced young man. She could almost imagine the hint of a curled tail poking out from his backside, and she'd taken an instant dislike to his tone and attitude. But he *was* qualified, and most of those with experience as a full purser were keeping their warrants aboard the ships in-ordinary, skimming what they may from the limited provisioning and hoping for another war.

There'll be no feeding at Mongoose's *trough for you.*

Alexis had Isom to keep a sharp eye on the purser's books, and the purser aboard a private ship held no warrant — the captain could dismiss him as readily as anyone else.

She held up a hand to cut off the man's next words — some protestation about the length of the line, she assumed. "I'm sorry, sir, but we'll get back to you after we've interviewed everyone."

Dursley *harrumphed,* as though offended at her refusal, but thanked her for the time and took his leave.

The next hopeful stepped into his place, but Alexis noted Nabb nearby gesturing for her attention.

"Excuse me a moment, please," she said to the applicant and motioned Nabb to come over.

Nabb bent close and whispered, "Begging your pardon, sir, but Mister Villar has a question."

She rose, grateful for the chance to stretch her legs. "I'll return in just a moment," she told the waiting man.

Nabb followed her back to Villar, who already had quite a crowd of selected crew members milling about behind him and partaking of the offered refreshments, though quite a larger crowd still waited for his attentions.

As she drew near, she was a bit surprised to see a group of four women in front of him and began to suspect his question. She smiled and nodded to them before approaching Villar, who stood and motioned her a bit away before speaking low.

"I wanted to ask you, sir, if you were bent on a, shall we say, traditional Naval make-up of the crew?"

Alexis grinned at his phrasing. Their long association and frequent dinners had certainly made Villar used to her opinions about certain Naval traditions, the dearth of female officers and crew in the Fringe fleet not least amongst her targets, as well as her belief that "tradition" was often a Naval term for utter madness.

"Are they qualified, Mister Villar?"

He nodded. "There were some few others earlier who were not, or not enough, I think, which is why I didn't ask for your wishes before this." He glanced at his tablet as though to confirm something. "These four, though — they're off a merchantman, but have sailed the Barbary often enough already. They know the systems — and the dangers, well enough. Seen some action as their ship is one to fight off pirates, with arms and crew to do so."

"So they've been in an action?"

Villar nodded. "Some — more running chases, but they've fought off boarders a time or two."

"And all four together?"

"A full mess — that's what we're seeing, sir."

He gestured toward the waiting crowd and she noted that it was clumped together in groups of four, six, or eight — the numbers of shipboard messes, depending on the ship's size. That made a certain amount of sense, as the Navy paid a ship off and sent the crew on their way after the cease-fire with Hanover, messmates would have stuck together as much as they could — those that weren't trying to make their way to their homes, that is.

There were a few groups with odd numbers, where a man might have done just that, or found a berth for himself alone, but for the most part they were full messes, and she could see that the pattern followed with those Villar had already selected, with clumps of men around the food tables and kegs brought over from the pub.

She frowned. Would that be a problem? Merging crew from so many ships, with so many groups of old mates possibly still identifying themselves as their former ship and not as *Mong* —

Gooses *or* Geese? she pondered. Well, it would be something to worry about later.

"I have neither objection nor preference, Mister Villar," she said finally, "so long as in your estimation they're qualified."

SEVENTEEN

Alexis was finding that an overabundance of candidates was as bedeviling as a dearth. She'd made no decisions about officers, telling those she found possibilities that they would be invited to a dinner that night where they might meet Villar as well. He'd have to share a wardroom with them, after all, and while competency was paramount, so was having a happy and companionable mess. There was no sense in starting things off with tension or dislike if it was avoidable.

With that put off, she merely lacked a purser to make her own choices complete and the group in front of her had shrunk considerably, as she'd announced that those seeking the filled positions could be about their business. That Dursley fellow was the best of the lot she'd interviewed so far, but something about him made her hesitate and merely take his name to be notified later. Perhaps it was only her general distrust of the position itself.

So, with only pursers and the remainder of the candidates for ship's officers remaining, she took a gulp of wine and pressed on.

"Next, if you please?"

"Lieutenant Estcott Hacking, lately third in *Forrester*," the next in line announced, rather more loudly than necessary.

He was in uniform, perfectly acceptable, regardless of his half-pay status, but Alexis couldn't help but feel he put a bit too much into it. Still, while there were many officers to choose from, she'd not been terribly impressed with any. She suspected that, given Penduli's state as a major Naval system, the best of those off ships laid up at the end of the war had been moved to other stations, while those on the cusp had likely made their way just a bit coreward to the nearest system with an Admiralty office where they might seek a place.

Those left here were either too junior or lacked the patronage to expect much else.

"Welcome, Mister Hacking. Tell me, if you will, what interests you about sailing with us on *Mongoose*?"

She noted the direction of Hacking's gaze, which was to her dangling feet. Feet, she noted, which she'd been idly swinging to tap against the crate. She stilled them, feeling her face grow hot.

Hacking laughed. "Employment, of course. Left idling with the cease-fire and not enough Naval berths."

Alexis smiled. "So why a private ship and not a merchantman?"

"Action and prize money," Hacking said. "I'm not one to plod about on merchant cruises, making do with a salary year in and out. No, with the war off, a private ship's the place for me."

It was a fairly standard answer and she'd not expected much different. Hacking's bearing was a bit off-putting, but his records showed a steady officer — with good reports from his last captain and nothing to show a problem.

"Very well, Mister Hacking. We are not selecting the ship's officers outright here, but rather inviting a select few to dine with me and *Mongoose's* first officer this evening. He and I will make our decisions after that — and I do mean that I wish to invite you to dine with us, if such was not clear."

"Of course," Hacking said. "Though I was hoping for a clearer answer here." He smiled widely. "There are other possibilities brewing, you understand, and I may not be available later."

He looked at Alexis expectantly.

That put her off. Even if he did have other offers to consider, which she doubted, she did not appreciate being pressed. Still he had good reports, and off a frigate which had seen its share of action, so he had experience on a fighting ship and had stood up well under fire. That was the sort of officer *Mongoose* needed.

"Do come to our dinner if you find none of those other possibilities brewed to your liking, Mister Hacking. Until then?"

Hacking's smile fell the tiniest bit, then widened again. He nodded and stood. "Of course. Until then." He cleared his throat. "Assuming I am still available, of course."

"Of course."

He turned to leave and the next in line made her way forward. Hacking, perhaps distracted at not being selected immediately, must not have noticed her movement and their shoulders collided. The woman next in line was driven aside by the blow, which Hacking acknowledged with only a curt nod and a muttered apology before moving on.

The woman glared after him for a moment, and Alexis considered calling him back to rescind her invitation. She wanted no such discourtesy or shortness amongst her officers, after all, but in the moment's thought Hacking was much of the way to the warehouse's hatch and the woman had approached. She would have had to call out loudly and that would both disrupt the proceedings and embarrass Hacking unnecessarily. She could sit through a dinner with the man, she supposed, given the half dozen others she'd invited, and then inform him that he would not suit — or perhaps send him a message that the positions had already been filled.

The woman's approach drew her attention from Hacking and she smiled welcome, though her thoughts were tinged with curiosity. Villar might have seen several women applying for positions amongst the crew, but there'd been none so far amongst the potential officers and warrants.

Most of those applying were off laid-up Navy vessels and, while women were common in the Royal Navy's Core Fleet, those ships had been recalled to the Core, not laid up here at Penduli. It was only Fringe Fleet vessels which had suffered that fate, and none of them would have had any women aboard. Alexis herself was a bit of a fluke in the Fringe Fleet — brought aboard her first ship by kindly-disposed captain and, she suspected, trundled along in part because no one was quite sure what to do with her.

"Fernleigh Parrill," the woman said by way of introduction. She was in her thirties, perhaps, with short-cropped, blond hair that would fit in a vacsuit much easier than Alexis' own ponytail.

"Good afternoon, Miss Parrill." Alexis scanned the proffered records, confirming that Parrill was off a merchant vessel, with no time in the Navy — and not one, as those Villar had asked about were, which prowled the Barbary. No, the routes laid out in these records were good, safe, New London shipping, centering around Penduli and Lesser Ichthorpe. She stifled a sigh so that the woman wouldn't see it — much as she'd like give her the chance, *Mongoose* was going into harm's way. She'd likely not take a man with no experience of action, so couldn't justify an exception.

"May I ask what's brought you here to us?"

She expected much the same answer as Hacking had given. After all, Parrill had a safe berth, one which she'd apparently held for some years, aboard her current ship, *Doggersbank*. The reasons to make a change from that to a private ship would almost certainly center around money or some misguided quest for glory.

"You," Parrill said.

Alexis blinked. That certainly wasn't an answer she'd expected. She shifted uneasily on the crate and wondered what the woman was about.

"What do you mean?"

Parrill took a deep breath and swallowed visibly. "I'm first officer aboard *Doggersbank* — you'll likely not recognize the name, I suppose."

Alexis' brow furrowed. Why would she? There were tens of thousands of little merchantmen prowling the Dark, it wasn't as though she'd encountered so very many of them. Then her blood chilled. There were, indeed, some ships she'd learned the names of — she'd only not expected to encounter them again. She should have, perhaps, in coming back to Penduli, so near Lesser Ichthorpe, and both so close to the Berry March.

"Giron," she said quietly.

Parrill nodded. "*Doggersbank* was ... next." Her voice was quiet and she spoke slowly. "We saw."

"Miss Parrill, I —"

"We saw your signals," Parrill went on, speaking faster now, as though trying to get something out before Alexis might stop her. "We saw the frigate come back on your ship. I tried to convince Captain Cantrell to come about. *Doggersbank* had only a few guns, but we could have been some help — perhaps ... I very nearly came to blows with Captain Cantrell over it."

Parrill trailed off, allowing Alexis to speak. She was uncertain of what to say and no little in turmoil herself to have that action brought up again. She forced the memories out of her head as she'd practiced, allowing herself to focus on the here and now.

"There was —" No, it wouldn't do to tell her there was nothing *Doggersbank* could have done to help in that action. One never wanted to hear that one was useless — though that wouldn't be the message she meant, it would be the one Parrill took from it.

"Your duty was to the civilians and soldiers aboard your ship," she said finally. "Getting them to safety was what you came for, wasn't it?"

Parrill nodded.

"And you did."

"Thanks to you."

"Thanks to all of us. You do see that, don't you?"

Parrill nodded again. "There's talk of a crest, you know? For the ships that were there."

"I'd heard." Alexis thought it was little enough recognition, come to that. She cleared her throat, hoping to steer the conversation away from such an uncomfortable topic. "Which brings us here."

Parrill smiled. "Yes, I'm sorry, but you did ask." She settled herself on her crate and Alexis noted with some envy that her feet touched the floor. "In any case, I'd thought since then that I might ... be of some more use than sailing crates of goods back and forth, you see? I looked into the Navy —" She shrugged with a wry grin. "— bit long in the tooth to go midshipman, though, and I can't see myself as common crew. The fleets here on Penduli or anywhere *Doggersbank* sails wouldn't have me, in any case. Have to go to the Core for that, and I haven't the means now. Wouldn't like it anyway, I suspect — the Fringe is more to my liking. Even Penduli's a bit too refined for my taste now."

Alexis raised an eyebrow at that. Penduli was really the first bit of the Fringe, almost Core in its attitude and infrastructure by now.

Parrill must have seen the question in her expression and went on.

"I like the freedom," she said. "I once sailed nearly two years in the Core and it's all so bloody the same, isn't it? If one wishes a pub, it's always a Waterhill's, no matter the world one's on. Need a pastry? Well find the nearest Scone & Crumpet — there's one on Penduli Station now, and how they made such a success is beyond me. Bloody cardboard and paste would make a better mouthful." She became louder now, and far more animated, as one did when let onto a favorite and familiar rant. "Why, I remember what settled me on leaving for the Fringe as though it were yesterday. I was on ... Kethfield, I think, and I only wanted some fish and chips. I took a bite and I realized it tasted the same — the very *same* — as the last round I'd had on Greater Maddock not two months past. And I thought to myself, I thought, *how did they do that?* Do you know what I found out?"

Alexis shook her head, fascinated despite herself by the tale.

"They ship it in," Parrill said. "Can you believe it? There's a whole bloody world, Huxford, I think, where they pull out tons and tons of the same fish every day. Then they cut it up into the same size pieces — what they do with the bits that don't fit, I have no notion — and then they toss on batter and freeze it before they load it into those massive Core ships with the bloody soulless mechanicals and hardly any crew to speak of and ship these little diamonds of fish and batter to hundreds of worlds. All that, so that whenever you walk into an Ashvale, no matter where, it's all the same bite, you see?"

Parrill looked around, blinking, as though not having realized she'd said so much.

"I'm sorry," she said.

Alexis grinned, quite taken with the tale and Parrill's passion.

"And so you came to the Fringe, and now seek to come aboard a private ship — are the merchantmen too much the same for you as well?"

Parrill flushed red, but Alexis held her gaze. She wanted an answer to that, a real answer about why Parrill wanted a berth on *Mongoose*. It was one thing to take on an officer lacking in experience, it was quite another to take on one lacking any real expectation of what the voyage might be like. Alexis might be taken with the woman's tales, but she didn't want some casual dilettante aboard *Mongoose* when it came to an action.

"I've enjoyed my time aboard *Doggersbank* quite a lot," Parrill said, "but I've always thought there might be something missing." She frowned. "After Giron, after seeing first-hand what the Navy's for — what you did, not the bothersome stops and searches of the revenue boats —"

Alexis' lips twitched in amusement, having only just come from commanding such a ship.

"I suppose that ... well, trade is necessary, certainly, but it never made me feel ... *useful*, if you can understand that. This voyage of yours, I know it's not a formal Naval expedition, but you'll be going after the pirates, not running from them as I've done all my life, yes?"

Alexis was silent, shocked a bit by the expression of the very sentiment that had sent her into the Navy — the very sentiment that made her reluctant to take over the running of her family lands, even now that she could. There were varying degrees of useful, she supposed, but what could compare, really, to taking one's ship into harm's way? Commerce might be the lifeblood of the kingdom, but what kept that blood safe was the ships and crews she'd commanded, laying themselves alongside the enemy and pouring hellfire from her guns into those who'd spill it.

"I'm sorry, but you did ask," Parrill said, standing. Alexis realized that she must have been silent for some time. "Certainly you're looking for those who've had experience with such things, not merely fancies."

"A moment, Miss Parrill, if you will — I'd like to invite you to dinner."

EIGHTEEN

The pub's common room was crowded and Alexis felt out of place. It was in the Naval section of the station — she and Villar had hosted the dinner for prospective officers here, it being familiar territory — but since neither she nor Villar were in active commission and were serving on a private ship, neither wore a uniform. Villar was in a generic ship's jumpsuit, lacking any patches or even rank insignia, while Alexis wore what she'd become comfortable in during the months at home: a white linen shirt and denim trousers.

They'd abandoned the private room upstairs where they'd hosted the dinner and sent the prospects away, the chosen officers to settle their accounts and any business aboard Penduli Station, while she and Villar stayed for a final drink or two.

"To a crewed ship," Villar said, raising his glass.

Alexis, reluctantly, raised hers in turn. There'd been more than enough at dinner, as well as food, and she was feeling full of both.

Still, the time would give their new crew a chance to settle into *Elizabeth's* ...

Mongoose's, *bugger it all,* Alexis thought, as the name had stuck and even those who'd sailed with her from Dalthus were using it.

In any case, with so many new hands, she'd decided to let Nabb and her former *Nightingales* have a free hand at settling the newcomers in. The officers' absence would make it clear that she had every confidence in her coxswain and the new bosun, Dockett, so there'd be no questions raised as to who was in charge — and any bruises come about as a way to make that clear could be raised without her official notice.

It was also their last chance to dine on any but shipboard provisions before reaching the Barbary, as Alexis planned to sail straight from Penduli now that the ship was fully crewed.

Fully crewed and more.

She sighed at the thought, both from satisfaction and bewilderment that Isom and Villar's bizarre advert had worked such magic — and lucky they were done and able to pull the advert from the station's newsfeeds as well.

So now she had a ship and crew of would-be *Mongooses.*

Mongeese? she wondered.

One more thing to blame on Isom, Villar, and the vile creature, now they'd named the ship that — there'd be no agreement amongst the men as to what to call themselves.

In any case, they'd had the pick of what she could only call the best of spacers left idle by the cease-fire with Hanover. Men who, for one reason or another, had taken no berth with a merchant ship since being paid off. Most, Villar'd discovered in his interviews, preferred the life of a warship and were simply waiting, idle or at whatever work they might pick up on-station, for the Navy to decide they were needed once more.

True, some had been refused berths on merchants for other reasons, but the experienced *Nightingales* like Ruse and Sinkey were able to suggest questions that ferreted those out of the mix.

Women, as well, which would make for a new experience — other than Marie, she'd never sailed with other women aboard as crew. Dansby's ship, when she'd sailed on that into Hanover, had some, but she'd not truly been part of that crew herself.

In the end, she had enough of a crew and turned away more who were equally suited to her needs — even after making clear to them that it was unlikely in the extreme that they'd be splitting some two million guineas in prizes, no matter what the bloody advert claimed.

Oh, there'd been some, many in fact, who'd refused to sign on. They'd taken a look at her, decided she was no fit captain, and gone on their way. But there were the others ... others, like Parrill, who'd wished to sign on because of her, and she wasn't entirely sure how to feel about that. Two old *Merlins* signed on, men from her first ship who'd grinned with pleasure as she called them by name. Then others that she didn't know but who felt they knew her.

"Served with a man who came back with you from Hermione, sir, and said I should follow if you're ever at the foe."

"Was on Swan under Cammack at Giron, sir, and I'll sign them Articles if you'll take me."

It was ... unsettling. Satisfying and frightening, both, to be known so by men she'd never met. Still, it had netted her a crew in the end.

A fine crew, she had to admit.

She grimaced as she took another sip of wine, determined to limit this to one glass, as she'd had her full share at dinner only a short time ago.

A fine crew, but, sadly, she wondered if the same could be said about her chosen officers.

Oh, they looked right enough on their records, all the ones she'd invited to dine with her and Villar, but issues soon became apparent over the meal.

Lieutenant Wooddell, who, after his first bottle, finished before the first plates were served, seemed to lose interest in all but the food and drink before him. Alexis suspected he'd not really been looking for a ship, not a private ship, at least, but was instead after the free meal and wine while on half-pay.

Lieutenant Byrd, who'd flushed red and clenched his jaw once he'd learned that Alexis was, indeed, captain of the *Mongoose* and it all wasn't some sort of joke by the real captain. He'd stayed, though, and eaten and drank his fill as well.

Lieutenant Hudkins, who'd nearly stormed out at hearing that Villar, a mere midshipman in the Navy, would be first officer of *Mongoose*. He'd made it quite clear that, private ship or not, it was simply mad not to carry the officers' Naval ranks over to the ship's wardroom.

A half dozen others who, when it came down to the questioning lacked, to use Villar and Isom's phrase, "a certain something."

In the end, it was Hacking and Parrill who Villar and Alexis had chosen. Hacking as second officer and Parrill as third.

While Hacking's attitude gave her pause, all the rest lacked sufficient experience to take a chance on.

"To a full wardroom?" Alexis offered.

"As fine a one as we might," Villar answered. He raised an eyebrow. "You have doubts?"

Alexis pursed her lips. She did have doubts.

Parrill lacked experience and had what Alexis could only describe as an inability to let a question she might answer pass by unnoticed.

During dinner, one of the others, a passed midshipman who might have been a match for the ship had he not drunk so much that he'd been snoring by the end, told a tale of taking a smuggler packed with sugar sailing for Wootwell, and marveled at why they'd carry such a cargo.

"It's an interesting system, Wootwell," Parrill said. "You see they were settled by this lot who think trade with other systems is never the answer — set up tariffs you'd not believe to protect their local business and jobs. Thing is, their world has trouble producing a single sweet — every bit of produce is lacking in sugars, you see? Not empty of it, only that it would take five times the produce to get a bit of sugar or sweetener. So they must import it, but they've put so very high a tariff on the stuff to protect their own farmers that it's dearer than gold almost. Padmouth, now, where your smuggler was likely coming from, has an abundance — seems all they plant there is beets and cane, likely because Wootwell has such a need and they've seen the profit in it. A captain can turn nearly ten times the profit if he puts sugar down without a tariff stamp on Wootwell, and, did you know, there's an active resistance to the Wootwell revenuers on the planet itself? A whole network of distribution taking sugars in from smugglers boats in the hinterlands and routing it to the cities — many of whom are the very farmers the tariff's supposed to be about protecting. Some make more off the smuggling of sugars than they do the growing of it."

She looked around at the others who'd gone silent and were staring at her, then hunched her shoulders and lowered her eyes to her plate.

"I'm sorry," she said, "but you did ask."

Alexis chuckled, though ruefully, at the memory. The first such outburst of such very detailed information had been surprising, the second amusing, but the third and fourth had made her share a glance with Villar over whether he'd truly care for such in the wardroom every day.

"Only what I've expressed already," Alexis said, answering his question about doubts.

"I'd certainly prefer to have Mister Spindler back with me," Villar said, "if only because I'd spent so much time with him, and he's a good lad, but he's off to home since *Nightingale* paid off. Of the lot we saw, I'm satisfied — though there's still Lesser Ichthorpe and a system or two else we could try."

"Do you wish to?"

For Alexis' part, she wished only to get to the Barbary and begin her search for Delaine. They'd managed to fully crew *Mongoose* with this single stop at Penduli, so any other would be solely for the officers.

"No," Villar said. "From what you said — and I saw at dinner — there're slim pickings for a wardroom. The crew are more willing to seek out a private ship, it seems, while the in-atmosphere lieutenants dream of advancing their careers and won't risk the chance their commissions will be reactivated while they're away with us."

Alexis frowned. There was that, and she was risking her own career a bit. If a call-up occurred while she was off on *Mongoose* and she was unavailable to answer it, then her own prospects would be dimmed — of course, she remembered, her own prospects in the Navy were likely darkened all entire, as she'd have to resign her commission to take her place on Dalthus.

That did, though, raise the question of Villar's career.

"And you?" she asked. "Suppose there's a call-up and you miss it?"

"Ah," Villar said, "you forget, from your lofty lieutenant's rank, that I'm merely an unpassed midshipman, so far as the Navy's concerned." He raised his glass to her. "I serve at the pleasure of my captain in any case." He grinned. "Besides which, Marie would never forgive me, did I leave you to your own devices."

Alexis grinned back. "And a bit of prize money will do you no harm in your plans with her, will it?"

"Indeed, sir." Villar sobered. "I do fear I've little to offer her, even with what prizes we took with *Nightingale*."

Alexis sobered as well.

"You've more to offer than coin, Whitley," she said, "and Marie's not one to weigh a man's purse against his other qualities."

"Thank you for that, and no, she isn't." He shrugged. "But I do wish to make my own way. A midshipman's pay only goes so far and that stopped these last months with no berth. The prices on Dalthus these days, as well ..."

Alexis nodded. While she, as a lieutenant, was on half-pay with no ship, a midshipman like Villar was left entirely to his own devices. And the cost of everything on Dalthus seemed to be going up as more and more cash from the gallenium mines flooded the system.

Villar brightened and raised his glass again. "To Captain Carew and four hundred pounds prize money the man."

"You and your bloody 'somethings.' Next the men will be asking about the split of those millions," Alexis muttered, then, "So you're satisfied with your wardroom, then?"

Villar shrugged. "As may be, I suppose. I've served in worse berths and not been in charge — before *Nightingale*. With only the three of us, we'll make do, I think.

"Hacking's a bit harsh and speaks his mind, while Parrill is ... well, one can learn to never ask a question one doesn't truly want the answer to, I suppose." He grunted. "They'll do. Hacking's experienced, for all he's full of himself, and Parrill ..." Villar grinned. "She does have a certain something."

Alexis laughed.

"So long as you're satisfied," she said. "I do fear they're the best we may find. And we have told them they're in, after all. It would be a fine thing to put them in-atmosphere now."

"True. So we're off, then?"

Alexis nodded. "A full crew. Enough officers that, with our new bosun, the watch billet is full, as well." She took a deep breath. "Day after tomorrow." She made the decision. "Time enough to bring aboard any last supplies, for the crew to say any goodbyes they have here, and for our officers to finish their business as well."

"Hacking did speak as though half the station were dependent on him."

"Indeed." Alexis drained her glass. "So we'll sail direct from here to the Barbary and be about it."

Villar refilled her wine from the bottle on the table, then his own, splitting what remained neatly between them.

He wiped at his mouth with a napkin and caught her eye.

"If you'll excuse me for a moment, sir?"

"Of course." She nodded.

Villar rose and made his way toward the heads.

Alexis took the opportunity to look around the pub.

The sight of so many uniforms did drive home her new status.

She was not, for the moment at least, a part of the group she'd grown so accustomed to.

"Your lad left you all alone, did he?"

Alexis raised an eyebrow as the speaker dropped into Villar's abandoned chair across from her. He was a lieutenant, younger than Villar, she suspected, only a little time into his commission, if the newness of his uniform was to be believed. Lucky in the war, perhaps, to be aboard some ship seeing enough action to raise him before the cease-fire.

"He'll be back in a moment, never fear," Alexis said, but could see in a moment that this wouldn't deter the man. She glanced back the way he'd come and saw a table of his fellows watching eagerly.

"I saw you come in," the lieutenant said, "and I said to myself, I said, Couchman, there's a lass come up from atmosphere and looking to see what the wider universe is all about."

"Did you?" she asked. "Well, that's quite perceptive of you, I'm sure, but as I said my companion will be returning shortly, so if you wouldn't mind —"

The lieutenant, presumably Couchman, nodded. He pushed Villar's plate to the side, took Villar's glass in hand, and leaned toward her.

"Have you ever been a'space before?" he asked.

Alexis resisted the urge to bark at him in her best command voice to get his bloody arse off her first officer's chair, leave their wine alone, and take himself back to his ship before she sent word to his captain. She'd try, once more, politely, at least.

"Mister ... Couchman, was it? My companion really will return soon —"

"Then I'd best hurry and win you away from him, hadn't I?" Couchman drained Villar's glass, then reached across the table and laid a hand over Alexis'. "Come on, then — first time a'space, yes?"

Very well, then, if the smarmy bastard wouldn't move on, then she'd see he regretted staying.

She lowered her eyes then glanced up at him and away again.

"Does it show so very much?" she asked.

Couchman grinned. "I knew it! From the first look I said that's a lass on her first time aboard station, even, I'll bet." He took up the bottle, frowned to find it empty, and set it back again. "Have you ever seen a proper ship before? Inside, I mean. I could give you a bit of a tour, if you like." He cocked his head to one side. "*Pembroke*, a frigate, best in the fleet, she is. Our captain's all-night-in down on the planet, so it would be no fuss at all." He made what Alexis assumed he found a seductive look. "You could touch the big guns, if you like."

Eager to show me, are you? Alexis thought. *I do not believe I've ever sat alone in civilian dress for more than ten minutes' time, before some lout takes it into his head that I might simply perish for want of his company.*

"I don't know if I should," Alexis said. "My companion's only left for a few moments ..."

Couchman leaned closer. "We'll slip out now, leave a bit of a note for him that you've found a better entertainment, eh?"

Alexis sighed — there was no getting rid of his sort short of bluntness. She caught her lower lip between her teeth. It was a habit she thought to break herself of, but Delaine had once called it adorable, so she assumed it had a certain effect on men for some reason.

"I suppose I might," she said in almost a whisper. "I could actually see the big guns, you said?"

"Touch them, if you like," Couchman whispered back, leaning closer. "Run your hands right along the barrel — feel how powerful they are."

"Oh, dear," Alexis breathed. "I ... I might like that."

"You will, I promise."

"I do have ... well, one question first, if you don't mind?"

"Ask away, dear, but quickly so we can be away."

Alexis sat back, fixed Couchman with a narrow-eyed gaze, and took a deep breath.

She reached for her best voice — the one she'd use on the gundeck, when the hull was shot through and the radiations of *dark-*

space killed the vacsuit radios. When she'd have to press her helmet against one of her lads' and make her words cut through the echoing, terror-filled rasp of his own breath to put steel in his core again.

"You are in command of a cutter, Mister Couchman, fore-and-aft rigged, with all plain sail and jib set — in pursuit of a merchantmen ignoring your signals to heave-to. To leeward are the system shoals of a heavy star, fairly visible to you they are so shallow, and to windward a squall is oncoming. What do you do, sir?"

"What?"

"What do you do, Mister Couchman? *The squall approaches!*"

"I —"

Alexis could see his bewilderment. Caught between his lechery and being addressed like the midshipman he'd likely been not so very long in the past, his own sitting for lieutenant and being set questions like this by the board of captains still fresh in his mind.

"The squall has struck, Mister Couchman, and your jib is torn through — in tatters and fouling your particle projector! *Your orders, Mister Couchman!*"

The poor man had drawn back in his chair, eyes wide, mouth agape in astonishment.

"Your quarry begins a turn to leeward, sir! Your orders?"

"What — I ... damn you what is —"

"Your chase has fired! Your port bowchaser is struck and dismounted! Shot slices through your rigging!"

Couchman's face was turning red, his initial astonishment becoming anger.

"The main force of the squall hits," Alexis said. "Your standing rigging, cut through and tangled by your jib, gives way, sir." She sat back and crossed her arms. "You are dismasted, Mister Couchman. Dismasted, adrift, and driven upon the shoals."

There was silence for a moment — too much silence, and Alexis looked around to find that she might have miscalculated a bit in her use of that particular voice, for the entire pub was dead silent and staring at her table. Couchman's face reddened further, then made a fair try at purple as the crowd burst into laughter. He stood abruptly, thrusting his chair back.

"You ... you *bitch*!"

Alexis shook her head slowly. "Dear lord, man, go and see your bosun for a proper curse, will you not?"

Couchman sputtered, glared around the pub, then turned for the hatch, his shoulders hunched.

"Oh, Mister Couchman?" Alexis called and he had the poor sense to stop and turn back. "Do think of me as you caress that great gun tonight, will you?"

NINETEEN

A lexis drove *Mongoose* hard toward the Barbary, exercising the crew and the ship itself as she had *Nightingale* in her first months aboard — and, now there was a full crew, putting everything to rights and doing away with the shabby façade of Dansby's tenure. The difference with this ship, from her first days aboard *Nightingale*, was that the crew responded immediately — more so than she expected and more so than she'd seen aboard other ships.

"It's the prize money," Isom said, when she mentioned it. "Profit drives a man."

Villar nodded. They were having dinner, something which became a regular event, though Alexis would sometimes invite a few of the master's mates and the bosun himself.

She wondered for a moment if bosun was even the proper term for that position aboard a private ship — but had no time and less inclination to find out. There were too many new things about this environment out of the Navy to keep track of.

There was no use of the cat for discipline — the men wouldn't accept it, despite most having served years in the Navy where it was common. Instead, much of the discipline was handled by the bosun and his mates, with the most grievous punishment to be simply kept in irons until *Mongoose* called at some system and then be put in-atmosphere.

Losing their place, and the chance at that prize money, was a more effective threat than any bosun's cat, it seemed.

One thing Alexis didn't care for was the lack of marines aboard. Not because she needed them to maintain discipline, but because there was no group of them to work out with every day. The spacers themselves thought little of exercise, much less unarmed combat drills — their idea of a fight was the brawling, wide-armed swings of a drunken melee in some pub.

Still, she had mats aboard and she practiced what she could. Villar sometimes joined her, but found it not to his liking. Many of the crew, while not joining in, took the time to stop and watch — some, she thought, were busy ogling one of the only women aboard, dressed as she was in shorts and a sweat-stained shirt, while others might have had an interest in learning if only their mates hadn't mocked it so.

"Looks a pretty dance, that," one of the hands had commented after they were a few days from Penduli.

"Belay that, Askins," Nabb said.

"Easy, Nabb," Alexis said, stopping her movements and stepping to the side of the mat. "It is very like a dance in ways, Askins. Would you care to try?"

"Not much of a dancer," Askins said. "Outside of the sheets, that is."

The watching men laughed and Alexis smiled, shaking her head at Nabb's scowl. The laxer discipline aboard a private ship extended to interactions between officers and crew — the captain, she'd learned, was not so much in command, as leading. These men were aboard for profit — partners, to an extent, in her enterprise, and not entirely subordinates.

She found that a bit easier than the strict discipline of the Navy as well, though she did wonder what it would mean should she have cause to give an order they might balk at. Would they follow or refuse?

"This is a different sort of dance than that, Askins — a bit more risk of injury, I think." She grinned. "Unless the lady's husband comes home, that is."

"Never saw no use in all that movin' about," Askins said when the laughter died. "Rush at 'em bellowin' an' pummel them's as haven't the sense to run — that's what my pap always said."

"Well, you've the size for that, no doubt." In truth, Askins was one of the larger men aboard — as tall as Nabb and broad-shouldered. He worked the heaviest tasks with no complaint.

"Aye, works for me," he said. "Doubt yer prettified dance'd do you honest in the sorts o' brawls we get on to."

"Do you now?" Alexis' interest perked. She hadn't had an actual bout since *Nightingale* paid off. All of the marines had made their way home after, and none of the crew was at all interested — Nabb occasionally made to copy her movements, but was reluctant to spar with her. She grinned, feeling the familiar stir of excitement at testing herself — whether it was the guns, an action, or a boarding, the thrill of pitting her mettle against another stirred her blood. "Care to wager?"

Her casual tone and the hoots and catcalls of the watching crew virtually guaranteed that Askins would accept. He made only a token objection.

"Ah, sir, I'd not wish to hurt a gi ... well, my captain. Not e'en on accident, like."

Alexis gauged the watching men. They were good-natured in their egging Askins on, and he was a steady fellow — not the sort to take defeat badly. She thought this might be a good opportunity to grow closer to the lads — one she wouldn't have aboard a Naval vessel. Whether she won or lost, and she was confident she could take the man, as she'd seen him move, so long as no one was angered it would be to the ship's benefit, she thought.

Also, she was bloody tired of being referred to as a girl when she was very nearly twenty years old and in command of a vessel of war — even if only a private one.

She knew Askins meant no harm by his slip, but the thought was always there, hanging over her — had been her entire career.

Likely always will be — save when I've beaten it down ... and so ...

She turned from him and walked to the center of the mats.

"Just as well, I'd not want to take good coin from a *boy* ... a member of my crew, that is."

She turned back and gave him a grin to ease the sting of it and show she held him no ill will.

Askins flushed at the calls of the watchers. He looked at her for a moment, then nodded.

"All right then. What's yer wager, sir?"

She'd already considered this and she wanted the terms to be dramatic if she lost — if she won, that in itself would fit the bill, but a loss was possible as well. A few shillings wouldn't be a tale the men told about their captain, and she wanted them to have a tale either way it went.

Much as she might hate to admit it, Villar and Isom had been correct about the advertisement and what would attract a crew. This crew, those willing to risk it all on a private ship, wanted more than a job — they wanted an adventure. Something larger than life and dramatic.

"Your share of the first prize," she said, pausing as the watchers' eyebrows raised. Askins frowned — it could be quite a large sum, depending on that prize, especially if there was a valuable cargo. Alexis waited until Askins seemed to be about to speak, and then continued, "Against mine."

Now there were shouts from the watchers, and further shouts to call those who weren't watching over. The stakes had just gone up considerably and in dramatic fashion.

The division of prize shares was spelled out in the ship's articles and was much like aboard a Naval vessel, except that the owners — in this case Dansby and, Alexis presumed, some dark corner account of the Foreign Office, would receive four-eighths of the value. The master's mates, bosun, and Villar, as her first officer, would share one-eighth amongst themselves. Not equally, but according to their station. And the crew would share two-eighths, also split according to their rating, be it ordinary, able, or some specialty. But the captain — well, the captain received one-eighth all to herself.

That could mean a thousand or more pounds, with little trouble.

Askins cracked his knuckles and flexed his neck, then spit in his hand and held it out to her with a wide grin. Alexis did the same, slapping her palm into his.

THE SOUNDS of the crew cheering and shouting, nearly all of them crowded into the space around the mats, echoed throughout the deck. Alexis suspected that even the quarterdeck watch was viewing on their monitors, and shrugged off the worry that they might miss something while the bout went on.

Mongoose was well away from any systems still, with no vessel in sight. She could take the risk.

Askins shrugged his shoulders to loosen them and stepped onto the mats across from her.

"There rules t'this?" he asked.

Alexis took the mouthpiece Nabb offered her and grinned at his worried look. He was about to have more to worry about, but her blood was up and she'd not miss a chance to spar as she liked to.

"As you would in the hold," she said, slipping the mouthpiece in place.

Askins' eyes widened, but then he nodded and grinned back.

The men would sometimes hold contests in the hold on long cruises, with simple rules — leave a man's eyes and bollocks be, and leave him breathing at the end. All other than that was for the ship's surgeon to patch up.

It might be a mistake on her part, but it did have her heart racing and her grin wider than she'd felt in months.

Askins moved lightly, squaring off and then circling her as the bout began, instead of rushing in with a bellow as his pap advised — it seemed the prospect of a captain's share in their first prize had made him more thoughtful.

Alexis was thoughtful as well, for the man moved lighter than she'd expected, lighter than she'd seen him move before, causing her to wonder if she hadn't just been taken in by the man.

They circled for a bit, edging closer.

Askins waved his left hand forward and she ignored it for the feint it was, still circling. She'd wait for him to make his move, which he did in a moment, rushing — without the bellow and quicker than she'd thought he'd be even after watching him.

His arms were stretched wide to catch her in a bearhug, which wasn't such a bad strategy, come to that. If he did manage to get at her like that, she'd have a time getting loose, if she could at all. For sheer strength, there was no doubt the man outmatched her.

But Alexis had no intention of trying to match Askins' strength.

She waited for him to feint again, catching on that he liked to, then went to that side as he shifted back for his real attack. Too quick, though, he caught her at it and she barely ducked away from his grasp. His thick forearm met her cheek with a heavy *thunk* as she dodged and she blinked tears away from that eye.

Damn me, but he's far faster than I thought!

She made the next move, darting in — using her size and quickness to avoid his grasp and get a blow in on this thigh, near enough to let him know where it would have landed if the fight didn't have *some* rules to it.

A few boos from the crowd at that, but Askins laughed.

Now he bore in, as though the blow had told him how much damage she could do and he was willing to take it on to finish the bout. Arms spread wide and low, and his reach was such that it was nearly half a meter wider than Alexis was tall.

Alexis threw herself to the mat, rolling, but Askins' foot lashed out and caught her in the hip as she went by. It was a hard blow and stung, but not enough to stop her from making her own in return. She caught Askins behind the knee with the side of her fist as she came out of her roll and the man's leg buckled.

She was up and turned to follow through in an instant, but Askins spun as he'd fallen to his knee and managed to face her, ready to grapple again.

Alexis backed off and Askins rose.

They dodged and swung at each other for a time, neither gaining the advantage and each taking hard blows. Askins favored the knee she'd first struck, as she'd gone for it more than once, while Alexis' eye was closing from a fist that'd caught her particularly hard.

By some unspoken mutual agreement, they each stepped back a pace and caught a bit of breath, then almost as one went back into their stances.

Alexis eyed him, set to end it on this pass.

There was a particular move she'd seen, then practiced, though never tried in a true fight — but it did have drama, and she felt this fight deserved to end as dramatically as it began.

And if it doesn't ... well, he'll likely remember to stop squeezing me before my head actually pops off, so there's that ...

Askins neared her, arms still spread, ready to grab her and trap her. Alexis made to dodge, but had no intention of following through — instead she rushed forward as well, gaining momentum and leaping. Askins' arms came together, but she wasn't between them.

Instead, she'd grabbed his left arm like it was a swinging bar, and swung under it, sweeping her legs up and over then wrapping them around his neck.

Askins' hand brushed against her leg, but only just missed the grip as she released his arm and twisted her body, using the full torque and leverage of her weight, slight though it was, to force him along, and, in an instant, Askins was on the mats, face bloodied from the impact, and Alexis' legs still gripping at his neck.

143

The crowd was dead silent, stunned by what they'd seen.

Alexis released him and backed away.

Askins shook his head, half rose, and coughed, then sat back and nodded to her.

She reached out and helped Askins to sit, then took an offered mug and handed it to the man. She could see coin being exchanged amongst the watchers — quite a lot of it going in the direction of Isom, Nabb, and the other former *Nightingales*.

Askins hawked up a mouthful of blood, spat, and drained the mug. He blinked a bit and rubbed at his throat.

"Are you all right?" Alexis asked, taking the empty mug from him.

Askins nodded, blinked for a time, then nodded again.

"Aye, all right, sir." He looked from her to the mats, then back again. "But I'll learn your bloody dancin', if you'll have me."

TWENTY

"Sail!"

Alexis heard the call through the image of the quarter-deck displayed on her cabin tabletop. It was a mechanism which allowed her foreknowledge of what occurred when she chose not to walk the quarterdeck itself, but there was a still a formality and ritual to it, in case she might be occupied with something else.

"Where away, Dorsett?" Villar asked, as he had the watch and was actually on the quarterdeck.

"Three points off the starboard bow and level, sir."

Alexis brought the corresponding image from the ship's optics up on her tabletop, as she knew Villar would be doing on the quarter-deck navigation plot.

Her tablet *pinged*.

"Aye?"

"Sail, sir, three points off the starboard bow and level," Villar told her. "I make it a merchant brig of some sort."

Alexis nodded. She tried to picture their course in *darkspace* in her head, but found it too much to manage. The calculations neces-sary to account for the warping of normal-space masses, as well as margin of error for the near dead-reckoning navigation *darkspace* required were best left to the computers in her opinion — not least because she could never get it quite right herself. There was something, she thought, about piloting a ship through bloody guesswork that her mind rejected as unnatural. Oh, certainly the ship's computers took it all into account — where they'd started, each day's charted progress of speed, winds, drift, and course changes, as well as expanding and shrinking the distances involved based on normal-space masses — but when one got right down to it, the uncertainty made her stomach churn.

Ships did get lost — especially in the bare space of the Barbary. Lost left a ship's occupants with but one option — sail on, usually with the winds, and hope that those winds' tendency to eventually blow directly toward a star system would bring one there. Then it was transition to normal-space where the stars were visible and try to determine one's position from that.

Not a comforting backup plan at all.

The computer's representation of *Mongoose's* course and the space around them was far better than her mental image would ever be.

She pursed her lips for a moment as she studied the systems which were closest. The Barbary was not one kingdom or nation as New London or Hanover was. Instead, each system was its own sovereign, unless some particularly strong leader took it into his head to unite, or conquer, his neighbors — usually for a quite short-lived time before rebellion or some other cause cast him down.

She wanted to reach the privateer rendezvous Eades had told her of during one of the appointed times, but three points off their course was not so much and the men could do with a bit of action. All of the surrounding systems, those that were inhabited, were on the list covered by her letter of marque, and so their merchant shipping was fair game for *Mongoose*.

"Fly Hanoverese colors, Mister Villar," she said. That was who the Barbary systems bore some allegiance to, after all, and the Chase might deem them friendly, she thought, "and bear down on her. *Interrogative* as the signal, I think. We'll let her believe we're a friendly ship in need of news."

"Aye, sir."

ALEXIS FELT pangs of uncertainty as they closed with the other vessel. Not anxiety over any action, for *Mongoose*, even without an inordinate number of guns for a schooner of her size, was more than a match for the dowdy, unknowing merchantman very nearly within deadly range of her broadside, but rather, over taking a merchantman at all.

Taking an enemy's warships was one thing, their merchant shipping in time of war another, but there was no formal declaration of war between the Barbary systems and New London — more, the Barbary consisted of so many nearly independent systems, that such a declaration would be meaningless on its face. Instead she must make do with Eades' list of "systems and nations known to engage in the despicable acts of piracy." All well enough for some functionary on New London to write up, but much different to the owner-captain of a small ship, trying to make do with cargo run to cargo run.

This *was* a thing which was done, however — letters of marque were not so unusual. And there was the chance, however small, that putting up with the distaste of this business might lead her to Delaine.

It was nearly time to be on with it.

"On my mark, Mister Villar," she said, "our true colors and run out the broadside. *Heave-to* is the signal."

"Aye, sir."

Alexis waited for the moment she felt might have the most impact on the other captain — the one which would make him feel hopeless and have no will to run or fight when he saw what he faced.

"Now."

THERE WAS NOTHING, really, the other captain could do but surrender – not a common merchantman faced, in-range, with a broadside of twenty-four guns and a faster ship by far.

Good sense prevailed and, after a moment's shock, the other ship struck, masts and hull, which had previously displayed the colors of a nearby system, going dark as the ship turned up into the wind and doused its sails as well.

"Bring us alongside, Mister Villar. I believe I'll attend the boarding party myself — this first time, at least."

"Aye, sir," Villar said.

ALEXIS' trepidations about privateering against honest merchants grew aboard *Beneghem*.

The ship's crew was a motley band, ill-dressed and scowling at the crew of *Mongoose* as they came aboard. The captain was little better, a man who looked as though he saved a few pence on his water recyclers by not bathing, and the smell as Alexis neared him merely confirmed that thought.

Alexis disliked him, but her fears about this enterprise only grew despite that, for this ship had all the look of an independent vessel, and dislike was not enough, she thought, to destroy the man's livelihood as taking it would do.

"See to the cargo, Reddish," she ordered, choosing one of the master's mates and one of the steadier hands of the boarding party, "while I speak to Captain ...?"

"Aksoy." His accent was harsh and guttural, a different accent and language than she'd found in Hanover proper, though he appeared to speak some English, so she wouldn't have to resort to her tablet's translation software, something she disliked. The disembodied voice in her earpiece always made her queasy when it didn't match up to the speaker's lips, but the Barbary's patois would eventually drive her to use it, she was sure.

Alexis nodded. "Captain Aksoy, *Mongoose* is a private ship sailing under letter of marque from New London. I am authorized to take your vessel and cargo, as the Kayseri system is known to engage in piracy and other infamous acts."

Aksoy spat. "'Authorized.'" He spat again, nearer her foot and Nabb fairly growled beside her.

"Easy, Nabb," Alexis said. "There'll be none who're pleased by our presence here and this won't be the worst we see, I suspect. Captain Aksoy, shall we retire to your cabin? I wish to review *Beneghem*'s records."

She followed Aksoy to his cabin, Nabb and two other spacers behind her. She might understand the other captain's anger, but that didn't mean she should be so foolish as to be alone with him.

Beneghem's records did nothing to ease her mind, for the ship was, indeed, owned solely by Captain Aksoy. How could she, in good conscience, take the man's livelihood like this?

This privateering may not be for me at all ... yet how would I get out of it?

She made a show of rereading the ship's records, hoping none of her concerns showed on her face. She felt both Aksoy's and Nabb's eyes on her — the one with anger and the other always seeming to know when something was bothering her.

It was somewhat with relief that she heard her tablet *ping* and Reddish's request that she join him in the hold.

She motioned for Aksoy to follow her and made her way down the nearest companionway.

In the hold, she found Reddish and four men reviewing the *Beneghem*'s cargo. Reddish came over at her entry and held out his tablet.

"Bit of a mix, sir, but some value."

Alexis reviewed the list and it was, indeed, a mix of cargoes. Condensers from Hanover, three materials printers from New

London itself, several crates of assorted machinery from *Hso-Hsi* — just the sort of thing one might expect being imported to worlds with a limited manufacturing base. For though the Barbary bordered on the Core, the worlds were so sparsely settled that she thought they'd likely be forever part of the Fringe.

"What are these ships' names here?" Alexis asked, pointing to a column.

"Looks as though these bastards didn't bother removing the original lading tags from the loads, sir," Reddish said. "Those are the ships these things come off of."

"Ah," Alexis said, "so the ships which brought them here in trade?" She wasn't at all certain that was useful information or why Reddish had included it.

"No, sir," he said. "That's off the lading tags — a proper delivery and the ship bringing it would've took that back with them as proof they'd turned it over. Next ship took the cargo on would have its own tag, see?"

Alexis thought she did see now.

"So this cargo was never properly delivered by these ships, you mean?"

Reddish nodded. "Proper pirates back someplace *civilized* would've stripped those off and made their own — this lot don't seem to care who knows."

"I buy!" Aksoy called out, speaking for the first time since they'd arrived in the hold.

"You may well have, sir," Alexis said. She believed that, for there was little chance *Beneghem* herself could act as a pirate. "But from entirely the wrong source, it seems, and that is to your detriment." She took a deep breath — this find did make her feel better about her actions. "Mister Reddish, stay aboard with your pick of —" She considered the size of *Beneghem*'s crew which would have to be watched over and the hands necessary to sail her. "— twelve hands, armed. Make ready to sail and trail *Mongoose*. We've still time to make our first rendezvous if we don't delay."

"Aye, sir," Reddish said with a grin. As the prize crew, he and any men he chose would have larger shares of *Beneghem* and the cargo was a decent one.

Alexis' tablet *pinged* for her attention.

"Aye?"

"Sail, sir," Villar said. "To windward, but coming our way."

THIS SAIL PROVED to be another merchantman. One which turned and ran at the sight of *Mongoose* and *Beneghem*, her captain rightly determining that two ships, sitting idle in *darkspace*, could not bode well for his own command.

Mongoose, though, proved her speed again, and quickly caught up.

There was no subterfuge of false colors necessary, as the Chase was already alerted and running, so Alexis had her colors showing from the start, guns run out and bowchasers manned.

It took only a single shot from those bowchasers, laid close along the Chase's starboard side, to bring the captain to his senses.

Alexis soon found herself boarding a strange ship for the second time that day, Nabb and the remnants of her *Nightingale* boat crew at her back, another grinning master's mate, this time Corrick Stott, leading the way, for he knew he'd have the prize crew's share of this one.

"This one", though, turned out to be the *Bisharet*, a shabby, decrepit bit of a ship, even after the standard for these worlds set by *Beneghem*, carrying bulk goods from Kayseri to Antalya. The captain spoke no English at all, and Alexis had none of his language, so she must resort to having her tablet translate, which introduced a slight, but frustrating, delay in their converse.

She supposed she'd have to begin wearing her earpiece as a means to better hear the translations, though she disliked it. Perhaps, if *Mongoose* were to spend more time near the portion of the Barbary

151

which bordered the former Berry March she might make use of her French, but her German was simply not up to the task of speaking with native Hanoverese, and as she understood it, there were more languages than German spoken in the Barbary, as well — far more. The systems here seemed to be a dumping ground for the unwanted of nearly the entire rest of settled space, and rather than settle on any one language, they often made do with bits of each. Alexis found that she could, at best, garner one word in five of the local patois, so resorted to her tablet's translation.

Alexis stared from the sacks of grain in the hold to the ship's records on her tablet and made a sudden decision.

"Captain Katirci?"

"Yes? You wish?" the man said, nodding nervously. He was fat and mustachioed, with metal beads tied into the ends of his waxed facial hair in a way that Alexis found comical, but she was certain must be the height of style on his home world.

"You see the *Beneghem* trailing after us and know what we're about, yes?"

Katirci sighed and nodded, his shoulders slumping. He murmured something and a moment later her tablet repeated, "You will take my ship because the *beep big man* takes yours."

Alexis sighed. There were some terms that simply couldn't be translated in any reasonable manner — the machine did its best, she assumed, but couldn't when the concepts were simply too alien. "Big man" must be some dialectical term for whoever ruled the system Katirci was assuming Alexis and New London were in reprisal against.

"Mister Stott?"

"Aye, sir?" Stott's grin was wide as he readied to take over the ship.

"Collect your prize crew and return to *Mongoose*, Mister Stott."

"Aye, si — wait, what?" He blinked and frowned. "Beggin' your pardon, sir, but ... what again?"

"Return to *Mongoose*, Mister Stott, we'll not be taking *Bisharet* — at least not today."

The hope in Katirci's eyes nearly broke Alexis' heart, for she thought he might still be wondering if she was playing with him — raising his hopes before dashing them again.

"*Beneghem* was carrying pirated cargo, Captain Katirci, and it appears you are not."

"No, lady" Katirci said. "We carry only grain to Kayseri and then *beep untranslatable local produce* to Antalya."

"So I see from your records and from your cargo. This is why, Captain Katirci, I will not be taking your ship."

"Blessings!" Katirci exclaimed. "You rain blessings upon me and my family's blessings shall fall upon you!"

"Captain," Stott said, looking around the hold, "do you really want to —"

"Easy, Mister Stott, you'll lead the prize crew for the next ship we do take — one with, perhaps, more than grain for its cargo, yes?"

Stott perked up at that. The grain wouldn't bring much at all at a prize court and *Bisharet* wasn't much of a prize herself, come to that. He could look to forward to a share of a much larger pie now, and that seemed to ease his disappointment at putting it off.

"Keep away from the pirated cargoes, Captain Katirci, and you'll have nothing to fear from *Mongoose*, do you understand?"

Katirci swallowed heavily and nodded. "Grain and *beep untranslatable local produce*," he said, nodding more. "Always grain and *beep untranslatable local produce*. Never anything for your great devourer of serpents to worry over."

Alexis stared at her tablet for a moment, lips pursed. Was that how the thing would translate *Mongoose* now, she wondered? Well, it could be worse — or more appropriate.

Defiler of boots, she mused, *or we could be known as stinking-bloody-nuisances.*

"See that you do," Alexis said.

Katirci nodded vigorously.

"Captain Katirci," Alexis added, deciding that she might as well begin her search with someone who owed her a bit of good will, at least, "I do have some questions. Have you, in your travels, come across word any foreign fleets?"

Katirci shrugged. "All fleets are foreign here."

"I suppose so, but some time ago — over a year now, I think — the Hanoverese and New London fleets may have crossed the Barbary, perhaps even battled here. Have you heard of such a thing?"

Katirci shook his head. "This is a thing you wish to know? The knowledge would be a blessing to you?"

"It would, indeed."

Katirci grinned. "Then I will find this thing."

TWENTY-ONE

Enclave was an odd world to Alexis' eye, with far reaching ice caps and what little land not covered in ice being desert. There were three settlements, all at the very edge of those ice floes, and spaced nearly equidistant around the globe.

Mongoose transitioned from *darkspace* and made her way toward the planet with no pilot boat and no challenge from the world itself. There was plenty of other traffic in-system, and therefore plenty of communication, but there seemed to be no one in overall charge.

Ships announced their intention to leave orbit, take orbit, or transition with impunity.

That was all well and good for a Fringe world with little in the way of traffic, but Enclave had nearly fifty ships in orbit, and the lines of their tracks cluttered the world's image on the navigation plot.

"Is this right?" Villar asked, looking up from his tablet. "A geostationary orbit?"

"That's what the sailing notes, what there are for this world, claim is best." Alexis said. "And over the territory of whichever of these towns you plan to visit. Apparently they are none too neighborly here."

Enclave was variously held by three other systems, and had been fought over by more for some time. Its location made for a welcome break through the Barbary, midway between New London and *Hso-Hsi*, and its makeup, with so much ice, made it a preferred place for taking on fresh water.

After years of fighting, those three systems had reached an uneasy agreement to share the system, hence the three different settlements. One of those catered primarily to Hanoverese shipping, another to *Hso-hsi*, and the third's, their destination's, custom came from New London ships. None of the settlements were official outposts of those governments — though with the entire Barbary being ostensibly Hanoverese, the argument could be made that the entire system was. In reality, it was simply that merchants of a given nation sought their own and this was how it had worked out here.

Enclave was also one of the systems Dansby had given her, a place where there'd be a contact outside of Eades' to gain information and perhaps sell their prizes.

"Make for the New London portion of their orbital, will you, Mister Villar?"

"Aye, sir."

THE FREEZING, dry air struck Alexis immediately on debarking from *Mongoose's* boat, tightening her skin and making the inside of her nose ache and itch. She sniffed irritably and looked around, noting that most of the people on the landing field — only a space of the ice flow kept somewhat flat and clear of snow — had a sort of scarf over the lower half of their faces, in addition to hurrying from one place to another. Many seemed to be wearing vacsuits, despite being on the planet's surface, and she supposed that made sense as the suits were quite good at regulating heat.

She and the others merely had heavy coats, and they quickly found these not nearly enough.

Alexis made her way toward the nearest structure, followed by Villar and Nabb, the rest of the boat crew staying behind and quickly raising the ramp after her.

The door, more of a hatch, really, despite their being on the surface, was closed when she got there and there appeared to be no way to open it — only a speaker and button mounted on the wall nearby.

A voice sounded from the speaker before Alexis could press the button.

"Twenty centimarks."

She blinked. "What?"

"Twenty centimarks for entry."

Alexis thought for a moment, calculating the Barbary's currency, loosely tied to Hanover's, into more familiar units — that was nearly a shilling. "So much?"

If a speaker mounted on a wall could shrug, this one seemed to. "It's twenty to open the hatch. Twenty or lift, your choice."

"What? A shilling each time?"

"Heat costs. Now do you wish to come in or no?"

"Very well."

The hatch slid open and then started closing again as Alexis and the others entered. She saw then that it was, indeed, a ship's hatch, not just made to look like one, and part of an entire airlock. The outer hatch closed and the inner opened, revealing a set of metal steps leading down.

The walls past the lock were bare ice with pipes and wires strung from hanging posts above their heads. Here and there other hatches and simpler doors were visible, their frames embedded in the ice that made up the corridor walls.

At the bottom of the stairs, some five meters down, a man sat in the corridor at a small desk with a set of hatch controls.

"You can take on water from the far side of the field," he said, after Alexis transferred the fee to him. "Three marks a boatload.

We'll know what you take, so don't try hiding it or you'll be banned from landing."

Alexis nodded. "Our purser will see to that."

"Right, then, all you'll want's down that way," the man said, pointing.

It was warmer inside, at least, though not what Alexis would call comfortable.

"We'll see this man of Dansby's," Alexis told the others as they moved off down the corridor, "sell our prize, then share out a bit to the men and have a day's leave."

"I could wish we had a man or two more along in this place," Nabb muttered.

Alexis was beginning to agree. She hadn't wanted to march in with a strong force at her back, but the look of this settlement did nothing to make her feel safe. There was a hard look in the eye of every person they passed and she thought those looks lingered on her group a bit too long.

These corridors were not at all what she'd expected, either. Given their proximity to the landing field, she'd thought they'd hold the typical pubs and other establishments catering to visiting spacers. Instead, the corridor was nearly empty, with closed off doorways and people scurrying hurriedly from one place to another.

She wondered where the crews of all those ships in orbit were, as the number of boats on the field indicated there were many on leave here.

After a few minutes of walking with no sign of a business establishment, she stopped a man who looked less angry than the rest.

"Excuse me, but where might we find a chandlery?"

The man shrugged, jerked his head in the direction they were headed, and muttered, "Where you find anything else here — the bloody Casino."

THE CASINO, when they reached it, was quite unlike the rest of the settlement.

It was as though every bit of merchanting, entertainment, and debauchery had been crammed into one place and not allowed elsewhere on Enclave. A pair of double-wide hatches allowed entry from the corridor, and where the corridor was dimly lit and quiet, the Casino awash with light, color, and sound.

The walls here were covered, not bare ice, and it was comfortably warm.

Voices, mere conversation as well as shouts of triumph and anger, vied with the sounds of the machines, and Alexis had to squint for a moment against the lights as they entered.

An attendant met them as they entered and offered to take their heavy outerwear, which they accepted.

They wandered for a short time, simply taking in the sight, which was far larger and more extravagant than the typical gambling houses on a station, where space was at a premium. It was only as they wandered farther that Alexis realized just how much larger, as the space wasn't all one. Instead their path twisted around walls of gaming machines, with each turn revealing yet another space and new, different machines.

Interspersed among it all were the other sorts of establishments she'd expected to see just inside the hatch from the landing field. The pubs, chandleries, shipwrights, houses of negotiable virtue, and all the other myriad sites and services a visiting spacer or captain might need to seek out. And all of them placed in and around the Casino, so that one simply had to pass untold numbers of games to reach them.

"One could become quite lost in here, I think," Villar murmured.

Alexis agreed. "I rather suppose that's the point."

"It explains where the ships' crews are, certainly."

"Yes," Alexis scanned the crowd. "And makes our finding of this friend of Dansby's — Remington Wheeley, his name is — the more difficult. Dansby said to seek him at the center of things, do either of you see a middle to this —" She broke off, realizing that Nabb wasn't listening. "Nabb? *Nabb!*" She grasped his arm and shook it.

Nabb blinked from where he'd been staring at the surrounding machines. His eyes darted to Alexis, then off again. "Sorry, sir, but that's a powerful lot of coin, that is."

Alexis followed his gaze to a bank of machines where a blinking sign advertised some sort of possible winnings. It was, to be honest, a very great deal of coin.

"And it'll cost you a powerful lot of your purse to try for it, I imagine," Alexis said.

"Aye," Nabb nodded, not looking away. "But if —"

Alexis grasped his arm. "Come on, then, perhaps you can have a go later when —" She broke off as she noted Villar was now staring at the same number. She could almost see the thoughts working in his head as he imagined what that amount would mean for him — concerned as he was over being able to provide for Marie.

She grasped his arm as well, and tugged the pair along.

"Did neither of you study maths at all?"

TWENTY-TWO

The center of things turned out to not be so central after all.

Alexis stopped an attendant to ask where the center of the casino floor might be, and the woman, scantily clad with an odd arrangement of studs and rings in her left ear, pointed out the way. When they arrived, though, they found a collection of restaurants ranging from food stalls to far more elaborate dining which gave no further clue to where they might find Remington Wheeley.

"Do you fancy a bite, sir?" Nabb suggested, nodding at a nearby cart selling skewers of meat and vegetables slapped into flat rounds of bread.

"I don't suppose it would hurt anything to eat a bit." She paid for food for all of them, noting that the vendor also had an arrangement of jewelry in his left ear. She waited until they made their way to an empty table before mentioning it.

"It's an odd sort of fashion," Villar agreed.

Nabb nodded.

"I note it's only the workers, and none of the patrons, who follow it," Alexis said, studying the crowd.

They finished their food — good and enough for a time, though Alexis felt they'd need a proper supper soon. She found one of the ever-present girls wandering the tables with a tray of drinks and this time Alexis asked specifically for Wheeley, which got them a bizarre bit of directions through the maze of gaming tables.

"It was around the great, spinning wheel game and past this place with dancing, yes?" Alexis asked.

Villar nodded absently, and Alexis noted the direction of his gaze was toward the place with dancing, which had nearly naked women dancing in silhouetted boxes out front.

Alexis cleared her throat. "Mister Villar?"

Villar jumped, then grasped Nabb's arm and tugged him along as well.

"We might never get the crew to leave this place once we've let them come down," Villar muttered.

"I imagine they'll have to once their coin runs out," Alexis said and moved on.

WHAT "THE CENTER OF THINGS" actually meant, it turned out, was a discrete, walled off portion of the casino intended for those who wished their gambling to be at higher stakes and in a more private setting.

A large man in a shiny, purple suit guarded the entrance, which had an actual velvet rope stretched across it as a barrier.

Alexis, Villar, and Nabb approached, Alexis very aware of the appraising look the man gave her group. Nabb was in a clean ship's jumpsuit, though bare of any insignia. Villar was in civilian dress, though Alexis had to admit it was of higher quality than her own linen shirt and denim trousers, brought from Dalthus. A ship's badge for the crew and any sort of uniform for her officers was something she still hadn't accomplished — but worrying about it now would do her no good in getting past this gate for a chat with Wheeley.

She stopped at the entrance, but the guard looked past her right shoulder to Villar.

Alexis cleared her throat and the guard looked down at her.

"We're looking for a Mister Wheeley, if you don't mind."

The guard raised an eyebrow. "Mister Wheeley is not one for being seen most days."

That, at least, settled Alexis' concerns about whether they'd be able to find this Wheeley, as he seemed known to the guard. Whether they'd be let in to see him, was another matter.

"I've come at the recommendation of an old friend of his," Alexis said.

The guard grunted. "Easy to say. Who should I say's recommended you?"

Alexis hesitated, not sure if Dansby would want his name bandied about except to the individuals she was to speak to, but if they couldn't get in they'd have to send some sort of message and there didn't seem to be any other way.

"Please tell him I've come from Avrel Dansby, I believe he knows the nam —"

The guard's reaction was immediate. He stepped in front of the roped off entrance, left hand extended at Alexis, as though to keep her from rushing forward, his right went inside his jacket.

His eyes scanned from Alexis to Villar and Nabb, then to the whole expanse of the room behind them as though searching for something.

"Scan the floor for Dansby," he said, eyes still moving.

Alexis noted his earpiece and assumed he was speaking to some unseen monitor and not to her, but the reaction amused her more than anything else — if for no other reason than to validate her own feeling that one should reach for a weapon the moment the man was mentioned.

"He's not come with," Alexis said.

"Aye," the guard said, eyes never ceasing their movement, "he'd have you say that."

She certainly hadn't expected this. Dansby'd said he wouldn't return to the Barbary for some reason, but this reaction spoke to a much larger tale than she'd assumed. It also appeared to frustrate her efforts to meet this Wheeley fellow.

"He's really not," she said, though what she could do to prove it, she couldn't think of.

The man's scanning eyes paused a moment, as though listening, then he grimaced, "Mister Wheeley'll see you."

He stepped aside and unhooked one end of the rope, but stopped Villar and Nabb from following. "Just her, he says."

Alexis nodded to them that she'd be all right and they reluctantly moved to the side to wait.

"That table there in the center," the guard said.

The indicated table had only a single gambler at it, a heavy-set man wearing a dark suit, in a chair at the center of the table's half-circle. Across from him sat a woman dealing the cards and before him were several large stacks of betting chips.

Even with the relatively few others in the room, Alexis noted that the tables surrounding Wheeley's were empty, as though allowing the man maximum space.

Compared to the main casino floor, this room was almost deathly silent, and she felt out of place as she crossed to Wheeley's table. The opulence made it clear that this was not a welcoming place for a Fringe landholder's granddaughter, no matter their wealth on Dalthus — and that made her wonder at how much wealth there might be here in the Barbary. How much, and its source.

Wheeley turned to face her when she was a few steps away. She stopped, meeting his eyes.

"You've used a name I haven't heard in an age," Wheeley said. "But not one I've longed to hear again. I'll give you a few words before I have you thrown out a lock onto the ice, so speak them quickly."

Alexis clenched her jaw on her first response. She was no longer a Naval officer and this was not New London space, so she had little authority — none, truth to tell — here and no way to object to the man's manner. She'd have to hope that Dansby hadn't steered her wrong.

It would be just like the snake to send me off to someone who hated him.

"Good afternoon, Mister Wheeley, I'm Captain Alexis Carew of the private ship *Mongoose* —"

"Those aren't the words that'll keep you inside," Wheeley said. "Dansby's an easy name to throw about, so why should I believe you've ever met him?"

"All right, then. Mister Dansby said that I should remind you of a debt to him, and —"

"Nonsense!" Wheeley turned his back to her and spoke to the dealer. "Call a floorman, will you, and have this bint tossed out on the ice."

Alexis stepped closer and raised her voice, if she was going to be thrown out she'd at least have the satisfaction of embarrassing this Wheeley fellow.

"Mister Dansby's exact words were, 'Tell that treacherous, cowardly bastard that he owes me and it's time he paid at least one of his debts.'"

The quiet room grew quieter and several gamers turned to stare at her. Others, she noted, directed their dealers' attention back to the game and paid her no heed.

Wheeley's shoulders shook and, without turning, he kicked the chair to his left back from the table.

"Sit down, girl, and tell me what the bugger's been up to, will you?"

Alexis sat and the muted sounds from the other tables resumed their previous levels.

"Mister Dansby told me —"

"It's a thousand mark minimum," Wheeley said, pointing to a spot on the table's felt top in front of Alexis.

"What?" Did he really expect her to join in the gambling just to

165

sit here and talk to him? And at a thousand marks, the wager was far more than she'd care to hazard.

"You sit at one of my tables, you'd best be playing," Wheeley said. "The game's pontoon, have you played?"

Alexis studied the table for a moment. It was a game she recognized, as she'd pulled more than one spacer out of gaming establishments to get them back aboard ship in time, but she'd never had the urge to play herself. It was something about getting closest to some number without going over, she thought she remembered, but didn't see the point — never mind that the thousand marks Wheeley was demanding came to over two hundred and fifty pounds.

She narrowed her eyes.

"I've seen it, Mister Wheeley, but is this some attempt to put off the assistance Mister Dansby believes you owe?"

Wheeley froze, then slowly turned to glare at her. "Are you calling me a welcher, girl?"

"I'm suggesting, sir, that there should be no conditions placed on speaking of a debt's repayment — one either owes or one does not, wouldn't you say?"

Wheeley turned from her to the dealer and his voice took on an unexpected whine. "But there's rules about sitting at my tables, isn't there, Afet?"

"There are rules, Mister Wheeley," the woman agreed.

"See?" he asked, turning back to Alexis. "There are rules."

Alexis nodded. "Of course, sir." She started to stand. "Perhaps there's another time we might speak?"

Wheeley grimaced. "No, I'll not have it hanging over my head to hear what the old serpent wants."

Alexis raised an eyebrow at hearing him characterize Dansby so — it was her own opinion of the man as well.

Wheeley sighed, then placed a chip on the felt in front of Alexis. "Come on, then," he said.

Alexis wasn't sure if he said it to her or the dealer, but sat back down again. If Wheeley wished to pay the cost of speaking to her here, then she'd not stop him.

"I'll not make your losses good, Mister Wheeley," she said.

"Just have your say." He motioned to the dealer. "Cards!" Then to Alexis. "What does Dansby want?"

"As I said, Mister Wheeley, I'm here as captain of a private ship —"

"Card?" Wheeley asked pointing to the table.

Alexis glanced and saw that the dealer was looking at her expectantly. "What —"

"Do you want another card?" Wheeley asked. "Keep up the pace, will you?"

The two cards she had seemed a small enough number. "Yes, fine, I suppose." Another card hit the felt. "Isn't that the sum we're trying for?"

Wheeley snorted and Alexis felt it must have been, for the dealer collected the cards and placed another chip in front of Alexis.

"As I was saying, a private ship, *Mongoose*, of which Mister Dansby is a principal. He believes you may have —"

"Do you wish to press, miss?" the dealer asked.

Alexis looked over, distracted. What did that even mean? "Yes?"

The dealer stacked the two chips one atop the other and went back to the cards. Alexis hurried on, hoping to get a full sentence in before she was interrupted again.

"I have letters of marque from New London, Mister Wheeley, to address piracy and smuggling in the Barbary —"

Wheeley laughed. "It'll take more than a letter to deal with that here. Cards!"

Alexis noted the dealer was again looking to her and wondered if that was how this conversation would go — half a thought before being interrupted again.

"Very well," she said, then to Wheeley, "Be that as it may, Mister Dansby led me to believe that you might be of some assistance in that regard — yes, press, or whatever it's called, thank you. Both with the disposal of prizes and with other information I'm seeking."

Wheeley grinned. "Aye, ships I can ... dispose of, aplenty. What information, though, I've my own reputation and business to look after — but I do owe Dansby, and if this is what he'd choose to settle the debt, what do you wish to know? Fat hunting grounds for your letter of marque?"

"No. Before the war ended — no, not another, thank you —" Alexis caught Wheeley's look of impatience and told the dealer before he could demand she do so. "— two fleets are said to have battled their way through the Barbary. I'm seeking word of them, if you have any."

Wheeley grunted. "There were wrecks from that all through this space."

"Why no certain word, then?" Alexis had to assume that either Hanover or New London or even both would have sent their own fleets to investigate if they'd known that for certain.

"This is the *Barbary*, girl," Wheeley said. "It was Barbary ships what spotted 'em and the Barbary don't share — not without reason. What the few merchants passing through might've seen, well, a merchant who wishes to last here learns to keep his visions to himself." He grunted as the dealer took his bet and paid Alexis, then he placed more chips for the next deal.

"Can you tell me where?" Try though she might, Alexis couldn't quite keep her excitement in check. If she could track down the battle sites, she might be able to find survivors in surrounding systems.

"Most were lifeless hulks," Wheeley said, eyes on his cards. "Some were salvaged before they broke up, but it's certain they're all gone by now."

"Where?" Alexis' heart skipped. They wouldn't be there still, as they'd have been broken up by the *darkspace* winds driving them against dark matter — without fusion plants or intact hulls, the ships would have been wrecked, torn apart, and the pieces compressed to nothing by those forces — but knowing where could help with finding any survivors. There were worlds in the Barbary where merchants seldom stopped and survivors, set down there in ships' boats, could still be waiting for rescue. It was a long chance that Delaine's ship might be one of those wrecked there, longer that he'd be among the survivors, if so — she pushed that thought aside — and longer still that she might locate him, but she'd do everything in her power to try. And any survivors might have further word — any word — of where Delaine might be.

"I've a list in my head this very minute, you think?"

He grunted again as the dealer took his bet. Alexis noted that the dealer had stopped asking her about the "pressing" matter, which she now took to mean leaving one's winnings in the betting circle. The stack there had grown considerably and Wheeley grunted yet again as the cards fell and the dealer added to Alexis' total without even asking if she'd like another — the total of the cards was the target from the start this time.

"Give us a new deck!" Wheeley said.

"Of course, sir." The dealer began shuffling a fresh deck of cards.

Alexis hoped the respite would give Wheeley the opportunity to talk, uninterrupted by the game.

"How long do you suppose it might take you to get me that information, Mister Wheeley?"

"Before you can get back to your ship, I suppose — what was it? *Mongoose?*"

"Yes."

"All right then. Now about this prize of yours, at least there's some profit in that for me."

TWENTY-THREE

"Did that go ... well, sir?" Villar asked.

His eyes were on Alexis' hands, which held a number of the betting chips. She and Wheeley had settled on a price for their prize, the *Beneghem* — a fair price, and fairer than she'd expect from a New London prize court. It had taken some further bargaining for him to agree to make the payment in coin rather than his casino's scrip, though. Both of them knew that exchanging scrip for coin at one of Wheeley's own agents would only profit the man further, and that her crew, knowing this as well, would be further tempted to spend it all here in any case.

It had taken another of those instances where the dealer paid her on the initial two cards dealt, and the stack of chips before her more than doubling, for Wheeley to stop insisting on scrip.

"All right, girl, coin!" he'd fairly shouted. "And then off with you — the profit's not worth the cost of having you at my tables, and if the rest of your crew's as bloody lucky, then take the coin and sail! Good bloody riddance!"

Their business done, she'd thanked him, but he'd refused to let her leave the chips behind, taking back only his initial bet on her behalf.

The dealer had exchanged the rather large stacks of chips for others of a different color and size — fewer, but still more than she could comfortably carry.

"Carry some few of these for me, will you, Mister Villar?"

"Aye ... uh, sir."

Villar stared at the handful of colored clay for a moment.

"So ... well, sir?"

"Aye. We'll have information on the fleet battles before we sail, and full value for *Beneghem* and her cargo — in coin and in hand this very day."

"The crew'll be glad to hear that, sir."

Alexis nodded. She scanned the area, trying to remember where the center of the place was with all the food, as she found herself quite hungry. Around her, machines buzzed and blinked while crews from a dozen ships sat before them or at tables.

For a moment, she considered seating herself at another table and having a go while she wasn't distracted by her conversation with Wheeley, but then her stomach rumbled angrily.

"Shall we have ourselves a bit of a proper supper, Mister Villar? My treat — Mister Wheeley's, rather," she corrected holding up the chips she still held.

Yes, a fine meal would sit better than more gaming, though she did wonder if she might do even better if she weren't distracted by a conversation. It did seem to be an easy game to profit at.

TWENTY-FOUR

Whatever else Enclave had to offer, its food was top notch.

Alexis, Villar, and Nabb found a place with nearly every dish she could think of set out for the taking, and many she'd never heard of. In fact, the only thing she'd not seen them offer was *currywurst* — and she'd looked more out of curiosity to see the thing than any real desire to try it.

Stuffed to bursting, they'd returned to *Mongoose*, by which time Wheeley, who was nothing if not efficient, had sent his own men to take possession of *Beneghem* and transferred the agreed upon amount to *Mongoose's* accounts. She'd added to those accounts the coin from cashing in her handfuls of chips — a goodly sum in itself.

She'd barely made it through the announcement to the crew of their share, and that they'd have it in hand, in full, for their liberty, as the rumble of their shouts seemed to resonate in her overfull stomach.

It was with a great deal of relief that she'd sent the starboard watch off for a full day on Enclave and finally settled into her cot. She was entirely certain her denim trousers must have shrunk between leaving the restaurant and arriving in her cabin, and it was a joy to be out of them.

"Will you take some wine before bed, sir, or a bit of bourbon?" Isom asked, retrieving her clothes from where she'd dropped them.

Alexis groaned, easing herself into her pillow and placing a hand on her stomach. "No, I believe I shall not eat or drink again for a fortnight." She took a deep breath — well, as deep as she had room for — and closed her eyes.

"When you take your own liberty, Isom, I do highly recommend the buffet ... only do be wary."

IT SEEMED Alexis had only just closed her eyes and managed to get to sleep before a hand on her shoulder woke her.

"Word from planetside, sir," Isom whispered.

Alexis groaned. She wasn't yet ready to give up on sleep, nor had her overfull stomach had time to settle, and word from any planet where a ship's crew was on leave could hold no good news. She rolled her shoulders to work out the kinks, eliciting a low chitter of irritation from the creature curled up in a warm ball on her chest.

Idly, she reached a hand up to stroke its fur. There were times she thought the thing might not be so vile as others. In truth, she did sleep better when it was loose in her compartment and chose to curl up with her — not dreamless, but without the horrifying nightmares she'd experienced in the past.

She opened her eyes to find Isom watching her pet the creature with an amused look on his face.

"Off!" she said, turning her stroking into a prod. It wouldn't do for Isom to begin thinking she wouldn't space the thing if it became too much trouble. "Bloody thing looks to steal my breath in my sleep."

The creature grudgingly leapt from her chest, planting a disapproving foot in her gut as it did so.

"That's cats, sir," Isom said. "The breath and all."

"I'll put nothing past the vile thing, Isom."

The creature made its way to a covered box Isom had convinced it to use — enough of the time to keep it from being spaced, at least — by the disturbing but expedient idea of including a pair of Alexis old, well-worn boots inside. There was a scratching sound and a spray of dried clay scattered across her deck.

"Sorry, sir," Isom said. "I'll get that cleaned up. Thought Boots' aim was getting better in there."

"I think its aim is better than we give it credit for." She slid out of her cot and began pulling on her uniform. "Who's locked up?"

If the planetary authorities were calling them, rather than *Mongoose* having to contact them to locate wayward crew, then the brawl must have been so egregious that the citizens wanted her spacers off-planet immediately.

"The starboard watch, sir."

"Yes, I recall it's the starboard on leave just now, but which of them are in cells?"

She put her arms through her linen shirt and began buttoning, thinking once again that she had need of some sort of proper uniform, but was uncomfortable at many of the designs she'd seen. They were too reminiscent of the Navy and seemed as though the wearer was playing dress-up — like some fringe world constable covering his chest with ribbons and badges in an effort to prop up his authority.

Isom stopped his sweeping of the deck and shrugged.

"Near as the caller said, sir, it'd be the lot."

TWENTY-FIVE

E nclave's casino security office was more like the rest of the settlement than the casino itself — dingy, ill-kept, and nearly freezing, with walls of sheer ice. Alexis supposed if one were to see the inside of it, then one's patronage was no longer desired by Wheeley and his partners, so keeping up the pretense of luxury was no longer necessary.

Still, she thought, stubbing the toe of her boot against a raised bit of grime on the metal decking laid over ice, *they might send a cleaning bot through once a fortnight or so.*

There were one or two others in the security office's waiting room seated on plastic benches — Alexis assumed they were picking up shipmates or loved ones, but was a little distressed at how resigned they looked. She hoped she wouldn't be kept waiting as long as they seemed to have been.

Already, the wait had been longer than she expected. After the apparent urgency of the call that one of *Mongoose's* officers was requested and required to attend to a security matter regarding the ship's crew on the planet's surface, her reception once she arrived was ... disinterested.

She cleared her throat again, but the woman behind the glass partition never looked up — she merely kept her eyes glued to her tablet and held up a single finger, clearly meaning *wait*.

The officials hadn't said exactly what happened over the coms, but she hadn't been required to come herself, which, thankfully, meant no one was actually dead. She could have sent Villar, as he was already on planet for his own leave, but she'd given him all-night-in and didn't wish to disturb whatever he was about — or know about it, if it was something Marie might disapprove of.

She didn't think Villar was the sort to hunt up a doxy, but months in *darkspace* with more months ahead was a hard thing to take. He'd gone off on his own for leave at Penduli, as well, with no word of what he was about. She shrugged. Marie was her friend, but Villar was her first officer — and a good one. Whatever he got about was between the two of them and none of Alexis' business.

She was still not sure enough of Hacking or Parrill to send one of them — they were decent officers for watch-standing, but Alexis didn't think they had the feel of a private ship's crew just yet. Parrill was still too much the merchant officer, not understanding the sort of men who'd seek out a battle, and Hacking had too much of the Navy in him yet. Alexis herself wasn't certain how she'd handle half her crew's being jailed.

The security officer behind glass finally looked up and edged closer to the glass.

"Ship or local?" she asked.

"Ship," Alexis said. "The *Mongoose*."

The officer's eyes narrowed and she frowned. "Whyn't you say so sooner? They've been asking to get your lot gone to free up space in the cells." She tapped at her tablet and the door next to the glass buzzed. "Through, left, right, straight, follow the signs to holding."

Her eyes returned to her tablet.

Alexis assumed those were some sort of directions, or what passed for them here, and led her group — Nabb and a few from the port watch who hadn't had liberty yet — through the door, past which there was a counter. The officer looked up again once they'd closed the door and frowned at Alexis.

"Thought they'd asked for a ship's officer — you his clerk?"

Alexis shook her head. "I am *Mongoose's* master." She held out her hand, thinking a bit of politeness might be in order — she'd found most magistrates and even station patrol or planetary constables found a bit of common courtesy from ship's officers a pleasant surprise. "Captain Alex —"

"Don't look like one." The officer returned her eyes to her tablet in clear dismissal.

"Is it really the uniform?" Alexis wondered aloud, moving on.

"A uniform does add a certain something," Nabb said.

"Speak me no somethings, Nabb," Alexis said. "I had enough of 'somethings' from Isom and Villar with their bloody adverts on Penduli."

"Aye, sir."

Still, it was tiresome forever being assumed to be some sort of messenger or servant rather than *Mongoose's* master.

She followed the officer's directions, such as they were, as best she could through a warren of corridors, until she finally encountered a sign affixed to the wall which directed them to the holding area.

"And why they couldn't have just put up signs the rest of the way, I'll not fathom," she muttered.

"The plodders're never helpful, sir," Nabb said.

Alexis agreed, but perhaps couldn't fault them. After all, their interactions with ships' crews *were* always after the trouble'd started, weren't they? And, while her own ship and crew might spend weeks between systems, the station patrols and constables knew that seeing the stern of one troublesome crew only meant the bowsprit of the next was rapidly approaching from the transition point.

She had to grin, though. Nabb might be coxswain of her boat crew, but he had little time aboard ship, and here he was talking about the local constabulary as "plodders" as though he'd seen a hundred systems.

"I hadn't thought you'd been in trouble often enough to think that of the authorities, Nabb," she chided.

"No troubles, sir, but it's more'n the bosun off to collect any waywards when we had *Nightingale*. I've seen my share of lockups from the outside."

Alexis nodded. Most often it would be the bosun and his mates who collected the drunks and laggards from wherever they'd been penned up for their indiscretions, but her boat crew'd brought their share back as well. It was only for something egregious that a ship's officer was required, much less her captain.

"I wonder if they asked for me as Mister Dockett wasn't aboard." It was an idle hopefulness, but she'd also had *Mongoose* call Dockett's tablet and he hadn't answered, which was quite unlike the man.

Ahead of them was yet another doorway with a windowed cube beside it and yet another bored and surly looking officer of Enclave's constabulary. Here the waiting area was somewhat removed from the window itself, so Alexis had Nabb and his lads settle themselves there while she approached the officer, fixing her face in what she hoped was an expectantly pleasant smile despite the early hour for her and having been dragged from her cot for this nonsense.

"Good ... afternoon?" she began with an attempt at estimating the time on Enclave's surface.

The officer looked up from his tablet — it seemed as though every security officer she'd ever seen sitting at a desk had their head buried in a tablet of some sort and never doing any actual work — frowned at Alexis, then looked her up and down, lingering a bit, as she'd come to expect, in inappropriate places. His eyes returned to his tablet.

"No visitation by unaccompanied minors," he said, voice flat and uninterested. "Come back with a parent or guardian. If your parent or guardian's the one in lock up, an uncle'll do."

Alexis took a deep breath, then let it out slowly. She really did need to come up with a uniform of some sort — the denim pants and linen shirt she preferred at home didn't identify her as a spacer, let alone a ship's captain. Add, she had to admit, her slight stature, and she still did look quite young.

"I'm not a child. I'm here for the crew of the *Mongoose*."

The man glanced up, shrugged, then returned to his tablet, mumbling, "No wives or sweethearts. Wives and sweethearts're on Thursday. Five centimarks and twenty percent of your fee." He looked her over, eyes lingering again, and shrugged. "Ten percent if you give a guard a go — first, mind you — but most of us like a bit more to hold on to, if you understand? Maybe Farnlea, he's got the look about him that may like your sort, but he don't work Thursday's until next month, so —"

It took Alexis some time to catch up with the man and rein her temper in. He'd gone from thinking her a child to thinking her a doxy in an instant, and blatantly stating that the guards would take a fee for such a visit — in coin or in kind — stunned her. Not that they did, but that they'd be so comfortable saying so outright.

Enclave must be the most corrupt system she'd ever seen — then she paused and thought again. Was it more corrupt to state it openly or to hide it behind a veneer of smiles and innuendo as they did elsewhere?

Regardless of that, she fought the urge to slam her palm down on the little ledge of a desk jutting through the window and cut the man to ribbons with a few choice words. She wasn't Navy and this wasn't a New London world, for all that its people might have come from there. There was no Admiralty authority backing her up, only her own, her ship, and what influence she might have through Wheeley's name and her association with him — something she hesitated to use, for such associations always came with a cost later.

She ground her teeth, face fixed as pleasant as she could make it, and laid her palm on the window's ledge — hoping he wouldn't note her slow placement there as the forceful slap she wished it was.

"I'm sorry I wasn't clear," she said as he went on to list others who might be interested in her charms. She began to wonder if she should be more irritated by him thinking her a doxy or that she might need such earnest assistance in finding clientele.

"Just come back Thursday, then, right?

I mean, it's not as though I couldn't make a living at it if I chose to, is it? I might even be quite good at —

"I'm captain of *Mongoose!*"

The guard's eyes widened. "Oh."

"Yes," Alexis said, thankful they'd settled that and she could stop thinking —

"Look, what make-pretend a man wants for his coin, I'll not judge — known many a spacer who'd like to bend his captain over and ... well, that don't change that this ain't *Thursday*, now do it?"

TWENTY-SIX

It took bringing up Nabb and the rest of the crew with her to convince the guard that Alexis was, in fact, captain of a ship, had, in fact, been specifically requested to retrieve her crew, and would not, in fact, be offering any services of an intimate nature within the Enclave constabulary's holding area.

When the guard, still obviously dubious of Alexis' status and intent, finally opened the doorway for them to enter, Alexis was fuming.

Bad enough to be mistaken for a doxy, but even after Nabb had confirmed she was *Mongoose's* captain, the guard had blithely continued to question *Nabb* and not her before finally allowing them entry. Never mind that Nabb was younger than she and not even a ship's officer.

"If *Mongoose* were a Navy ship ..." she muttered, striding down the hallway toward the holding cells, Nabb at her side. But *Mongoose* wasn't and Alexis had only what authority she could muster on her own, without the backing of Admiralty, which had just been shown to be very little off her own ship. She supposed this must be how merchant captains and ship's officers felt all the time, at the mercy of the petty bureaucrats in whatever systems they visited.

She flung open the last set of doors and entered the cell area itself.

If Enclave as a whole, outside of the Casino, was a bit dingy, then this could only be described as filthy.

The stench hit her first — stale beer and what her old *Nightingales* might have referred to as *afters*. There was more than one way a spacer might not be able to hold onto his drink, and all of them seemed to be represented here — years of it, layered into an almost physical presence.

The lighting was dim, with nearly two in three of the overhead panels dark — why that might be the case, she couldn't guess, as the panels themselves were cheap and should last for years, while their power use was negligible. Alexis wasn't certain if Enclave had its own fusion plant or if they relied on the planet's geothermal, but either should have made power plentiful.

The noise, though, was enough to give even a seasoned spacer, used to the shouts and cries of a crowded berthing deck, pause.

"Sweet Dark," Alexis murmured, "how many do they have crowded in here?"

It was difficult to tell, for they'd entered a sort of alcove before a long corridor lined with bars on both sides. There were doors in the bars every four meters or so, and the corridor stretched a long way into the distance.

"Give 'er up, you poaching rodents! Or we'll do fer y'again!"

"It's not us yer'll do, y'bluddy doxies! Here's a pence'n show us yer knickers!"

Alexis frowned, wondering if the enclave officials had locked up a bunch of negotiating ladies and what for — there weren't many worlds that frowned on such things to that extent, and Enclave certainly didn't seem like one of them.

She edged farther in and peered into the gloom, trying to catch sight of where her crewmen might be. Her eyes hadn't quite adjusted to the gloom.

"Bend over for the next gent what wants a piece!"

That voice Alexis recognized, just as Nabb murmured, "It appears we've found our bosun, sir."

At that, Alexis' jaw clenched and she strode forward, blood hot. She'd not have any of her crew speak so to a woman, no matter her profession, and was shocked to hear *Mongoose's* bosun do so.

"Mister Dockett!" Alexis' voice cut through the din and there was sudden silence. Spacers, no matter their ship and no matter their state of intoxication, could recognize an officer's voice and tone, and Alexis' tone made it clear that someone was in for no good.

She made her way down the corridor to where Dockett's voice had come from, past cells occupied by one, two, or more spacers. The bulk of the noise seemed to have come from midway down the corridor where two facing cells were packed to bursting.

She noted the patches on the ships' jumpsuits the occupants of the cells she passed wore and that the authorities seemed to have segregated the arrestees by ship. Something that gave her pause when she grew close enough to note that one of the crowded cells, with Dockett and some few others at the bars, held nothing but the crew of *Mongoose*.

It could well be the entire watch — what could they have possibly done all together?

That question became clear when she noted that the opposite cell also held all crew from a single ship, not one she recognized, but they held the same positions has her lads — and lasses, she noted, as there were more than a few of her women crewmembers in the cell as well.

So where're the doxies they're berating?

She strode to the midpoint between the two cells, gave the other ship's crew a cold glance to let them know she wasn't there for them but would brook no disruption there either, and turned to face hers.

"*Mister* Dockett," she said, "and whichever of you it was offering pence for a knickers show, I'll *not* have such behavior from anyone aboard *Mongoose*. Negotiating ladies offer ease and comfort after weeks a'space, and you should bloody well know better! Now point the lasses out and apologize for your behavior, *this instant!*"

There was silence for a moment, then every one of *Mongoose's* crew, and no few of the other spacers paying attention, burst into laughter — save those in the crowded cell behind her, which echoed with cries of outrage.

Alexis' jaw clenched tighter, as she'd clearly misunderstood something — which made no never mind to the situation at hand. She caught Dockett's eye and he sobered instantly, cutting off his own laughter and elbowing those to either side of him. In a moment, her crew, at least, had quieted.

"Weren't no *ladies* involved, sir," Dockett said, having the grace to at least cast his eyes down at his boots as he must have realized how things looked.

It was up to him to keep order and set an example, after all, but here he was in lockup with the rest of the crew — and, Alexis noted, now that her eyes had adjusted to the dim light and she could make out faces farther back in the cell, at least two of his mates, which meant fully half the ship's petty officers were in lockup with the rest of the starboard watch.

Dockett nodded toward the other cell. "It were them we was telling off, sir."

"*Bloody bugger-catchers!*" someone at the rear of the cell shouted.

"*Poachin', theivin', rats!*" came from behind her.

"*Boots ain't no rat, y'molly!*"

Alexis drew breath, but both Nabb and Dockett were there before her, bellowing, "*Quiet!*" in unison.

"Mister Dockett," Alexis said calmly, though not easing her glare, "will you be so kind as to explain why half of *Mongoose's* crew is behind bars with you, then?"

"Aye, sir," Dockett nodded. "We'd all just got down, see, and stayed together for a pint or two, as to celebrate the prize money comin' in so quick and all."

"Poached coin what be our'n!"

Alexis whirled on the other cell. "Whatever ship you lot are from, is your captain so lax that he'll tolerate you interrupting another, for I'll surely have words for him if a one of you does so again!"

That cowed most of the lot, who shrugged and backed off from the bars, looking down and away. Some few stayed where they were, though, meeting Alexis' gaze with anger and defiance. Likely she would have to have words with their captain, if only to sort out what had happened between the two crews and where the blame was to be laid. She took note of the faces of those who remained at the bars, so that she could name them to that captain when the time came — regardless of the strife between the crews, the men should show *some* respect to another ship's officers.

She stepped closer to Dockett at the cell's door, hoping they could speak softer and quell any further outbursts from the other crew.

"Go on, Mister Dockett, and quietly if you will."

"Aye, sir." Dockett sighed and scratched at his neck. "Well, sir, we were more'n a few pints in, what with all the toasts an' all."

"Toasts?"

"Aye, sir. We was all feelin' our good fortune, y'see? What with signin' aboard a ship with so many still sittin' idle aboard stations, and with so lucky a captain ... not to blow smoke up yer ... well, not to seem like I'm flatterin', sir, but y'do have a reputation an' all."

Alexis nodded, hoping the heat she felt in her face wasn't showing. What reputation she should have, she didn't know, but with so many dead marked to her account she didn't agree it was something to toast to.

"Go on."

"Well, and lucky to take prize on her way here, and so easily done, sir," Dockett said. "Then the share out o' the prize money so quick, when no one were expecting t'see a pence fer months from those pinchin' buggers."

And they wouldn't have if she hadn't gone outside the normal prize courts to deal with Wheeley, but the crew didn't know the details of that so might bless their luck that a court had moved at more than a snail's pace for once in their lives.

"So there was toasts, sir. Toasts to *Mongoose*, a fine ship, and toasts to you, sir, a fine captain. Then there was toasts to the prize's captain fer givin' in so easy, and to the pirates what took the loot, and to the merchantman what shipped the lot first, and to you again, sir, fer pickin' the route and takin' her so easy-like, and —"

"Yes, I see."

"— and to Boots, of course, sir."

Alexis sighed. "Of course."

"More'n one to the wee devil an' the luck he brung us."

"Of course, yes, and then?"

"Well, sir, we was just toastin' that — Boots, you see, and the luck he brung us — when *that* lot come in." Dockett nodded to the other cell.

"And then?"

"Well, they was all friendly and smiles at first, sir, for we — all us from *Mongoose*, you see — was feeling right generous and when that lot says they're of a private ship as well, well, we might've toasted them, too, and offered a pint to give 'em a bit of our luck an' all."

Alexis raised an eyebrow at that. She'd have expected a bit of rivalry between the crews of private ships, not that hers would buy a round for what appeared to be several dozen off another ship.

Dockett must have seen her skepticism, for he hastened on, "It were full toasts, sir, not no raise a glass an' sip a bit, you see? The lads were in, well, a generous state, as it were."

"Of course, and then?"

"Well, sir, after that it were all oy-mate-and-glad-ter-meet-ya for a pint or two, but then theys starts with their questions, sir."

"Questions?"

"Aye, sir, friendly at first, and all, but then soon's they ask where we took that ship, and Creasy, he outs with it like it's nothing before I could shush him, not wanting to give away a good hunting ground, if you see, sir?"

Alexis nodded. She wasn't entirely certain how this private ship thing must work, but it made sense to not tell others where a favorite hunting ground might be — aside from the competition itself, word might get around to the merchants shipping pirated goods and they'd start to avoid the place.

"Creasy, of course," she said. Creasy and his Dutchmen and spirits of the Dark. At least he hadn't gone and told the other crew about his beliefs that the vile creature was —

"An' then Creasy, sir, well, he says we took that ship without a shot in return, and it being —" Dockett's eyes fell to the cell's floor again and his hand worked at the back of his head, scratching. "— Boots' blessing, an' all like he does, sir."

Alexis scanned the crew, who were now crowding the front of the cell. She couldn't spot Creasy, though anyone whose gaze she met looked away quickly and shuffled back into the crowd.

"And then?"

Dockett sighed and then went on in a rush. "Some o' them lot're lookin' angry, sir, an' I'm wondering why and what's up, you see? But others o' them, they ask, 'What's a boots, then?' and Creasy, he says to them, he says, 'Well, he's our mongoose, isn't he?' and then one o' thems says, 'What's a bloody mongoose?' and another o' thems says, 'It's a giant rat, I thinks,' an' then, Creasy, he stands up and cries, 'Boots ain't no rat! He's our'n mongoose and we love him!' an' why he sees fit to say that last, I'll not fathom, but then, one o' them, he stands up and yells, 'They's rat-buggers an' poachers!' pointin' right at Creasy, you see, so there's no doubt it was us he was calling that, an' no cause to, for Boots ain't and we never and what's all this about poachin' anyways, I'm thinking, do you see, sir?"

Alexis paused for a moment to take it all in.

"And then the fight started?" she asked.

Dockett shrugged. "Well, sir, there were some hemmin' and hawin' back and forth a bit, an' I tried to settle it some, I did, sir! I says to thems, I says, 'Look, lads, sit back an' we'll buy you another pint and talk on what's bothered you, see?' but one o' them —" Dockett narrowed his eyes, looking past her at the other cell. "— that big feller grinnin' at the bars, there — no, don't look, sir, as that's what he's after — well, he stands up an' pours his beer out, real slow like, with that big, shite-eatin' grin like he's got now, sir, an' he says to us, 'I'll not drink with any rat-worshipin' poachers!' an' then Creasy, well, he stands up an' pours out *his* beer an yells back, 'I'll not drink with any as don't believe in Boots!'"

Dockett paused, frowned, and then, even more quietly, as if he hoped the rest of the crew wouldn't hear, "Which was not so well of Creasy, sir, for there's half the crew as don't believe the whole of what Creasy says — only that Boots is, well, lucky, sir."

Alexis took a deep breath, held it, and let it out ever so slowly. She'd found that was best done before speaking whenever Creasy and his followers in the crew were involved, else she'd say something that put a wounded look on the men's faces.

Speak ill of the creature, or even the bloody truth, and they look as though you'd kicked a puppy down a well already full of kittens.

She shook off the implications of Dockett's words, that half the crew didn't take to Creasy's words couldn't possibly mean that half *did*, now could it? The Dark did breed a certain credulousness, but the bloody creature couldn't even be trained to stay out of her dining cabin during dinner.

"And then the fight started?" she asked.

"Aye, sir," Dockett nodded. "Oncet beer's on the ground, there's no comin' back from that, sir."

"I see. And these allegations of 'poaching' you said they made?"

"Near as I can tell, sir, they thinks Kayseri's their own private hunting ground."

That did make sense, and she could see why they might take exception, whether such were the case or not. "No such designations were made clear to me in our letter of marque, so I suppose I'll have to speak to their captain about that."

Perhaps she could clear things up with the other captain and leave with no real ill-will between the crews. They'd likely be encountering the other crew in some systems more than once before this cruise was over, and she didn't want to be paying the magistrate for a full-on brawl every time.

"*Oy! Bouncy-bits!*" came a voice from the other cell, and a coin, a single pence, *clinked* to the jail floor beside her foot. "Give over that lot and I'll have a go, me!"

TWENTY-SEVEN

Dockett scowled and there were angry murmurs from within the cell. Nabb let out a low, guttural growl and made to move toward the other cell, but Alexis laid a hand on his arm. She glanced down at the coin, then back to Dockett.

"What was that bit about doxies the lads were yelling when I arrived, Mister Dockett? It seemed to goad that lot to no end."

Dockett had the grace to flush red and look away. "Weren't no slur on any real lady who negotiates proper, sir, but it were that lot's ship name, you see? *Bachelor's Delight*, it is."

"I see." Well, that did evoke certain images, didn't it? And an odd name for a private ship, she thought.

A second coin, another pence *clinked* to a stop next to the first.

"Best offer, lass! A bony little chit like you'll do no better!"

Alexis sighed. She really couldn't fathom how spacers would visit the ladies every time in port, treat them well and appreciate their services, then use the label as an insult to other women. Marie, her dear friend back on Dalthus, had made some arrangements with captured midshipmen back on her homeworld of Giron — though Alexis was never sure if it was for coin in hand or merely favors, it

193

had certainly gone far enough to get her a child out of the bargain — and Marie was the sweetest, most level-headed girl she could think of.

Well, save when Villar is about and she goes all addle-pated and pudding-boned.

The growls and mutters made her scan the assembled crew of *Mongoose*, now crowding the bars of the cell and looking not at her but glaring across the way to the other crew. She'd let it go if it were only her, but she could tell the crew'd not accept it.

The first lieutenant on her first ship had once told her that she, as a newly minted midshipman, held in her person the honor of her ship, her captain, and New London's Queen. She'd since come to realize that as captain her crews held their own honor tied to hers as well — and to their ship. And, in this case, for some reason only the Dark and Creasy's delusions knew, to the vile creature likely making free with her cabin and bedding this very moment.

What she might laugh off for herself, they'd hold as a dire wound, and there'd be no peace between these crews ever again. The *Bachelor's Delights* — and wasn't that a crew's name begging for punches to be thrown — would see that as well, and take every opportunity to tweak her lads on it from that moment on.

She placed her boot over the two coins, metal grinding against the cement floor of the jail block, and with a twist of her ankle sent them sliding back to the other cell.

"Ah, look, lads! She's of a mind t'give it away — knows a good ride when she sees one, she does!"

Alexis turned and stared down most of the laughter. Only a half dozen or so continued, crowded around the speaker — a large, red-haired young man leaning close to the bars, one arm casually through them and resting against their outside.

Nabb was near shaking in place, held back only by the light pressure of her hand against his arm, and Dockett and the others had taken her turn to mean they were free to yell back at the other crew. Epithets and threats filled the small space between the two cells.

Alexis considered. Words wouldn't do, not with this lot, and their captain might be of the same ilk — she couldn't be certain speaking to him would do a bit of good. No, this would likely need to be handled here, and between her and the speaker.

If these were Navy crews, it would be a different matter, and she once again cursed the end of the war and her half-pay status. She'd never realized just how much of her authority rested in that uniform and the clear backing of Admiralty. Without that discipline, things were ever so much more complicated.

"Is that how you speak to a ship's captain?" she asked, beginning the dance.

"Don't see no captain, just a tiny tart up from the farm for some fun!"

"You tell her, Little Mal," one of the others called out.

She stepped closer to the other cell, Nabb following. He wasn't exactly pushing against her restraining hand, but clearly wishing to rush the bars of the other cell.

"Comin' to show us the goods, tiny tart? See if we'll up the offer?" Little Mal asked.

Alexis put pressure against Nabb to stop him coming farther with her and he obeyed, but was clearly displeased to do so.

"Stay, doggy!" one of the *Bachelor's Delights* called out.

As she neared, Little Mal's smile widened. He was young, but large as she noted before, nearly two meters, if she was a judge, and with broad shoulders.

"Come on, tiny tart, the bogeys had us a'fore there was a bit of fun and we're ready for you."

Alexis raised her hands and laid them lightly on his arm where it rested on the bars, one at his elbow and one at his wrist.

"Are you?" she asked.

"Oh, aye, we'll —"

Alexis grasped his hand and twisted, keeping pressure on his elbow as well.

"Really?" she asked.

"What's — *ow!* Bloody —"

Slowly, almost casually, she put more pressure on his arm. Some of his mates started to reach for her through the bars, but she shot them a warning look and twisted more so that they backed away as Little Mal cried out.

"In future, Little Mal," she said, returning her gaze to him, "I'll expect you'll have a bit more of a respectful tongue in your head when you speak to a ship's captain, yes?"

Little Mal nodded, head jerking up and down quickly, his eyes wide.

"And your captain and I will settle whatever this 'poaching' business is, so I suspect it'll be no more of your conc — *urk!*"

TWENTY-EIGHT

A lexis broke off speaking with a startled sound as something grasped the back of her linen shirt and lifted her up. Up, past standing and off her feet all entire.

She lost her grip on Little Mal's arm as she grasped at the cell's bars in search of something solid while her feet dangled, but not before he'd quickly scrambled up as well, dragged painfully by her grip on him.

"Haur noo, 'en, who's puttin' hans oan mah wee bairn?" a deep voice asked.

Alexis' view of the cell block spun as she was twisted in midair to come face to face with the speaker. Eye to eye with him, she realized, and that with her feet nearly a meter off the ground.

Sweet Dark, he's a bloody giant!

Broad as he was tall, and as strong as both, for he held her easily suspended at arm's length, he had long, bushy red-hair much like Little Mal's and ...

A naked bloody giant! Alexis thought in astonishment, for though the man's torso was covered in heavy, reddish hair, he was, indeed, unclothed save for a pelt of some kind thrown over his shoulders.

Naked from the waist up, at least, for a large paunch spared her the view of anything below that.

The man shook her once, to the sound of her shirt's stitches ripping, then glowered at her.

"*Noo who're ye tae pit hans oan uir wee bairn?*"

Alexis blinked and her tablet's earpiece *pinged* followed by a message in her ear: *Untranslatable - possibly indecipherable gibberish.*

"What?"

"Bloody hell, but she hurt me, Da!" Little Mal cried, standing. "Kill the tart!" He pressed himself close to the bars and glared at Alexis.

The giant looked from him to her and shook her again.

"*Weel?*"

That she understood well enough, though it was garbled and indistinct.

Nabb looked ready to throw himself on the giant, which she thought wouldn't end well for either of them. Between remaining silent and angering the brute by admitting she hadn't understood a single word, she wasn't entirely sure which might have the better outcome.

"I didn't —" Another shake cut her off.

"*Ire saw!*"

"*I can't bloody well understand you, you great oaf!*" Alexis yelled, angry now. If her end was to be pulled limb from limb by a giant ginger in the bowels of a Barbary constabulary, she at least wanted to know why exactly. "Speak the Queen's English or some other human tongue my tablet can translate, will you?"

She managed to raise her arms and get a grip on the giant's own as he held her, which at least relieved some of the pressure on her shirt.

The man's eyes narrowed further until they were mere slits and he took a deep breath.

"Who're you," he said, slowly and distinctly, but still with a heavy accent, "t'be pootin' 'ands ... on our wee bairn? Didja get that, lass, an' they're the last 'Queen's bluddy English' yer ever 'earin."

That, at least, she could understand, and the accent came clearer once she could identify it.

New Edinburgh — much like that family who plays the pipes grandfather once called a "cat-juicer."

She took her own deep breath. Perhaps there was hope she wouldn't be dismembered just yet.

"Captain Alexis Carew of the private ship *Mongoose*," she said as calmly as she could while suspended in midair.

The man's forearm beneath her hands was bigger around than she could encompass and like a length of cordwood wrapped in sponge — large as he was, there was naught but muscle beneath a thick outer layer of flesh, and all bound with wiry red hair. She might be only a bit over forty kilograms, but he kept her suspended as though it were nothing.

"Would you mind putting me down?" she asked.

"Y'poot 'ands on me bairn," he said slowly.

"Kill the tart, Da!" Little Mal repeated, fairly hopping up and down at the bars.

They're related? Alexis nearly groaned. She'd grown up on tales of her grandmother, a native to New Edinburgh herself, and the familial feuds running through centuries. *I may just have doomed Dalthus all entire ...*

She cleared her throat, drawing the giant's attention back to her.

"He did — your son, is it? Your son did make some rather lewd suggestions and offers."

The man's eyes narrowed further, but darted toward Little Mal and Alexis took that to mean his ire might be redirected.

"Threw two pence at my feet and called me — what was it, sir?"

"Tiny tart, you tuppence slag," Mal said, grinning, "and not worth that once my Da's done with —."

His voice cut off as the giant's fist, the one not holding Alexis lashed out, barely clearing the space between the cell's bars before striking Little Mal square in the nose.

"I told y'lad," the giant said without turning to watch as Little Mal was flung back from the bars, knocking over those crowded behind him. "Y'pay more'n tuppence, y'speak respectable, an' y'thank 'er an' add a bit when yer done." He sighed. "I'll not 'ave the ladies blacklist the *Delight* o'er yer lackwit self." He nodded to Alexis. "I'll say sorry for mah bairn, lass."

"It *is* captain, actually," Alexis said again, a bit put out that he'd struck Little Mal for a perceived insult to the negotiating ladies, rather than to the captain of another ship.

The giant cocked his head.

"You weren't foolin'?" He frowned. "Dressed like that?"

IT TOOK a few more moments to settle things out to the giant's satisfaction.

He did lower Alexis back to the floor, rather than drop her as she half expected, and she was quite relieved to discover that the lower half of him, hidden by his paunch while she was suspended, was *not* as bare as the upper — though the skintight breeches of some animal hide with a grain unlike leather weren't much better.

"Ha!" he said when she pointed out that her choice of dress at least provided more coverage than this own. "I was occupied when the call came, an' couldn't find the rest."

Occupied with what, she didn't ask. Now that she'd identified the accent as a rather thick New Edinburghan, she was following his words much easier.

"William Malcomson," he said, holding out the hand he'd struck Little Mal with. That worthy was still on his backside within the cell, head tilted back and holding his nose while blood dripped off his chin. "Captain of the *Bachelor's Delight*, an' yer off *Mongoose*, eh?"

Alexis nodded.

"I am — and I do regret this incident between our crews. It seems to have been —"

Malcomson waved her apology away.

"The lads'll be lads," he said. "I don't hold with these 'territory' mouthings of our commodore, eh? We hunt where we hunt and whoever's there first gets the game, eh?"

Alexis frowned. "Commodore? Is there a Navy presence, then?" Even with the cease-fire, perhaps especially with the cease-fire, she couldn't imagine Hanover allowing the Royal Navy so deep into what was, after all, Hanoverese space. No matter that they took such a lackadaisical view toward policing it themselves. Given the tensions between the two realms, she would have thought such would be a step too far.

Malcomson laughed. "Haven't met our fair commodore, then, lass?" He spat. "Get y'to our little rendezvous and I'll not be the one to spoil the surprise for you."

He turned to the cell holding his men.

"An' you lot!" he bellowed. "What're y'aboot, losing such a fight?"

Little Mal was on his feet again and grasped the cell's bars, though keeping a bit of distance between them and his face.

"We weren't losin', Da, we was —"

Malcomson spat again. "If yer in the tolbooth, you've lost, laddie. Finish it an' get away, or don't start it, I've told you."

There was a sound from the lockup's entryway, and Malcomson turned as Alexis looked that way. One of the guards had entered.

"Will you be speaking to the magistrate?" he asked. "Or leaving them to us?"

TWENTY-NINE

The magistrate's office was little more than a cubby off the corridor leading to the cells and the "magistrate" himself was, Alexis suspected, whichever of the guards happened to have the luck of the draw that day. The whole business fairly screamed that it was unofficial, though she suspected Wheeley would have a cut of whatever the "magistrate" got off them as his fingers were everywhere.

The magistrate, who'd not even bothered to remove his guard's uniform, looked up as they entered, eyes widening as Malcomson followed Alexis and loomed over her, and nearly everything else. Given the room's small size and clutter — the "magistrate's" desk, being an empty container and his chair being a smaller one — Malcomson might have filled half the available space on his own.

The magistrate swallowed, visibly gathered himself, and glanced at his tablet.

"Public drunkenness, disorderly conduct, brawling in public, damage to property — both public and private." He shook his head sadly. "Captains, it appears you might have to sail without half your crews —"

"Bawbags," Malcomson growled. "What's the price and nae more said aboot it?"

The magistrate looked offended, but went on with what Alexis suspected was a prepared speech — in fact, she thought she could see his eyes moving as he actually read the words from his tablet.

"Ah, you appear to be in luck today, as staffing issues have pre ..." He frowned. "Precloo ..." He shrugged. "Kept us from beginning the processing of your spacers. There being no *formal* charges at this time —" The man actually felt the need to tip them the wink at that, in case they were so dense as to not see the game. "— and in the interests of ex ..."

He frowned again.

"Exped ... bloody Charlie and his words," he muttered, then shrugged. "Look, there ain't no records in the system yet and we're short-staffed, see? Could be days before we get to it — weeks before you see the magistrate ... the *other* magistrate, I mean, see?" He winked again. "And he ain't so understanding as I am, so —"

"How much?" Malcomson asked.

"Two marks the head."

Alexis sighed as she did the conversion to shillings. It was high, she thought, but not so much as it could be, though it was a fair chunk of what each crew member had received from their prize — if they had any left. If not, *Mongoose* would pay it against their accounts aboard ship. Two marks per head was nearly a crown each. "Any discount for the emptier ones?"

"They've nearly all emptied. We'll have a time cleaning those cells."

"I meant — No, never mind." Alexis transferred the total from her tablet, from the ship's accounts, not her own, and made a note to see that Dursley saw the ship repaid from these men's next prize money.

Honor of the ship or no, Barbary or no, there's no world that looks kindly on a hundred drunken spacers tearing it up.

ALEXIS SENT her crew off to reboard *Mongoose* under the supervision of Dockett, little though the bosun's oversight had done before. Malcomson had made it clear to his crew that there was to be no more talk of poaching, so the two groups might be thought to make it to their respective boats without further incident.

Alexis and Nabb went along with Malcomson and, to Alexis' concern, Little Mal, to the nearest pub.

"Sit, Captain Carew," Malcomson said, then called out loudly, "*Pints!*"

"Tea, please," Alexis called, gesturing to herself and Nabb, it still being quite early in *Mongoose's* day, whatever it was for Malcomson.

Alexis sat, Nabb beside her, as Malcomson and Little Mal did across from them.

"So," Malcomson said as a harried server placed mugs in front of each of them, "let's talk a bit, shall we? An' build a base o'beer afore we're on to business."

She added milk and sugar to her mug, then took a sip, Nabb following suit, while the other two quaffed half of theirs in one go.

"Where're y'from, lass?" Malcomson asked.

"Dalthus. It's a new world off toward —"

"Oh, I ken Dalthus. There're Malcomsons on Dalthus, are there not?"

Alexis nodded. "I believe so. We've not had much trade with them, but —"

"Dalthus, eh?" Malcomson's frown deepened. "Why does that ring a bell?"

"Well, you just said there were Malcomsons there, so —"

"Carew. Your people from New London?"

Alexis nodded. "My grandparents, before settling Dalthus."

Malcomson narrowed his eyes. "Heard there was more than Malcomsons on Dalthus. That a New Londoner'd married a New Edinburgher and was maybe a Carew sounds right."

205

Alexis nodded again. "My grandmother, Lynelle."

"What was her clan?"

"Ah ... Sheehy, I think? I'm not certain —"

"Y'dinnae ken!"

"My grandmother died before I was born. Should we not, perhaps, discuss our crews and their —"

"Sorry for that." Malcomson frowned further, his brow furrowing. "So yer a Sheehy? Let me ponder a bit."

"What difference does that make?" Alexis asked. She'd thought at first that the relation might build a bridge to Malcomson, but she was beginning not to care, the more the man interrupted her.

Malcomson looked at her as though she'd asked why one wears a helmet in vacuum. "Why, all of it, y' dinnae ken? How can y'not?"

"Ken — know what?"

"Whether I'm bound to kill you or feast you, o'course." He put his fingers to his temples. "Hush, noo, while I figure on it." He took a deep breath. "Kill y'fer the Bruce —" He shrugged. "— feast y'fer changin' on the Bruce ... important I get the first bits right, y'see, or it'll throw the whole lot off ... kill ya, feast ya, kill, feast ... feast, feast, kill ... Lichenburry Tor were a mess an' I never can tell ... kill, feast, feast, kill ... Second Bannockburn were a wash, I think ..."

He went on mumbling to himself for some time, leaving Alexis to be torn between amusement and real concern that the massive man would decide he was somehow honor-bound to kill her. She'd always thought the tales of her grandmother's feuding nature were exaggerated, but she now might have to apologize to her grandfather for doubting him.

Finally, Malcomson looked up, eyes bright.

"Aye, lass, we're friends!" He shrugged. "'Til the next mails come in, o'course. Never can tell what they'll bring."

"Of course," Alexis said. "And glad I am that I'll not have to kill you back."

Malcomson's face fairly split in a wide grin. "That's the clan spirit, lass!"

THIRTY

Mongoose left Enclave the next day, making her way to fresh hunting grounds. Malcomson gave her a list of systems which he considered good sport, but wouldn't have time to visit himself, and advised she make the next rendezvous of the private ships at Carina, an empty, worthless system chosen for that purpose.

He spat as he said it, and Alexis suspected he'd not make these rendezvous himself if it weren't the place where the most recent information from New London could be had. If a war started up again and New London added the foe to their letters of marque, none of the private ship captains would want to be late learning of it. The thought of a fat, enemy merchant getting away would surely make Malcomson's teeth ache.

Those systems, though, proved to be less than ideal hunting grounds.

Mongoose sailed nearly a fortnight before spotting another ship, which proved to be only a half-decrepit luggar, carrying passengers and no cargo to speak of. A week later, the crew began muttering, and Alexis couldn't blame them. After getting a prize so soon after their arrival, and giving up the bulk of that prize money to Enclave's vendors as most of them had done, they were more than ready for another and more.

She began to suspect that these worlds were not so much the fresh hunting ground Malcomson described, but rather the dregs of the Barbary where none of the other private ships wished to hunt.

Worse than the lack of prizes, at least for Alexis, was the lack of information. Wheeley had not come through on his promised word of where ships from the warring fleets had been spotted. He'd sent only a terse, "My sources need more time. Perhaps when next you return."

Now they faced foul winds that seemed to have them beating to windward at every turn. Whether they'd reach the rendezvous in the allotted time was more and more in question with every chime of the bell, and the heavy work of tack after tack, all with no sign of a prize, was wearing on the crew.

Alexis gathered Villar and her other officers around her plot table to discuss plans.

She nodded absently as Isom set a freshly filled glass at her side. Across the table, Villar was similarly distracted by the images of *dark-space* charts covering the table's surface. Parrill and Hacking looked on from either end.

"It's possible," Villar said, tracing their route with his fingertip, "if the winds stay as they are and move to be in our favor only a little just here." He tapped a spot where the charts indicated the winds couldn't be predicted well — there appeared to be an even chance that they'd work for or against *Mongoose* in that bit of space.

"And if not," Hacking put in, "we'll have to sail through all this empty space to get back to any sort of chance at a prize."

He was right in that, Carina was far from any inhabited system, which was likely why it had been chosen as a rendezvous point — little chance of the private ships' spot being found out by others.

"Would it not," Hacking went on, "be a better use of our time to find a prize?"

"In fact," Parrill said, "as I assume we'll want to hunt in some systems with more traffic than those we've just left, Carina could be well on our way to them. If the winds where Mister Villar points out are fair to us and we leave Carina after only a few days in-system to confer with the other captains, then we may leave by this route —" She traced a path on the plot, "— and find ourselves with a fine wind the whole way. Even from where we are now, it will take nearly as long to get back to any system that stands a chance of us gaining a decent prize. See here, how if we were to turn about this minute, we'd still have nearly a month's sail to the established trade routes?"

Hacking grunted and clenched his jaw, which caused Parrill to look up. She saw the look on his face and lowered her eyes. "I'm sorry, but you did ask," she said.

It was not that Parrill was often wrong at all, Alexis thought, for her information and opinions had proved spot on, it was only how she presented herself that seemed to put others off.

Alexis traced the route as well. The predicted arrival time in their destination system — Carina, the rendezvous point for New London's privateers provided to them by Eades — and confirmed by Malcomson, though why he spat every time he mentioned it or the "commodore" she couldn't say — was in the second half of the next possible rendezvous period. No one could predict what the winds might do to a ship's progress, so an exact date was never possible — each rendezvous was a full week's time in which they might expect to meet others in the privateering force at Carina.

She frowned. "And if the winds are not in our favor, then we've missed it all entire until the next time. With Captain Malcomson's talk of a commodore being involved, I'll not want to keep him waiting, I think. It's all well and good for a full-time privateer like the *Delight's* captain to speak ill and spit at the thought, but I've a Naval career to think of — as do you, Hacking."

There was no need, strictly speaking, for *Mongoose* to make the rendezvous at all. She could, if Alexis wished, work entirely on her own, given their Letter of Marque, but the notion of this commodore did change what she thought prudent. She thought it might be well, also, to at least meet the other captains involved. As well, the rendezvous point allowed for any prizes to be consolidated and sent in convoy to a more established and conventional prize court than on Enclave — though with the attendant delays and lesser valuation that a formal court would give over Wheeley.

Malcomson had been surprised at that, when she'd told him that Wheeley had bought her prize at a premium and immediately, and she thought it might have been a mistake to mention it. The man might have done it only because of his debt to Dansby, after all, and she didn't want to impose on him by sending every privateer captain in the Barbary to his door.

Still, Malcomson had been so understanding about the fight between their crews, and if she could curry more favor by imposing on Wheeley, she supposed there were worse ways. The man would make his own profit on the transaction, after all.

They had no prizes to show for their efforts now, and what might the other captains — or this commodore — think of her and her crew if they showed up empty-handed?

She took a deep breath and held it. Make for the meeting with no prizes in tow or double back farther into the Barbary and take more ships, delaying until the next rendezvous time?

There was a chime from the cabin's hatch and Isom came out of the pantry to answer it. A marine at the hatch to announce visitors was something Alexis hadn't thought she'd miss, especially one as she'd last had whose every word was a puzzle of an indecipherable accent. Still, she did. It would be comforting to know who was bringing her a bit of *Mongoose's* troubles before the hatch opened.

And certainly, it would be trouble, for as Isom slid the hatch open she saw that it was the bosun, Dockett — he was a steady man, despite being caught up in the brawl on Enclave, and wouldn't bring something trivial to her, not if it could wait until she was on the quarterdeck herself.

"Bosun, sir," Isom said.

"Come through." Alexis gestured for Dockett to sit. "A glass, Mister Dockett?"

"Thank you, sir, I will, as you're offering."

Alexis nodded and Dockett sat between Villar and Hacking, then waited for Isom to pour.

"What is it that brings you, Mister Dockett?"

Dockett sighed. "It's the crew's food, sir."

Alexis raised an eyebrow at that. The one thing she'd not thought to hear as a complaint aboard *Mongoose* was the food, as she'd made clear to her new purser that she wanted the crew well-fed. She knew for a certainty they'd taken aboard fresh provisions at Enclave, for Isom had brought her the bill to approve, and he'd certainly have checked that those provisions arrived, in addition to Dockett doing so.

"What about it?"

"The vat beef, sir," Dockett said. "Cook brought it to me last week and I spoke to Dursley, but it's gotten worse."

"Worse?" Alexis wasn't entirely sure how the vat-grown beef that made up the bulk of the crew's diet could, at its best, ever become worse. "In what way?"

"Hard to describe, sir, but the crew's bound for dinner soon and Cook called me in to look..." He shrugged. "Cook's not keen on serving it."

Alexis shared a look with Villar, whose eyes were wide. Shipboard cooks, save those serving the officers, were not known for their discretion in what they put before the crew — especially in the way of the vat-beef. There wasn't much that could be done with that at its best, and it was often the better choice to simply ensure each member of the crew got their fair measure of a half kilo per day, leaving it to the men to have something to pour over it in an effort to make it palatable. In a storm, the berthing deck fairly rattled with the sound of ill-wrapped condiment bottles in the spacers' chests.

"Isom," Alexis said, "go and see Cook and have him fix me a plate of what he'll be serving the crew, will you?"

"Aye, sir."

"Mister Dockett, my compliments to Mister Dursley, and I'd admire it did he attend me here at his convenience."

"Aye, sir."

Villar waited for the hatch to slide closed behind Dockett before speaking.

"How could the stuff ever be worse?" he asked, echoing Alexis' thoughts.

Alexis shook her head. "I can't fathom it, myself. Nor can I imagine Dursley running some game that would be so obvious — I did tell him quite clearly that I'd share the crew's meals at times and hold him accountable. If he's tried to shave a few pence on the men I'll put him in-atmosphere at the next port."

That threat was far more serious aboard *Mongoose* than a navy ship. Royal Navy pursers purchased their warrant from Admiralty and only Admiralty could dismiss them — a captain's recourse was far greater. Her authority — sole master after God, as it went — might not go so far toward the lash as a naval captain's might, but she could put any man she chose in-atmosphere. With every man aboard, including the purser, after profit from this voyage, that threat was serious indeed.

Isom quickly returned and set a plate before Alexis. "Cook says it's not his fault."

"What's the matter with it?" Alexis studied the plate. The "beef" was much as it always was — more than a bit grey, more than a bit slimy-looking, no matter how it was cooked, and with more than a bit of the odd, not-quite-off odor of the vats wafting up to her.

Villar leaned over the table, peering. "Is it green?"

"More orangeish, if you ask me," Isom said.

"Nonsense," Hacking said, "it's clearly black now."

Parrill cocked her head. "How interesting."

"What are you all on about?" Alexis looked down and closer. "It's the normal sort of grey ..." She paused. Were their flashes of color as she moved her head? "Well, perhaps, it's a bit ..." She edged to the side, rounding the table to where Isom was standing. "I suppose I do see some orange, must be a trick of the light."

"Now it's green," Isom said. He'd circled the table to Villar's side in response to Alexis' move.

"Blue," Villar said, from the far side of the table.

"What could cause this?" Hacking murmured.

Parrill crouched down and eyed the slab of beef from table-level. "Light refracting from the cut edges at different angles through the varied layers of oil on the surface." She glanced up at Hacking's grunt of disgust. "I'm sorry, but you did ask."

"Not you," Hacking said, for once. "I turned my head a bit and the bloody rainbow's made me dizzy."

Alexis snorted and circled to where Villar had started, Isom and the rest circling as well.

"Oh, that is disturbing," she said.

"Quite."

"Put a man right off," Hacking agreed.

"Do you suppose it's really just the light hitting the ..." Alexis trailed off, not sure of what to call the bit of a sheen that sometimes covered vat-grown beef.

"Does it put the taste off, do you think?" Villar asked.

"I should think the larger question would be if it's at all safe," Alexis said. "Taste's never in it to begin with."

"Well, if it wasn't safe the vat controls would tell us, wouldn't they?" Hacking leaned closer, sniffing. "I mean, it smells all ri ... it smells as it should, at least."

"The vats will signal if something's gone dangerous, of course, but their sense of that is quite liberal. And they can be adjusted, so if the purser's determined to keep a vat going and the ship's willing to accept a probability of no more than ten-percent of the crew needing the heads in a given watch, then it's allowed. Most people, you see, have a bacteria in their guts which can handle a certain amount of ..." Parrill paused and glanced around the table. "Well, and ten-percent do not, you see, so ..." She sighed and stood up, eyes downcast. "You did ask."

"Yes, clearly, I'm at fault," Hacking sneered at her, "and not your —"

"Mister Hacking," Villar said quickly.

Hacking stiffened and glared at Parrill, whose shoulders hunched even further.

Alexis had a feeling this must be what life in the wardroom was like, and felt a flash of sympathy for Villar, having to ride herd on the others so much. Then for Hacking and Parrill, both, for they were clearly ill-suited to live in close proximity for so long and it appeared to be wearing on them. She might have to speak to Villar about it and decide if one or the other of them should be let go, though where she'd find another qualified officer in the Barbary, she couldn't think of. Perhaps one of the other private ships would have a likely fellow she might trade him for.

Or, she thought suddenly, *perhaps this commodore will have a lieutenant chafing a bit under a flag officer and wish a man like Hacking in his place.*

That was a possibility she might bring up with the commodore when they arrived at Carina — for now, though, there was the matter of the beef.

Alexis started circling the table again, Villar and the others following suit. She paused, and moved back a bit, then forward again. The change from green to blue was really quite something. "I've never seen the like before."

"It is worrisome," Villar said. "I can understand the crew's concern."

"Yes," Alexis frowned. "I wish there was some way other than just the vat sensors to reassure the crew that it's only a, well, visual disturbance."

There was a soft chittering from underneath the table and Alexis leaned down to look. She reached under and came up with the lithe, flowing armful of fur that always seemed to be underfoot.

"Exactly what I was looking for," she said, setting the mongoose on the table near the plate.

"Sir!" Isom said. "Not Boots, no!"

"Now, look, we've just said the sensors say it's perfectly all right, yes?" Alexis pushed at the creature's backside to edge it closer to the plate. "So it can't do it any harm. *And —*" she stressed, cutting Isom off as he started to speak again. "— with the crew so enamored of the creature they'll surely eat their share on its say-so, won't they?"

"I'm not sure that's the best way," Villar said. "I mean, they do like him, but 'Go on, eat this green bit, as the captain's pet says it's quite all right,' might not be the most convincing take."

"Go on, little creature," Alexis muttered, ignoring Villar. "Try a bit." She edged the plate closer to him. "Good stuff, fresh from the vat."

Boots turned and bared his teeth at her before leaping from the table and dashing into her sleeping cabin.

"Little bugger," she muttered.

The hatch chimed and Isom went to answer it, but not before giving her a disapproving look.

"It's not my fault, sir!" Dursley, the purser, exclaimed as he was ushered through.

Alexis pointed at the plate. "Well, whose is it, then?"

"I topped up our stores at Enclave," Dursley said, "as we do in every port, and now —" He jabbed his finger at the plate. "It's gone all rainbowish on me! Every vat, the same!"

"But it is safe to eat?" Villar asked.

Dursley started to speak, stopped, then looked from Villar to Alexis and back again.

"All of the vat sensors say it's the finest," he said finally.

"So it is safe to eat?"

Dursley shook his head. "It will not harm a soul."

Alexis frowned. "That's not quite the same thing, is it?"

Hacking looked skeptical as well. "Is it just the color that's off?"

Dursley licked his lips. "It weren't so bad before, sir, really.

Started with the color, then the color got brighter, see? And the brighter the colors, well, the worse — I've spoken to Cook and we've seen that it's perfectly all right when it's sliced off the vat and after it's cooked. So long as it's not further disturbed, the only difference is the color. So, yes, right?"

"'Not further disturbed'?"

Dursley shrugged. "Well, you know ... disturbed." He swallowed. "Not broken up no more after it's cooked. You have to just ... let it be, like."

Alexis glanced at the half kilo chunk of beef on the plate.

"'Broken up'? Do you mean ..." She frowned. "Cut, you mean, or possibly chewed?"

"Eaten." Villar said. "You mean it's fine once it's cooked so long as it's not actually eaten?"

"I spoke to Cook," Dursley said, "and he was to make the pieces smaller before cooking it, sort of a stew, like? So one could just ... well ... swallow it?"

"Are you mad?" Villar asked. "Tell the crew to just swallow their beef whole so it'll not ... what is it that it does besides the color?"

Alexis picked up the knife and fork to apply them to the hunk of beef.

Dursley held up a hand.

"I'd not —"

Alexis sliced off a bit of the beef and held the fork up to examine it.

"The insides are no different," she observed. "Still that odd shifting of color in the light and it —"

With an almost living quiver, the hunk of beef on the fork dissolved, turning into a liquid that ran down the fork and over Alexis' hand. With a muttered curse she flung it away.

"I warned you," Dursley said. "Next comes the sm —"

Alexis, Villar, and Isom stepped back from the table, hands to their faces, gagging, as the remaining half kilo of beef on the plate dissolved as well, and the cabin was filled with the horrible, overpowering odor of decayed flesh.

To Alexis' dismay, the hand she raised was the same one which had held the fork and which was now covered in similarly odoriferous goo.

She flung her hand out to the length of her arm, suddenly wishing she was taller so she'd have a bit more distance from her hand.

Dursley's shoulders slumped. "Damned hard to get a man to eat once it does that."

AN HOUR LATER, having inspected the vats and told the crew that their supper would be as a Naval banyan day, with no beef and mostly porridge and cheese — an announcement met with surprisingly little in the way of grumbling from the crew — Alexis reconvened her officers in her cabin.

"So," Alexis said, "we have only two containers of nutrient solution that weren't topped off with some vile stuff at Enclave."

Villar nodded. "I inspected all of them with Mister Dursley, and the other six containers are ... well, contaminated, I suppose we must say."

"And worse, the vats themselves?"

"Yes, sir." Villar shrugged. "The two containers of good solution will grow nearly two months of beef, so we're in no danger of starving."

Alexis grimaced. "That's far from the margin I'd prefer." Poor winds could add weeks to a transit time already long in the sparsely populated Barbary. She'd never yet had to put a ship on short rations, and didn't relish the prospect.

"The true difficulty, though," Hacking said, "is what's already in the vats."

Alexis nodded. Dursley, as most ship's pursers would do, had topped off all of the growing vats when in port — with the very solution now posing them the problem. With all of the growth vats contaminated with — whatever it was — adding fresh solution wouldn't solve the problem. They'd have to be emptied and sterilized, a process best done outside the ship.

"The crew'll not like doing that in *darkspace*," Isom noted, filling their glasses.

"I'm aware," Alexis said. She ran a finger idly over her table's surface, bringing up information about the nearest systems. "No matter there's no evidence of harm, they'll not want to eat anything grown in a vat exposed to the Dark."

Villar grinned. "Perhaps we could have Boots give them a runaround and declare them safe?"

"I'll thank you to not encourage that sort of thing, Mister Villar," Alexis said, ignoring the fact that she'd suggested the very thing about the contaminated beef to begin with. She thought that was certainly different, as it had the possibility of ridding her of the vile creature as well.

She sat back and drained her glass at one go. She set it back on table with a sharp *click*, then caught the expressions on the faces of Isom and Villar.

"What?" Villar and Isom looked away, but not before giving her glass a guilty glance. "Oh, for — look, you two, I had enough of my every glass being measured back on Dalthus. If I wanted a mother hen aboard, I'd have brought one."

The two had the grace to look uncomfortable, but Villar looked about to say more.

Hacking and Parrill merely looked puzzled, while Dursley continued to look as if he'd like to melt into the bulkhead and disappear. The man had been muttering, "It weren't my fault," the entire time they'd inspected the vats and Alexis was beginning to fear for his strength of mind.

Alexis eyed her empty glass and the state of the others'. Perhaps she had downed a bit more than usual during this meeting. She sighed and pursed her lips.

Will that be forever second-guessed now?

A quick tug at her pant leg took half her attention as the vile creature chose that moment to crawl to her lap. Much as she might wish it gone most of the time, it was a bit of a comfort at stressful times and she absently made to stroke its fur.

"Ow!"

A sharp pain in her finger, and more in her thigh, as the creature launched itself away made her rise from her seat.

"The little bugger bit me!"

Isom frowned.

"He's never done that before, has he, sir?"

"No, and I'll not have it. I —" She raised her hand to her lips to suck at the bite — two drops of blood showing where the thing had caught her — then winced and extended her arm away from her.

Despite her best attempts at washing and the use, she was certain, of nearly a quarter of her water ration and nearly every sort of cleaning solution aboard, the smell of the deconstituted beef still clung to her hand. She sighed. "I suppose I can't blame it for not wanting to be petted with that odor about me."

Isom was hiding a grin, while Villar, at least, seemed to be sympathetic to her plight.

And the distraction had ended what certainly would have been an uncomfortable exchange between the three of them. Alexis eyed her empty glass. She'd kept her own measure of her drinking, both at home and now aboard *Mongoose*, and was satisfied that there was no problem such as she'd had aboard *Nightingale*. Neither was she using it to numb herself or deaden her sleep, as she had during that commission.

To be honest and fair, the creature's presence did help with that somehow. Vile as it might be, and its penchant for her boots notwithstanding, she had to admit that it was a relief when she woke rested and dreamless with its warm body curled next to her on her cot. Still, she'd never admit that to Isom — there was a certain decorum she must maintain as captain, after all.

"Even so, if it does that again I'll see it spaced, do you hear me?"

Isom nodded, still with a hand over his mouth. "Aye, sir. Of course."

Alexis tapped her tabletop, indicating one of the systems between them and the rendezvous point and not too far away from their path. If the winds stayed as predicted, it would be the least impact on their travel time and they might still make the window for meeting any of the other private ships.

"Here, the Deluvia system," she said. "We'll drain and sterilize the vats in normal-space, then be off to Carina and our meeting."

THIRTY-ONE

T he decision was easier than the act.

They made Deluvia without further mishap, though the crew's initial acceptance of a banyan day grew less so as it became two, four, and then a full week of them. Alexis finally made the decision to share out her own stores, and those of her officers, with the crew, something Villar and Parrill accepted readily enough, but Hacking balked at.

"It's not the cost, sir," Hacking said, "but what good can my few kilos of frozen meat do for so many?"

"It's the principle, Mister Hacking," Alexis said. "A bit of shared sacrifice, if you will — and your cost will be made whole from *Mongoose's* funds when next we take on stores. Mister Dursley will compile a list of all you donate and replace it then."

Hacking huffed.

"Still don't see what good a few shreds in their porridge will do, sir."

"It will show them that *Mongoose's* officers face the same deprivation they do in the coming weeks — all the more important on this ship, as we're not under Naval regulations."

Hacking agreed, but didn't look happy about it.

Mongoose transitioned to normal-space at a Lagrangian point deemed near enough to Deluvia's primary to have enough heat and radiation from the system's sun to do a proper job sterilizing the vats.

It was an uninhabited system with no habitable planets and nothing at all of interest. Once in a stable orbit around the chosen planet, though, they were able to be about setting the vats to rights.

To get rid of — whatever it was causing the issues with the beef — they'd have to sterilize the tanks, but doing so with chemicals would leave a residue to interfere with the new growth solution. Getting rid of the residue with a good rinse, as might be done on a station or planet's surface, wasn't an option as the ship didn't carry nearly enough water to do the job properly. Even leaving aside the need for the water to run through the recyclers, which were nowhere near efficient enough to keep up.

Instead, the vats would be sealed, moved outside the ship, and their contents expelled. Then the empty vats left to bake in view of the primary for a time, until vacuum, heat, and radiation sterilized them.

It was hot, heavy work in the hold, even with the ship's lowermost gravity generators off. They opened the hold's loading hatch and carefully worked the massy vats out into open space, then unsealed them to void the contents. That was a tricky task, as the stuff would turn to either ice or vapor, depending on its exposure to the sun, and a vat of expanding nutrient solution could act very much like a conventional rocket as its contents vaporized.

To be safe, they had to brace the sealed vats against a ship's boat and counteract the solution's thrust as necessary. Then, once all the solution was emptied, they opened the full top of the vat and left it to bake in the primary's rays for a day, until they could be sure that every drop was gone and every bit of the surface was as lifeless as may be.

Even with that, many of the crew watched the vats come back inboard with a chary eye.

The vats cleaned, all of the containers of tainted solution given the same treatment, and the ship put back to rights, they were ready to sail on. Still, no one breathed easy until they were nearly four days out from Deluvia and the first vat produced enough beef to cook up and see the results.

There was a bit of a ceremony about it, as Cook set the first serving before Dursley, nearly the full crew crowded around him on the mess deck, and Dursley took up knife and fork. The slab before him *looked* as fine as vat-grown beef ever might, with, at least, a consistent grey color to it and no more than the usual sheen of grease.

The purser looked about at the watching crowd, swallowed heavily, and cut his eyes to Alexis and her officers, but there was no mercy to be found there. If the newly grown beef were found to have the same issues as before the cleansing, then the whole crew would be on short commons until they could find a system in which to fully replace the vats — which might mean sailing right out of the Barbary altogether. It might not be his fault in truth, but the crew would never trust the purser again thereafter, so he'd be out of a position, at the least, and walking small about the ship until set in-atmosphere to avoid a beating.

Dursley set his fork to the slab of beef and raised his knife in a trembling hand.

"Such a production," Hacking muttered, though Alexis noted that his own eyes never strayed from the little drama unfolding at the crowd's center.

"For Dursley, I imagine it is," Alexis said. "If we're on short commons and with no beef at all while we leave the Barbary, that's weeks of sailing — and weeks with no prizes, mind you. We'll likely have to seal him up in a wardroom cabin to keep him safe until we reach some system."

"And would any Navy ship take him on after?" Villar mused.

"Not even a merchantman," Parrill said. "Not with the reputation he'll have."

"*Carve the bloody roast, Mister Nipcheese!*" someone in the crowd bellowed.

"Belay that!" Dockett yelled.

Dursley closed his eyes, his lips moved in a mutter Alexis would swear must be, "It's not my fault," and he sawed at the hunk of meat.

The watching crowd seemed to sway forward as one to hover over Dursley and the plate. The deck went silent without the sound even of a breath.

The low, scraping grind of the knife making it through to the plate came a moment later.

"*Eat it!*"

"*In yer mouth, you!*"

Dockett and his mates tried, though half-heartedly, to calm the crew, but they still shouted.

The purser, eyes still closed as though he didn't wish to see what was coming, slowly raised the fork, which showed a goodly hunk of beef, still grey and in one piece, so there was that.

He opened his mouth.

"*In or we'll do it fer ya!*"

Dursley shoved the beef into his mouth and tossed the fork to the table.

"*Chew it! No, bloody swallowing whole, you thievin' bastard!*"

"Do you suppose we should have done this first test in secret?" Villar whispered.

Alexis shook her head. "There're no secrets aboard ship, and they'd want to see regardless, not trust anyone's word for it."

"*Open! And show us it's chewed good!*"

"You see?"

Dursley chomped loudly, mouth open but eyes still closed. Alexis thought she caught sight of a small tear on the man's cheek and hoped it was from relief and not some sign that the beef's taste was off ... more than to be expected.

Finally, the men nearest him became satisfied that the meat was sound and the crowd's grumbles changed to cheers. They seemed to all want to clap Dursley on the back, which nearly made the man choke on the unswallowed beef.

Alexis breathed her own sigh of relief, as this meant *Mongoose* would not have to turn aside and seek aid from a planetary base.

———

MONGOOSE MADE Carina and the rendezvous time with mere days to spare.

Alexis eased into the system slowly — Dansby had not been exaggerating when he said the system shoals in the Barbary were more pronounced and shallow than elsewhere. Enclave had been a difficult system to approach, but it was near enough several others that even the larger merchant craft on their way to and from *Hso-hsi* were able to make it through. Carina, though, was more remote, allowing more dark matter to accumulate in one place instead of being spread over multiple systems.

It was a binary system, as well, doubling the accumulation and with a dozen gas giants and no habitable planets. The sheer amount of mass in the system's normal-space attracted a like amount of dark matter, which formed a dense halo around the system in *darkspace*. Too much of it would react with the ship's mass, overcoming the charged gallenium of the ship's hull and trapping *Mongoose* until she could work herself free.

Much like an electrostatic field or a planet's magnetic field may affect water or a star's radiation, the charged gallenium in the hull was particularly effective at repelling both dark matter and the radiations of dark energy that permeated *darkspace*. Too much of either, though, could overcome that field and interact with the ship directly.

With so much dark matter, too much and too long and the hull itself might be breached or crushed.

Mongoose had a shallow draft, being not too massy herself, but even with that Alexis kept a close eye on her course toward the nearest Lagrangian point. Aside from the shoals at the

225

system's edges, the dark matter collected around the corresponding planets as well, creating shifting bars of the stuff which moved along with the planets' orbits, and as those masses became more than the planet could carry along with it, they broke off and moved about the system until they dispersed.

"There's nothing from either Eades or Malcomson about *where* in the system we might rendezvous with the others, so we'll transition as first we're able and get out of this mess."

"Aye, sir," Villar said, nodding, his eyes on the navigation plot, as well.

The ship's computer could predict, as best it was able, where some of the shoals and bars would be, based on what it knew of the system's planets and their orbits, but it was always possible for a storm or some other effect to break a bit off and leave it behind in the orbital plane. Carina had so much mass, in any case, that the trails of dark matter behind some of the larger planets ran fully half their orbits.

The only ways to detect the stuff were visually, looking for a darker mass against the blackness of *darkspace* itself or firing off a laser ahead of the ship and observing how the masses of dark matter might twist and deform its bolt.

"I believe I'll have a man on the bow, firing the lead, if you will, Mister Villar."

Villar nodded, a slight sheen of sweat on his brow. "That might be best, sir."

Within a few minutes, there was a vacsuited figure on *Mongoose's* bow, and a moment later a short, bright bolt of light leapt forward from the ship. Smaller than one of the guns, the "lead" was a handheld laser and gallenium-encased capacitors which shot a small bolt into *darkspace* ahead of the ship.

The typical amount of dark matter, present everywhere in *darkspace*, effected even the laser's light, compressing and foreshortening it as it did the guns' shot. More of the stuff, though, would affect the light to an even greater degree, curving and warping it away from its straight path and shifting even its color.

This was what Alexis and Villar were looking for, using the bolt's path and color to gauge how much dark matter might be built up ahead of *Mongoose* and avoid the worst of it.

"I've never seen it so dense before," Alexis murmured — she had an unexplainable urge to keep her voice down, as though *Mongoose* were sneaking past some sleeping giant she feared to wake.

"Most systems haven't so much," Villar agreed, his own voice muted as well. "Enough to worry a heavy merchant or ship of the line, perhaps, but nothing so light as *Mongoose*. I understand it has to do with the systems here being so far apart, as well?"

"Yes — it does make sense that more would accumulate where it can, when there are fewer places for it to do so."

They crept on, altering course as the flying shot from the lead indicated more dark matter ahead than Alexis was comfortable taking *Mongoose* through, until they finally reached the closest Lagrangian point viable for transition, the solar L3 of the outermost gas giant. There had been a few bodies farther out, but they were small rocks, barely worth the name, and their Lagrangian points were weak.

"Transition," Alexis ordered, when they were well situated, and sighed with relief a moment later when the stars appeared and *Mongoose*'s normal-space consoles awoke.

"There's still the getting out through that," Villar reminded her.

"Ever ready to cheer my day, eh, Mister Villar?"

"A first officer's job, sir, I'm sure."

"Ship in-system, sir," Dorsett announced.

"Where away?"

"Farther in," he said, transferring the data to the navigation plot, "in orbit about the sixth planet off the star's port side."

Alexis nodded. True, stars had no real port or starboard, but from *Mongoose*'s position and orientation, the planet was to port of the star. It served to form a mental image while the more accurate data appeared on the screen.

"She's a big'un," Dorsett added. "Second, maybe first rate."

"That is large," Alexis agreed. "And may be our commodore."

She'd have expected a frigate or a smaller ship-of-the-line, especially given the shoals they'd just come through. A first rate would have had a harder time of it.

"We have, perhaps, four hours until they're aware of us, sir," Villar said.

Alexis nodded. One of the advantages a ship transitioning from *darkspace* had was that the light from *Mongoose*, and the knowledge of her presence, would only begin to spread through the system once she transitioned, but the light from every other ship was already detectable by her — though some four hours old, having traveled so far, as in this case.

"Send a signal with our identity and intention to return to *darkspace* and close with her, Creasy. This is our rendezvous system after all, so I presume she's friendly. Lord knows our foes have no cause to frequent such a desolate place."

THIRTY-TWO

Mongoose returned to the shoally confines of *darkspace* and made her way to the L1 point of the planet the other ship orbited. She closed with the other ship and received, after a bit of a delay, notice that it was the *Hind*, a Marchant Company ship, along with the rather terse instruction *Captain to Repair Onboard*.

"A merchantman — a stores ship, do you suppose?" Villar asked. "It would be good to retop our vats and storage with good, safe, New London solutions."

"Indeed," Hacking agreed. "Though we appear to have missed our commodore."

"Perhaps next time," Alexis agreed. "A support ship is as welcome, I suppose."

"We can hope. It would be nice to refill our vats with solution we can rely on. But what's this signal? A bit pushy for a merchantman, don't you think, sir?"

Alexis nodded. It was the sort of thing she expected from a senior Naval captain, not from one private ship to another, but she supposed the other captain might well consider *Mongoose* to be his inferior, given the *Hind's* size.

"She's bloody huge," Villar murmured, as more data came in about the other ship.

"Indeed," Alexis agreed, studying the plot. *I wonder at how she made it so far insystem with that mass.*

The *Hind* was as large as a first-rate ship of the line. Nowhere near as many guns, of course, but pierced for enough — nearly fifty guns. Where a Naval vessel would carry more guns, the Marchant ship would carry cargo, Alexis knew, and in fact could see that the ship was pierced with only two rows of gunports, the third deck, presumably, being taken up by additional cargo space.

"Largest merchant I've seen outside the Core," Villar said. "It's a wonder they can sail her without mechanicals."

"They may have some," Alexis mused. "It would take a valiant pirate to take her on, after all, so the risk might not be so great as we think." She raised her eyebrows giving voice to her earlier thought. "It's a real wonder her captain made it in here through the shoals though."

That must have been a sight to see, for the *Hind* was actually shorter than *Mongoose*, though with far more volume and mass — built for strength to carry so much mass, rather than the speed of *Mongoose's* construction. With the other ship drawing so much more mass, she'd be that much more vulnerable to the accumulations of dark matter around this system.

"Hadn't thought of that — I know I wouldn't want to try it. I wonder at why they'd send such a beast to the Barbary, then, given the conditions?"

"I suppose it makes sense to someone."

It was hours of travel under the conventional drive before they reached the *Hind* and came to rest relative to the other ship. Alexis took the opportunity to nap, then showered. She wrapped a towel around herself, lost in thought about meeting another privateering captain, if such *Hind* was and not merely a stores ship, as well as wondering at where the Navy ship and the expected commodore might be, then stared at her bunk in consternation.

"Isom! What the bloody hell is this?"

"Uniform, sir!" Isom called from her pantry without returning to the cabin, which showed, Alexis thought, that he knew well how she was going to react to this latest nonsense.

Brown breeches, which looked far too small even for her, a white, blousy shirt which looked too large, by far, a vest of some sort of skin that was almost scaled, and boots of the same material as the vest — boots which, if they weren't taller than Alexis' legs, were certainly damned close.

She had no idea where the things had come from, having expected her usual dress of denim trousers and linen shirt. If the commodore had been in-system, she might have worn her uniform — appropriate for meeting a senior officer, no matter she was on half-pay — but that wouldn't do here at all now.

She picked up the vest, which glittered blue to purple in the light — disturbingly like the changing colors of the bad vat-beef in a way. It was also lacking in any sort of strap to go over one's shoulders, making it not a vest, but —

"Isom, get in here!"

The clerk's head appeared in the pantry hatchway. "Sir?"

"I'm not wearing this — where did it even come from anyway?"

"Picked up on Enclave, sir. The lads come up with it themselves."

"The crew is aware of this ..." She waved her hand at the clothing, words failing her.

Isom nodded. "There's some few, sir, made a comment or two — after we took that prize. And after all those others remarked on your dress."

"Comments?"

"Only as to how you and the ship were so disrespected, sir, by that Malcomson fellow at the first, though he turned out all right, but then Nabb talked of the guards at the jail thinking you were ... well, not rightly seeing you were a proper ship's captain and all." Isom shrugged. "The lads figured it weren't right, you having to go aboard prizes and meeting others like them captains dressed as you were, sir. Thought it didn't properly represent *Mongoose*, you see?"

"I do not see, not at all. I went aboard the prizes in a bloody vacsuit. What on earth could be wrong with that?"

"Well, sir, it's that this ship's different than the Navy, right? They're all good lads, proper Navy lads if they were aboard such, but *Mongoose's* not, see?"

Alexis gestured for him to continue.

"They've their ideas for as how things should go — and, well, there was talk that proper privateer captains don't go over in the first boarding party. A proper private ship captain should wait, see, until the ship's took and all under control, then make ... well, an entrance, I suppose."

"I bloody well did enter, so what's their complaint!"

"No, sir, an *entrance*, see? With, well ... style?"

Alexis stared at him for a moment. "*Style?*"

"Not that you're not stylish at times, sir, only that —"

"'At times,' is it?"

"Ah ... in your proper lieutenant's uniform, assuredly, sir, or them dresses you brought back from Hanover, but you can't wear them here, can you? They're different, see? And all else that's brought from home are those linen shirts and denim trews — not proper style as the lads see it at all."

"I see."

"So, then, Coburn, sir, she —"

Alexis raised an eyebrow at that. Coburn was one of the women they'd taken aboard at Penduli, and she wondered at her being involved in this foolishness.

"— says, 'Well, look at that Malcomson fellow,' she says, and the lads do and see what dress *he* has, what with that great fur cape of his and them tight leathern pants what shows his —" Isom cleared his throat and his face went red. "Well, what shows he's ... mean to say ... well, he's a well put together sort of man and that sends a certain message, that does."

Alexis did have to admit that. When Malcomson walked into a pub, the place grew quiet and he received a wide berth until he'd chosen a place and settled in. How the lads thought she might have the same effect, she couldn't say.

"And so you've come up with this?"

"The lads did, sir ... Nabb, he talked to that Malcomson's coxswain and asked about the other private ship captains."

"*Nabb* was a part of this?"

"Aye, sir, and it's the same as Malcomson to hear talk of the others. They've a certain style, sir, each of the private ship captains."

Isom came farther from the pantry door now, as though becoming reassured that he might not need to duck behind the hatch. Alexis was not so sure of that, but both Nabb and Isom were steady and had nothing but her interest at heart, she was certain, so she was willing to listen at least.

"The lads, sir, they put their own coin together for it, as well, you should know. They came to me for sizes and such, which I have for your uniforms. It was all them, though."

"Really." She stared at Isom for a moment and thought she caught a twinkle in his eye that belied his claims that it was *all* the crew and none of his doing. She took in the clothing again, it gaining nothing from a second look in her opinion.

"Aren't the trousers a bit small?"

"Ah ... I'm told they stretch, sir."

"*Stretch?*"

Isom nodded.

She held up the not-vest. "Stays, Isom, really? Am I some pub girl on a colony world needing to tote and carry all day?"

"It's said that skin there'll turn a blade, sir."

Alexis sighed. "Tell the lads they've had their joke, will you, and set me out some proper clothes."

Isom hesitated. "It's no joke, sir."

"Oh, this is a joke, believe me. They've had their fun and I'll laugh along with them, but I draw the line at wearing this nonsense even for a moment."

He hesitated again and Alexis began to suspect he was quite serious that the lads weren't joking with her. She frowned.

"Get me Nabb, will you?"

In a moment her coxswain was in the cabin. The lad came to a dead stop, flushed deep red, and fixed his gaze on the aft bulkhead. It was only then that Alexis remembered she'd come from the shower, hadn't dressed yet, and was clad only in a towel. She was so used to Isom being about her cabin that she hadn't noticed — the tight quarters made modesty an impossibility, in any case. She'd expected Nabb to have come to the same conclusion below decks, what with *Mongoose* having a number of female crewmembers now, but he was young and it might be taking him more time to acclimate to the idea.

"Nabb, what's this rubbish about the crew buying me a bloody costume?"

Nabb took a deep breath. "It was a sort of general idea, sir, but the detail started with Creasy, I think."

Alexis closed her eyes and rubbed at her temples, where she was certain she could feel the start of a headache. Creasy, the signalsman from *Nightingale* come along with the rest of that ship's quarterdeck crew. Creasy with his superstitions, his Dutchmen and other terrors of the Dark. She sighed.

Nothing good ever started with Creasy.

"What's he done?"

Nabb grimaced. "Told a tale or two of *Nightingale* to the new lads, sir. About the Dutchmen we faced and —"

"There were no bloody Dutchmen! They were suicidal religious fanatics who sent themselves off to God knows where by transitioning outside a bloody Lagrangian point! They were done in by *bloody science* not some ... some specter of the Dark!"

Nabb nodded. "There is that, sir, but Creasy ..."

"Aye, 'but Creasy'." She sighed. "What else has he told them?"

"Boots, sir, and *Nightingale's* last battle with the *Owl*."

Alexis turned her gaze to her bunk, where, surely as if conjured by his name, the vile creature was sitting next to the bloody costume, sniffing at the stays.

"How Boots was loose before the fight, sir," Nabb went on, "and how old Garbett died. Slipping as he did in what Boots left behind and knocking his gun just so, as to put the final shot of his life dead into that breach in the *Owl's* stern, straight into her fusion plant and saving *Nightingale* as he did."

"It didn't *save Nightingale*," Alexis said, though she knew the reality would make no difference to Creasy or his tales — nor to those who heard them, in all likelihood. "*Nightingale* had already battered the *Owl's* stern so badly it was breached — she'd have taken the ship regardless."

"Only after a bitter fight still, to hear Creasy tell it, without old Garbett's sacrifice."

"It was no sacrifice," Alexis whispered, though she thought she could hear a distant voice muttering "it doesn't matter" over and over again as she spoke. A crew would believe what they would. "It was coincidence. No spirits of the Dark or whatever else Creasy's come up with involved."

"Aye, sir, there's them that sees the truth of that."

"And those that don't," she finished for him.

"And those that agree Boots is just lucky — lucky for a ship named after him and lucky for a crew of ..."

Nabb trailed off and Alexis opened her eyes to stare at him. He'd taken his eyes from the aft bulkhead and was staring at the deck near his feet, flushing again and not from the sight of Alexis' towel, she suspected.

"Sweet Dark, there's more isn't there?"

Isom cleared his throat and looked away, then darted toward the pantry.

"Just tell me and get it over with, please?"

"It was the translator, sir, your tablet?" Nabb explained. "Back on *Bisharet*? That ship we took but you let go." He paused for a moment. "Word of how that captain muddled the ship's name ... well, it rather set right with the lads. To have a nickname, and all."

"A nickname?" Alexis asked, certain she couldn't bear any more.

"Snakeeaters, sir," Nabb said. "The boots and stays there are some sort of scaly beast, you see?"

Alexis looked back to her bunk and could now see that the odd pattern was quite scaly. Also that the vile creature was out of hiding and sniffing at the boots — for once, she could almost wish the thing would destroy the pair all entire, and save her from having to wear them.

For that was where she saw this going. If the crew felt strongly about it, she'd acquiesce, she knew — to do otherwise would damage morale. And they were a good bunch — odd though the outfit might be, if both Isom and Nabb were unopposed, then she could be certain there was no ill-will in the gesture.

And she had been thinking she needed a uniform of some sort, with no doubt that Malcomson, as well as some of the other captains, even merchantmen, she'd seen in Enclave's casino, each had a certain ... style, as Isom said, about their own.

"Snakeeaters," she muttered.

Isom poked his head in from the pantry. "More than one new tattoo's come out of our visit to Enclave, sir, if you'd like to see."

THE OUTFIT DID HAVE, Alexis had to admit as she regarded herself in the mirror, a certain something.

The trousers had indeed been too small and did indeed stretch —

to a quite alarming degree, which made them fit with an equally alarming snugness. The boots, Isom informed her, were not to be worn at their full length, but with the tops turned down — which placed them at only mid-thigh. They did fit well, as Isom had all of her sizes and measurements available through her tablet for ordering uniforms.

The boot material, though, was astounding, and Alexis found she quite liked it. They were made of a skin native to Desva here in the Barbary, and very much like a serpent, which is why the men chose it. It consisted of small, close knit scales with five sides, each of which caught and reflected the light in hues ranging from deep purple to a dark watery blue.

The stays, of the same skin as the boots, fit snugly over the far looser blouse and its billowing sleeves. It also had an ingenious little pocket at the small of her back which would keep her flechette pistol discreetly tucked away, while still allowing her to draw it quickly — something the crew would have had to have custom made.

She turned to the side and observed herself from that angle.

It was not, perhaps, the very worst thing the crew could have come up with. In fact, it was ... flattering. Far from the slightly baggy ship's jumpsuits or the straight-lined uniform of a Naval officer, certainly, but Alexis did have to admit she looked ... quite good in it.

"It does have a certain ... flair, doesn't it?" she muttered.

"It does, sir," Isom agreed. "Wouldn't work aboard a Queen's ship, of course, but ..."

"But *Mongoose* is not a Queen's ship and I am not a Queen's officer at this time," Alexis agreed. She thought of the huge fur cape worn by Malcomson, and of the other odd styles she'd seen at Enclave. "I am captain of a private ship in the Barbary, after all."

"Aye, sir."

"Well, then." She straightened her shoulders, feeling how the stays did aid her in keeping a straight back. There was a reason women working farms wore them, after all, even on Dalthus still. She sighed. "Let's go show the lads what they've wrought."

"Don't forget the hat, sir!"

Alexis turned. "Hat?"

There was indeed a hat, wide-brimmed with the sides turned up and ...

"Is that a feather?"

THIRTY-THREE

Nearly the entire crew was assembled on *Mongoose's* main deck as Alexis exited her quarters. She strode to the edge of the platform from which she could address the crew, boots *clicking* on the hull and hat, feather and all, atop her head. She stopped and stared out at them.

Some were smiling, others appeared a little nervous, as though suspecting they might have gone too far, but they relaxed when she tipped the hat and grinned at them.

"Well, lads, I'll thank you for your gracious gift," she said. "It's *not* what I'd have bought myself, but it does make a statement and it's a fine addition to represent our ship after our first prize." She smiled at the cheers and applause. "The first of many more to come, I hope, after I've gone aboard the *Hind* and met one of our fellows. We'll be back after prizes soon, and make back the cost of this and more."

With that, she made her way to her boat, Nabb and the crew following her.

The boat made its way to the *Hind* and docked, after which she made her way through the docking tube.

Up close, the *Hind* was even more impressive than at a distance, a solid wall of gallenium-laced hull was nearly all she could see through the boat's viewscreen.

It might even be larger than a First Rate, she thought.

She'd be a slow ship, certainly, with that mass and beam — hard to sail into the wind, such as when leaving a system, but the devil herself running, with four masts rigged, she suspected, for royals.

A smaller crew than a first rate, though. Certainly not large enough to fight both sides of the ship at once — perhaps not even enough to fight and work sails at the same time. She'd rely on her size and the fear of that first broadside to stave off pirates, who'd likely go looking elsewhere for a prize, rather than risk a taste of that.

The crew she saw as she came through the docking tube was not what she'd expected at all. Despite being a Marchant Company ship, she'd expected the *Hind*, being here at the privateering rendezvous, to be much the same as the others she'd encountered.

Instead of the ill-matched ship's jumpsuits and rather scruffy lot of the others, the crew of the *Hind* had an eerie precision. The crew's jumpsuits were all far too tidy and pressed for Alexis' comfort and they went about their work with an even more eerie silence. There was none of the hustle and bustle and shouted orders that came with most ships, nor even the hushed murmur of conversations one might encounter on a ship's make-and-mend day.

An officer, Alexis wasn't certain of his rank as his uniform bore an insignia she wasn't familiar with, met her at the hatch.

"Welcome aboard *Hind*," he said, then paused. "Captain?"

Alexis nodded. There were no colors as there would be aboard a naval vessel, but there was a large image of the Marchant Company logo, blue waves against a red circle, filling the aft bulkhead. She settled for doffing her hat to that, as she would her beret aboard a Naval vessel, while thinking it did strike one a bit pretentious for a private company to so mimic a nation's navy.

The uniforms, she noted, mimicked the Royal Navy as well, but with more gilt and ornamentation than she'd typically expect to find on a Naval officer, even one so enthralled with such things as her former Captain Neals of *Hermione*.

"Captain Alexis Carew, of the private ship *Mongoose*," she assured the officer, wondering for a moment what she should do with her hat now that she'd doffed it once. It was far larger than her Naval uniform's beret and the feather would almost drag the upper bulkhead as she walked. She settled for that, rather than leaving it in hand.

"I see," the man said. "I'm Lieutenant Hudnall of the *Hind*, Marchant Company."

Alexis nodded greeting, wondering about the "lieutenant" bit and frowning.

"Has the *Hind* been brought into the Service, then?" That might explain it, if the Navy were making use of a merchant ship as a sort of irregular sidestep of sending a vessel into the Barbary, Hanoverese space — one could always disavow such a thing if it were found out, much as Alexis and the other privateers could be.

Hudnall flushed and his jaw tightened, so Alexis assumed she'd gotten that wrong. Quite wrong, given the tone of his answer.

"The Marchant Company is not 'brought in', as you say, *captain*."

"I'm sorry. It was only your rank and uniform that made me think —"

"The Marchant Company, at least the branch to which the *Hind* reports, prides itself on its bearing," Hudnall said. "Perhaps you and your ... *private ships* may find your own attire, but the Marchant Company maintains a respectable image."

"THE COMMODORE WILL SEE you in a moment," Hudnall told her after leading her aft.

Alexis frowned at that. No self-respecting Naval officer would take up his flag aboard a merchantman, so what *was* this commodore about?

Hudnall gave Alexis another appraising look, which she met with a stare of indifference, but inside she was regretting her decision to wear the new garb. Or, rather, part of her was — while another part was wishing she had the fur cape and skintight leathern breeches Malcomson wore.

The *Hind* was not the privateer she'd come to expect and thought it to be. Instead, the officers she'd seen, not just Hudnall, wore neat, matching uniforms of the Marchant Company, as did all the spacers. It was quite like the Royal Navy in that regard ... in fact, it was more like the Royal Navy *than* the Royal Navy, if one got down to how the Navy actually looked.

Her outfit hadn't seemed so out of place aboard *Mongoose*, with the crew in a motley collection of whatever they'd collected over the years, but on the *Hind*, she stuck out distinctly — not least because of the number of shined surfaces on the *Hind's* quarterdeck from which the colors of her boots and stays were reflecting.

Hudnall's words also gave her pause about this meeting, as if this "commodore" was aboard a Marchant ship, a private ship, no matter their airs, then she rather expected she wouldn't get on with him at all. Hudnall's claim of a lieutenancy and, more, this commodore-nonsense, was striking her as disrespectful to the Service, and she didn't like it one bit.

Her greeting was also not what she was expecting, as it wasn't typical, outside of the Navy where a superior might make a point of it, to have a visiting captain cool her heels before being greeted. At the least, she should have been seen into the *Hind's* master's cabin and offered refreshment while the ship's *captain*, saw to whatever business he was about.

She'd worked *Mongoose* hard to arrive here within the rendezvous window — her crew had worked hard to do so — and to be kept cooling her heels by some self-styled commodore was —

A man Alexis instantly took for an officer's steward poked his head through the hatch to the *Hind's* master's cabin.

"Captain Carew?"

Alexis nodded, though she wondered at the question. Were there so many strangers standing about *Hind's* passageways that he'd felt the need to confirm her identity?

She shoved that question aside, noting her irritability and determined not to let it show.

"Commodore Skanes will see you now," the man said.

Alexis followed him through to another surprise. She wasn't expecting to find a woman behind the table in the *Hind's* master's cabin ... and that woman was, by all indications, not expecting to see Alexis. At least not as she was.

They stared at each other for a moment, before the woman motioned Alexis to sit.

"Carew, was it?"

"Yes."

"Commodore Alurea Skanes, Marchant Company. Please, do sit. Tabron! Wine, please."

The man who'd ushered her in hurriedly placed a glass before Alexis and poured, confirming his role.

"Thank you ... ah, sir."

Skanes' head came up at that. "Navy, were you?"

Alexis nodded. "Yes, sir. On half-pay now, though."

It occurred to her that Skanes might be as well — a thing that might go a ways toward explaining the woman's attitude and claim of rank — but was soon disabused of that notion.

"Well, I'll have none of that 'sir' nonsense here, if you please. The Marchant Company doesn't stand by that foolishness."

"I see ... ma'am, then?"

"That'll do — or Commodore Skanes or simply commodore, if you must. So, do you have a report for me?"

Alexis blinked. Eades had said nothing of commodores or reports, only that those private ships in the Barbary might, from time to time, meet and exchange news at this particular place.

"I'm sorry, ah, Commodore Skanes," Alexis said, still finding, oddly, that "ma'am" did not come at all naturally to her after so much time in the Navy. "I wasn't aware that we'd be reporting on anything."

Or to anyone, she thought, but did not say aloud.

"I want reports of what's going on, so kindly have something of your actions so far written up and delivered to the *Hind* before you sail, will you? Fill me in now, though."

Alexis did so, explaining *Mongoose*'s encounters so far.

"So, this merchant ship, *Bisharet*, you just let him go?" Skanes asked.

Alexis nodded. "He was carrying no cargo that would indicate involvement with piracy, nor was he a warship of any of the systems on my list, so I thought it best."

"Hmph. In future, I'll have you think twice on that," Skanes said. "I want every ship possible taken, so that we might show these bastards not to harass honest shipping."

Alexis nodded again, but didn't understand what difference an honest, or relatively honest man, losing his livelihood would make to the pirates and system leaders who supported them.

"And you passed your prize off to some fellow on Enclave? Well, you'll bring prizes here, from now on, rather than any of the Barbary systems. The *Hind* has enough crew to send them on from here, and the Company will give you credit immediately. You'll have your crew back aboard and be able to return to your cruise that much the quicker."

As Skanes talked, Alexis became more and more skeptical. This all sounded very much like it would be to the profit of this "commodore" and the Marchant Company, rather than the privateer crews, and it was nothing like what Eades and Dansby had led her to suspect.

"We have a fair amount of supplies aboard, as well," Skanes went on, "so you may resupply here, rather than any of the Barbary systems — and ensuring that none of these systems profit by it."

Alexis raised an eyebrow at that, but remained silent. More to the Company's profit, though she did like the opportunity to resupply from a source she could rely on and avoid another fiasco as with *Mongoose's* beef vats.

"In addition," Skanes said, "I'll be sending you a list of systems to patrol — these will be your areas of operation. I'm afraid your first prize might be considered poaching by the fellow who has Kayseri as his grounds, but I'll try to smooth things over. Tell him you're new and didn't yet understand, if you see."

"I did speak to Captain Malcomson already, sir — Commodore Skanes. He, at least, seemed unconcerned about territories."

That was true so far as it went, though the *Delight's* crew might not be so unconcerned. Still, Skanes' attitude grated on Alexis and this whole privateering nonsense seemed to be getting far more rules than she'd been led to believe.

"Malcomson, yes," Skanes said, drawing out the name. "Not a great believer in following instructions, that one."

Skanes took a deep breath and ran her eyes from the tips of Alexis' boots to the space above her head.

That would be the feather ...

Alexis turned her head just a bit in order to watch Skanes' eyes follow the feather's tip as it bounced.

"Excuse me, Commodore Skanes," Alexis said, "but I was not given to understand that there was quite so much structure to this business when *Mongoose* sailed. In fact, having spoken to Captain Malcomson of the *Delight* and —"

"Malcomson! That — Look, Carew, it's possible your principals didn't yet know that the Marchant Company was involved or that the *Hind* would be here. She's the largest, most powerful ship in the Barbary right now, so it's only right she should bring some structure with her."

"I see."

"Part of that structure will be the specific systems which each ship will patrol — in order to better cover the whole of the Barbary, you understand. You will patrol those systems, preparing a full report of your activities so that I may better allocate our force. In addition,

I'll have your prizes *here* for transfer to a proper Marchant crew to take them to a legal prize court. Do you understand?"

Alexis nodded. She understood, but bridled under the order. Skanes might think she had the authority to order these things, but there was no requirement in *Mongoose's* Letter of Marque to back it up.

"Now I'll expect that full report, in writing, before your ship leaves. In the meantime, you may speak to Hudnall about resupply and I'll have him send you a list of systems which you may patrol. You're dismissed."

Alexis opened her mouth with the thought to question Skanes' authority over *Mongoose*, but then closed it again as the realization came that there was nothing to say. She determined, though, to speak to Malcomson and the other private ship captains at the earliest opportunity. So, instead, she nodded again, and rose to leave.

As she reached the hatch, Skanes spoke again:

"And when next you report to me, Carew, wear a proper uniform, will you?"

THIRTY-FOUR

"**I**som!"

Alexis tossed her hat and stays onto her bunk and began stripping off her boots.

"Sir?"

She studied the boot in her hand for a moment, rather liking the play of light across the skin's scales.

"I'm afraid the crew's choice of uniform for me, while quite pleasing to myself, did not go over well with the Marchant Company's commodore."

Isom frowned. "The Marchant's commodore? What's that then?"

"A pretentious bollocks washer who fancies herself a proper officer, that's what."

Isom sighed, clearly disappointed. "I see, sir, so we're back to the farm clothes? Or will it be your uniform?"

Alexis tossed him the boot, which he caught, surprised.

"Oh, no," she said. "It's only that what the lads picked out for me lacks ... a certain something."

"It does? I mean ... the hat even has a feather, see?"

"The next time I meet with Commodore Skanes, Isom, I wish to look the proper private ship captain. Will you see to it?"

"So ... more something?"

"Indeed."

ALEXIS WASTED no time in driving *Mongoose* out of orbit and back to *darkspace* via the same L1 transition point she'd arrived from. Mere hours after taking on such stores as *Hind* had to offer — and hearing Dursley's assertion that while the nutrient solution was of good quality it was also priced so as to guarantee *Hind* a large profit — they were back in *darkspace* and beating their way out-system.

"That doesn't sound at all like privateering," Villar said after being informed of the content of Alexis' meeting with Skanes.

"It is nothing like it, and I begin to wonder at what authority she thinks she has," Alexis said. "*Mongoose* is not owned by the bloody Marchants, after all."

Alexis had to admit that her prior encounter with a Marchant ship and captain might be coloring her opinion, but the whole mess smelled rotten to her. Add to that her immediate dislike for Skanes and offense at the woman's presumption to a rank she didn't, couldn't, hold, and Alexis had no interest at all in following the Marchant's "structure".

"No," she said, "*Mongoose* is a private ship and I'll sail her as such." She didn't add that she couldn't imagine Avrel Dansby putting up with any of Skanes' strictures. Not that she felt herself bound by what Dansby might want, nor that how he might act would at all color her decisions, but, still, it was his ship after all.

At dinner that night, hosting her officers, she found that Hacking and Parrill both agreed as well.

"What possible right does she have to tell us where to search for prizes?" Hacking asked as the port was served.

"None," Parrill said. "*Mongoose's* letter of marque specifies the systems of the Barbary, and while 'Barbary' is not an official designation, it is in common usage and well understood to mean those systems past the Haguenau system and prior to Clonalin to fringeward — bounded by the New London border to one side, *Hso-hsi* to the other, and the French Republic above ... there being no lower boundary other than the common agreement that the space ends with those worlds over which Hanover exerts any sort of direct governance, rather than a mere territorial claim. There's neither mention nor implication that the ship must heed any other privateer's instructions. Every ship with a letter is an equal to the others so —"

She broke off at Hacking's snort. The man stared at her for a moment, then shook his head.

Parrill's face grew red and she looked down at her glass. "I'm sorry, but you did ask."

"Thank you, Parrill," Alexis said. "It's good we know where we stand with this 'Commodore' Skanes, after all, and that we're all in agreement that she has no true authority over *Mongoose*."

"You've decided our destination, then, sir?" Villar asked with a smile.

Alexis nodded. "Yes. Something Captain Malcomson mentioned when he dismissed our 'poaching' as being of no concern. He said that there were some places he could only take a prize or two, as all the other ships would scatter and there was no time to take more — then they'd return once he was known to leave the area. This has made me think that the captains involved in this may take the 'private' business too much to heart. We all might do better to concentrate on those areas where the shipping is, rather than spreading thin in an effort to not step on one another's toes."

Hacking frowned. "That sounds rather the opposite of what that Skanes has ordered."

Alexis met his gaze levelly.

"Why, yes, it does, doesn't it?"

THIRTY-FIVE

Enclave's landing field was as cold as always, but Alexis chose to wait outside the large doors.

The wind was up, whipping what little snow there was about in flurries and funnels, and more of it kicked up by the antigrav fields and engines of those boats setting down or taking off.

Villar and Parrill were with her. She'd left Hacking aboard *Mongoose* and come down herself to meet Malcomson after her repeated signals that she wished to speak to him had gone rebuffed.

"I've bin a'ship a month an' we'll gab when I've sat in a pub a while."

Then he'd cut signal and refused her calls for the remainder of *Delight's* approach to Enclave.

She couldn't blame him, she supposed, as she'd granted liberty to *Mongoose's* crew, as well. The port watch was down even now, and up to who knew what.

Still, her own crew was on edge for more than the time a'space. They'd not taken a single prize on the way from Carina — barely sighted one, and Alexis was anxious to speak to Malcomson about her idea to pair their two ships. Her crew, at least, badly needed a prize, and it would be either pair with Malcomson or hunt the systems "assigned" to him or one of the other ships even without the *Delight*.

Otherwise, the muttering of her crew might turn to more.

Already there was talk of ill-luck falling on the ship for this or that act. Everyone seemed to have an opinion on what to do about it — from the more amusing notions that they must begin spinning the ship end for end, clockwise, three times at the end of each watch, to the more disturbing view that the women aboard had brought on the ill-luck. Both of those were rare, thankfully, though Alexis was near to putting one man in-atmosphere for the latter — she did note, with some amusement, that his views did not extend to leaving a comfortable berth and seeking a new ship himself.

Then there was Creasy, as there seemed to always be, and his talk that —

"There, sir," Villar said, voice heavily muffled by his coat, collar turned up and his head lowered so as to breathe into it.

Alexis followed where he was pointing — well, shrugging, as he kept his hands in his pockets and sort of gestured as best he could with an elbow before clapping that back tightly to his side.

The *Delight's* boat came into clearer view and set down lightly on the field fifty meters or so from the hatch in a fresh flurry of blown snow. The ramp was lowering before the snow cleared and Malcomson was first down. His size, great beard, and fur cloak making him both recognizable, even through the blowing snow, and seeming like some mythical beast out of frozen legends.

He reached the bottom of the ramp, caught sight of Alexis already moving toward him, and shook his head.

His voice bellowed and cut through even the gusts of Enclave's winds.

"Not a bluddy word, lass, 'til I've a hot pie and a cold pint before me and half of each within, y'understand?"

Alexis shouted back to be heard. "It's important!"

Malcomson was close enough to be heard easier, even over the wind, but still bellowed. "Priorities, lass! Pints and pies and priorities!"

"I'd think profit was a priority!" Alexis yelled back.

Malcomson scowled. "Dinnae speak to me o' profit this trip! We've three prizes in tow, but the lads —"

He was interrupted at this point as the settlement's hatch opened and figures rushed out, all screaming and bellowing at the top of their lungs. Dozens, in a thick stream which broke around the group of four officers only to rejoin on the other side.

Malcomson, Alexis, Villar, and Parrill stood frozen while the wild, ululating group passed around them, then turned to watch.

Malcomson's men were ten or so meters from their boat, thirty from Alexis. They didn't stay frozen like the officers did, but immediately reacted, rushing the oncoming group with cries of *"Delights!"* the war cry of their ship.

It was only as the two groups met that Alexis recognized the cry of the attacking group. Perhaps she'd missed it because it was so drawn out. Perhaps because of the winds howling about her head. Perhaps only because she couldn't believe it and didn't want to.

"*Booooooooooots!*"

Alexis shook her head as the two crews met with fists and feet flailing to strike the other. Bodies fell entangled to the snow-covered ice and rolled about until they were so covered in the white crystals that there was no telling them apart. Red spattered the white landing field as noses and lips were crushed. Shouts of pain and outrage began replacing the war cries, but were soon drowned out by renewed efforts from both sides.

Alexis sighed.

"Bloody Creasy."

———

MALCOMSON SPUN from the fight and glared at Alexis.

"What's this then, lass? Word come from home while I were away? Are we feuding, us?"

Alexis shook her head. "No, it's —"

She wasn't at all certain how one could explain Creasy and his ideas, nor how they seemed to infect the crew like some sort of plague of idiocy and delusion. She was certain Creasy's thoughts, dim though they be, were behind this, though. His talk of displeased spirits from their not defending the vile creature's dubious honor in the face of the *Delights'* taunts were certainly the source of this.

"I'm sorry," she said finally. "Mister Villar, Miss Parrill, get our lads under some sort of control, will you?"

Before the pair could move off to do so, though, Malcomson bellowed again.

He turned to glance at the fighting spacers then back to Alexis, his face twisted in an odd combination of anger and anticipation.

Alexis barely had time to recognize the slight shifting of his feet before his fist lashed out and he bellowed, "*Delights!*"

For a moment, she was somehow outside the hull. Without her vacsuit, curiously, yet not lacking for air — or, perhaps, the gravity generators had failed and she was floating within her quarters. Yes, that must be it — she'd been sleeping and something had happened to the gravity, allowing her to float free of her cot. That was the only thing that would explain why she was in the air with no memory of how she'd got there.

Then her body slammed to the ice and snow, driving the breath from her and spoiling her thoughts.

HANDS HELPED HER TO SIT, then to kneel, then to stand. She was grateful for that, as she thought she might have fallen without all those hands on her upper arms supporting her as she swayed. The shouting she could do without, though, as her head hurt.

Well, not so much her head as her face. The left side seemed to have doubled in size and was throbbing with her every heartbeat.

She blinked, trying to clear her vision, which didn't, then raised a hand to tentatively touch her face. She was relieved to find that her nose still protruded what felt like the appropriate distance — she'd been a bit worried from the pain that she might find she now looked like one of those little flat-faced dogs the women on *Noveau Paris* all fawned over.

Her hand did come away wet and sticky, though — and red, she noted as her vision did clear and she could see once more.

She swayed to the left, back to the right, steadied by Villar and Parrill to either side, then managed to find a bit of equilibrium again.

Malcomson stood before her, fists raised and scowling.

"One blow? I dinnae ken, lass, how y'ever made —"

Alexis shrugged off her officers' hands. Her mouth widened in a grin even as her eyes narrowed, then she lunged at Malcomson.

For the three steps it took to reach him, she felt free. Free from restraints of command, free from the restraints of propriety, free from cares about anything but the foe before her and bringing him down. It was as though all of her frustrations and cares — from Skanes and *Hind*, to somehow managing Creasy's delusions, to the myriad tasks of commanding *Mongoose*, to her worries about Delaine which preyed every moment at the edges of her thoughts, to, even, her growing certainty that her place was in *darkspace* and not bound to Dalthus, no matter how she did love her home, and how ever would she tell her grandfather that?

Everything disappeared into the simple, clear, and, somehow, clean desire to pummel Malcomson into the ice-covered surface of Enclave.

Three steps.

With the first step she exulted as the weight of all those cares lifted.

With the second step she drew breath for her own cry — though she'd be damned if she'd stoop to that vile creature's name, not that it had one, truly, for she'd not accept the crew's naming of it ... ever. But she did have a ship she loved.

"*Mongoose!*"

With the third step she reached Malcomson.

THIRTY-SIX

The pub was loud, raucous, and filled to overflowing, with spacers in every seat and nearly every bit of standing room available. The servers and pubtenders rushed about, sliding through openings in the crowd that existed for only a moment's time, in an effort to place a glass or mug before every spacer in a timely manner. They'd seen enough bruised and battered crews to know that the line between another pint and another brawl was measured in dry seconds.

As it became clearer that the two crews were only interested in drinking for the moment, the staff closed off the hatches that opened onto the casino floor, meaning that the crews of *Mongoose* and *Delight* comprised the entire clientele and that they'd not disturb those wishing to game. It seemed an act the publican was not entirely unfamiliar with.

Alexis eased herself into her chair, wincing. Her head felt three times its normal size, and not from the result of any drink. Her left ear was swollen and she couldn't hear through it — which was a blessing, honestly, as some of the spacers were singing — and did offer a certain symmetry, she supposed, to her right eye which she couldn't see out of at all. Her jaw ached and her lips and nose were as swollen as her ear. A full accounting of what was scraped, battered, bruised, or aching would take far longer and far more attention than she could spare. At least nothing was broken, she thought — though her left pinkie was stuck in an odd bend that should, if she were not so dulled in thought, disturb her.

She felt wonderful.

There's something to be said for draping one's frustrations over another and battering the bloody piss out of him.

The singing grew louder, though not any better, and she glanced that way. Dockett and Little Mal were in full voice, one arm each raising a mug while the other was around the other's shoulders. They swayed together, giving voice to one of the lewder shanties in the bosun's repertoire — the lyrics not made any more respectable by the lisp through Little Mal's newly missing teeth nor the hollow, foghorn effect of Dockett's taped and cotton-stuffed nose.

She raised her glass, dribbled as much wine as she could through her swollen lips, and wiped at what had made it to her chin, then grinned across the table at Malcomson who'd just done the same with his beer.

If a grin on her battered face looked half as frightening as one did on his, it was a wonder the serving folk hadn't run screaming from the pub already.

Villar and Parrill, similarly battered, rejoined the table, having valiantly fought their way through the crowd to bring back another round.

"Och, but yer a game bunch, you *tri*," Malcomson bellowed. "Nigh had me fer a moment!"

He slid his chair to the side to offer Parrill a bit more room as she sat and winced, bringing a hand to his side, which brought a wince from him, and his opposite hand to his shoulder.

Alexis was rather proud of that, for she suspected it was her hanging on his arm by the elbow and kicking at his ribs which had caused both hurts. That he'd subsequently plucked her from his side and hurled her nearly over his ship's boat — or so it felt at the time she slammed into the hull and slid to the ice — wasn't in it.

At the end of the fight, it was only Malcomson left standing, which, he charitably allowed, made the whole dust up a draw.

The rest of both crews were left prostrate on the ice and snow, either unconscious or too exhausted to do more than roll about nudging their foes. Villar and Parrill ended things grasping Malcomson's calves and weakly punching at his ankles in their attempt to bring him down, and Alexis herself was still crawling her way back from her third — she thought, though it might have been more as things did blur together — trip to the side of *Delight's* boat.

Enclave's Patrol did them the courtesy of dragging them all inside before they froze to death, then left them to make their own way to the nearest infirmary — or pub, as they'd chosen, knowing that any proper spacers' pub would have the necessaries for most of their hurts.

It was good to know, she supposed, that the Patrol didn't seem to care if they beat each other senseless out on the landing field where they couldn't damage any citizen's property with their antics.

Malcomson drained his mug, took up the fresh one Parrill set before him, and drained half of that, dabbing at swollen and split lips in a manner laughingly dainty for such a massive man. He frowned and his cheek bulged out before he opened his mouth wide and reached inside with two fingers.

There was a bit of a sodden *pop* as he pulled out a tooth.

Malcomson held it up for a look, a broken bit of a metal stud gleaming at the bottom, then tossed it to the table between Villar and Parrill.

"That's the work o' one of you," he said, "but it's th' third in 'at place, so dinnae be too prood o' it."

He took a long draught again, swishing the beer about in his mouth.

"Sae whit is it ye wished tae speak aboot, lass?"

"Well, Captain Malcomson, when last we spoke — before you

259

sent me off to your 'suggested' systems for *Mongoose's* hunting, that is
—"

Malcomson laughed. "Found any geese, did ye?"

"Next to nothing, as I'm sure you knew."

"Allow a man his jokes, lass," Malcomson said with a shrug. He winced again and rubbed the shoulder Alexis' had tugged on with all her might during the fight. "Y'got yer revenge in fine fashion."

"That's not what —"

Alexis stopped herself. Better, perhaps, if he did think she'd planned the fight herself as payment for his sending her off chasing phantom prizes.

"Let it be a lesson to you," she said.

"Aye, t'will," Malcomson said, but there was a twinkle in his eye that told her she might wish to watch carefully for his next "joke."

"In any case, you did say that you've sometimes encountered too many ships to take."

Malcomson nodded. "Aye. This very cruise again — took some, but the rest scattered an' *Delight* cooldnae make after 'em."

"How many were the rest?"

"A round dozen in line." He frowned. "Thrice I've seen as mony together, too."

That was surprising. There wasn't so much traffic in the Barbary for so many ships to be encountered together that many times.

"All with pirated goods?" Alexis asked.

"All pirated hulls," Malcomson said. "Goods an' all. An' Ah ken whit yoo're thinkin', lass. Convoys of pirate prizes, an' that's no good. Means there's a powerful lot of them bawbags out there somewhere, an' they're takin' ships as they like."

"That would take a powerful force," Villar said. "A dozen prizes would mean a large crew."

Malcomson nodded. "Near *tois* hundred men, if they're crewed as the ones I took are. Ten or twenty men each, and nae a body who'll tell you his home."

"A dozen ships taken," Alexis mused. "No, three dozen, with

those you've seen before. Is that more piracy than the Barbary typically sees?"

"The Barbary's reputation is somewhat misleading, from what I've read," Parrill said. "While the number of ships going missing each year is significantly higher than in other areas, much of it *could* be writ down to natural causes — with so much space between systems and so little traffic, relative to the volume of space, a ship blown off the established lanes in a storm has much less chance of being assisted by some fellow coming along than in other sectors. Also, with fewer habitable planets, a ship in distress has less chance of finding a system to make repairs in on its own. Most of the losses, therefore, are likely attributable to that, and much of the talk of piracy could come down to nothing more than breakers — folk from the systems finding a hulk in *darkspace*, all its crew dead, and towing it home to make use of what they can. Piracy, true piracy, likely takes up no more than forty percent of the losses — which is still a great deal, but —"

Villar cleared his throat and Parrill broke off. She gave Villar a nod and a small smile, as though of thanks, but still hung her head and said, "I'm sorry, but you did ask."

Malcomson stared at her for a moment.

"Aye," he said, "mair than usual an' mair than one band should take."

Alexis pursed her lips. "So, a large band, larger than usual, and mair, *more*, than one ship — one private ship — should consider taking on, perhaps," Alexis said. "Both the convoys, for fear of losing the prizes when they scatter, and certainly the main pirate force. If they can afford to send off two hundred men in prizes, then any one of our ships is certainly outmanned."

Malcomson frowned at her. "Yoo're pokin' aroond a point, lass. What is it?"

Alexis phrased her next words carefully, knowing Malcomson's independent frame of mind. All the private ships' captains, she supposed — hadn't she, after only a short time in command of

Mongoose and out from under the weight of an Admiralty, bristled under *Commodore* Skanes' dictates?

"Suppose you'd had another ship when you'd encountered that convoy of prizes, would the action have gone differently?"

"Oh, aye," Malcomson said. "Anither ship, put him near out of sight to windward an' he falls off when he spots the jobbies. Let 'em come down to *Delight*, then he's t'windward of 'em when they scatter." He shrugged. "But I've nae other ship and nae lads tae crew one, e'en if I did keep a prize for it."

Alexis raised her brows and gazed at Malcomson expectantly. A further suggestion wouldn't do, she thought, he'd have to come to it on his own.

"What, lass?" Malcomson asked.

"I believe," Parrill said, "that Captain Carew is sug — *ow!*"

She reached down to rub her shin and glared at Villar, who leaned close to whisper in her ear.

"Oh, really?" she said. "But why would he not just listen to — *ow!*"

Another whisper from Villar.

"But it's self-evident that we should — *ow!*"

More whispering.

"If you say so," Parrill said. "But it seems —" She broke off and held her palms toward Villar while turning in her seat to move her shins away from him. "Never mind, no need."

Malcomson watched the exchange, brow furrowed.

"Do you nae allow the lass tae talk, then?"

"Miss Parrill has some difficulties with conversation," Villar allowed.

"I fear I will never understand people," Parrill muttered, face despondent.

Malcomson grunted. "If the wallapers won't ken you first, lass, then they're nae worth the bother."

Villar frowned at that and Alexis did, as well.

True, Parrill's conversational style was a trial at times, but what must it be like for her? With Hacking's open derision in *Mongoose's* wardroom? Villar's usual method of signaling her that she'd gone on too long, or down a conversational road she shouldn't, was gentler than the kicks to the shins he'd just delivered — Parrill's usual digressions not being such that they'd be to anyone's real detriment, as might have been the case here — but what must it be like for her to be constantly told that the words coming out of her mouth were somehow wrong or annoying to others?

Alexis had been happy to leave most of dealing with Parrill to the ship's wardroom, relying on Villar there and limiting her own interactions with the woman to either ship's business, where Parrill was entirely competent, or suppers with all *Mongoose's* officers, where the verbal ticks were few enough to be amusingly tolerated.

What must it be like to be so constantly made aware that you're saying the wrong thing in the wrong way? Alexis thought of Parrill's last comment. *And, possibly, to never truly understand why that's so?*

She'd have to think on that, and speak to Parrill some, as well as Villar. Hacking she could still leave to Villar to manage in the wardroom, at least.

"Thank you, Captain Malcomson," Parrill said.

"Yer welcome, lass."

Parrill frowned, then, possibly emboldened by Malcomson's support, "May I ask you a question?"

"It's only that I wish to know things, to understand them," Parrill said. "But I was under the impression that a New Edinburghan such as yourself would wear a kilt and not ... well ..."

She gestured at Malcomson's tight leathern trousers and fur cape.

"Miss Parrill —" Villar said.

"No, lad, 'tis all right." Malcomson leaned close to Parrill and said softly, "It's for mah crew I've given up the kilt, lass."

Parrill frowned. "The crew?"

"Aye," Malcomson said. "For their spirit, ye ken?"

"How does a kilt —"

"It's not wearin' the kilt, lass, it's the not wearin' else."

Malcomson grinned at her. "Think on it — we're in action an' the grav's burst, aye? Weel, up goes mah kilt, an' then the crew's all in a cringe for seein' what they lack."

Parrill glanced down at Malcomson's lap, then fixed her eyes on the far wall, swallowing hard and flushing red.

Malcomson grinned.

"Aye, lass, cannae expect a man tae fight when he's feelin' all inadequate abit himself. Best I keep it hid."

"I see," Parrill said, growing so red that Alexis thought her head might burst.

"I'm sorry, lass," Malcomson said, patting Parrill's leg, "but y'did ask."

Villar cleared his throat.

"Oh, aye," Malcomson said, "we were talking abit how grand it would be for me tae hae another ship." Malcomson turned his attention back to Alexis and sighed. "In any case, lass, I've only the one ship and nae extra crew, sae it's —"

He broke off and frowned, brow furrowing.

"Yes?" Alexis prompted after a moment.

Malcomson held up a finger. "A moment." He pursed his lips and rubbed his chin. "Noo here's a thing I've just thoght of —" He pointed to Alexis. "What if yer *Mongoose* were tae sail with *Delight*, eh?"

"What? You mean sail together and share in the prizes?" Alexis asked.

Malcomson nodded.

"Noo Ah ken it's a thing we private ships don't dae sae much, but think on what we coods dae together, comin' across sich convoys as Ah have."

THIRTY-SEVEN

Mongoose's quarterdeck was tense with excitement from the chase. Alexis and Villar bent over the navigation plot, while the spacers at the consoles flicked their eyes over images from outside the ship and readouts from the systems within.

The plot itself was cluttered with over a dozen ships, even excepting the tracks of *Mongoose* herself and the accompanying *Bachelor's Delight*.

Malcomson had not been exaggerating when he'd said that there were sometimes more targets than the *Delight* could take herself, and Alexis could feel the crew's excitement over the rich find they'd made.

A convoy, looking for all the world like any legitimate group of merchantmen bound farther into the Barbary, but scattering for cover when *Mongoose* and *Delight* began flashing New London's colors and demanding they heave-to for inspection.

"They're dropping the gunboat and splitting up," Villar noted.

Alexis studied the plot. The pair of ships *Mongoose* was after had indeed split up, with one veering off to run for the nearby system — perhaps to hide within its shoals or transition and go dark in normal-space if she could get out of sight of her pursuers for just a few moments.

Her captain had made a mistake, though, in Alexis' estimation, of cutting the lines to the gunboat he towed behind. Several of the ships had similar vessels in tow and, while they were of little use in the open chase, the little vessels with their low mass and single lugsails could play havoc with a larger ship once amongst a system's shoals.

"We'll leave her to *Delight* and stay on the other," Alexis ordered, then to the helmsman, "Two points to port, if you will, Layland."

"Aye, sir."

When the convoy scattered at their approach, some toward open space and others toward the nearest system, *Mongoose* had been closer to the outside — by design and agreement with Malcomson, for while the *Delight* was the larger ship with heavier guns, *Mongoose* was the faster and her sail plan allowed her to come more fully up to the winds.

Delight would therefore take the downwind chase toward the nearest system, while *Mongoose* took the upwind targets.

To all appearances it looked to be the best of plans, as the navigation plot was now predicting that both private ships would be well able to catch up with nearly all their targets, provided they took no more time than expected to force each one to strike.

"Have the bowchaser put the next one into her," Alexis ordered.

"Aye, sir." Villar nodded to Creasy, who passed her word on to the guncrew in the bow.

A moment later, the flash of a laser came, striking the fleeing ship dead in her stern.

"A hit!" Villar cried, grinning widely.

Alexis struggled to keep her own grin under control. They might be playing the wolf, but it wouldn't do for her to look like one and she was fairly concerned that Villar's tongue might start lolling out, so widely was his face split with delight.

"Her helm's off, sir," Dorsett announced, his nose almost touching his screens as he squinted to make out details of the images of the fleeing ship. "Rudder or planes, one — hard to tell."

"The next alongside," Alexis said, "but close enough to make them understand it was no miss."

"Aye, sir," Creasy said, working his console to relay the order.

The entire quarterdeck crew seemed to hold its breath, waiting for the guns to fire — then waiting more, as they didn't. Alexis caught her lower lip between her teeth and held back the urge to query the bowchasers as to the delay. She had the two best guncrews there, manning the pair of long nine-pounders in *Mongoose's* bow, along with Hacking who'd shown himself a dab hand with the guns, and they knew their task well enough without her jostling them.

A few moments later and her confidence was vindicated as both bowchasers fired as one, their bolts lashing out, shortening and condensing as the dark matter affected them, but arriving true to flash close along either side of the fleeing ship.

"There'll be no misunderstanding about that," Villar said with a laugh.

"She's struck!" Creasy announced.

Alexis nodded with satisfaction. "Mister Villar, I'll have —" She thought for a moment of the master's mates, as well as Parrill and Hacking — who could be spared first from the rest of the chase and who might be needed later? As well, who might keep their first prize safe and under control as *Mongoose* sailed on after the rest? "Stott and a crew of seven others. He's to have that small cutter we took on from *Delight* and follow along in the prize as best she's able. Signals as discussed, mind you, and you, Creasy, keep watch on her as well as ahead — I'll not have one of our prizes retaken and disappear with any of our lads."

The chorus of "aye, sirs" sounded and Alexis turned her attention to the plot again. The ships of the convoy might have scattered, but there was an order to it — there were only so many points of sail that might allow for the possibility of escape, after all, and the trick now would be for Alexis to determine the path *Mongoose* might follow that would allow for taking as many of these as she could.

"Four points to port, Layland, and up ten — we'll take this one next." She tapped the plot over the next target, which would highlight it for the rest of the quarterdeck crew, as well.

"A brig, sir," Dorsett said, his tactical console already having analyzed the images of the next target. "Eight guns — no more'n six pounders, if I'm any judge, and a small crew. Twenty men at most."

Alexis nodded. The estimate of guns and men would be just that. Correct if these were merchantmen carrying pirated goods, but off by quite a lot of they were the pirates themselves. Or prizes with pirate crews, though any prize crew should still be small in numbers, as the pirates would want to keep as many as they could on their main ship for future targets.

Much as we must, she thought as a low *thump* announced the detachment of a ship's boat with Stott and his crew for their first prize. That boat was borrowed from *Delight*, where Malcomson seemed to have a penchant for collecting them from his prizes. The *Delight*, and now *Mongoose* in turn, looked much like some sea-going predator with a full dozen boats latched onto her outer hull like lampreys.

Malcomson had taken one look at *Mongoose's* original complement of ship's boats and scoffed.

"Och, lass, are y'on a bluddy outing or is it real business yer aboot?"

At first, she'd been amused, but now she was glad for them. The delay in coming alongside a capture to transfer a prize crew likely would have meant losing two or even three of the prizes she pursued — with the added boats, she could drop a prize crew for the latest and never slow in pursuit of the next.

One of the women who'd come aboard at Penduli had come along well and had been made master's mate — she'd do for the brig's prize crew and it would be a fine test of her to command it.

"Coburn and a crew of five to our smallest boat, Mister Villar," she said aloud, eyes already on the maneuvers *Mongoose* would have to make once the next prize in line surrendered.

THIRTY-EIGHT

Mongoose's second time cruising with *Delight* was not so successful in the way of prizes.

The crew was a bit sullen as they broke orbit around Enclave, despite the week's liberty Alexis allowed. Wheeley was unable, or unwilling, to front the prize money for all the prizes, saying that he wished to consult with the Hanoverese and *Hso-hsi* settlements before finalizing an offer. It had only taken the one quick settlement of their first prize for her crew to set that as their expectation and they'd been looking forward to time on Enclave with individual fortunes to squander.

Wheeley'd offered casino scrip again, and Alexis had, again, declined, but managed to get him to settle immediately on those ships of New London registry, at least. That gave the spacers prize money from three of the prizes, and enough for a fine run on the pleasures of Enclave without being cheated too badly.

Mongoose and *Delight* sailed again in concert and both Alexis and Malcomson were wise enough to discuss setting other expectations for their crews, as well.

"We'll not see a convoy like the first one each cruise, certainly," Alexis put forth the night before they were to sail.

She, Malcomson, the officers from both ships, and Little Mal, who seemed never far from his Da's side, were meeting to discuss their next cruise over supper. The particular pub had become one of their favorites, set off a bit from the casino floor and, oddly for an establishment of Wheeley's, having no gaming devices built into the tables. Alexis found it easier to concentrate on the task at hand if she weren't tempted to think on odds and systems.

Though — her eyes wandered to the pub's doorway — *if we're finished early enough, there is that one bit I want to try. Just a few hands to prove it out ...*

She'd had moderate luck at the tables during this visit, neither losing nor winning any large sum, and thought that was certainly a sign that her understanding of the games had improved. As well, the little thrill she felt when the cards turned was somewhat more alluring than the thought of another cruise aboard *Mongoose*. Despite the collection of so many prizes, their taking had lacked a certain ... something. They weren't warships, after all, nor even the pirates' main vessels — only thin-sided merchantmen with ill-kept guns and lightly manned.

Not a one of them fired back at us, and Mongoose *barely ran her full broadside out, much less fired one.*

No, profit aside, the cruises had been less than satisfying, and Alexis found herself longing for an action that would let her put *Mongoose* alongside some other and truly test her.

There was a twinge of guilt at that, for a real action would put her lads at risk, but she knew some few of them felt the same way. Picking up ships and their cargoes so easily was little better than going a'merchantman oneself, and if that, then why bother with a private ship?

"It's rare, aye," Malcomson was saying in response to her, "but fine to get the like noo an'again. They'll shift their routes noo, I expect, and one ay the others might see profit frae it."

Little Mal drained his glass and called for another.

"Perhaps we could enlist the other private captains?" Alexis suggested. "To find where they may shift this route and —"

Malcomson laughed and Alexis realized her mistake. She'd made the suggestion rather than merely hinting at it, and Malcomson was one who'd rarely accept an idea not his own.

"Better herd cats than that lot," he said with a further laugh.

THIRTY-NINE

W eeks of disappointment followed.

The space they'd formally patrolled seemed empty and abandoned, with nary the sight of a sail, much less close enough to pursue. They moved on, Alexis letting Malcomson set the route, as he'd hunted this area longer than she, and putting ever more space between their ships in order to cover as much of *darkspace* as possible — until even *Mongoose's* finest optics and computer enhancement could barely make out the lights of *Delight's* masts and hull.

It made *darkspace*, somehow, lonelier than she'd experienced before, to have just that one bit of light in view. The full, featureless expanse of it, with nothing but the far off, roiling storms to break the other darkness, was somehow more intimidating with another ship just barely in sight.

Or, perhaps, it was that pinpoint of light offset against one of those rolling masses of dark matter clouds that did it. Pointing out just how small her own ship must be in the vastness.

Worse than monotony and lack of profit the failure to take any prizes brought was the corresponding lack of information about the fleets. With no merchant captains to question, Alexis was left to ponder the possibility that this whole venture – at least the possibility of finding Delaine, which was what had drawn her to it – was a wild goose chase. So far, there'd been nothing but rumors as to the warring fleets and their passage here – rumors which gave her no clear direction to take her inquiries.

Alexis squinted at the plot. Come to that, that particular roiling mass was one they'd hoped to avoid, skirting its edges at a safe distance, but it seemed to have grown larger and its path —

"Winds' shifted, sir," Layland said from the helm. "Two points to starboard and down ten ..." He paused. "*Three* points to starboard and down *fifteen*, sir."

Alexis glanced at him, then back to the plot. Even as she watched, the winds shifted further — strengthening, too, until they settled again.

Now *Mongoose* was nearly directly upwind of *Delight*.

Alexis caught her lip between her teeth and worried at it. That was a rapid shift in the winds, and more than she liked. The plot showed the winds strengthening as well. That, and the speed of the shift, might mean the storm was stronger than they'd thought, picking up more and more dark matter and that mass sucking the dark energy winds into itself, further strengthening the storm.

"Any signal from *Delight*?" she asked.

Malcomson was closer to the storm and would surely have noticed the winds' changes before *Mongoose*.

Then again, the mad fool's more likely to leave it longer, as well. Probably puts on a vacsuit and lashes himself to the mast for every storm, screaming at it to do its bloody worst.

"No, sir," Creasy said.

"Well, signal to *Delight*, then. Ah, *Storm to Leeward* and ... well, leave it at that. If we suggest he come up to us it'll likely make him sail directly into the damn thing just to be contrary."

"Aye, sir."

"Ease us to windward, Layland."

"Aye, sir."

Mongoose came up to the wind, making as much way as possible away from the oncoming storm. *Delight's* image showed the other ship was doing so as well.

"Signal from *Delight*, sir," Creasy announced a few minutes later. "Ah ... *Have Eyes*, sir."

Alexis shook her head. "Then he should have used them before this, I should think."

They sailed on, the winds ever strengthening and changing to bear directly toward the oncoming storm. *Delight* came closer, only because *Mongoose* was forced to bear off those winds and was making ever more leeway herself, despite having her keel fully extended to bite into the surrounding dark matter. They'd soon have to bring that up some, as the forces being exerted on it were growing, as well, and things could soon warp or even snap off due to the stress.

More, the stress on *Mongoose's* masts and spars was increasing with the stronger winds.

"We'll want to reduce sail, Mister Villar," Alexis said, "and strike the topmasts altogether, I think." Alexis watched the image of the storm, which seemed to grow and pulse with malevolence. "The morning watch might see us under bare poles if this keeps strengthening."

IT DID NOT QUITE COME to bare poles, but both *Mongoose* and *Delight* bore mere scraps of sail before too long.

Malcomson worked his ship upwind and nearer to *Mongoose*, but maintained a distance out of respect to the storm. Both ships were being tossed and knocked about, even before the full force of the storm reached them.

That full-force was visible now, still past *Delight* on *Mongoose's* navigation plot, so close now that the entire image was nothing but the oncoming storm, it's face rolling like a wall of shadows.

There was no doubt, either, that both ships would soon feel its full force. The winds being sucked into that mass were such that they could make no way to windward, away from the storm, at all, and were forced to crab their way along its face, hoping to eventually edge around it until they found some reduction in the winds.

Even the image of *Delight*, though she was close enough now to make out her gunports and rigging, was occasionally obscured by blown drifts of dark matter — picked up and made visible by the winds.

Mongoose had barely a scrap of sail on her poles, just enough to keep her helm answering, and even that, Alexis feared, might be too much, but the sail crews were already inboard and the hatches closed. She'd not risk any of the crew on the hull until they were past the outer wall of the storm.

The winds and dark matter being drawn into that mass would accelerate once past the wall, flowing and accelerating around the storm's center mass to pick up even more energy, as from a body in normal-space sling-shotting around a mass. Every bit drawn in then shot out again before being drawn back. That reversal formed the storm's wall and the worst of its might.

"Signal from *Delight*, sir," Creasy said. "*Making for Vendrizi. All luck.*"

That was the nearest system, and they might, with that luck, make it there with enough control of the ship to transition to normal-space and sit out the worst of the storm.

"Acknowledge it."

"Aye, sir."

And all luck to you, too, you daft giant.

The wall of the storm came closer, engulfed *Delight*, and rolled on, blocking her view of the other ship.

Dockett came through the quarterdeck hatch, vacsuit helmet under his arm from his time at work on the sails, and approached the plot.

"All our hands inboard, Mister Dockett?" Alexis asked.

"A short crew in the sail locker, should we need anything cut away, sir," Dockett said, "and the rest nearby."

"We'll hope they're not needed and we may ride this out."

"Aye, sir." Dockett stole a look at the images on the plot. "It'll be on us soon."

Alexis nodded. The storm's wall, which had already driven *Delight* completely out of sight, was nearly upon them. The quarter-deck lights flickered and she felt the first tremors through the deck as *Mongoose* was tossed about so much by the storm as to overcome the inertial compensators.

"For what we are about to receive ..." Dockett muttered, and Alexis took no heart that it was a saying for a ship about to be the target of a broadside from a stronger foe.

FORTY

A *darkspace* storm is like a shadowy, malevolent tumbleweed; a globular hurricane scouring all before it with a torrent of dark energy and dark matter.

It started as a tiny, compressed bit of dark matter — small in size but large in mass.

Mass enough to begin attracting the winds, pulling the dark energy radiations toward itself with ever-increasing force until they wrapped around the core like a spacecraft sling-shotting around a body in normal-space.

As those winds came on, they picked up more bits of dark matter, leaving some behind to fall into the core and enlarge it, which brought on more and faster winds in an orgy of each feeding off the other.

Those winds, faster and stronger after their trip around the core, were eventually pulled back in, reversing course at the storm's outer edge, the wall. They might have slowed then, for their return trip around the core, but their energies were still enhanced and they carried all the mass of the dark matter they'd picked up along the way.

As the storm became larger, it attracted winds from farther and farther outside its wall, overcoming even the attraction of normal-space masses until huge compasses of *darkspace* were all winds rushing toward the storm as though eager to become part of that roiling mass, strengthening the forces that looped from wall to core and back again.

Stronger winds, though, did not give up their bits of dark matter easily. Instead they began to tear at the very core of the storm, destroying what strengthened them, until they'd ripped it apart and distributed its dark matter across space, until both the winds and core were dissipated to nothing.

Then the bits of dark matter would begin to form again. Tossed about by the gentler winds, attracted to each other by their own, nearly undetectable mass, until there was enough together to begin again.

THE STORM'S wall took *Mongoose* from above, driving her down and away from her track. Layland, on the helm, let the planes and rudders run free for the moment, else they'd be snapped off in trying to fight so great a force. The ship lurched and shook, nearly knocking Alexis and her officers to their knees. The quarterdeck's lights and instrument panels went dark for several heart-wrenching seconds before the worst of the wall moved on, then only flickered as gusts of dark energy were able to penetrate the hull and interfere.

For a time, the ship spun and whirled like a bit of flotsam caught in a storm driven river, then the wall passed and they were well within the storm itself.

Layland measured the stresses on the rudder and planes and, gradually, eased them into play again.

"I've a bit of bite, sir, without ripping the pintles out of her," he called.

"Ease us back to our course, then," Alexis said. "Handsomely, mind you."

"Aye, sir."

"Any sign of *Delight*?"

"Nothing, sir," Dorsett said.

Mongoose jerked to the side and Alexis' knee struck the navigation plot. She took a moment to curse the Navy's tradition that officers walk their quarterdeck instead of having seats as the watchstanders did.

Bugger tradition, and the whole, daft lot who came up with it.

The lights flickered again. Alexis maintained her feet, eyes on the images from outside the hull. The winds were tearing at the bits of sail still on *Mongoose's* masts, filling them then sending the woven, metal mesh aback as the winds shifted direction in the chaotic torrent that was the inside of a *darkspace* storm.

With each change in the wind, the masts and booms shook and bowed

"Halve the projectors, Layland," she ordered.

"Aye, sir. Halving — nary five-percent now, sir."

The sails dimmed, barely glowing, with the reduction in the particle projectors, which charged the gallenium-laced mesh of the sails to allow them to better catch the winds. With that and the reduced sail area, *Mongoose* was at little better than bare poles, and still the masts and booms bowed under the pressure.

"What do you think, Mister Dockett?" Alexis asked. "Will she stand it?"

The bosun was at the plot as well, watching what occurred outside the hull with the same intensity as Alexis.

"The masts won't bow, but I'd worry about the hinges," Dockett said. "More stress than I'd like to see there."

Alexis nodded. There was not enough sail high enough on the masts to make them bow, bend in such a way that the upper masts couldn't telescope in and out as they should, but the forces were working the hinges. Those, where the masts met the hull and could be folded down to lie flat, were the weakest points, and difficult to repair. They'd have to detach the mast and hinge entirely from the hull and fit new hinges, else run the risk of the damaged hinge breaking and leaving *Mongoose* dismasted at some crucial point.

Alexis took a deep breath. She hated to do it, hated to require her crew to go out on the hull in those conditions, with the winds so strong and carrying so much dark matter along with them. The effect would be the same as going off the ship entirely, even staying close to *Mongoose's* hull, with the feeling that one's very thoughts were being slowed by the dark matter pressing around. And with the added strength of the winds blowing one about.

She couldn't say so, though. Couldn't tell even Dockett that she wished she didn't have to do this — that she was sorry. Certainly couldn't show that she feared for those she was about to send out into the teeth of the storm to risk themselves for their ship and their mates.

"I fear I've left too much sail on, Mister Dockett," was the best Alexis could do.

"Storm's stronger'n I thought," was the most acknowledgment Dockett could make that he understood her.

"Storm trisail and jib?" Parrill said. "We'd have little choice in where we go, but may ride it out."

Alexis frowned. The trisail and jib might not hold up themselves in these winds, but they were needed. *Mongoose* would have to ride along, rather than letting the storm pass over, as the winds at this storm's core would likely be much stronger than they'd yet experienced.

"Those to keep us running with it," Alexis said. "Do you suppose the masts might maintain themselves with a single reef, Mister Dockett? We're running nearly direct toward Vendrizi — if we have even a bit of control then we may be able to transition to normal-space and find shelter there."

"No choice but to chance it, is there, sir?" Dockett said. "We'll need a bit of control to avoid the shoals there, all regardless."

ALEXIS GRIPPED the navigation tightly as the evolution was made. Not for the shaking and knocking about of the quarterdeck, which was bad enough, but for what the images from the hull showed.

The crew, *Mongoose's* crew, *her* crew, outside, battling to rig the storm sails and take in all but a scrap of the mains. Men and women, their vacsuits sometimes obscured from the camera by flows of dark matter picked up and made visible by the winds, leaning heavily to make their way across the hull. Sometimes knocked aback and sent to their knees or backs, only maintaining their place by the grace of the magnetic boots and their safety lines clipped to the hulls cables.

She was only grateful that *Mongoose's* sail plan, and what sail she'd taken in already, removed the need for any of them to climb the masts.

Once the spacers pulling on the boom to angle it to take the winds more easily were knocked into each other by a gust. They lost their grip on the line, only for a moment, but it was enough to let the boom swing and strike the group working on the sails.

Bodies were flung about, some coming free of the hull and would have been blown aside if not for their safety lines and their fellows trusting their own lines to fling themselves after and grasp an arm or leg to pull the floater back to the hull.

"REDDISH HAS A BROKE ARM," Dockett reported after all was complete and the crew was inboard once more. "Stott and Wood-ham're a bit woozy — didn't duck near fast enough when the boom went and took it to their noggins." He sucked air through his teeth. "They'll know better next time."

Alexis had no doubt of that. Stott was one of Dockett's master's mates and would likely hear from his superior about paying more attention once his eyes unglazed.

"Thank you, Mister Dockett."

Alexis eyed the plot. If it was all representative of their position — which was not a bet she'd make, it being even more of a bit of guesswork than usual when hit with a storm — they should be able to run freely for several hours before sighting Vendrizi, if they didn't miss it, and have some chance of making a transition point there.

"See the crew's fed and has a tot to strengthen them."

"Aye, sir."

THEY DID SIGHT VENDRIZI — barely visible through the dark matter fog stirred up by the storm — but only when it was close upon them.

A mad scramble of orders sent the crew back to the hull and worked the sails, taking in the trisail and jib so that *Mongoose* would not make so much way in the face of the storm, then raising the gaff to shake out more of the mains, and finally hauling on lines to bring those sails about and tack the ship.

Layland laid on the rudder and planes until Alexis was certain she could hear the hull creak and groan in protest, but *Mongoose* answered. She turned and made for the transition point they were lucky enough to spot before being driven upon any heavy shoals.

"Douse sails and transition as soon as you may, Layland," she ordered. "Don't wait for the way to come off her."

"Aye, sir."

It wasn't strictly proper; a ship was supposed to get as near the center of a transition point as practical and stop before transitioning. Especially in a system with no pilot boat, there was the possibility of another ship having just transitioned and not cleared the point in normal-space yet. As well, motion didn't carry over well from *dark-space* to normal-space, and that would stress the hull and inertial compensators.

Still, with the storm, *Mongoose* would never come to a stop at all, so there was no point trying or they'd be driven past and miss it.

The ship jerked, nearly throwing Alexis off her feet, as another gust of winds struck, and then came the slight blur of transition, as Layland didn't wait even for the center of the point, only for *Mongoose* to be enough inside the point to make it.

A BLINK WAS all it took to miss the change, but in the next moment the ship went peaceful and quiet. The creaks and groans from the hull, the high-pitched, nearly inaudible whine of the compensators, the certainly imagined howl of the winds and rasping grate of dark matter blown across the hull, all stopped.

There were some muted *clicks* as monitors and sensors, all dormant in *darkspace*, sprang to life and began their work once more, and, perhaps, a collective sigh of relief from the two hundred odd souls aboard *Mongoose*.

Alexis' shoulders slumped as some of the tension was released, and she eased her grip on the plot's edge. Beside her, she saw Dockett's knuckles go from white to red as he eased his own grip. She shared a look with him, then he turned his head to glare at the quarterdeck hatch where it seemed half the crew had gathered, vacsuits on, helmets in hand, to see them safely transition.

"All right, then, back to stations! Y've all seen worse, y'bloody lubbers!"

The crew scattered and Dockett turned back.

"Secure the hull, sir?"

Alexis smiled, her own relief at being out of the storm's rage evident. "Aye, Mister Dockett. Secure the hull and see what damage's been done."

FORTY-ONE

There was more than *Mongoose* seeking shelter from the storm in Vendrizi.

As the normal-space sensors came to life, nearly two dozen ships appeared on the navigation plot. Scattered about the system at the transition points they'd entered from, but mostly around the four outermost planets, depending on where they'd entered the system in *darkspace* and which was closest to them as the storm approached.

Mongoose had come in from the outermost planet's L4 point and Alexis immediately saw that *Delight* had made it to the same planet's L5. Bracketing two of the planet's largest Lagrangian points and likely sending some worries through the four merchantmen also there. Those at the other planets would have a good chance of escaping, should the pair of privateers decide to ply their trade here, but those nearest would not.

"Lay a laser on *Delight*, will you, Creasy?" Alexis asked.

"Aye, sir."

There was a delay, as the planet was a large, gas giant and its Trojan points quite distant from each other. Distant and cluttered, as, in addition to the other ships, there were a number of large asteroids captured at each. One would soon move between *Mongoose* and *Delight*, and Alexis wanted contact established so both ships would know to move and maintain the laser link.

"'Y' made it, lass!" Malcomson's voice was happy. "Found our own wee huntin' ground, tay, dae you see?"

Alexis had to smile at that. She felt a bit of a qualm at targeting these merchants who'd only been seeking shelter from a storm, but if they were carrying pirated goods, then they were not so honest and it was their own bad luck to have chosen the same shelter as *Mongoose* and *Delight*.

"Only those we're sure of piracy," she responded, settling back to wait for Malcomson's reply and a report from Dockett on what repairs would have to be made.

It was odd to watch the bearded giant on her plot going about the business of setting his own ship to rights while he waited to hear the words she'd already spoken. Odder still to see his attention turn back to her as the message arrived and watch his lips purse and flutter as he *harrumphed* at her words. Malcomson's level of proof for a merchant's having conspired with pirates, she'd found, was not nearly so strenuous as her own, and he seemed to be wondering now if *Mongoose's* appearance might not be a boon.

With obvious reluctance, though, he agreed, as he'd already discovered that Alexis was inflexible on the point.

They took their time about it.

The storm would still be raging in *darkspace* and few of these ships would risk returning there.

So, *Mongoose* and *Delight* both put themselves to rights, then laid communications lasers on those ships nearest and informed them they were to be inspected for pirated goods.

It was when *Mongoose* had a crew aboard the second for inspection that Malcomson messaged her again.

"Lass, why is thaur this Barbary savage at my port askin' if Ah eat snakes — and while I'm guilty ay enjoying a braw haggis come Burns Nicht ... I dae hae a bluddy line."

IT TOOK MANY, maddening minutes for Alexis' response, asking for the name and ship of the captain asking, to make its way to *Delight* and for Malcomson's response to return to *Mongoose*. Minutes in which Alexis cursed *Delight*'s captain for not providing that information in the first place. It was as though he took a deliberate joy in holding it back and drawing out the conversation — which was more deviousness than she could credit the bluff Malcomson with, but anything was possible.

The answer, when it came, was that one of the ships near Malcomson was the *Bisharet* and Captain Katirci, whose ship she'd not taken on their arrival in the Barbary.

More minutes passed as Alexis' response of, "Well, what does he want of me — no, never mind that, if he's at your boarding hatch then bring him to your quarterdeck, please, that I might speak to him myself?"

Additional minutes while Malcomson did that, and all the time she couldn't help but think he was grinning at her behind his beard.

When Katirci did arrive, his errand aboard *Delight* came out all in a rush, with the ship's translator barely able to keep up with him and the mishmash of dialects and language the patois of the Barbary systems became.

"Oh, good Captain *Cahroo* and the devourer of serpents. I, Katirci, humble master of the *Bisharet*, and your grateful servant for the kindness you have shown me, bring you tidings. When you so kindly allowed *Bisharet* to keep her cargo of *beep untranslatable local produce*, little did you know how the gods guided your hand. With fear and *beep poor translation trembling awe* I steered *Bisharet* from those systems, though it meant a loss of many marks on the *beep untranslatable produce* we carried.

"Instead, we sailed to Erzurum in search of some answer to your question. There we found such an answer — at great expense and no little danger, which we hold prayer you will take to your heart and speak for us to this —" Katirci nodded to Malcomson. "— great bear and captain of the *Catamite* —"

Malcomson frowned. "What?"

"— for I fear my poor *Bisharet's* cargo does not, at this time, carry the innocence of *beep untranslatable produce*, as I once promised you. Instead we carry, as we must, goods from Erzurum — and the markets of Erzurum have become the marvel of the poor Barbary, with goods from a thousand worlds, such as we seldom see."

"He's a bluddy hauld full ay modern farm equipment," Malcomson growled. "All more'n a Barbary world'd take on."

"The market of Erzurum teems with such now," Katirci went on. "I assure you, great bear of the *Catamite*, no ship sailing from there will come away with less, for they have had nothing of interest for export since the world was founded and it sits behind a wall of shoals the likes of which are rarely seen."

Malcomson's eyes narrowed and he looked from Katirci to his own translation system, as though unsure which to pound with his clenched fist.

"Now, though," Katirci went on to Alexis, "the market teems with goods. It is said, and I swear to you, devourer of serpents —"

"'Ere now," Malcomson said, "why's she gie that an' my *Delight* gets — what's that mean, anyway?"

"— that I believe this to be true, ships without number swept past Erzurum in a great battle, leaving wreckage in their wake. The people of Erzurum stirred themselves to plunder the wrecks of both goods and men, for that cursed system has always had a hunger for slaves. Though nearly all those ships were beyond hope and broke themselves upon the system's shoals, one was repaired. A ship of many guns which, now in the hands of the men of Erzurum, takes as it will from the wealthy worlds who ply our space and leave us their crumbs."

"What kind o' ship?" Malcomson asked.

"*Firkateyn.*"

Neither Alexis nor Malcomson needed the translator to work on that, for the meanings was clear.

"A frigate," Malcomson muttered. "A bluddy pirating frigate loose in the Barbary."

FORTY-TWO

"**A** bluddy *frigate*, lass!"

News of the fleets — and the possibility of captives from those fleets — drove all else from Alexis' mind and she ordered *Mongoose* to close with the *Delight* and *Bisharet* so as to end the delays in communication.

Once aboard *Delight*, she heard from Katirci little more about this Erzurum system. Only that he had not, personally, seen the frigate, but how else would such a small, unimportant system suddenly become the hub of pirated commerce in the Barbary? They, Erzurum, had always engaged in *some* piracy — and more wrecking, as their system shoals were the bane of any ship caught in a storm nearby — but more along the lines of a ship or two a year, with the goods being kept in the system itself.

Now there were more goods in-system than they could reasonably use and a thriving market for the surrounding systems and merchant ships willing to brave the space.

Unlike the frigate, though, Katirci had some personal knowledge of the captives, having been able to recognize English, German, and French being spoken amongst the marketplace slaves.

That latter piqued Alexis' the interest the most, for if there were crewmen from the Berry March worlds' fleet speaking their French on Erzurum, then there might be word of Delaine — or he might be there himself, which was something she barely dared think, for fear the thought might make it untrue.

"It might not be," Alexis said. "I mean we've only the tale of a tale that they have a frigate, yes?"

They'd sent Katirci back to his ship, with strict instructions not to make way just yet, and gathered in Malcomson's cabin.

The *Delight's* master's cabin was larger than *Mongoose's*, possibly to accommodate its occupant, who still seemed to fill the space to overflowing — not least because he was clearly angry.

The storm had passed and Alexis' rendezvous with his ship had allowed all but the two ships he'd taken in prize to escape — and then she wouldn't allow him to take the *Bisharet*, because of Katirci's service.

"Oh, aye," Malcomson said. "These savages micht mistake a frigate — coods be a sloop." He snorted. "Or a bluddy first rate, come tae that. But a frigate're better's whit explains all these ships we've seen took."

"Well, whatever she is, she wouldn't be at Erzurum, in any case, would she? The pirates would be off working at taking more merchantmen, not hanging around their home system."

"Hae tae gie th' lads a rest same as us."

"Which would be better done in a system *not* described in the sailing notes as 'a fortnight's sail past the sphincter of the arse-end of nowhere,' now wouldn't it? A pirate crew'd want better entertainments than they'd find in such a place, no matter it's their home."

Malcomson scowled and crossed his arms over his chest.

"A frigate'll make cuttie work ay *Delight* an' *Mongoose* baith. I'll nae risk it an' my crew'd hang me frae th' mast by my bawbag if I asked it ay them. We're nae the bluddy Navy, lass."

Alexis knew he was right in that — neither *Mongoose* nor *Delight* was a match for a frigate. Even together they were outmatched. She'd fought a frigate from a smaller ship herself and, while she'd "won", it had been at a cost no privateer captain or crew would wish to pay.

Still, she had to go and investigate — if there was a chance to find any of the fleets' crew still alive, she had a duty to do so. And if there was a chance there might be word of Delaine, she had no real choice.

The captured frigate was likely not there — that much of what she'd argued to Malcomson was almost certainly true — but if it was, then she'd need more than *Delight* with to help. She'd need a larger ship, much larger, and more guns might be in order, as well.

FORTY-THREE

The *Hind* seemed little moved or changed since Alexis' last visit. To all appearances, the ship had rested in the same orbit for all the time *Mongoose* had been chasing prizes with *Delight*, and Commodore Skanes hadn't stirred from her place behind her desk.

"We've seen nothing of you since your first visit, Carew, and now you return with no prizes in tow? An unsuccessful cruise, was it?"

Alexis flushed. She'd scoffed at Skanes, derided her, even, in conversation with Malcomson, and ignored the woman's orders — not that she had any authority to give them — but she was now in need of Skanes' help. That was both embarrassing and galling.

With Malcomson's refusal to go up against a pirate Frigate, Alexis had left him to his merchant-hunting and sailed for the one source she thought might assist.

"We, ah, found an outlet for prizes closer in ... commodore," Alexis said.

Skanes nodded. "So I've heard. Wheeley, on Enclave. Little better than a pirate himself when one gets down to it. The Marchant Company, you know, has better things to do with a ship so prominent as *Hind* than leave her sitting here as nothing more than a stores ship for your group — without those prizes, I might as well go back to carrying profitable cargoes and leave you to resupply from your Mister Wheeley and his sort."

"It is a better use of your ship, your fine ship, Commodore Skanes, that I've come about," Alexis said, wincing at the need to satisfy Skanes' ego.

It's for Delaine — if I have to piss down her back and tell her it's raining, then so be it.

Skanes raised an eyebrow. "Really? And now you know better what I should do with my ship than I? Such a clever girl you are."

"No, sir — ma'am — commodore —" *Damn me.* "No, that's not what I meant, I'm sorry. It's only that I've come across some information — which we've not had before, and which might, if you think it's wise, give some greater ... no, *different* use for *Hind*."

Damn me twice, but I'm bad at this. She's not one for an appeal to duty or grand deeds and the Dark knows it's the ship itself I need and not her.

"What sort of information?" Skanes asked.

Alexis marshalled her arguments as though they were ships to be taken into an action.

She laid out the existence of Erzurum and how it was now a sort of central hub for the disposal of pirated goods throughout this section of the Barbary. The pirate frigate, and how it must have come from the missing fleets. She even went so far as to tell Skanes how she – Alexis – had come to be here in the Barbary; not about her search for Delaine, as that would be too personal a thing to share and unlikely to sway the ostensible commodore, but about the Foreign Office's interest, without naming Eades.

"The Foreign Office?" Skanes asked, and Alexis could fairly see her ears twitch with interest.

"Indeed," Alexis said.

"And they enlisted you?"

"Among others, I'm sure," Alexis said, trying to keep a scowl off her face.

"A frigate, though," Skanes muttered.

"Likely off hunting," Alexis said.

"True," Skanes agreed, "and if not, then manned with pirate rabble and not a proper crew."

It bothered Alexis a bit that Skanes was coming around to her own arguments, and she wondered if, perhaps, that was because she herself was trying to talk her way around to making the endeavor seem less than it was. Malcomson had not been swayed, after all.

"*Hind* does carry nearly the same weight of guns as a frigate," Skanes was saying, "with a crew to man them." The commodore paused for a moment, thinking.

"Yes," she said, finally. "I think this is just the thing the Marchant Company should look into."

FORTY-FOUR

Erzurum was remote, even for the Barbary, with no systems, even those with no habitable planets, within a fortnight's sail.

It was also a shallow system, with numerous gas giants creating *darkspace* shoals that were actually visible in the images brought inboard by the ship's optics. Multiple crescents and swirls of obsidian, pulled along by those planets in normal-space, obscured the view of the roiling dark energy clouds behind the system. Like deeper shadows upon the already black void of *darkspace*.

Villar stared down at the plot for a moment, shaking his head.

"I've never seen the like before," he muttered.

Alexis nodded agreement, as did Dockett, who'd joined them at the plot. Hacking and Parrill remained silent, but stared as well. Alexis could imagine what they were thinking — the ship-handling alone to enter such a system, at least with a ship of any size, would be a formidable feat. The visible shoals were only the worst of them, there was no telling how many smaller shoals had broken off the main ones and cluttered the system — nor where they might be.

"Any signs at all of a pilot boat or beacon?" she asked.

"No, sir," Creasy answered from the signals console. "Nary a glimmer."

"Well, we can't have expected them to lay on a welcome for us, I suppose."

"Oh, I'm certain they will once they know we're here ... sir," Hacking muttered.

He was still not taken with the plan. None of them were, truth to tell, and Alexis was no different. Especially on seeing Erzurum now for herself, she'd rather have Malcomson and his *Delight* along, or nearly any of the other private ships, than the *Hind*.

"That lolling cow'll never make it through," Dockett said. "Her arse's so heavy it's a wonder she's not bottomed out here already."

"*Commodore* Skanes has assured me that her sailing master is quite experienced with taking the *Hind* into even the shallowest system of the Barbary," Alexis said, still finding herself stressing the woman's self-appointed rank with a bit of irony she couldn't help. "Though I believe Erzurum may force her to admit some inability at last."

"Signal from *Hind*, sir," Creasy called.

"Speak of the devil," Dockett muttered.

"Yes, Creasy?"

"*Captain to repair on board*, sir."

Alexis sighed. "Of course she is."

HIND WAS a flurry of activity when Alexis arrived, with crew rushing about to strike everything unnecessary for an action down into the hold. A bit more of a task in *Hind*, what with every nook and cranny crammed with supplies for the private ships. As Alexis watched, waiting again on the quarterdeck for Skanes to admit her to the master's cabin — and she wondered, yet again, if the woman had some sort of plan for how long she made a person a wait or if she simply was so disorganized that she couldn't see one upon arrival —

she noted that some spaces were cleared only to be filled up again by some other group of crew.

She began to wonder if the *Hind* had ever truly cleared for action before — leave aside why they were doing so now, when the ship was still hours away from the outermost reaches of Erzurum and with no enemy in sight at all. Before leaving *Mongoose* she'd set her own crew to a hearty supper.

Finally, Tabron, the steward, opened Skanes' hatch and invited her in. He pressed a glass into her hand as she neared Skanes' desk and Alexis was pleased to find it held her preferred whiskey — at least her preference from what Skanes had available. The man was nothing if not efficient and Alexis wondered at his service to such a disorganized mistress as Skanes appeared to be.

Skanes' cabin, though as cluttered as before, was an oasis from the chaos of the rest of *Hind*, with no sign of being cleared. In fact, it appeared that her table was being set for a full supper of her own, as Tabron returned to that task after Alexis was seated.

"Ah, Carew, a moment, if you please," Skanes muttered without looking up from her tablet.

Alexis sat, idly, and sipped at her whiskey.

Finally, Skanes set her tablet aside and looked up.

"The burdens of command," she said with a small smile.

"Indeed," Alexis allowed.

"So, then." Skanes lifted her own glass of wine and raised it. "To our coming victory, yes?"

Having now seen Ezurum, Alexis was rethinking their strategy. The shoals here were so much more than she'd imagined and the thought of her ship becoming trapped in those, with virtually any opposition, made her doubt the outcome. Had they found they were able to simply sail in and transition, then *Mongoose* and *Hind* were a match for any pirates they might find, but as it was – Alexis thought they might be better served to seek the other private ship captains, perhaps try to persuade Malcomson again, and come at the problem with more in the way of force.

"Commodore Skanes," she began, carefully keeping the bit of stress she found herself wanting to put on the rank from entering her tone. "I think we may have overstepped things with regard to the shoals here. Perhaps we should return to Enclave and seek assistance from the other private ships? With more ships we could map out routes through the shoals and spread the gunboats thin. *Hind*, powerful as she is, must certain draw too much mass to enter these shoals."

Skanes waved a hand. "Nonsense, Carew. Other than your mythical frigate, these pirates are said to have, what, some few gunboats and a sloop or two? Enough to take those smaller merchantmen you've retaken, but nothing to challenge *Hind*, surely? There's a *reason*, you know, that Marchant Company vessels are so seldom troubled by pirates. Larger, more heavily armed, and, frankly, better crewed than others. Why, I expect our mere entry into the system will see the blaggards surrender in an instant!"

"With respect, commodore, such might be the case if *Hind* were a Naval vessel, but your crew has seen no action while the pirates —"

"*Hind* drills her guns weekly, Carew, as any Marchant ship must. Your fears grow tiresome." Skanes glared at her a moment, then seemed satisfied that her point was made. "Now, as to the approach, my sailing master has recommended that your ship, being of less mass, scout the approaches for us. For myself, I think this unnecessary — my crew's well-drilled and able to back and fill with the best of them — but he's a cautious fellow and I'll humor his wishes."

Alexis nodded, glad that at least one man aboard *Hind* was not prepared to rush the massive ship through those shoals with nothing but a leadsman to guide them. She didn't relish the role of scout, but would like *Hinds'* guns to be of some use, not laid up in the outer system and beat to pieces by the winds.

"So," Skanes went on, "*Hind* will remain at the system's edges, just inside the halo, while your *Mongoose* lays out our course through the shoals. We'll want to transition at the habitable planet's L1, so make your way there. Then we shall see if your information is correct and *Hind* shall put paid to any piracy hereabouts, yes?"

THE SLOW, creeping approach through Erzurum's shoals had the entire crew on edge. Those on the quarterdeck, Alexis included, spoke in hushed whispers, as though the Dark itself were alive and they wished not to draw its attention. For all Alexis knew, some of the crew might actually believe that — Creasy being the most likely, and he did seem to hunch unusually far over his signals console, calling out the fall and curve of each shot of the lead in a harsh whisper.

"Pulled to starboard ahead and down," he said.

Alexis watched that herself on the plot's images and noted where more of the hidden dark matter might reside ahead.

"A quarter to port and up five," she ordered.

"Quarter port and up five," the helmsman repeated, easing his controls.

"Lighten sail by a third, as well," she said after a moment's thought. Despite *Mongoose's* already negligible speed, she could almost think they were traveling far too fast.

"Aye, cut projectors by a third."

The sails, what little *Mongoose* had on, were already sparsely charged, barely glowing at all in the images from outside. The cut to the particle projectors lowered that further, and the ship slowed quickly, dragging through the accumulated dark matter.

There was a sudden jerk, more sensed than felt — at least by those on the quarterdeck inside the hull with gravity generators and inertial compensators. Outside, the sail crew stumbled, some losing their footing altogether.

"Back sail!" Alexis ordered. "Quarter charge when they're backed!"

"Aye, sir!"

On the bow, the two leadsmen acted as quickly and without

needing orders, firing their laser charges to either side. The one to starboard curved almost immediately, warped away by some mass of dark matter they hadn't noted before.

The sail crew heaved the boom around, taking the winds on it in such a way as to stop *Mongoose* in her track and even back away a bit.

The hull groaned and creaked as the ship neared, then backed away from the unseen pressures.

"Hard a'starboard, roll forty-five to port. Bring her back."

"Aye, sir."

Eased away a bit, *Mongoose* resumed some forward motion, rolling away from the shoal and turning to port. Her long keel, fully extended for better maneuvering and lacking any gallenium at all to shield it from the effects of so much dark matter, caught the edge of the shoal and the ship jerked again, then again with a low, creaking groan that sent shivers down Alexis' spine.

With a shudder she couldn't be certain was the ship or herself, *Mongoose* was past and back to edging farther in-system.

Alexis shook her head. There was no way that the *Hind*, as massive as she was, would be able to follow through that turn. *Mongoose's* task was to seek out a path the larger ship could take, and this was clearly not it.

"Prepare to come about," she ordered. "We'll rejoin *Hind* and try another way."

"Aye, sir."

With that began the laborious task of retracing their route, save, at least, the false turns and reversals of their attempt at entry.

"Is it any wonder no one wishes to come to the bloody Barbary?" Alexis muttered, studying the plot for their next try.

"Civilized systems would have pilot boats and beacons out," Hacking said with a sneering curl to his upper lip.

"Signal from *Hind*," Creasy said. "*Captain to repair on board.*"

Alexis sighed.

"IS it truly so very much to ask, one wonders," Skanes said, "to find a simple path of entry to this one system?"

Alexis, kept waiting and without benefit of being offered a glass or even to sit on this visit, had had nearly enough. *Mongoose's* crew was exhausted from the constant sail changes and the stress of keeping to such narrow channels, her sail crews and leadsmen even more so, for it was upon them to remain outside the hull, receiving the full brunt of so much nearby dark matter with only the little protection their vacsuits offered, and *Mongoose* herself was showing the stresses as well. Lines were worn, her hull was stressed, and the bottom of her keel was certainly damaged from dragging through so many shoals.

All to no good end and with never a sight of any other ship near Erzurum.

She was beginning to wonder if this "pirate base" were some fantastical imagining of Captain Katirci, as, if *Mongoose* could find no way through the system's shoals, how could these pirate crews manage it with a bloody frigate?

"Well?" Skanes prompted.

"Perhaps on the morrow," Alexis said, voice as tight as her shoulders and jaw.

"On the morrow, of course." Skanes traced figures on the copy of the navigation plot shown on her tabletop. "Perhaps *Hind* should find her own way in, since your little ship has had no success."

"The shoals are quite extensive, commodore, I would truly not advise it."

"It's not your place to advise or not, though, is it?" Skanes rose. "It's your fancy, this 'pirate base,' this supposed location of, what, thousands of men off warships? All while no ship can apparently even enter the system? How is it, then, that they even got there?"

"I don't know."

"No, you don't. All you know is what some merchant captain told you — told *you*." Skanes' voice dripped scorn. "A merchant captain, I'll add, who's likely involved with the very pirates we seek. A merchant captain you've let slip through your fingers — *twice*, mind you. And one who's now sent us on a wild goose chase, leaving the systems I've ordered you to patrol entirely free for these pirates and their vessels!"

Skanes stood, strode to her sideboard, and poured herself a glass of wine, pointedly not offering any to Alexis.

"So you don't believe there's anything here now?"

Alexis wondered at Skanes' rapid change in mood. She went from enthusiasm at the prospect of taking Erzurum to doubting the information that brought them here in so short a time.

"No, Carew, I don't. I now believe you were deceived by this Captain Katirci and sent off here to no good purpose." She paced the limited space behind her desk like a caged animal. "I should not have listened to you, but you were so certain you convinced me of this ... this fancy. Drawing *Hind* off her proper station to no good ends. Clearly due to your youth and inexperience — oh, I know you've had some small success, or luck, in your Naval career, but now?"

Skanes looked her over with such contempt that Alexis flushed.

"Now it's clear that you are just a little girl ... playing *dress-up*."

Alexis felt her face burn further at that, but bit her tongue.

"No, Carew, you've delayed me enough. I will now take *Hind* in-system myself — show you how it's done — and prove your fancies for what they are, a trick of this merchant captain you've let go for some ends of your own. Then *Hind* will return to her proper station and you may be sure my report to my superiors will make clear her absence was entirely upon your head."

"WHAT DO WE DO, SIR?" Villar asked.

Alexis watched the plot, along with her officers and Dockett. She noted that the rest of the quarterdeck crew had at least a small copy of the plot displaying on their own monitors.

It's rather like watching from a hundred meters away while a man walks straight at a pigsty all engrossed in something on his tablet ... one wants to stop it, but there's little one can do and, after all, shouldn't the fool know a bit better?

"We wait, I suppose, Mister Villar."

"They're going for that bit we tried at the last yesterday," Dockett said.

"She'll tear her bottom out on that last turn," Hacking predicted.

"Oh, the money's on her quagging down long before that, sir," Dockett murmured.

Alexis looked up at that. "The 'money,' Mister Dockett?"

"Ah, not that there's a book aboard ship, sir, certainly," he said quickly. "I mean as to say, it's a prediction of sorts."

"Of course."

FORTY-FIVE

Alexis could feel the tension on the quarterdeck as the *Hind* neared the last of the bit *Mongoose* had scouted the day before, the sharp turn to port where she'd given up and turned back. Hours had passed since *Hind* first entered the shoals, pulled along by Erzurum's outermost gas giant, and *Mongoose's* officers had come and gone from the quarterdeck — sometimes attending to other bits of ship's business but, like her, drawn back to watch.

Hind rolled, as she must, and began her turn.

"She's too much way on her," Villar said.

"Far too much sail," Parrill agreed.

Alexis could see it too. The larger ship was moving too quickly for the sharp turn she was coming to. The roll would help, but not enough, and there was the other, indisputable fact — that the *Hind* was larger than *Mongoose*. Larger by far and carrying far more mass, with taller masts and a deeper keel.

That channel and that turn had almost caught the livelier *Mongoose*, and the larger ship had no chance.

Mongoose's quarterdeck echoed with a collective groan as the

Hind's sails and masts shook — once, twice, and then the huge ship simply stopped. The hull, at least, as the sails, still set and charged and far too much of both continued their pull. The masts twisted, pulling at their stays and, for a moment, Alexis was certain one or more of them would snap, but then *Hind's* sails went dark as someone in command had the sense to cut the ship's projectors.

Alexis sighed, wondering if that had been at Skanes' order or if her ship had been saved by a quicker thinking officer. One who might, even at this moment, be feeling his "commodore's" wrath despite having saved the ship.

"See to preparing tow lines, will you, Mister Dockett?" she said. "We're some hours from her, but I'll want to waste not a moment when we arrive."

With the expected end to the day's excitement and with the expectation of a great deal of work to come in pulling the massive ship out of the shoals, the group clustered around the navigation plot began to break up.

"I believe I'll take a nap before our next labor," Alexis said. "Mister Hacking, you have the watch, do you not?"

"I do, sir."

"In your hands, then."

"Aye, sir."

"Sail, sir!" Dorsett called from the tactical console.

"Bloody hell," Villar muttered. "Is that fool going to try and work her way off?"

"Not the *Hind*, sir! New sail — three ... four ... ten, I think, sir, all in-system of the *Hind*, but making way!"

Alexis rushed back to the plot, as did the others, in time to see the new ships appear as Dorsett confirmed them and transferred the data.

"Gunboats, sir," Dorsett said.

Alexis expanded one of the images, zooming in on the other ship to find Dorsett was correct. More like a ship's boat than a proper ship, the single-sailed, lateen-rigged gunboats carried a minimal crew, but placed either a large gun or a pair of smaller ones in the bow.

Their small size and low mass made them perfect for systems such as Erzurum, as they could easily sail through shoals a more massy ship couldn't, allowing them to outmaneuver better armed foes, even if that foe wasn't dead in space as the *Hind* now was.

"Beat to quarters, Mister Dockett," Alexis said.

MONGOOSE'S own preparation for battle might have been as premature as the *Hind's* the day before. They were still some time from the *Hind*, and while the gunboats were not limited by the heavy shoals, they were also not limited in the foresight to see that coming out to meet *Mongoose* was the poorer of their choices.

Like a pack of dogs harrying a larger beast, they stayed in-system of the *Hind* and the shoal she was stuck fast to, sometimes darting in to just within range of their guns and taking a single, poorly aimed shot before scurrying back again.

Nonetheless, Alexis kept a keen eye on their locations as *Mongoose* made her own way into the system.

"Another miss," Hacking muttered as a gunboat sailed just within range of *Hind* and began its turn away even before firing. The gun, jerked away from its targeting by the boats change of course, fired far wide of its target. "One wonders why they don't simply mass as one and attack her from all sides."

"Their boats are quite fragile, I imagine," Parrill said. "And these are pirates, after all, with only a thought to their purses and none for duty or their mates. Were they to mass and close, *Hind* would certainly get off a broadside and her guns are heavy enough that even a single shot might do for one of those boats all entire. Then, of course, there's *Mongoose* — and we're almost within range of *Hind*. Another hour or two yet, surely, but to truly surround their target would mean coming within range of our guns — or come about *Hind* so closely that they'd be easy prey to her broadsides." Parrill squinted at the plot. "Still, they might shoot *before* turning aside as that last one did and have a far better chance of a hit."

"Yes, of course," Hacking said. "How could I have missed all that?"

Parrill hunched her shoulders. "I'm sorry, but you did ask after all."

The quarterdeck crew was all in vacsuits, though without helmets yet, and both Hacking and Parrill were present with Alexis. Villar had taken command of the leadsmen in the bow himself, not wanting to waste a moment nor rely on the men themselves. Alexis thought it an unnecessary precaution, but did appreciate his diligence.

Dockett was on the hull minding the sail crew, and he was a better sailor than either Hacking or Parrill, so neither of them were needed there. The gundeck was still sealed against *darkspace*, though prepared to fling the ports open in a moment should the guns be necessary.

This left Hacking and Parrill at loose ends, so to speak, with nothing to do but mind the plot with Alexis, and Alexis was nearly at wit's end with the pair. She was half determined that Hacking dangled such question in front of Parrill so that she might bite at them in her — admittedly annoying — way, thus giving him something to sneer at. A thing the man seemed to live for.

"There's a boat leaving *Hind*, sir," Dorsett said.

Indeed there was, as the images of the other ship showed.

Skanes had launched one of her boats, little lugsail raised and making way slowly away from the ship. It sailed back toward the outer system, until just within the last, thick bank of shoals *Hind* had made her way past before sticking fast.

Vacsuited figures poured out of the boat and the craft's large cargo hatch opened. The spacers hitched and shoved a large block out of the boat.

"They're dropping a kedge," Parrill noted.

"As we can all see," Hacking said.

"A bit of decorum, Mister Hacking," Alexis said, as there'd been no cause at all for his comment, despite that everyone on the quarter-deck had been expecting Skanes to attempt this very thing for some time and was perfectly aware of what the *Hind*'s crew was about without Parrill's pointing it out.

The kedge, a large block of the thermoplastic that made up most of a ship's hull and bulkheads, but without the embedded gallenium that insulated from *darkspace*, would stick fast in the shoal — more solidly than a much larger ship, in fact, due to that lack of gallenium or any particle charge to enhance it as a ship's hull had. Once the boat moved off, as it was now, there'd be no hope of moving it except at the whim of the shifting dark matter that held it fast.

A thick ship's line trailed from the boat back to *Hind* and was now looped through the kedge and doubled upon itself as the spacers made their way back to *Hind* and threaded its other end through the ship's stern to within the hull.

Hind's hull fairly burst into light as the ship's particle projectors were turned to full upon it with an effort to enhancing the embedded gallenium's repulsion of dark matter, and within her stern's engineering spaces a heavy winch began to draw upon the line.

Now it was a test of strength. On the one hand, the block of the kedge held fast to the far shoal; on the other, the far more massive *Hind* held fast to hers.

The ship was larger, with considerably more mass than the kedge, but she was lightened by the charged gallenium in her hull.

There was, of course, a third hand beside the kedge and *Hind*, which was the line itself, and in the battle between the three, that was the one which finally lost.

It was hard to tell if the *Hind* had moved at all, perhaps she had or perhaps it was only a bit of shifting in place, a realignment of the hull within the shoal. The line drew tauter, strained, and broke, its ends snapping back toward ship and kedge as all of that energy of attempting to pull the two together was released at once.

For the kedge, it was no matter, for the *Hind* it was another small disaster in a day of them.

The snapped line came snaking back to the ship, coiling and tangling about itself as it drew its whole length through *darkspace*. Spacers dodged and flung themselves across the hull in an effort to avoid it, but the ship's masts and rigging had no such recourse.

From what Alexis could see at the end, no spacers had been killed or even injured, but the *Hind's* rigging was a lamentable mess. The towline draped and wrapped the sails and yards. She thought two or even three of the mainmast's standing lines might have been snapped by the force of the incoming towline — or perhaps that was simply bits of the towline itself she was seeing floating free in the image of the other ship.

She sighed. It had been a valiant try, she agreed. Perhaps with two kedges and two lines to distribute the mass better, it might be done. Or perhaps not, given the *Hind's* size. It was not only the ship itself, but all of those stores and supplies aboard, adding to the ship's mass and being drawn on by the surrounding dark matter of the shoal.

"Gunboats making another run, sir," Dorsett said.

And they were. Three of them this time, closing with the *Hind* — closer than before, and three at a time, but not so close as to have any real chance of their shot striking true.

Lights, signals, flashed on the middle boat, perhaps in some attempt to coordinate fire, but the shot when it came was ragged, with first the middle, then the left, then finally, some few seconds later, the right boat firing.

All of their shot went wide, with none coming so close as to even threaten *Hind*, but there was a message to it, Alexis thought — the gunboats might be content to harry the larger ship from afar, but only so long as she remained stuck fast. Skanes had likely got the message as well, and knew that her crew was not so large as to be able to both work the ship, even with the help of another kedge to wiggle out of the shoal, and fight her. The gunboats might hold back for fear of the *Hinds'* guns, but they were smart enough to know when those guns weren't manned as well.

What they would do as *Mongoose* drew nearer, Alexis wondered at.

FORTY-SIX

"Well, there's that question answered," Alexis muttered.

As *Mongoose* neared a particularly tricky stretch of the shoals she'd mapped the day before, four of the gunboats moved as well.

The pirates clearly knew Erzurum well.

The four boats sailed around the *Hind*, out of range of her guns, and took position between *Mongoose* and the larger ship, bracketing the bit of shoal *Mongoose* would next need to traverse. Their own small ships allowed them to set themselves nearly within the worst of the surrounding shoals, both where *Mongoose* herself could not go and where her shot would be warped and nudged by the surrounding dark matter so as to make aimed fire nearly impossible.

The gunboats' shot would be affected as well, but once *Mongoose* entered the coming channel she'd be traveling slowly, stern and bow to the gunboats, and unable to respond with any but bow- and stern-chasers.

"An hour here and another when we make the turn," Dockett said, having come in from the sails to consult. Villar had returned to the quarterdeck as well, as Alexis had *Mongoose* lying idle — out of range of the gunboats, but moving no closer to *Hind*.

"Two hours of raking fire, if they can reach us," Villar said.

Alexis caught her lower lip between her teeth and chewed on it for a moment before speaking.

"Dorsett," she asked, "do we know the armaments on these four boats?"

"No, sir," Dorsett said. "These four haven't fired yet — the boats themselves are a bit larger than the others, though."

"Saved their best for us, do you suppose, sir?" Villar asked.

Alexis nodded. "Or their largest."

It made a bit of sense. She'd got the impression that the pirates really hadn't been trying to strike the *Hind* with their repeated attack runs, merely harry her. They fired from so far out that a hit would be difficult in the best of conditions, which Erzurum's shoally space was certainly not. The dark matter of the shoals affected the light shot of the gunboats almost as much as it did that of the leadsmen — warping and arcing the fall of shot so that it might land anywhere other than where one'd aimed.

Larger shot, though, with more energy behind it, would track truer. *Mongoose's* main guns, for instance, or that aboard these larger gunboats.

Mongoose would spend nearly two hours sailing slowly through the coming morass, able to bring only her two pair of bow and stern chasers to bear on the gunboats. Even if Alexis were to move pairs of the ship's heavier main guns to replace the lighter in bow and stern, it was still only the two that could fire from each, while each of the large gunboats might have a pair of equally matched guns to fire back at her.

Outgunned two to one, at best.

At worst, those gunboats might mount a single, larger gun. The thought of what a twenty-four or, Dark forfend, thirty-two pounder might do to *Mongoose* in a raking strike to bow or stern wasn't to be thought on long.

"Signal from *Hind*, sir," Creasy said.

"If it is *Captain to Repair Onboard*, I feel I should be quite cross, Creasy," Alexis said.

Her officers laughed at the weak joke, if joke it was, for she could very well see Skanes making such a signal and expecting Alexis to make her way there somehow.

That she would be disappointed would not put her off, I am certain.

"No, sir," Creasy said, "it's *Engage the Enemy More Closely*, sir."

Alexis sighed.

DARKSPACE AROUND *MONGOOSE* was fairly blossoming with laser shot. What with the leadsmen firing to either side and ahead with only the interval of reloading, and her bow and stern chasers doing the same, all added to the shot from four gunboats, and with all of those making a stronger, if not much more effectual, attempt to actually strike her than their brethren had with *Hind* — one would almost think two ships were exchanging broadsides, rather than mere chasers.

Not that there was much *mere* about two of those gunboats — one to either end of *Mongoose* and both with what Alexis did judge to be thirty-twos aboard.

That shot stayed truer to its course than any other, and, though none had struck home so far, each was closer than the last.

"Steady, Layland," Alexis murmured to the helmsman.

"Aye, sir."

She needed his, and the whole crew's, attention on the upcoming turn, where *Mongoose* would come about, reversing direction and ending the first of their two hours in this narrow bit of shoal.

Mongoose's own guns were speaking in return, of course, but the gunboats were so small, barely three meters across at the fore, that the target was nearly impossible to hit as shot was warped and drawn aside by the dark matter shoals.

The boats had crept ever closer, perhaps emboldened by the misses. They seemed curiously less hesitant to actually hit *Mongoose* than they were of *Hind*. Perhaps they wished to take the larger ship whole, as it was the more valuable.

The quarterdeck was blissfully quiet and uncrowded for once in the endeavor, for all her officers were fully engaged in the maneuver. Parrill was on the hull with Dockett, working the sail to ensure it came around lively and caught the winds for their reverse of course. Villar and Hacking, though, were on the gundeck, ready for their part in the turn themselves.

"On my mark, Layland," Alexis said.

A groan from the hull close to the turn, *Mongoose's* bow already nearing the heavier collection of dark matter ahead which they'd be turning from.

The next shot from the leadsmen showed the heavy shoals close ahead and Alexis nodded.

"Now, hard a'port!"

Layland played his controls and *Mongoose's* bow swung around, pivoting nearly in place so hard did he put the rudder over.

"As you bear — fire!" Alexis ordered, and Creasy passed that along to the gundeck.

While the bare three-meter target of a gunboat's bow across such an expanse of shoals might be difficult for a single gun to hit, it was not so for a full broadside. Two targets, as both *Mongoose's* flanks rippled with action as her gunports came up.

Crystalline barrels poked forth and paused for the barest moments as gun captains carefully adjusted their aim, guessing at the effect of the intervening shoals, stepped back, and slapped hands on the buttons to discharge their guns.

Bolts of light exploded from *Mongoose*, streaking away toward the gunboats to either side. Their course was neither straight and true, nor the more expected gentle curve of light being bent by the ever present dark matter.

No, these put on a show across the shoals, twisting and curving around each other and the masses of the shoals as though dancing to some tune only they could hear.

Most would miss — drawn aside as all the rest had been — but two, finally, struck home. Both on the nearer gunboat to port, one of those with a thirty-two, and that would be no more worry to Alexis and her ship.

The first bolt struck the gunboat's bow dead on, possibly through its own open gunport. Alexis could only imagine the chaos that might cause. If it struck the gun's barrel then the bolt would fracture, its light splintered by the tube's crystal and split into dozens of smaller bolts, each of which was perfectly capable of killing a man or destroying some part of so small a boat.

The second struck near the boat's stern, wafted away and then back in a gentle curve that was at first lucky and then decidedly un-so for the little boat. Any strike away from the bow would be fatal for the fragile craft, decimating the helm or destroying the air supply, it would certainly send the boat scurrying back to the safety of a system and repairs.

This boat would never have the chance, as that shot struck far enough aft to find the fusion plant, coming in from the side as it did, the heavier hull gunboats had to the fore of the plant did no good at all.

There was a moment's cheering on *Mongoose* as the quarterdeck crew and the gun crews saw they'd struck one of the boats at all, then silence as the boat's fusion plant went in a ball of released plasma that consumed the little boat all entire.

After that the cheers redoubled, but combined with grunts of effort to reload the guns. They'd not have time for another broadside before *Mongoose* completed the turn, but they'd be ready for the next.

FORTY-SEVEN

That bit of luck, though, was the last bit *Mongoose* had.

The gunboats, as though angered by the loss of one of their number, increased their efforts — and, as though learning something from the success of *Mongoose's* broadside, they increased their numbers as well.

All but two of the boats, those left to continue harrying *Hind*, made their way out-system to join in firing at *Mongoose*.

Now fire was coming in not only from bow and stern, but from multiple angles as the gunboats spread out in a cone to either end of Alexis' ship.

They were making hits now, too. Not so very damaging ones, but *Mongoose's* hull occasionally *thwumped* with a resonating blow as its thermoplastic vaporized under the pirates' shot. The respite for the sail crews between the evolutions necessary to slow or hasten the ship or to make the myriad little turns of the channel, became fewer and shorter as they were also called on to splice rigging and repair sails struck by the gunboats' shot.

Outgunned three to one now, *Mongoose's* answers went largely in vain. Some few of her return shot struck home, but not with the success of her broadside. Those gunboats hit took the blows, for the most part, on their heavily armored bows and shrugged them off to continue their harassment of their larger foe.

Alexis more and more felt the constraints of the Erzurum shoals. It was as though her ship were stuffed into a basket, unable to move and beset from all sides. She longed for open space where she might twist and turn at speed to come at her attackers and bring her full armament to bear.

Instead she was stuck nearly immobile, creeping along at such a petty pace that she could barely tell their movement on the plot.

"Two points to port and down thirty, Layland," she ordered as they came to the next twist in avoiding the masses of dark matter that surrounded them.

"Aye, sir."

Mongoose swung ponderously, more so than could be accounted for by her low speed and the surrounding shoals. Alexis frowned and instinctively reached for navigation plot to steady herself before the ship lurched. A long, low grinding sound echoed from the hull.

"It weren't me, sir!" Layland said quickly. "The helm's off — she's slower to answer."

"A message to Mister Dockett, Creasy," Alexis ordered, wincing as another moaning shudder ran through the ship. "The helm is slow to answer and he's to discover to me why."

"A DAMNED UNLUCKY SHOT, SIR," Dockett said, pointing out the damage on images displayed in Alexis' cabin.

He and *Mongoose's* officers, along with the carpenter, Mister Marton, were clustered around her table. The images were of the ship's stern, deep inside the massive plates of rudder and planes, where the broad, flat surfaces were hinged to the hull. Those surfaces, with no embedded gallenium, were, along with the keel, what allowed *Mongoose* to maneuver. Where the hull itself allowed

Mongoose to glide through the dark matter with ease — when it was not so thick as within these shoals — those surfaces dug in. They turned the ship, in the case of the rudder and planes, or offered resistance, as with the keel, to allow the ship to sail somewhat into the winds rather than solely with them. Without those, the ship was entirely at the mercy of the winds.

In this case, the hinges and mechanical aids, some of the only ones aboard, and one reason a ship's stern was so vulnerable, had been damaged by a single shot from one of the gunboats. Rather than spending itself on the rudder where there'd be only the loss of some easily replaced thermoplastic to deal with, it had somehow made its way in past to strike at those more vulnerable parts.

"Indeed," Alexis murmured.

One of the hinges was shot through and the mechanicals were damaged, leaving the rudder with less range of motion than it should have, and that slower as the parts ground together.

"How much will it affect our maneuvering?" she asked.

Dockett sighed. "It's not just that, sir, but this here." He pointed. "The mechanicals are wearing with every turn, and the rest of the hinges and pinions as well." He traced two lines with his fingers. "Here's where she should set, and here's where she is, see? The mechanicals'll seize from the stress after a time, and have to be replaced."

"How long will that take?"

Dockett looked to Marton, who frowned. "No more'n a bell for the mechanicals t'be replaced — we've a ready-made in stores. Just a matter o'pulling the old and sliding in the new, but the new'll last no more than a watch. Two, if we're lucky."

Dockett nodded. "That's the thing, sir. With the rudder so far off true, it'll only put stress on the replacement as well, and the wear'll do the same to it. If we weren't in such a place as this, with only the normal pressures of the dark matter on things, then the replacement would last longer. But as it is, here, it'll wear faster with every turn."

"And how long to repair it entirely?"

Dockett took a deep breath and shared a look with Marton.

"We'll be a full day, sir — have to unhinge the rudder, pull it out, replace the bits on the hull, see it true again —"

"Might be another day for that, sir, if she's as bad as I fear."

"Could be two days, then, sir," Dockett said. "Then to rehang the rudder and work her in."

"Gentlemen, we cannot be a single bell, much less two days, lying idle here while those gunboats are about," Alexis said.

"Work'd be hard here, sir, and longer, I think," Dockett said. "Have to pull the rudder away and work it — that means lads in suits, away from the hull. They'd rather do it in normal-space, certain, out in the deep Dark, if they must, but here?"

Alexis closed her eyes for a moment and ran through a litany of curses she'd heard from a parade of bosuns over her career. She found the exercise calming and hoped the others would think she was finding some solution, rather than what she was about.

For there did seem to be no solution — no good one, at least.

"What are our chances of it holding until we've cleared this shoal, and the next, and can give some assistance to pulling the *Hind* off of hers?"

The silence was much the answer Alexis suspected she'd receive.

FORTY-EIGHT

"Another signal from *Hind*, sir," Creasy said.

"Respond again, Creasy," Alexis ordered.

No doubt Skanes would find this response to her demands that *Mongoose* do this or that or, frankly, she suspected, anything other than what *Mongoose* was about, no more to her liking than those which had preceded it.

Alexis found it no more to her liking than she suspected Skanes might — nor did *Mongoose's* officers or crew.

Neither Dockett nor Marton, even pressed for their most optimistic prediction, thought there was any chance the rudder would hold through the remainder of the laborious journey to *Hind's* side. Faced with that, the inability to repair it here within Erzurum's shoals, and the further inadvisability of attempting those repairs while under fire from seven gunboats, Alexis reluctantly ordered *Mongoose* put about.

They'd had that unexpected opportunity to throw broadsides at the gunboats again, with results very much less spectacular than the last — a few hits, but no damage to speak of, as all of their targets remained on station and in working order.

Hind had quickly sussed out the change in *Mongoose's* course and begun a flurry of signals, first demanding to know what Alexis was up to, then demanding that *Mongoose* return and engage the enemy, and then a few choice epithets laboriously spelled out letter by letter.

Alexis was reluctant to signal an explanation of her ship's status, as Skanes, commodore though she might name herself, had neither the Navy's private signals nor come up with any of her own. Their communications, therefore, were almost entirely open to being read by the occupants of all the nearby gunboats.

Hello, pirates, my rudder is damaged, I'm slow to maneuver, and one more good hit there might leave us entirely helpless — not the message I'd like to put out there.

Instead she'd done the best she could to both inform and reassure Skanes, but *unable to comply* and *will return* were not appeasing Skanes — and Alexis could not, in good conscience, blame the woman. From her perspective, it must appear as though Alexis and *Mongoose* were running off and abandoning them.

It looked a bit like that from Alexis', as well, and she still wracked her brain to find some way to turn this bit of bad luck around. Dockett and Marton were aft, both keeping an eye on the state of the rudder and its mechanisms and seeing if there was anything else they might do. Both had agreed to think on it, but both had given Alexis no cause to hope there was any other solution than what she'd ordered.

A day, perhaps two, to sail far enough from Erzurum that we'll be safe from the pirates while we do the work; a day, perhaps two, to do the work itself; and then a day, perhaps two, to return. Return and work our way through all this mess again, and that's if Hind *can hold out for nearly a week on her own.*

The larger ship had the guns for it, the gunboats had still largely left her alone, concentrating on *Mongoose*.

Would Skanes have the nerve to do so, though?

What signal could she send that might reassure Skanes while still not endangering *Mongoose*? Even if she signaled that she was going for help, if any such help were closer than a fortnight's sail, would such a message not only embolden and encourage the gunboat crews to harry *Hind* more aggressively?

"Movement on the *Hind*, sir," Dorsett said.

Alexis brought up those images and watched.

"She's backing sail," Dorsett told her, "and waving her rudder and planes to and fro. Keel's full up, as well."

"Trying to wiggle her way out of the shoal," Villar said.

"Too massy," Hacking muttered.

Still, despite none of her officers believing the *Hind* would manage freeing herself that way, they all watched, desperately hoping, even while shot from the gunboats peppered *Mongoose* and her chasers returned fire. If *Hind* *could* free herself, then there might be a very different circumstance. Those great broadsides, freed to fire against the gunboats, would surely drive them off.

All those hopes were in vain, though, as the *Hind* remained mired where she was.

Hours later, even the signals from *Hind* had stopped, as though Skanes had chosen to forget that Alexis and *Mongoose* existed at all.

Hours after that, *Mongoose* was nearly out of the last planetary shoal of Erzurum, nearly free of the system itself, with only the dark matter halo to traverse before the freer and more open range of *darkspace*.

"Movement on the *Hind*," Dorsett announced once more.

The images now were blurry, at the extreme range of *Mongoose's* optics and their ability to discern detail. It was hard to tell just what was happening, but there were figures on the other ship's hull, it seemed, and ship's boats sailing away then back again.

"Those boats're leaving things behind, here —" Dorsett sent an enhanced image to the navigation plot.

"More kedges?"

"Lightening ship," Hacking said. "Dumping all their stores and supplies — do you suppose it could work, if she were close enough to be able to move through that muck she's stuck in?"

"Unlikely," Parrill said. "The hull, masts, and sails are most of the ship's mass — true, the stores are still a great deal, but given how surely the *Hind* is stuck, when the attempt to use a kedge broke her doubled line, I believe she'll see no luck with this. A simple calculation of the hull's mass, alone, would indicate she must lessen even that to move on her own. A great deal of sail and several of those gunboats pulling forward, with the wind, might do it, but then she'd only be farther in-system and under the control of the gunboats."

Hacking slammed his palm down on the plot. "Of all the —"

He broke off, glanced at Alexis, then mumbled an apology and left the quarterdeck.

"He did ask," Parrill said.

Alexis laid a hand on the woman's shoulder. "It is sometimes comforting to give question to a hope, no matter how unlikely it may be."

Parrill frowned. "I don't understand that at all. The hope would be entirely false."

It was not so long before they all saw that the hope, possibly the last for the *Hind*, was not to be.

Alexis and the others watched as boat after boat of stores were dumped into *darkspace*, then images that Dorsett was certain would be the *Hind's* guns followed suit, all until there must not have been a piece of bedding on the berthing deck or a gram of beef in the vats — or rather the vats themselves, for those were seen to be taken off and dumped as well.

Then all those ship's boats returned and took up lines, throwing their little lugsails into the effort to pull *Hind* from her resting place.

Alexis had *Mongoose* tacking off and on just before the system's halo shoals, ready, no matter the risk, to come about and return if *Hind* really were to free herself.

Dorsett set up measurements in the images, telling Alexis that he'd see the moment she budged and by how much, but it was not to be.

"Signal from *Hind*, sir," Creasy said at last. "Not our number, just a general signal. She's struck, sir."

FORTY-NINE

T he mood within *Mongoose* was reserved, almost sullen, as all aboard dwelt on what had occurred. Bad enough they'd been forced to flee — for though, as privateers in search of a prize, they might prefer a merchant foe who'd strike at their first shot alongside, they were a fighting crew from fighting ships and it galled to retreat at all, much less leaving an ally behind to be taken. Even so impugned an ally as Skanes and the *Hind*.

But flee they did, putting the ship back to rights from her long time at quarters even as they cleared the dark matter halo around Erzurum, leaving behind not only the *Hind* and Skanes, but no little bit of their pride, as well, along with their hopes for the fat prize of Ezurum's markets and any merchantmen unlucky to be found in orbit there.

That last was making the crew mutter about where their luck had gone, and Alexis was wondering herself. The weeks without a prize, then the retreat in the face of those gunboats – small foes which it irked the fighting men and women of *Mongoose's* crew to flee from – came together to form an almost intolerable situation.

Alexis found it no more tolerable as she watched the dimming, shrinking images of the *Hind* and the gunboats, no more than blurry dots now at the most extreme magnification *Mongoose's* optics were capable of.

"We'll wait until we're out of sight, then tack so that we can't be followed and be about repairing the rudder," she said.

"Aye, sir," Villar acknowledged.

Even that seemed to be a cursed endeavor, for the winds were up and against them, keeping them within sight of Erzurum for some time. Once she was confident that her ship could not be seen from any trailer, even if they had, by some miracle, optics as fine as *Mongoose's*, Alexis set course in a random direction.

Then, if not within a system and normal-space as the crew might prefer, at least well away from any enemy, they set about repairing the ship.

Hot, heavy work that Alexis joined in. Not that her assistance was needed, nor even very helpful to be honest, but because she wanted to throw herself into something, anything, that would exhaust her. The alternative was to stare at the navigation plot, either on the quarterdeck or her cabin table and wonder at what she might have done differently.

Perhaps if she'd set the ship to veering from side to side in the already narrow channels? Then might that cursed, fatal shot not have struck elsewhere? Might they then have been able to reach the *Hind*?

It was a useless exercise, she knew, for any veering that might have put them away from the one shot might have put them in the path of another. She could see, of course, in the repeat of the action on her plot what she might have done. Exactly when to have veered and when to have sailed straight on, so as to have made it through, but that was always the case — one could tell very well after an action where the shot would be flying.

"But not during," she muttered.

She sat away from her table, back aching, and checked the time. She'd been staring at the plot here for nearly four bells, she found. At least the watch would be over soon and she could return to the quarterdeck.

Creasy had the current watch and had begun his muttering again. Not Dutchmen this time, thank the Dark, but merely that it had been an unlucky blow and how had they displeased some idle spirit?

Despite his inanity, she didn't want to become a captain who ordered silence on the quarterdeck. The watches were long and some conversation passed the time, but her temper was short and ill-suited to Creasy's musings at this time.

She eyed her glass, half full of wine, and sighed.

The feelings were recognizable, at least, though what to do about them was less clear. Poulter, the surgeon on *Nightingale*, had given her some thoughts before *Nightingale* paid off, though his main suggestion of talking through her fears was less than helpful. There were no doctors with his training on Dalthus, after all, and Merriwether, the surgeon she'd taken aboard *Mongoose*, while a fine man with his tools, was less accomplished with his words.

That bit of talking out her feelings wasn't a thing she wanted bandied about the crew, in any case — not the proper image of a captain, certainly. None of the officers were confidants of that degree either — perhaps Villar, but he was overburdened with his own concerns at the moment, what with *Mongoose's* repairs. Which left ...

"Isom!"

She eyed the glass again — there was a tug at her pant leg, then another, and before she knew it the vile creature had swarmed up into her lap. Where it would stay, and return even if dumped to the deck, for as long as it wished if she stayed in her cabin. Even moving to another chair or to her cot wouldn't put it off, the thing would only follow her until, having got its fill of her, it slunk away again.

"Bring my vacsuit, will you? I believe I'll assist with the rudder for a time."

WHEN THEY RETURNED, Erzurum appeared much as it had when they'd first laid eyes on it.

Dark and, to all appearances, uninhabited, with no beacons or pilot boat — nor with any gunboats in sight, and certainly with no evidence of the *Hind* left. The pirates must have got her off the shoals and into normal-space within the system, as even Erzurum's winds and shoals couldn't have broken the big ship up in so little time.

"Once she struck, I imagine the gunboats were able to pull her out of the shoal," Villar said.

Alexis nodded, but caught her lip between her teeth and worried at it. She caught Hacking's look of amusement at that and stopped.

She wasn't certain what she'd expected to find upon *Mongoose's* return — or what she planned to do. Frustration and guilt filled her in equal parts, for she knew she couldn't now take *Mongoose* through those shoals alone and she felt responsible for whatever fate had befallen Skanes and the crew of the *Hind*.

"Sir?" Villar prompted.

Alexis realized she'd been standing silent and contemplating the navigation plot for some time as *Mongoose* stood on toward the first of Erzurum's shoals. They'd have to turn soon or make the attempt again.

"Prepare to come about and make for Enclave," she ordered. "We have need of more ships."

FIFTY

T he entryway to *Hoof & Turf*, what Wheeley assured her
was the finest restaurant in the Casino, was as staid and
gentrified as Alexis had imagined it would be.

Dark wood paneling, which she suspected was real, coated the
walls and the narrow podium behind which stood the *Hoof & Turf's*
host. The lighting leading into the interior was dim, and they'd used
some of the space to install a short hallway to the dining area, leaving
those not allowed entry only the barest glimpse of the interior and
diners. Rough as the Barbary might be, the *Hoof & Turf* offered some
luxury to those captains or passengers who'd relish such after a
long sail.

Alexis squared her shoulders, hoping for the few millimeters'
more height and added authority that gave her. She was outfitted in
her full "uniform," hat and be-damned feather included. It wasn't so
much the restaurant's host she hoped to impress — she had Wheeley's name and backing for that, after all — but the other private
captains. And they were a curious lot themselves, so perhaps a
feather wouldn't go amiss.

"Of course, miss," the host said, "anything for a friend of Mister

Wheeley." He looked down his nose first at her, then at the podium's surface, keeping his back and neck ramrod straight. She suspected he did so to facilitate looking down his nose at everyone and everything, though she did fancy him trying it once Captain Malcomson arrived.

Likely fall over backward in the attempt.

"A room for twelve," he continued, fingers flicking across the podium's surface. "Of course."

She was certain he was scrambling, without actually saying so, to move other diners about in freeing up the room, and she felt a bit bad about inconveniencing them, but this matter was most important. *Osprey* was in, under Captain Kingston, and the last of the four private ships Malcomson recommended to her. They'd been three weeks now at Enclave, fairly begging those captains to delay departure and meet with her all at once. She wanted to lay out her proposal as one to the group, though Malcomson already knew her purpose. The captains only stayed because she'd hinted at profit and some embarrassment to Skanes and the *Hind*.

That last piqued their curiosity. None of them was fond of Skanes and they were eager to hear something to her detriment.

So, Alexis had wheedled each into staying a bit longer, so that they all might hear together.

First Malcomson, who seemed most amused at the prospect of her trying to get the captains of so many private ships to coordinate on anything at all. He, at least, was in no hurry to sail again, so long as there was such an entertaining prospect in the offing. He'd even agreed to sail for Ezurum with her – provided she convinced the others.

Then Pennywell, captain of *Gallion*. A rather reserved man whose personality was quite at odds with the garish, striped coat he wore.

Captain Spensley and his *Oriana* were next to arrive. An officious little prat, in Alexis' opinion, who dressed all in black, thought little more of Alexis than she did of him, and made no secret of it. But he seemed to dislike Skanes even more and was anxious to not miss what Alexis had to say about the putative "commodore."

Scorpion and Captain Lawson — another woman, but one whose habitual dress made Alexis a bit uncomfortable. The skintight jumpsuit of some iridescent hide made Alexis thankful the worst she'd gotten from her crew was the feather.

That very afternoon, *Osprey* and her captain, Kingston, whom Alexis had yet to meet, made orbit and Alexis sent her invitations.

Six ships, with *Delight* and *Mongoose*, if she could convince them all. That might be enough to make it through Erzurum's shoals and gunboats to rescue *Hind* and find the truth to the rumors about crews from the fleets.

Now she only had to convince them.

A shout from one of the casino's nearby tables drew her attention and she had a sudden thought. A bit of coin to sweeten the deal up front wouldn't go amiss with these captains, either. Pulling from *Mongoose's* accounts to give to the other captains might be an investment in the endeavor, but it wouldn't reap enough to pay back the coin given.

There was some time, though, before the other captains would arrive.

"Mister Villar," Alexis said, "would you see to the room and preparations with Isom? I'll be just over there — no more than a few minutes, I'm sure, and the captains aren't due for some time yet."

"Aye, sir."

Alexis ignored their looks and made her way to the nearest table. There was no dealer here, as there'd been in the room where Wheeley played. No cards, either, only the table's surface displaying the images of them. Four players sat at the table in a circle, which was also a differently shaped table, but she supposed that made sense if there were no need for a place for a dealer to stand.

She pulled up a chair and sat, also taking her tablet out as it *pinged*. The table had apparently recognized her seating and was asking her tablet to transfer funds.

Well, she had no need of the stakes Wheeley played at, even if the table allowed it, which she saw it didn't.

She thought of the amount she might need to offer the other captains and transferred half that. Not an excessive payment, not with the prize money and reward held out to tempt them, but just enough to take the edge off the risk.

She tapped the table to place her bet and a single chip rose from a recess in the table — odd to use a real chip when the cards themselves were merely images on the table's surface, but she did like the tangible feel of it. She noted a raised eyebrow or two amongst the other players. The man to her left, but separated by one seat, nodded to her and she gave him a small smile in return.

"You're holding up play," the man across from her muttered. He raised his glass and took a long drink, adding to the brew which was causing his flushed, sweaty appearance.

"I'm sorry," Alexis said. She glanced down and saw that the table was also asking her if she was ready to proceed. She tapped that button and the cards began appearing.

There was a collective groan and Alexis' cards disappeared and her chip was swallowed back by the table.

"What happened?" she asked, frowning.

"Dealer won," the man next to her muttered.

She saw that the dealer's cards were still illuminated in the center of the table, showing the target sum of the game. She knew that meant an immediate win, because she'd received it herself several times at Wheeley's table, but she'd not seen the dealer receive it before.

"Oh, it works that way for the dealer too?"

The two men who'd acknowledged her presence grunted and glanced her way, the others toyed with their glasses. A thin woman to Alexis' right drained her glass and tapped the table to signal for another.

"Waiting for your bet," the man across from her said.

"Oh, yes," Alexis said, tapping at her tablet again. Now she'd either have to wager twice as much or play two hands to both recoup her unexpected loss and gain enough to bribe the other captains. She had time, though, she thought, before they began arriving.

"You can transfer more than a single bet to the table, you know?" the man across from her said as she took her chip and placed it in the wager circle.

"I thought as much, but I've never needed more than the one before."

That got her more looks from the other players and the woman tapped the table, grasped her tablet, and walked away.

Alexis considered the table — she had time enough for the two hands, and doubling, then redoubling, would recoup her loss and leave her with a bit more she could bribe the captains with.

The cards fell. She saw she needed only a small amount to reach the requisite number and flicked her fingers as she'd seen Wheeley do. Another card appeared — too large by far.

"That was my ten!" the man to her left nearly yelled.

"Well, I'm sorry, but it was my turn." Alexis frowned at the cards displayed in front of her. "I'm not at all certain what went wrong — every other time I've received a three for that ... well, twice a two, but it was sufficient."

The others stared at her.

A HAND on her shoulder some time later broke her concentration. She was trying to decide what to do with these cards, and history was no help.

"Sir," Villar said from behind her, "the other captains are assembled."

Alexis narrowed her eyes. Perhaps there was some sort of pattern. Would the computer that dealt these cards have something like that? Could it be why her experience at this table was so different from that at Wheeley's?

"Yes ... have a drink served, will you, and I'll be along presently?"

Villar cleared his throat. "Ah ... that's what you told Isom twice now, sir — they're several glasses in and growing restless."

Alexis looked up, noting that she had the gambling table to herself now. Through a haze of card images and frustration, she remembered the man who'd been seated next to her leaving after several instances of going on about her taking his this or that, or the dealer's whatever. She'd soon grown tired of that and he hadn't thought much of her response that the next bloody card was hers until she decided not to take it, so clearly, he had little knowledge of how the game was played, now didn't he?

This had been some time after the man across from her left with a muttered oath at her only transferring enough coin to the table for her next bet, but he clearly didn't understand how it was supposed to work either — though she had to admit he had a bit of a point and she'd begun transferring enough for several wagers some time after he left. Which, when one thought about it, reflected poorly on him for his lack of patience, didn't it?

When the others had left, or why, she had no recollection.

Perhaps that was it, though — when she'd played with Wheeley, it had been just the two of them at the table. Could it be that ...

"Mister Villar, would you mind having a seat here." She patted the chair to her right. "I just want to try something."

Yes ... if I can remember how Wheeley *played and then instruct Villar in which cards to take ...* She frowned. *Perhaps that man had something in his thought that I'd taken his card ... I wonder if I can track him down and ask him a question or two ...*

"Sir, if you wish to speak to the other captains before they're all topgallants- and royals-full, then you should come now."

Alexis sighed. No doubt Villar was correct. She stood and gestured over the table for her last card of the hand — it was a poor pair of cards when one got down to it, and ...

The next card fell and, to her surprise, gave her the requisite number, which triggered the dealer's play, which failed. A chip matching her wager rose from the table.

"Well, now, that's more like it, isn't it?" She pulled her chair back from the table and started to sit.

"Sir? The matter of Commodore Skanes?"

She glanced at Villar and felt her face grow hot at his expression — a mixture of amusement and concern, tinged, she thought, with a bit of reproach which he must have learned from Isom but wasn't quite as good at.

She pushed the chair back and swept up her chips — a paltry number, even given the last addition. A check of her tablet sent a small shock through her. She'd wagered, and lost, a goodly portion of the personal funds she had on hand *and* her share of the prizes. She hadn't thought she'd done *that* poorly at the table, nor been there so long as to have lost all that.

She'd have to contact a reputable agent here, if she could locate one in the Barbary, and have her accounts replenished from those held by her prize agents back in New London. In the meantime, they'd have to be more conscious of the cost of her personal stores and Isom would likely be giving her that look Villar had yet to master.

There'd be no bribes for the captains, either, unless she drew on *Mongoose's* funds, and she regretted having put those first winnings into the collective pool, no matter how it had cheered the crew.

She glanced back at the table.

I believe I have the hang of it now — there's only the need of suffi-cient funds to see it through.

FIFTY-ONE

The other captains were, indeed, several sheets-full, with the normally reserved Pennywell and the hide-clad Lawson engaged in a rendition of a shockingly bawdy romantic ballad, arms about each other's shoulders, and showing little or no respect for the intended genders of the parts they sang.

Alexis entered to Lawson leaning close to Pennywell and giving full-voice to a desire which was anatomically unlikely.

Spensley, Kingston, and Malcomson cheered them on, while Isom and one of the *Hoof*'s staff rushed about refilling glasses and mugs.

Upon entering, Villar made his way to the room's corner where the other captains' first officers were grouped and joined them.

At first glance, they seemed simply more reserved than their captains, but a closer look showed Alexis they all held similar expressions combining reproach, tolerance, and resignation. Looking about at the antics of the five privateer captains, she could understand it, but was a bit put out that Villar saw fit to join them.

Bad company, I imagine — I'll have to speak to him about it.

Isom hurried up to her, a pitcher of beer in one hand and a bottle of wine in the other.

"Oh, thank the Dark, you're here, sir. The place's management's been in twice now about the noise. There's soundproofing, but when —"

There was a horrid, grating screech from the singers and Alexis, after the initial shock, realized that it was Pennywell reaching for a note he had no business being near ... and that the note was part of a word describing something he did not possess.

"Aye, sir, that one. Makes it right out to the main dining room, it does, and I imagine they'll be along any moment to complain again." Isom gave her the look he usually reserved for when she'd just suggested the vile creature be spaced, as though it were her fault — which she supposed it was, given her tardiness.

"My apologies, Isom, for leaving you to deal with this ... this."

Isom nodded, apparently mollified for the moment.

Alexis cleared her throat, hoping to gather the captains' attention.

Lawson gave full voice to an act which would be improbable no matter who was involved.

She strode to the center of the room's large table and looked around expectantly.

Spensley shoved Kingston, who shoved him back, which caused the former to rise, hand at his belt knife — until Kingston poured half of his mug's contents into Spensley's glass, and the two sat again to watch the performance.

Villar appeared at her elbow. "Perhaps hold the refills until they give you their attention, sir?"

Alexis glared at him, not least of which because she felt it poor advice.

Likely be off to sack the Casino if I did that.

Also, though, because of the look of amusement on Villar's face. She drew a deep breath.

"*Stop your gobs, you cack-handed lubbers!*"

Her voice cut through even Lawson's chorus about a third-mate named Morgan and his captain's ...

"Oh, dear," Alexis muttered.

"Och!" Malcomson said. "It's aboot time oor tawdry host arrived!"

Villar stiffened, and Malcomson's own first officer, perhaps seeing the look on Villar's face, stepped over and whispered to him.

"Perhaps you meant 'tardy', sir?"

"Nae if she means to be part o'this lot!" Malcomson waved his hand at the others, who joined in his laughter.

Alexis sighed and laid a hand on Villar's arm to let him know she took no offense.

"If we might have dinner served?" she suggested. "And discuss our business? Let us set some sort of base and reason for the night's remaining drinking, eh?"

ALEXIS WAITED until dinner was done and the other captains settled into their port before coming to the point.

The meal, fine though the food was, had been a rowdy affair, and loud, but now the full stomachs seemed to have dragged them all into a semblance of calm.

She laid out the *Hind's* situation, waited for the laughter to die, and then made her proposal.

These pirates had gone too far, taking a Marchant ship, for everyone knew the reprisals the Marchant Company might make. Wouldn't it be better, she argued, for them — the private ship captains — to show their own worth before that happened? There was a standing reward offered by Marchant for coming to the aid of one of their ships in need — so profit there. And the pirate market, with goods from dozens, perhaps more, merchantmen traversing the Barbary — all sitting planetside at Erzurum for them to take and condemn as illicit. Who knew what merchantmen might, even now, be in orbit around that planet to take on those goods — and liable for taking as prizes themselves?

It was, when one thought about it — *but not too thoroughly mind you and here's a full glass yours seems to be empty* — a tempting fruit, ripe for the picking and not too terribly dangerous with only a few gunboats about.

A frigate? Well, perhaps.

But likely away, don't you think? Taking more ships and sending them back to Erzurum to wait for us?

When you think about it — *here, let me fill that for you* — that frigate's a boon, yes? The more she takes the more there'll be for us!

Hadn't *Mongoose* and *Delight* taken a convoy of a full dozen ships on their way to Erzurum? All unescorted by that frigate, which was certainly off hunting more?

Why, think about it — *another round of bottles, Isom, this one's empty* — a frigate could send two such convoys home before depleting her crew too much. Two dozen taken ships in orbit, waiting to be rechristened and sold? As many merchantmen come to buy cargoes? The reward from the Marchants for so large a rescue as *Hind*? And, yes, there could be members of the fleets still on Erzurum — there'd be money from Admiralty for their rescue. Not a lot, perhaps, but the icing — no, let's call it the sweet, sprinkly bits on top of the icing, shall we?

All there for the taking. *Someone's* taking.

Hadn't we better be on our way before someone else gets it? No, here we go, and take the bottle with you!

FIFTY-TWO

The six private ships scattered while out of sight of the system and approached from different vectors, each toward their agreed upon point. At nearly the same time, as such things could be measured and planned in *darkspace*, each worked her way through Erzurum's halo and began the laborious task of sailing to and then working her way through each of the shoals.

From her plot, Alexis watched them all as *Mongoose* made her own way.

It might make more sense for them to approach as a single force, at least for dealing with the gunboats, but then each would have to make its way through the masses of shoals to different Lagrangian points regardless. They had no knowledge of what waited for them *inside* Erzurum, after all. What Alexis could recall of the Navy's doctrine for attacking a system called for multiple ships scattered at transition points throughout the system, so as to take defenders in-system from many positions at once.

She didn't know if that doctrine changed when attacking a system so shallow as Erzurum, though. None of the other captains had objected to the plan, but she wondered if that was due to their own propensity toward independent action.

In any case, the plan was made and agreed to.

Osprey had the worst of it, she thought — least massy of the group she might be. Erzurum's halo was thick above and below the ecliptic, and Alexis could almost see *Osprey* shudder again and again as even her mostly-retracted keel and hull were affected by the thick dark matter there.

Kingston was game and a proper ship handler, though, and brought *Osprey* about over and over to try again, never allowing her to be held fast.

The coordination of their approach soon disappeared, as ship after ship was either forced to fall back and find a different route through the shoals or found one and advanced farther than the others.

Alexis ordered a near constant rotation of the crew. Sail handlers back inside after only half a watch, to be replaced by others. Those inside sent to rest and have a hot meal. The schedule was grueling, but the crew on the hull had told stories of how their minds had felt dull during *Mongoose's* last approach and she wanted no one exposed to so much dark matter for too long at a time.

She set the same rotation for the leadsmen in the bow, though at some stretches of the shoals she had four men there firing their beams at once. These shoals were so windy and broken up in places that two clumps of the dark matter might pull a beam between them, tricking *Mongoose* into thinking the way was clear while the channel's sides waited to entrap her or crush her bow.

The ship, and the whole crew, were nearly at quarters, with all, even those with no duties on the hull, in their vacsuits, though without their helmets affixed.

Three times in the first few hours, she was forced to come about, retrace her steps, and seek another route from some previous branch.

The other private ships fared no better, each finding some new success or failure at every turn, with every ship-length of advancement.

The respites, once through a shoal and into the clearer space between planets' orbits, were fraught with peril as well, for those spaces were full of chunks and invisible strands of thick dark matter spun off what trailed along with and behind each planet's course. And there the temptation after so long a time of the creeping pace required by the shoals was strong. More sail, more speed, with the system's winds running strong toward Erzurum's center, and less time to react and turn aside should the leadsmen uncover one of those shoals dead ahead.

Gallion signaled that they'd found a clear way through their shoal and for the others to follow if they liked, but Pennywell spoke too soon. He was deceived by a long channel with gradually narrowing borders and barely escaped with his ship as the edges closed in.

He wasn't stuck fast, but the angles were such that he couldn't back into the winds and had to finally work his ship back, laboriously, with his ship's boats and kedges to either side.

Osprey abandoned the attempt to make it through the halo away from the ecliptic. Such was an iffy proposition in most systems, and Erzurum was worse. The mass of dark matter there so great that even a ship so lightly burthened as *Osprey* could not make it through. Kingston brought his ship about, exited his latest attempt, then made his way around the system to the ecliptic plane where the normal-space mass of the planets pulled the halo to bits.

He followed the channels already marked by Lawson's *Scorpion* and took up station following and supporting her.

The *Delight* took the first real damage of the foray, scraping too close to a mass and dragging the ship's plane. *Delight*'s image spun wildly, as though on a pivot at the rear, and figures scrambled up her masts to reduce what little sail she had on, even as her helm cut the particle projector to send them dark.

Still, stays snapped as the winds pushed at those sails and the sails pulled at masts suddenly stuck fast and dead in space.

Within a bell, though, her sails were lit again and Malcomson worked her free. He signaled, in the private code they'd all agreed upon, that *Delight* was sound, though Alexis wondered at that. The impact had appeared more severe than he seemed to indicate, and she worried for his foremast's hinge, for that was where *Delight* had carried the most sail.

She zoomed in on the images until she could watch a host of blurry figures on *Delight's* hull, all clustered around the fore, as she'd expected. She couldn't make out detail of the hinge itself, that bit which allowed the mast to be unstepped and swung down to rest upon the hull, but so much activity there made her think she was correct.

It would also, she suspected, be as clear a message to any watching gunboats as if *Delight* had passed her status on with no private codes at all.

Surely the pirates, and she was certain they were out there, ships dark and hidden, but watching all the same, would be assessing the damage each of the private ships might take from the shoals.

As though summoned by her thoughts — and she cast a quick glance to Creasy at that, for his bits of superstitious nonsense were making inroads with the crew — new lights appeared on the plot.

"Gunboats, sir," Dorsett said from the tactical console. "Seven ... twelve ... more than last time, at least."

Alexis nodded. There were already more than the twelve lights appearing, but the full number and scale of what they faced would take minutes to make itself clear as the light from each of the gunboats' now-charged sails would take time to reach her.

"Pack up the galley and finish putting us at quarters, Mister Villar," Alexis ordered. "The guncrews to see to their charges, if you please."

"Aye, sir."

"Mister Hacking, Miss Parrill, to your places. You are our legs and teeth, I'll remind you."

"Aye, sir," Hacking and Parrill echoed, the latter fitting her helmet in place and heading for the sail locker to oversee the sail crews on the hull, the former to the gundeck and *Mongoose's* teeth.

Creasy was muttering at his console as he exchanged signals with the other private ships, each sharing what the others might not be able to see — more gunboats farther away, but lights obscured by the system's thick dark matter. She caught a familiar sound and listened closer. He muttered the words even as he worked his console, like an incantation.

"Turn for turn and twist for twist — run and hide thee, Nag."

Alexis closed her eyes and fought back a groan. She recognized the words from a bit at the beginning of the story she'd looked up after Dansby began calling her Rikki — and had hoped the crew, with their interminable fascination with the vile creature, would never discover it.

Oh, sweet Dark, they've found the bloody book.

FIFTY-THREE

The gunboats wasted no time in pressing their attacks, perhaps fearing the size of the oncoming force, despite outnumbering the private ships. There were fifteen in all, when they stopped appearing on *Mongoose's* plot — at least fifteen that had showed themselves. There could be others still lying dark and silent amongst the shoals, and no telling how many or what other ships might await the attacking force in normal-space.

The gunboats split up, pairs approaching each of the private ships, with the three extra heading for *Scorpion* and *Osprey*.

Those two, sailing almost together, were clearly the first real targets, with the others to be only harried.

"I'm surprised they've not used the *Hind* to attack us," Villar said. "Why do you suppose that is, sir? She's guns enough to take on any two of us."

"Guns, yes," Alexis agreed, "but we saw what happened the last time she went amongst these shoals. Following a gunboat captain who knows the channels is one thing — that must be how they get their own ships and visiting merchants past this mess at all — but fighting a ship is another. With her guns and stores she'd only become stuck fast again in any kind of action, I imagine."

She paused.

"I do hope they've not put any of the *Hind's* spacers aboard their boats, though," she added.

That was not so uncommon a thing, for pirates to offer captured spacers a place — joining was better than some other fates, but once a man had sailed under the pirate flag, he'd be marked for life by the authorities.

"Or spacers from the fleets," Villar added, giving voice to a greater fear.

What if there were New London Navy men aboard those ships? There for no other reason than that their ship was disabled in some fight and the pirates came along first.

What if Delaine is there?

Alexis shut down that avenue of thought immediately. It wouldn't do to think on. Surely Delaine wouldn't have joined the pirates, even at the cost of his own life?

No ... but for his men's lives, perhaps. Or to stay alive long enough to escape, he might play along ...

She clamped down on those thoughts again, furious with herself for following them.

I may not change what I may not change, she reminded herself.

Poulter, on *Nightingale*, had reminded her, time and again, that one could only do one's best. Told her to remind herself, rather, for that was the point he'd driven home. Worrying at what was done had no value past the lessons to be learned, and worrying at what might come had less past the planning.

Isom entered the quarterdeck wearing his own vacsuit. He carried her sword and firearms, a chemical propellant pistol for use in any boardings, and her tiny flechette pistol, which would be useless in a ship opened to *darkspace*, but might be handy if they were somehow captured themselves. Under his other arm he carried the vacuum-tight crate housing the creature, which would soon be secured in the hold near the magazine and fusion plant — the most protected part of the ship.

Alexis stripped off the upper half of her vacsuit, her underthings already damp with sweat from wearing the thing so long. With the stress of an action, she'd soon be soaked through. She slid the flechette pistol into its place within the suit. She might not be able to get to it in vacuum, but if she was ever taken then it might be overlooked in any search that didn't strip the suit itself from her.

The chemical pistol went into her suit's holster and the sword at her left side. It was lighter and shorter than the rough chopping blades the crew was issued — more suited to her small frame and muscles — but she'd become skilled in its use.

"I'll take Boots below now, sir," Isom said after he'd helped her shrug and wiggle her way back into her vacsuit.

"Yes, do, and yourself as well."

Isom was always the last of the ship's servants below in an action, taking it upon himself to see to both the creature and to ensuring that none of the other noncombatants — the cooks, stewards, and all those who had no place in sailing or fighting the ship — had somehow overlooked the call.

"Signal from *Delight*, sir," Creasy said.

"Yes?"

"*All ships*, sir, then ... ah, *Engage the enemy more closely*, followed by ... y - o - u - h - a-c - k - i - t - j - e - s - s - i - e - s ..." Creasy frowned. "I have no idea what that means, sir, and the computer tells me it must be an error on their side."

Alexis grinned. The reminder of the coming fight putting her out of her former melancholy. Whatever else, she was aboard a ship of her own about to engage the enemy — soon her guns would speak for her.

"I'm sure it means something to Malcomson, Creasy, though perhaps it's best if we not know." Her grin widened. "Acknowledge the signal and send this: *All ships - a hundred guineas that* Mongoose *takes the first foe.*"

ALEXIS LOST HER HUNDRED GUINEAS.

Kingston and Lawson engaged the enemy first, with a bit of coordination she'd not have expected from private ships.

Osprey and *Scorpion* leapfrogged each other through the channels, with never both of them moving at the same time, and each stopped to cover with her main guns the space the other could not while moving.

Despite this, the gunboats, seven in all, made their way closer until they were within range.

The gunboats fired the first shots of the day, ranging in on *Osprey* as the weaker of the pair and mapping out how the shoals might warp their shot.

Shot after shot flashed out from the boats with no answer, until finally *Scorpion's* sails lit from where she lay still. Just an instance, just a bit, but enough to catch a bit of wind, turn the ship, and present her guns.

While *Osprey* continued mapping the channel ahead, calmly as though sailing toward a pilot boat, *Scorpion's* guns flashed in response.

Whether by chance or whether Lawson had learned something from the gunboats shot, three of her shots struck home.

The gunboat's bow crumpled and her sails flickered. Their azure light returned for a moment, but dimmer and flashing as though the ship was signaling. Any observer could see that it was not intentional.

"Power routing," Villar muttered. "Or her projectors."

"Let's hope it's the projectors," Alexis said.

Those would be harder to repair in *darkspace* and with so small a crew as the gunboats could carry. Their damage would make the boat more difficult to sail.

That thought seemed to be confirmed when the damaged boat broke off, making, it appeared, for the nearest Lagrangian point and the safer confines of normal-space.

One less to contend with here, but they'll be waiting for us.

Alexis returned her attention to *Mongoose*. The gunboats targeting her had come within range and begun firing. These two seemed to have only nine-pounders or so mounted, but their fire was still a danger to the ship and the men working the sails.

Mongoose returned fire from bow and stern, but the captains of those gunboats seemed to have taken previous lessons to heart. They kept their boats out of the worst of the shoals, in the relatively clear space between planetary orbits, and broke off whenever *Mongoose* made to turn herself and bring her broadsides to bear.

It was a frustrating, time-consuming dance, for each turn to present her broadside lost *Mongoose* some travel time through the shoals — there was a risk, as well, in the narrow channels she had available — yet she couldn't simply carry on and allow the gunboats to pepper her without threat.

"Signal from *Oriana*, sir," Creasy said.

Alexis glanced at Spensley's position on the plot and found that quite a lot of time had passed while she danced with those gunboats.

Oriana had made it to the first of her stops, the L3 point of Erzurum's outermost gas giant, and returned from a transition to normal-space there.

"Two ships," Creasy continued. "The *Hind* and ... a frigate, sir? That can't be right, can it?"

"Send *Interrogative*, Creasy."

"Aye, sir, I'll ... no, *Delight's* beat you to it, sir ... *Oriana's* responding ... frigate confirmed, sir. *Oriana* says, estimated forty guns."

Alexis felt a chill. The frigate was here and in normal-space around the planet? They'd planned — hoped — for it to be away on its pirating cruise. Why, if they had the frigate here and could navigate it through this mess, was it not in *darkspace* and joining the attack now?

FIFTY-FOUR

Mongoose took another hit, this one through her sails and the men working them.

Alexis flinched and closed her eyes at the sight, but opened them an instant later. The quarterdeck crew would be looking to her for orders and she had no time to wonder or worry about who the dead and injured were.

"Steady on," she said.

"Aye, sir."

That had likely been the last hit for some time, as the private ships were all very nearly through the worst of this ring of shoals. They'd soon be in the relatively deep and uncluttered space between orbits, and the gunboats were even now pulling back.

"Signal from *Delight*, sir," Creasy said. He waited a moment, so the signal must be something they didn't have codes for, at least in part, and he waited for the letters to be laboriously spelled out. "*Note their course* and *Interrogative*, sir."

Alexis nodded. She'd been wondering much the same herself.

The gunboats were falling back past the next line of shoals, their course through the maze of dark matter clear to anyone with decent optics. That would show the way, or at least one particular way, but it was a way for the light, shallow-drafted boats. With so little mass they could go through bits of dark matter that would stall or damage one of the larger private ships.

It would be just the thing for the pirates if they could lure one or more of the attackers into getting stuck fast.

"Send *Be wary*," she said.

"Aye, sir." His fingers slid over his console, then stopped. "Signal from *Oriana*, sir. *All ships, Captain to repair on board*, then our number at the end, sir."

Alexis frowned and damned the slow, laborious signaling of *darkspace*. One couldn't just flash and set one's lights too quickly, as the dark matter between ships bent and blurred even the lights of a ship's hull and masts. The more highly spread photons of a ship's light might be affected less than the concentrated bundle of a laser, but they were affected nonetheless.

Just what did Spensley mean with that? For her to come aboard his ship, *Mongoose's* number should properly precede the signal, not *All ships*.

"Is he proposing some sort of meeting, do you suppose?" Alexis asked.

"That would be my interpretation, sir," Villar said.

Alexis frowned. It was an odd time for it and would pull all of them out of position as the private ships would have to be very near for a ship's boat to safely go between them — too far and it would give those gunboats time to attack.

"Creasy, send this. Oriana's number, *All ships. Form line ahead. Interrogative*."

"Aye, sir."

Alexis caught her lower lip between her teeth and worried at it as she pondered if she'd got Spensley's meaning or was only embarrassing herself.

"*Affirmative*, sir," Creasy said a few moments later.

"Very well, then, he thinks we should all have a bit of a chat." She frowned, then shrugged — if he had some concern he wished to voice, then she'd have to hear him out. None of the other captains were under any obligation to be here, and it wouldn't do to offend him. Delaying a bit more wouldn't necessarily be a harm to them either. It would give them all a bit of time to repair what damage had been done — better than they could while under fire — and the gunboats wouldn't attack them. Not concentrated together where they could maneuver.

"Layland, come about. Put us on the starboard tack, a beam reach, and keep us there."

"Aye, sir."

That would set *Mongoose* running perpendicular to the system winds, sailing easy down the center of what passed for clear space between planetary orbits. It would also, not accidentally, allow all of the private ships to present their full broadsides to the gunboats further in-system. Even if the gunboats went off the ecliptic plane, the little fleet would have but to roll and take them under fire.

"*All ships. Form line ahead. Captains to repair on board.* Send that, Creasy."

She had to admit to a certain thrill at that. For a moment, she imagined herself a proper commodore, with a real fleet under her command and not this ragtag lot of private ships. Would that ever happen? It would mean years more in the service, of course, and she'd not be able to manage the lands on Dalthus during that time. The question of that still gnawed at her.

She loved both, but the nearly overwhelming urge to throw up a new signal once the other ships formed their line caught her a bit off guard.

Fly Engage the enemy more closely, *Creasy,* she thought, careful not to give voice to it. Set her lads and her ship against the enemy and shoulder the challenge.

Much as she loved her grandfather and her home, she loved this more — it filled some void she doubted anything else could — and that would break her grandfather's heart.

Villar caught Alexis' eye and grinned.

"Perhaps you ought to have borrowed a pennant from Skanes, sir."

FIFTY-FIVE

The captains and their first officers were all aboard and seated around Alexis' table, Spensley wasted no time in getting to his point.

"I'll not take *Oriana* back into that muck!" he yelled before the wine was even served.

Lawson nodded, while Kingston shrugged — *Osprey* was the lightest of the private ships and he appeared content to follow along with Lawson, who, for herself, was nodding along with Spensley.

"My hull and masts are at risk with every turn, it's a wonder this system was ever settled to begin with! Any sane transport captain would have run for an easier place at the very sight of it! Transport, hell, the *surveyors* should have written it off as a bad bet from the start!" He snatched his half-filled glass from beneath Isom's pour, nearly dumping the wine in the process. "This lot should give off pirating and sue the buggers who sold their ancestors the sodding place!"

"Captain Spensley," Alexis said as he paused, "perhaps something stronger — to settle your nerves? You seem ... overwrought."

Spensley slammed his glass down and waved his finger at her. "No, none of that! You'll not get me in the cups and going along with this madness again, that's what you did the first time!"

Alexis caught herself before responding. As she remembered it, Spensley had been well into his cup and excavating the bottom so that it would hold more when she'd just arrived at that meeting, so there was no cause for the man to blame her if he regretted going along now.

"Yer committed," Malcomson fairly growled, his accent thicker with irritation. "Nae sense girnin' abit it noo."

"I'm committed to nothing!" Spensley shot back. "And speak Queen's bloody English, you highlands bog-monger." It was a measure of Spensley's upset that he didn't notice the lowering of Malcomson's brows and ease off a bit. "*Oriana* is a private ship — I've letters of marque which *allow* me to seek out pirates. *Allow*. At my bloody discretion and judgment as to what I do with my own ship! This is madness now!"

Spensley looked around at the others.

Malcomson made to speak, but Alexis laid a hand on his arm and squeezed gently. Better to let the others talk this out — Malcomson was viewed too much as her man and anything he said would be suspect.

"Hours of working our way through the next shoals, then on to the next, and the same again? All the while being pricked with shot from those gunboats? And waiting for us in normal-space, what's there? The bloody *Hind*, bigger than any of us, *and* a thrice-bedamned *frigate*!" He slammed his hand down on the table. "Which of you wouldn't turn tail at sight of a frigate? Tell me true, for there's not a one of you would take the damned thing on if you came across it in your cruising!"

There was silence for a moment and Alexis knew it to be true. Even if at war and their letters of marque named the Queen's enemies as valid targets, the private ships would avoid true warships even then. There was more and safer profit in the enemy's merchant shipping than in their navy.

"This isn't an enemy frigate, though," Alexis said, hoping to convince them that this situation was quite different. "Yes, we all heard these reports that the pirates had one, but, look — where'd they get it, do you think? One of the ships from the two missing fleets, it has to be, yes? Well, this lot didn't take it from a full crew, now did they? There're these rumors of wrecks and disabled ships scattered all along the fleets' path — most broken up by the winds and shoals, but it was always certain *someone* would come across a hulk that could be saved, isn't it? That's all that's happened here — they towed her, or got her fusion plant working somehow, and brought her back here, but could they have repaired all the damage that wrecked her in the first place? Could they *crew* her and fight her, with whatever other ships they have and these gunboats too? Or merely use her presence to frighten gullible merchantmen into striking at the mere sight of her?"

"Aye," Spensley said, "but it's *you* who suggested she'd not be here in the first place. Off taking merchants, you said, with the other pirate ships, and only the gunboats here. So you were wrong about that and what's to say you're not wrong about how well she's manned, eh?"

"I think that she's even there in orbit speaks to that," Alexis said. She wasn't entirely sure herself, but it was a reasonable assertion and there was no hope for the *Hind's* crew — or of finding out if Delaine had passed through this world — unless they continued. "If that frigate were whole, if she were sound and fully crewed, she'd be here in *darkspace* with her broadside in our teeth, not sitting idle in orbit."

Pennywell was nodding and spoke for the first time.

"The images show her just sitting there along with *Hind*. In orbit and masts not even stepped. This frigate could be nothing more than a hulk —"

"Or they could be waiting to use her against us in normal-space, rather than here where the bloody thing couldn't move a bit without sticking fast!" Spensley said. "As any sensible person would do, mind you." He shook his head. "No, once we transition to normal-space, whichever of us haven't been disabled by those gunboats, we'll be heading right for the planet — right into the guns of that frigate and *Hind*. They don't need full crews for that, or anything working but the fusion plant, guns, and a few thrusters."

Alexis couldn't argue that. The defenders in orbit around a planet would have the advantage as the attackers came in, unless they could make it all the way in-system to the Lagrangian points around that planet — transitioning anywhere else, which they'd planned to do, would mean a long transit time in normal-space.

Their guns might have greater range and accuracy in normal-space, where the dark matter couldn't warp the lasers' paths, but greater range took time to cross. A ship with heavy, normal-space thrusters, like that frigate or even *Hind*, needed to move only a little bit — a ship-length or two — to avoid the shot from an approaching ship's bow or stern chasers.

Meanwhile, the defending ship could present her full broadside and bracket a much more specific target area, as the approaching ships, no matter their maneuvering, still had to *approach*.

There was an art to assaulting planets — one very different than the more familiar ship battles in *darkspace*, and one that she'd only just started learning about when the war ended.

Malcomson snorted. "Thes wee lass has taken a frigate by 'er lonesome, an' here's th' a lot ay us girnin' loch beaten dogs."

"I'm no beaten dog!" Spensley shouted.

Malcomson grinned and cracked his knuckles. "Ah can fix 'at."

"Gentlemen," Alexis broke in. A fight between the private ship captains would do no good at all, might even drive the others farther to whatever side of the debate they'd already leaned toward — and, in truth, Spensley had valid points. She'd rather they find a solution that addressed those.

"Fighting amongst ourselves will benefit no one but the pirates," she went on once she had their attention. "We made our plan of attack based on the information we had at the time. Information which we now find to be wrong — *I* was wrong," she added with a nod to Spensley. "The question, though, is what we will do about it. Captain Spensley favors retreat —" Spensley bridled at that, but Alexis pushed on. He might not like her phrasing, but that was what he proposed. "— perhaps that is wise, but I do not think so when we've come so far already. We may need to change our plan of attack, but the presence of a, likely undermanned and, as yet, unrepaired frigate does not change why we've come here."

"Th' bluddy bunsens," Malcomson said.

"Yes, the money." Alexis sighed. She'd been thinking of the rescue of the *Hind's* crew and any New London or Berry March worlds spacers held captive — captive merchant crews as well, come to that — but Malcomson had his finger on the private ships' pulse and lifeblood. "The *Hind* is still there, with her cargo and salvage fees from the Marchant Company. The gunboats, the pirate ships when they return and we can ambush them — head and gun money and cargoes, all. The naval captives, and the coin for freeing those. *And now*, what's the head and gun money for a pirate frigate, captains, when she's sitting there in orbit with her masts not even stepped?"

Lawson pursed her lips at that and Alexis could almost see the calculations. There were few enough frigates in the Navy — never enough for all the tasks they were suited for, even in peacetime — and there was no doubt a proper prize court would buy her, whichever this was, right back in to service. There'd likely not even be the most typical of delays in their decision, as the Navy would want the ship overhauled and outfitted instanter.

"We have only to alter our plan a bit," she went on. "We are still six ships, experienced and heavily crewed, against a handful of gunboats, a former merchantman, and a frigate so badly damaged in battle that she was left behind by her fleet to be taken by rabble."

She had them, she could tell, as she stopped talking and looked around the table, meeting each captain's eyes in turn. Spensley was still skeptical, but Pennywell was with her — as was Malcomson, she knew, as he was grinning like a wolf who's just sent the sheepdog off after a goose. Kingston was looking at Lawson, and her narrowed eyes and pursed lips told that she was calculating the returns already.

Alexis' tablet *pinged*, but she ignored it. It was more important to keep the mood around this table right now. If Spensley left, one of the others might as well — if that happened, the others might follow. For all that they were captains of their own ships, they did seem to follow another's lead far more than she'd have expected.

Her tablet *pinged* again and she caught Villar's eye. He nodded and stepped back to use his own tablet and see what was so urgent that their conference should be disturbed.

"Well," Spensley muttered, casting a look to Pennywell as though for confirmation of his thoughts, "there is something to the idea that they wouldn't leave a working frigate behind when they were cruising for prizes."

Pennywell nodded and looked to Lawson. "It'd do our reputations no harm, I think, to sail a lost frigate into Penduli."

Lawson nodded in agreement. "Reputation spends as well, in some circles, never mind the coin."

Alexis had been so intent on the other captains that she didn't notice Villar at her elbow until he whispered in her ear.

"Sir, the message was from Dorsett —"

"What is it then? No whispering about!" Spensley said. "I don't like secrets in conference!"

Villar looked to her and Alexis nodded permission. Dorsett was on the tactical console, so it was likely some movement of the gunboats and the other captains should be aware of that anyway.

Villar sighed and ran fingers over her table's display, changing it back to the surrounding *darkspace*, rather than the images of the ships in orbit around Erzurum they'd all been examining. It wasn't until Villar zoomed the display out to show all of Erzurum, right out to the system halo, that she saw it. There were the dots of the gunboats, all milling about to leeward of the line of private ships sailing on their beam reach — but just at the edge, making their way through the halo and into the first set of shoals, were new dots.

"It would appear the pirates have returned with prizes, sir," Villar said. "Four sloops, seven merchantmen, Dorsett believes —" Villar took a deep breath. "— and a frigate."

FIFTY-SIX

The uproar was immediate and loud.

The captains all rose to their feet, all but Alexis and Malcomson, and Spensley pounded the table.

"*Two* frigates! Why didn't we know this?" He clenched his jaw and looked around at the others. "And here we are, between the bloody pot and the cooktop!" He fixed his gaze on Alexis. "One could almost think it were planned."

Malcomson growled and half rose, but Alexis placed a hand on his arm again. He seemed to more and more be taking on the role as her protector of sorts, and she wanted none of that. She might need his aid in battle against the pirates, but not against this sort of thing.

"Captain Spensley," she said, and, though softly, it cut through the outbursts of the other captains and caused them to stop and stare. "Do you wish to rethink your words?"

Spensley slammed the table again. "We should *all* think on them. Who are you? Newcome to the Barbary and all of an instant you're leading us here? Into this trap? Why —"

"Sir —" Spensley's first officer said.

"Shut up, Wakeling, I've had enough. If the others want to follow this child, they may, but I have some questions about where she's brought us." He looked around at the others. "Do none of you find it suspicious how she turned up here and suddenly we're in this mess? She's either a fool or in league with the damned pirates herself!"

Alexis watched Spensley, her eyes narrowing. She was angry, but also calculating the looks of the other captains. Pennywell and Lawson appeared to be considering Spensley's words. If their force broke now, many of them would likely be doomed. But there was little she could say to offset Spensley's accusations — one couldn't prove a negative, after all.

Lawson looked from Spensley to Alexis. "Will you leave that lie there unanswered?"

"Captain Spensley is clearly overwrought," Alexis said. "As we all are, I'm sure, by this new development. I'm certain he doesn't mean to —"

"Don't mistake what I mean," Spensley interrupted. "I'll speak it plainly. You got us drunk and agreeing to this — showed up late so we were well into our cups. Now we're here, drawn midway in-system, too far in to flee, with all those gunboats to leeward and a bloody *fleet* to windward — it's all too pat and I name *you* in league with them!"

Alexis scanned the others' faces. They didn't show agreement, but neither did they seem to discount Spensley's accusation. Even Malcomson was giving her a speculative look, as though wondering at her reaction to Spensley's words.

No, there was only one thing these captains might accept when such words were said, and she hoped her own desire for it wasn't coloring her decision.

"Mister Villar?"

"Sir?"

"May I impose upon you in this matter?"

Villar looked at her questioningly for a moment, then raised his brows and cocked his head at Spensley. The other captains and their officers were dead silent, seeing what Spensley couldn't through his own anger.

"Enquire of Captain Spensley on his desire for a meeting, if you will."

Villar looked as though he might question her, then, "Indeed, sir."

Alexis locked her eyes on Spensley, who seemed to just now be realizing that he might have overstepped. Alexis had settled into that bit of calm space she felt when the battle was inevitable, but not quite arrived. Care and thought of the approaching pirates disappeared for a moment, leaving her at peace. Now might not be the best time to fight a duel, but she felt Spensley was lost to her force in any case — whatever she and the others might decide, he would likely take *Oriana* and flee as best he could.

He'd doom himself and his ship by doing so, though they had little greater chance staying together in the face of such a force.

Damned if I'll meet my end leaving a man who's called me a betrayer still breathing.

"Sir," Villar said to Spensley, "do you desire a meeting with my principle? Will you name a man to speak for you?" He glanced significantly at Spensley's first officer who glanced away.

"What?" Spensley said. "Now? Are you mad?"

Alexis sighed. There was that bloody question again, and she was beginning to wonder.

"We are, indeed, tossed into the fire here, Captain Spensley," she said. "If *Mongoose* is to be taken by this lot and myself killed or made captive — I should desire to finish as much of my business as I may."

Spensley looked around at the others.

Alexis saw little support for him there, but perhaps he saw something different — or wasn't a man to back down even in the face of no support.

His eyes narrowed.

"You think I'll back down to a strutting child?" He stood straight and gestured at his first officer. "Wakeling! Deal with the arrangements for this meeting — I'll be in our boat, preparing."

With that, he turned and left Alexis' compartment. His first officer, Wakeling, mumbled something Alexis couldn't catch and then nodded to Villar. The two of them retired to a corner of Alexis' compartment for a moment.

"Captains," Alexis said, returning her attention to the table's plot and the enemy ships. "Shall we return to our plans?"

Malcomson drained his glass and waved it at Isom.

"An' Ah was afraid this meetin' would be borin'."

MONGOOSE'S BERTHING area was already cleared of loose items, the ship being at quarters. All of the bunks were folded to the bulkheads and the crew's chests were struck down into the hold.

Had Spensley chosen pistols of some sort, they might have had to use the gun deck, with its open space that ran nearly the full length of the ship, but for the chosen swords the berthing area would work well.

Bulkheads lined two sides of the space, but it opened fore and aft — which allowed the crowd of watchers to close in. This left the space, perhaps, five meters by three meters, with bulkheads along the longer sides and the bodies of the watchers crowding the shorter.

One crowd was fronted by the other captains and their first officers, and Alexis allowed Spensley to have that end of the space — she doubted he'd be comfortable beginning with her crew crowded at his back.

She'd removed her vacsuit for the occasion and dressed in her captain's garb, which, she thought, accounted for the grins and nods of approval she got from the crew as they made a lane for her to make her way through them — at least the outfit was what she attributed the whistle or two she heard from the crowd to.

That would never have happened on a Naval ship — though she'd not be fighting a duel or dressed as she was on one, either.

It did, though, bolster her spirits in an odd way.

On a station or planet, from strangers, it would certainly have been unwelcome, but here, from her lads, it was very different, and she realized she'd added a bit of a cocked hip to her stance that was quite unlike her.

She glanced down at herself and suppressed a grin.

Perhaps the something is catching.

Across the open space, Spensley stood with Wakeling, and behind them the other captains, save Malcomson — more of *Mongoose's* crew behind them, but not crowding. Malcomson waited with Villar on her side.

Villar leaned close as she reached the front of the crowd.

"Do you think this wise, sir? Perhaps an accommodation given the circumstances?"

"Is Captain Spensley prepared to withdraw his accusations?"

"No, sir, but —"

"Mister Villar, this is not merely about his accusations, though I take them to heart. Did you see the other captains when Spensley spoke?"

Villar shook his head. "Not to speak of, I suppose — I was listening to him."

"As were they. If Spensley sticks to his accusations and withdraws *Oriana*, it's possible either Pennywell or Lawson will as well. If one of them does, then both of them will — do you see? It's like the gundeck in action when one man breaks — should he be successful, not stopped and given heart by an officer, or stopped with more force by a marine at the hatch, then another will go after him. And another and another — and then comes the rout.

"First Spensley and *Oriana*. Then Pennywell, I think, would be next, and after him Lawson would see no profit in staying with us. Kingston will follow Lawson, no doubt of that, and so our entire force will be broken up."

"Ah note ye make nae mention ay me," Malcomson said.

Alexis regarded him for a moment, then grinned. "You'll be where you think you can find the best fight, won't you?"

Malcomson shrugged. "Transparent as all 'at, am Ah?"

Alexis laid a hand on his arm. "Reliable, I'd say."

Malcomson laughed.

"What they don't understand," Alexis continued, "as they've never worked as a fleet before, is what we're facing here. Those gunboats coordinate their attacks. The newly arrived ships as well. Other than Lawson and Kingston who've worked together a bit, and Malcomson and I, the other captains have worked singly always. They're thinking of their odds to escape, which might be good — for one. Most of the others, though, will be overwhelmed and outnumbered. Each of these captains, Spensley especially, thinks they'll be the one and cares not a whit for the others."

Villar frowned. "I wouldn't think we have that great a chance together, either."

Alexis shrugged. "We don't, I agree. We're outnumbered and outgunned, facing a superior force who's used to working together. But we have a better chance for more of us if we stay together."

"So you're doing this to keep the force together?"

"And because the smirking bastard named me betrayer." Alexis shrugged. "There's a good chance *Mongoose* will be taken by this lot within the next few days — I'll not go to my fate hearing that and not responding."

Malcomson laughed again. "That's a proper Sheehy lass!"

"I see," Villar said, then, "Sir, if this should go poorly —"

"You have *Mongoose*," Alexis said. She'd thought of that, and what she should order Villar to do, but if this did go poorly then her cares would be over — Villar would have his own, not least of which would be ensuring that he returned to see Marie again. Whatever her desires in getting to Erzurum and finding out Delaine's fate, Villar would have to make his own choices. "I trust your judgment Whitley, and the ship will be yours. Do as you think best in the circumstances you face."

"Aye, sir."

FIFTY-SEVEN

There were more hoots from the watching crew as Alexis
stripped her tight stays off, but she put a stop to that with
pointed look. No sense letting the lads think they could go
quite too far with their fun. Spensley had chosen blades, possibly
thinking that Alexis' slight form would make her more skilled with
firearms. The stays themselves did offer some protection against his
blade, but it was also rather form-fitting. Without it, the loose blouse
offered fewer hints at the target beneath.

She kept the boots. They were well-made and a bit of scuffing
against the deck proved to her they'd grip well enough to serve.

The hat was a different story and she made to remove that too,
but hesitated. It sat firmly, without obstructing her vision, and might
prove a distraction to Spensley, what with its wide brim and dancing
feather. She kept it on, reasoning that she could always doff it if
necessary.

Let Spensley think her a bit foppish and underestimate her more.

Villar and Wakeling were conferring at the center of the open
space. Spensley was *swishing* his blade through the air in preparation. He'd sent back to his ship for it, as he had only a boarding

cutlass at his hip through the action. That alone gave Alexis a bit of a pause about this fight, for the blade he bore now was clearly for duels, not an action.

It was longer, lighter, and thinner than would be useful in an action with no gravity and the need to hack through thick vacsuits. It was the blade of a man skilled in its use for other purposes than battle.

Alexis' blade worked well for her in both battle and against a single opponent, but it was less-suited for both than others. Longer and lighter than a cutlass, but shorter and heavier than a blade like Spensley's — it suited her frame and build, but offered her little else in advantage.

Across the open space, Spensley rolled his shoulders, then *swished* his blade through the air again. Alexis did the same, ensuring she could move freely and nothing would bind. Her lads, by accident or design, had chosen well in her costume, at least. Spensley kept his waistcoat on, which seemed odd, as it had the same effect as her stays would — to outline his form and restrict his movement somewhat.

Their seconds, Villar and Wakeling, had agreed on the *Mongoose* as the site of the duel in the interest of time, though it was anything but neutral, and on Pennywell as the master of the field, in the absence of any truly neutral party.

Pennywell made his way to the open space between them and cleared his throat, gesturing for Villar and Wakeling to join him.

"Captains," he said, "are you intent upon your course?"

There was more to it that should have been said and asked to follow the proper code, but no one wanted to waste any more time than was needed, not with a fleet of pirate ships bearing down on them.

"Is an apology to my principal in the offing?" Villar asked, answering for Alexis so she might concentrate on preparing.

Wakeling shook his head. Alexis thought he looked a little sad to do so. "There is not."

Villar shrugged, turned, and walked back to Alexis. "Then

Captain Spensley may apologize to God in a moment for the false witness."

Alexis raised an eyebrow.

"'Apologize to God?'" she asked. Villar's face went sheepish and Alexis clapped a hand on his shoulder. "It did have a certain something."

Villar smiled and made to speak, but then gave a short nod to Alexis' other side where Dockett had elbowed his way through the crowd and looked to get her attention. She couldn't think what the bosun might have to say at such a time.

"Yes, Mister Dockett?"

"Ah, sir, but I wanted to let you know the lads are behind you and certain you'll take the bugger down."

Alexis smiled. "Thank you, Mister Dockett. Do tell the lads I appreciate their confidence."

"Aye, sir." Dockett glanced over at Spensley and licked his lips. "It's only, sir, that if you were to take the bugger down ... *slowly*, as it were, then it would properly thank the lads, I think."

Alexis frowned. "What do you mean?"

Dockett's face turned red. "Well, I hate to mention it, sir — to bother you at a time like this — but it's that there's five other ships and, well, coordinating things takes time."

"'Things,' Mister Dockett?"

"The signals, sir."

"What signals?"

"To broadcast the fight, sir." He smiled. "It's Creasy what worked it out. He's set a code, see, with numbers for you and Captain Spensley there, and then all the different parts — where a body might be cut and poked, you understand. I seen him send a test and it'll be a right proper description, it will. The other crews'll think it's good as being here."

"I see." Alexis sighed. Well, she shouldn't have expected that the crews of the other ships would be less interested in the duel than her own. If they were in normal-space it would have been broadcast as video, and planetside the field would have been crowded with them all to observe first hand. She couldn't fault Creasy for his efforts, much as she might like to.

Then she frowned, wondering at Dockett's other words.

"What does that have to do with my being slow about it?"

Dockett cleared his throat. "Ah, sir, but it's only that, what with how quick the thing's been set up and then the signals between ships taking so long and Creasy's descriptions, fine as they may be, needing to be sent ... well, it takes a bit for a man to process it all and make his predictions, you see?"

Alexis thought she did. "'Predictions', Mister Dockett?"

"Aye, sir." Dockett nodded. "And there's some won't make a prediction until after the fight's started, so, see, there's time for them to see how it goes and time for it to be made clear to a man with a ... different sort of prediction, you see?"

"There's a bloody book on this duel?" Alexis asked. "And being run through our signals?"

Dockett shook his head. "Oh, no, sir." He shrugged. "There's six. Each ship has its own book, of course. It's the laying-off to the other ships that takes the time, see?"

Alexis closed her eyes and hung her head, but Dockett went on.

"Then there's the side bets — those over the winner, you understand?" He began ticking on his fingers. "First blood — our lads have you drawing it, sir, so we have to lay-off to *Oriana* or there'd be no coin on the other bugger at all. Then there's how many bloodings before it's over." He frowned and looked away, thinking. "There's disarming and *where* you're each blooded, of course."

Dockett stopped and leaned close, whispering, "If you were to do that flying, spinny, round-the-neck thing, as you did to Askins when you was showin' him those things, then our lads'll clean the others out — odds on that're bloody staggering, sir."

"Mister Dockett, are you suggesting this duel be *fixed*?"

"Oh, no, sir!" Dockett said, his face full of outrage. "Never that."

He glanced around then leaned close and whispered again. "Only that you might, you know, *poke* the bugger a time or two first."

ALEXIS AND SPENSLEY met Pennywell at the center of the open space.

Pennywell looked between the two of them, silent for a moment, and Alexis could tell what he was thinking.

Spensley was nearly half a meter taller than she was, as well as being heavier. He had several centimeters' reach on her, even without the longer blade.

Pennywell shrugged. "I'm sorry, Carew. I'll see it's as fair as I may, at least."

Alexis nodded while Spensley snorted.

"Can we get on with this, so that I might depart this bloody system?" Spensley asked.

"Captains," Pennywell said, then stepped back, "begin."

FIFTY-EIGHT

Alexis' hand went numb for a moment at the first blow, as Spensley batted her blade aside with more force than she expected. Apparently the man had no intention of feeling out her speed and strength as most opponents might, but was going for an immediate win. That spoke of an assumption that she was somehow unworthy of his concern.

She stepped back, half-hopping to avoid Spensley's backswing, and returned her blade to guard her. Spensley pressed forward, driving her back again and again.

Alexis allowed him to bat her blade aside each time, though controlling the force better than the first exchange, and when her hand recovered, she twisted her wrist just enough so that Spensley's blow missed.

She darted her own blade at him, but her reach was short and he was able to dance back before the tip could bloody his forearm.

Spensley backed two steps farther, *swishing* his blade and narrowing his eyes.

Alexis pursued him and this time he was less aggressive, feeling out her skill and strength.

She met his new tentativeness with her own for a few blows, then made her own attacks, but each blow was met with Spensley's blade, either blocked or turned aside, until, as though by some agreement, they both stepped back a bit and eyed the other.

Three more exchanges had as little effect, and then came first blood.

Alexis twisted her sword around a blow from Spensley's and darted forward, but the man was even quicker than she'd thought him and the tip of his blade found her thigh even as her own found his forearm. They both stepped back even before Pennywell could call "*Hold!*" and thrust his arm up.

"Captain Carew, is honor satisfied?"

"I've heard no apology," she said.

"And will not!" Spensley called back.

Alexis hoped her own voice was as steady as his, for the man didn't seem to be breathing as heavily as she was trying not to. She began to wonder if she'd misjudged things — no, she was certain she'd misjudged Spensley, as he was a far better fighter than she expected, but a quick glance at the other captains firmed her resolve. She had to keep them with her, at least, even at the loss of Spensley, for he and his ship were already lost. If the others broke off their force as well, then many of them were doomed.

Far more than just herself.

If she were to fall, Villar would serve to give *Mongoose* and her crew a chance to escape, but the chance was better if their force was stronger and working together, rather than scattered.

"There is no satisfaction," Alexis said.

Pennywell shrugged. "Very well. Continue then."

Alexis had taken the brief interlude of Pennywell's questioning to test her leg. It hurt, but the wound didn't seem deep. It was on the outside, away from the big arteries, and the tight leggings of her outfit, though cut, still pressed firmly against her, keeping the wound closed. She realized that her crew must have thought of that, as well as the style, in selecting it, and she smiled.

"Smile while you can, Carew," Spensley muttered, advancing on her.

He'd wiped his forearm clean, but fresh blood was oozing from the shallow cut.

The next series of blows almost ended things.

Spensley made much the same move as he had in their last, and Alexis made to pink his arm again, but without so much of a lunge as before. Spensley, though, was expecting that and his own return was at her belly.

Alexis twisted and Spensley's blade went through her loose blouse like paper, missing her flesh by so little that she could swear she felt it touch her side.

Pennywell looked to stop the fight again, thinking her struck, but there was no blood and Alexis spun away and back.

The sweat on Spensley's face mirrored what she felt on her own, and the ship's cold air chilled her. It crept through the rent in her blouse and hit her side like the steel she'd just avoided.

Another ringing exchange, this time with Alexis meeting and turning Spensley's blows with more force than she had before. She wanted him to suspect he'd misjudged her strength and speed as much as she'd misjudged him, and then, when she saw the realization on his face and the moment's concern of what else he might have misjudged and by how much, she made her own real attack.

Her blade suddenly didn't meet his. Instead she twisted to avoid it and lunged forward, not for his arm or body, but for his face.

Time seemed to slow. Her lunge was quick, but overextended. Spensley's eyes widened as the tip of her blade came straight for them. He jerked his head back, and Alexis saw his expression turn to fear as he realized that he, himself, was just as overextended, with too much weight on his foreleg to avoid the thrust.

Or would be, save for his opponent's shorter sword.

The tip of Alexis' blade *snicked* past his face. She knew that she'd have had him if she'd committed just a bit more, but she hadn't. She'd held back just enough to recover from her lunge and back outside the sweeping arc of the return of Spensley's blade.

She was torn between disappointment at not reaching him and the knowledge that doing so would have doomed her as well. That thought was on Spensley's face, she saw, as he came to the same conclusion and she set her own face in determination. Let him see that she might not make that choice a second time — that she was set on his destruction, no matter the cost.

It was the same message one sent an enemy captain when the time for clever maneuvering was done and she set her ship alongside.

She saw that Spensley understood, and he moved, driving forward even as she made to meet him.

This time the blows were furious and with more than swords. Their blades met with a *clang* and bound together between bodies pressed tight.

Spensley's off-hand struck her head a glancing blow, even as her knee came up. He twisted to avoid the knee to his groin, which sent her to bring her boot heel down on his foot as Spensley used his weight to shove her off balance. Shoves, kicks, knees, elbows, all flew between them, as though the blades were forgotten for a time. Alexis used every bit of what she'd learned from the Marines to avoid being overpowered by Spensley's weight, and every bit of nastiness they'd ever shown her to get a gouge or poke in at the right spot.

In the end, her size gave her away.

Spensley took it all, though not without his own grunts of pain, and finally forced her off balance.

Alexis stumbled backward, her sword flung from her grasp by a last, clever twist of Spensley's blade, and she fell to the deck. Her training helped her absorb most of the impact, so it was the sound of her sword clattering against the port bulkhead that drove the air from her lungs in a gasp of despair.

Time seemed to slow as she scrambled to her feet, with everything appearing to move far more slowly than she knew it was.

Spensley was closing the distance between them. Her sword was too far away for her to reach it in time, and doing so would expose her side to his coming strike.

He drew his sword back to thrust and without thought Alexis moved toward him. If she could get inside the tip of the blade, then she might take a cut, but could still grapple with him — that might give her a chance.

Before she could think why, her hand went to her head and grasped the brim of her hat. The silly thing, wide-brimmed with the ridiculous feather, was no weapon, but it might serve to distract him. She waved it toward him in a sweeping arc and, remarkably, Spensley stopped his rush. He leaned back, body tilted awkwardly and grimaced in anticipated pain as the very tip of the feather fluttered across his face.

Why he'd reacted so — whether he thought the feather was more than it was or simply feared that Alexis had some other trick in mind — she didn't know, but neither did she ponder it too long. She flung the full hat at Spensley's face even as she leapt for her sword, thoughts of grappling forgotten in the instant's chance to re-arm herself.

Sword in hand, breath knocked out of her as her roll to retrieve it was stopped short by the bulkhead, she clambered to her feet with her back to it.

Spensley spared only a moment to blink and realize his face was unmarked, then leapt for her again, blade outstretched.

Alexis twisted, smacked his blade with her own, and extended hers as she pushed off the wall.

Pain lanced her side as Spensley's blade slid along her ribs, parting flesh. The grating of steel on bone seemed to fill her body, vibrating through her, even as her own caught Spensley under the jaw.

Spensley's own momentum drove him onto it. His initial spasm away caused it to exit through his mouth, then the edge caught his face, raking at his cheek and eye as he thrashed.

Alexis' sword was torn from her grasp even as Spensley dropped his.

The man turned away, grasping first at his face, then at the blade. Blood flowed from both face and hands as he tried to pull the blade free and cut his hands to the bone as well, all the time giving voice to a horrifying howl of agony.

Alexis, through those horrible moments, grasped her side. The cut was bleeding and painful, but hadn't pierced her ribs. She doubled over, more to catch her breath as the fight's exertion caught up with her than from the pain.

Around them, the crew and other watchers were silent, staring on as Spensley fell to the deck, still writhing and howling from the pain of the blade through his face. Blood pooled around him, then spattered as he thrashed.

"You need to finish this, Carew," Pennywell said, coming to her side. "If you're able."

Alexis nodded. She picked up Spensley's blade and made her way toward him.

She could see that nearly everyone was watching her, though some had their eyes fixed on Spensley. Every movement, every cry, caused more damage to the man.

Pennywell winced at the sight. "It'll be a kindness, Carew," he said.

Alexis laid her — Spensley's — blade against the man's throat. Her vision blurred a bit, shadows creeping in from the edges, and a chill went through her. Her leg, the one Spensley'd pinked, went weak and she had to shift her weight before she fell to the deck beside him. It might be that she was injured worse than she'd thought. Pain from both her leg and side washed over her.

She raised the blade from Spensley's throat, wondering that the man's thrashing about hadn't slit it for her while she stood there.

"Mister Wakeling," she called, though it was an effort to be heard over Spensley's screams. "Fetch your surgeon and see your captain back to *Oriana*." She tossed Spensley's blade to the deck. "We're done here. You may take *Oriana* and leave if you wish, but alone and separate we'll be picked off one by one by those pirates." She met the gaze of each of the other captains in turn. "The rest of you, as well. We've enough of a fight in store for us without doing it amongst ourselves, so those of you who are with me will meet in my cabin in twenty minutes' time."

She forced herself to straighten. That pulled at her side and made breathing harder, then forced a step from her injured leg — then another, and another, though each became more difficult than the last.

Flashes of images made it through her rapidly blurring vision. The other captains, faces blank and calculating for the most part. Her crew cheering, though here and there she saw a more sober face and wondered if some had bet against her. Dockett, his face colored red as he seemed to be arguing with Isom and Nabb, both whom wore amused looks — but she had no time for that.

She strode, as nearly as she was able, aft toward her cabin, and toward the other private ship captains at the fore of that crowd, keeping her eyes on them the entire time.

"For those of you who wish to flee, you may get your cowardly arses off my ship."

She took another step, then stopped.

"And Mister Villar?"

"Aye, sir?"

"Be sure to retrieve my sword before Spensley makes off with it, will you?"

FIFTY-NINE

"Will he live, do you think?" Alexis asked.

Mongoose's surgeon, Merriwether, looked up from his work on her leg.

She was flat on her cot in nothing but her bloodstained under-things as the man worked. First on her leg, for that was the worst of it, despite her not having felt so during the fight. Her outfit was in a ruined heap — soaked in blood, both hers and more than a few spurts from Spensley's thrashing about — and in tatters. There was more than one cut to both her clothes and body that she didn't remember getting, though her leg and side were certainly the worst of it, and then Merriwether and his loblolly boys had set to cutting what remained off her.

"This would go easier if you'd come to the sick berth," Merri-wether muttered. "Those stretchy trousers did a fine job of holding the bits of you together, but this one's deep."

Indeed it was. Alexis swallowed heavily as she saw just how deep. She couldn't feel the pain from it, not with the anesthetic Merriwether'd applied — couldn't feel her leg at all, come to that. It was as though her whole leg from the thigh down belonged to someone else. Someone with a large, yawning slice in their flesh, as though a butcher'd set his mind to boning the meat.

"If I won't die from doing it here, it's best the others think I'm not too badly hurt."

Merriwether grunted. "You'll not die and you're *not* too badly hurt. So you can put on your show for the others with no worries."

Alexis swallowed hard as the surgeon sopped up a bit more of the blood that was flowing far too easily for her taste and pressed the wound closed.

"Give the sealant an hour before you go jumping about on it again, will you?" Merriwether said. "And easy as you can for three days. It's going to ache — if you feel a sharp pain, then you're tearing something apart again, so stop it."

He sprayed something on the wound, which was now reduced to a thin, red line with coating of clear paste over it.

"The tearing part would be bad, if you were wondering," he said. "Let's see to your side there."

He moved her hand from where she held a thick wad of blood-stained cloth to her side and tossed that to one of his assistants. There the numbing was more localized and she could feel the cold over-spray as he first spread the wound and sprayed on several liquids from his kit, then closed it and sprayed on another.

"That'll offset the coagulant and prevent infection," he said after one. "Get the blood flowing again, now that I can seal it. You'll want a laser treatment every few days to accelerate the healing."

Alexis nodded. "You didn't answer — whether you think Spensley will live?"

"I didn't treat him," Merriwether said, "so I can't rightly say. I expect he will, though. The blade went through his lower jaw and out his mouth, so none of the damage was what I'd call life-threatening. It'll likely seal up fine, but he'll have scars until he can reach somewhere to reconstruct things." He frowned. "His tongue and eye'll have to wait until then as well, unless his ship has better facilities than I'd expect."

Alexis winced.

"That's that, then," Merriwether said, closing his kit and rising. "I'd tell you to stay in your cot 'til next watch, but that won't happen, will it?"

"No." Alexis was already rising. "The other captains will want to meet and we have pirates coming closer every moment." She swung her numbed leg over the cot's edge and her foot *thumped* heavily to the deck. It seemed she had no control over her leg at all below her wound.

"That'll leave a bruise," Merriwether muttered.

He shook his head in resignation and left, replaced at her side by Isom who carried fresh clothing.

Alexis flushed as he had to help her change her bloodstained underthings — they were used to living in close proximity aboard ship, not *this* close — but Isom seemed to take it in stride. He'd brought her an old ship's jumpsuit from her time on *Nightingale*, rather than anything from home. That went on easier – with her dead leg and being unable to raise her arms too high for fear of stretching the cut in her side – than the denim trousers from home or the other pair of tight leggings.

"Thank you," Alexis said once she was dressed and standing, one arm around Isom's shoulders as she hopped toward her table.

"Of course, sir. I'll get the bloodied things cleared up quick as I can, but the other captains are waiting."

"I'm sure."

She settled into her chair and scanned the plot displayed on her tabletop.

Things were not so very different than she imagined. The oncoming pirates had spread out, working their way through the shoals in several different places, all the better to cut off any escaping ships. She'd expected that — and that their travels through the shoals would be quicker than any of Alexis' forces had been able to accomplish. They knew *darkspace* around their system, after all, and would have all the best paths marked on their charts and updated as they changed.

The gunboats had spread out too and were also making their way through the shoals inward of the private ships, which cut off most flight in that direction.

A quick look at the prevailing winds told her that none of the ships — perhaps *Mongoose*, which she thought to be the fastest, but still unlikely — would be able to get past the farthest of either group. They'd do no better than to become bogged down in an engagement at the very edges and then be caught up by the rest of the pirates.

As a group, some might make it past, but that would mean abandoning their engaged fellows. Or counting on being able to disable or destroy the farthest enemy ships without any of their own being similarly struck.

Her hatch opened and Isom ushered in the other captains and their officers — all except Spensley and Wakeling, of course.

They settled themselves, each scanning her tabletop plot as she had and she could see the same conclusions coming to them. Their faces sobered more.

"This is a fine pickle," Lawson muttered, her mouth twisting in a wry grin.

"Indeed," Kingston agreed. He pulled out his tablet and began tapping at it.

Malcomson leaned forward, causing his chair to creak — something Alexis had never heard of from the sturdy, ship-built thing. "Buggered guid an' stoaner."

"Buggered good and hard at the start," Alexis agreed. "Even if we'd scattered or stayed together to flee when they arrived, we'd be facing the same."

The others nodded.

Kingston tapped the tabletop in several places.

"Here, here, here, and here would be the farthest we'd have got as a group," he said, glancing at his tablet. "The fastest of us would have got here." He tapped the table again.

They could also see that none of those places would have done well enough to avoid engagement with the oncoming ships. The new arrivals had the advantage of being outsystem, with the wind gauge and better knowledge of the shoals.

"We're trapped," Pennywell muttered, then met Alexis' eyes. "Not that I'm accusing anyone, mind you."

"Only a body hin' tae dae when yoo're trapped," Malcomson said, his accent thicker.

The others stared at him for a moment.

Little Mal, his first officer, sighed. "There's only one thing to do when you're trapped," he explained.

"What's that?"

"I'm not chewing an arm off," Lawson said. "Unless it's Spensley's arm, at least."

"*Oriana* hasn't left yet," Pennywell noted, pointedly ignoring Malcomson, with a glance at the plot.

Indeed, *Oriana* was still sailing along with the rest of them.

Lawson tapped her tablet. "Do you suppose Wakeling's had a change of heart and intends to stay? There've been no signals since they returned to their ship."

"It will depend on Spensley's time to recover himself, I think," Pennywell said. "Wakeling might see the sense of it." He met Alexis' eye. "I'll admit I wondered at whether we should all go our own ways, myself, but I've run some simulations and you were right from the start — the pirates would have picked us off one by one."

Kingston sighed. "So, we've five ships against twelve, then the gunboats. What do we do?"

"Soond th' bags an' gang reit at them."

"No," Pennywell said. "We're outnumbered in ships and men, both. Going right at them will only get us killed the quicker."

"And keep your bloody bags on your own ship," Lawson said. "I'll have none of that caterwauling aboard *Scorpion*."

Malcomson sighed and looked down at the table, shaking his head.

Alexis laid a hand on his thick forearm. "You may send a piper aboard *Mongoose*, if you like, it may — Mister Villar, are you quite all right?"

Villar stopped shaking his head in a rapid, narrow arc and caught Malcomson and Little Mal glaring at him. "No, sir, nothing."

Alexis studied the plot then tapped it a few times to display what they knew of normal-space within Erzurum — merely the planets in their orbits and the pair of ships around the inhabited planet, along with a few other gunboats spotted by their one, brief glimpse into normal-space. She brought that up in overlay of the *darkspace* plot.

"Go right at them," she said.

"Told you it was contagious," Kingston whispered to Lawson.

SIXTY

"Look," Alexis said. "Their fleet outnumbers and outmans us here in *darkspace*, but not a thing's changed about our original plan. There's still only *Hind* and the frigate guarding Erzurum itself."

"Aye, a frigate we didn't think would be there when we started," Pennywell said.

Alexis nodded agreement, but tapped the other frigate's icon on the *darkspace* plot.

"This one's appearance makes it even more likely that the one in orbit isn't fully functional or manned. If it were, then they'd have had it off collecting prizes, wouldn't they?" She looked around the table, catching each pair of eyes in turn.

"Are we all agreed that if we attempt to flee separately in *darkspace* we'll each be caught?"

She waited for them to nod.

"And if we attempt to fight our way out as one force, we're likely to lose as well?"

More nods.

Alexis tapped Erzurum's habitable planet on the plot.

"Then our original plan stands. We take Erzurum." She nodded to Malcomson. "Go right at them, bags caterwauling —"

"Not on *Scorpion*."

"— and take their base. Once in orbit around Erzurum, *we* hold the ground they want and they must come to us. Facing our broadsides, and only being able to respond with their chasers."

The others stared at the plot, Pennywell tapping at his tablet the whole time.

Malcomson clapped her on the shoulder.

"It's a Sheehy plan, true. Yer a credit tae yer clan."

"It's madness," Lawson muttered.

Pennywell shrugged. "No more so than any other."

"And how do we get to the Lagrange points?" Lawson tapped the plot. "We'll still have to get past the gunboats, and through these shoals, then the next — all with that frigate and the other ships chasing up our skirts."

Alexis shook her head. "We won't transition there — we'd never make it through the shoals. The pirates know the shoals better, they'd have their ships on the other side before us and pound us to pieces from both ends." She pointed to the plot quite near their ships. "We'll transition here."

Malcomson leaned over to whisper, "Aam nae likin' thes plan, lass."

"That gas giant's L2? True madness!" Lawson said. "We'll be days in normal-space before reaching the planet!"

"A week," Pennywell said, not looking up from his tablet. "And that's assuming all your ships can maintain *Gallion's* speed in normal-space."

"A bit less," Kingston added, "as *Osprey's* compensators are smaller, but not so much as to make a difference."

The others nodded agreement. Their ships were never meant to do much more in normal-space than transition and make their way from a Lagrangian point to planetary orbit. The normal-space engine mass and shielding to accelerate and maintain any greater speed simply wasn't worth hauling around *darkspace*.

"Longer," Alexis said.

Pennywell raised an eyebrow. "Really? I'd have expected your *Mongoose* to be faster."

"We won't be making a least-time course," Alexis said. "If we do that, they'll simply sail straight to Erzurum in *darkspace*, and we'll be facing all their broadsides as we come in."

She stood so that she could reach all around her table and traced a glowing route that zigged and zagged toward each planet in turn.

"It'll drive 'em a bampot," Malcomson said with a grin.

Lawson frowned, then nodded.

"What?" Pennywell asked. "Other than wasting —" He consulted his tablet. "— nearly a fortnight more?"

"Not this exact course," Alexis said, "we'll have to figure that, but close. We transition to normal-space, then head for a planet — *not* Erzurum, the habitable planet, just yet. The pirates will think we plan to use Lagrangian points there to return to *darkspace* well away from their fleet in an attempt to escape."

Now Pennywell nodded as well.

"They'll have to send their own ships to cover it and intercept us there — they can reach it quicker in *darkspace* than we can in normal, afterall."

Alexis nodded.

"Meanwhile, we veer off toward yet another planet and possible transition points," she said, tracing her line.

"All the while, they have to watch us in normal-space, transition back to *darkspace*, and pass our course changes along — might even have to set some ships to hanging about in between as relays for their signals." Alexis tapped some places on the plot where she was certain the shoals would interfere with a signal being seen through it, as well as where the distance between planets would be too great without such a relay. "So much dark matter will play havoc with their lights."

Malcomson stood and leaned his massive form over the plot,

causing the others to lean away in their chairs. He stabbed his finger on the course Alexis had painted, then drew four new lines from it, each snaking from planet to planet as Alexis' original did, but all different, then he sat back and grinned.

Alexis grinned as well, as she thought about what *that* would do to the pirates and their attempts to catch the private ships.

If they each took a different course in normal-space, the pirates would have five times as many sets of transition points to be concerned over. They'd have to split their own forces even more.

"We're still weaker individually," Pennywell said, "that doesn't change."

"They'll hae tae catch us first."

Alexis nodded and Lawson with her.

"Here in *darkspace*, they have the wind gauge and better knowledge of the shoals. The gunboats can sail right through bits of the shoal that would rip *Mongoose's* keel right off and stick her fast." She cleared the plot of all but normal-space. "In normal-space, they face the same limitations we do with our engines and shielding — likely more, as they're mostly converted merchantmen."

Lawson nodded. "The frigates will be the only ones faster than us in normal-space, and there're but two of them, one if we're right about the one in orbit not being functional."

"Einstein wept, but Newton was a right bastard," Kingston said, echoing the motto of New London's Darkspace Research Institute, and the caveat its students had tacked on.

Darkspace might defy the laws of physics and drive some nearly mad, what with its expanding and contracting distances and the very nature of its winds, but normal-space was as rigidly inflexible to those laws as *darkspace* was contrary.

Once transitioned, the pirates, if they chose to pursue one of the private ships, would be bound by those same laws — the same limits on acceleration, speed, and maneuvering that applied to the private ships would apply to the pirates.

In *darkspace*, a ship with the wind-gauge, or one rigged more efficiently for a given point of sail — or even one whose captain or crew set those sails just a bit better — might catch up to another. In normal-space the conditions were different and the ship which maneuvered first — the one avoiding an action — could lead the pursuer a merry chase for very nearly as long as they liked.

"Sweet Dark, but they'll be exhausted," Kingston muttered.

Alexis frowned, then smiled as she understood and agreed.

In normal-space, the massive crews of the private ships would be idle, with no sails to trim or set. The conventional drive would simply push them along without the effort of sailing in *darkspace*. The pirates, on the other hand, would have to work those sails hard, flitting from Lagrangian point to point and back again in their efforts to intercept Alexis and the others.

The pirate crews would all be standing watch-and-watch the whole time, while Alexis' and the others' would be well-fed and rested when they finally met in an action.

Alexis looked around and saw that the others were all nodding slightly with thoughtful frowns.

Malcomson stood again and set his fingers on the lines he'd drawn, then drew them in toward Erzurum's habitable planet with a mighty clap.

"An' then reit at 'em."

"Aye," Alexis said. "We spread them out, tire them, wear them out — then right at them."

The frowns turned to grins.

"It's decided, then?" she asked. "Good, then let's be about it."

SIXTY-ONE

The private ships made for the transition point in line ahead, which put *Mongoose*, as the titular flagship, at the rear.

The surprise was *Oriana*, which stayed in line, following Alexis' signals as closely as any other. They'd flown, briefly, a signal, *Interrogatory*, perhaps wishing to know the results of the conference, which were more than either Alexis or Creasy could figure to communicate with their limited signals.

In reply, Alexis had simply had Creasy send *Oriana's* number and a repeat of her last signal — *Form line ahead. Make for transition.*

Whether it was Wakeling or Spensley in command, she didn't know — nor did she, mostly, care. They could make their own way or come along with the rest, as they wished, and she'd fill them in on the plan once they were all in normal-space and a proper communications laser could be laid between their ships.

One by one, the other ships made their way into the Lagrangian point and transitioned to normal-space, all keeping a wary eye on the two nearest gunboats making their way through the shoals. Neither was in range to fire on the private ships, but neither were Alexis and the other captains of any mind to ignore a danger.

The oncoming frigate and three of the other pirate ships had made it through the nearest shoals and were making their own way toward Alexis and her fleet, as well. Any delay in transitioning only brought those, and the danger they bore, closer.

"*Delight's* through, sir," Dorsett said.

"Thank you, Dorsett. Bring us about, Layland, and transition as soon as we're within the point."

"Aye, sir. Come about and transition instanter."

Mongoose had been standing off and on as near to the transition point as Alexis dared without interfering with the other ships. Now she came about, sails filling again as she caught the wind on the opposite tack, and headed back toward the point.

"Gunboats're putting on sail, sir," Dorsett said.

"Of course they are," Alexis muttered.

It wasn't entirely unexpected. With the rest of the private ships gone and facing only *Mongoose*, the gunboats might think to take her on. They were certainly outgunned and *Mongoose* was in relatively clear space, not all mired in the shoals as they might like, but if they could delay her, damage her, only a bit, then that frigate might catch up and make short use of her.

"Alert the gundeck," Alexis said, "Load the guns with roundshot and if they're within any range at all before we transition, fire at will."

The gunboats were so fragile that she wanted their hulls targeted – a decent hit or two might take one out, and that was one less they need worry about.

"Aye, sir," Creasy said, turning to his panel to pass the order along in a whisper through his microphone.

Alexis heard Hacking acknowledge the order over her own feed. It crackled with static, telling her that the gunports were open, strung with gallenium netting to keep out the worst of the *darkspace* radiations and let the crew's suit electronics work for at least a while more. Until there was return fire, at least, if that came.

The feeling on the quarterdeck was tenser than it should be. The gunboats were only a little danger and the frigate was hours away, perhaps more given the winds, which had fallen off some.

Perhaps it was only anticipation of the coming days trapped in normal-space, playing hide-and-seek with the pirates, that made it so.

Light flashed across the images displayed on the navigation plot, and a beam raced away from *Mongoose* toward the gunboats.

It was a long shot, arcing its way across the intervening space, and pulled this way and that by clumps of dark matter along its way. The two gunboats had come close together and were angling to pass behind *Mongoose* and take their shots at her stern. The lone shot passed close to the starboard boat — a miss, Alexis thought, until she saw the boat's sail go slack and realized it must have cut rigging. An impressive shot even without that bit of a strike it made.

"Up four notches and a spit aft!" Hacking's voice came over the radios, passing along how that guncrew had laid their shot. "And *fire!*"

Not all of the broadside was laid true, of course. A guncrew might have been a bit off in their initial lie, a bit slow or inaccurate in the changes Hacking called out, *Mongoose* had moved on in her position from the first shot, even as the gunboats themselves had — a broadside at any range farther than one could make out the opposing gunports themselves with the naked eye was always prayer fired nearly blindly into the Dark.

Nearly every eye on the quarterdeck followed the fall of shot on their monitors, just as Alexis was certain those on the gundeck made more than one glance away from their task of reloading to follow their shots' path.

There was a muttered, "C'mon, Boots," from the signals console.

Alexis turned her head to regard Creasy for a moment, opened her mouth to speak, then jerked her head back to the plot as the quarterdeck erupted into cheers.

She'd have to review the recording to determine how many of *Mongoose's* guns had found their mark, but the aftermath showed clearly that it had been enough.

The gunboat's sails, what was left of them blowing from the half-mast the boat had left, fluttered and sparked, going first dim and then dangerously bright as whatever damage had been done to the boat's particle projector ran its course. The holes in the hull itself looked huge, and one had to remind oneself that this was a small boat and not a ship so as not to wonder what it had been struck by.

The gunboat fell off its course, the winds playing havoc with the remnants of its sails and setting it back toward the shoals.

"Safe to transition, sir," Layland said.

Alexis counted to three, giving her crew a bit longer to savor the sight of an unexpected victory, then nodded.

SIXTY-TWO

A lexis yawned.

A great, wide-mouthed, throat-aching yawn that seemed to fill her lungs and then expel some block caught in her throat. A great, hulking, dense block of boredom, if she were to tell the truth.

She blamed Creasy.

Every ten minutes for this entire watch — she'd broke down at one point and put a timer at one side of the navigation plot — Creasy's shoulders would hunch. He'd swallow hard, then glance about the quarterdeck, cover his mouth with a hand, and take in a gulp of air. The covering hand did little to hide the sounds of either his breath or his jaw cracking — something Alexis resisted the urge to suggest he see Merriwether about, for no joint should ever make such a sound.

Creasy's yawn would make its way to Layland, who made less of an effort to hide it.

Thence to Dorsett, though, to his credit, he did turn as far away from the rest of the quarterdeck crew as he could.

Alexis and Villar received it last, and it was a toss-up as to which got it first.

If they were lucky, and Alexis thought she might consult Dockett for the bosun was certain to have the book odds on it, Creasy would be paying attention to his console and wouldn't catch sight of the last in the chain. Otherwise he'd be triggered again himself and start the whole mess up for another round.

This time, as it came around to the navigation plot, it was Alexis who got it first and she watched as Villar struggled against the urge, but there was no use fighting it — nor any denying it.

Normal-space is bloody boring.

They were four days in. Four long, idle days, after the initial flurry of unstepping the masts was done. *Mongoose* had cleared the transition point and the crew swarmed her hull. All sail down, rolled tight, and stored in the forward sail locker; rigging — standing and running, both — down and coiled, also stored away; the masts themselves lowered, each segment telescoped into the one below it, then the last bit folded down to lie flush against the hull.

They'd have no need of the sails for some time, and all those bits were so very vulnerable to damage.

Still, she wished the masts were back up and *Mongoose* back in *darkspace* where she belonged, not puttering along in a straight line, driven by a conventional drive, never varying in her course or speed.

All so very predictable.

Alexis glanced at the plot, then at the quarterdeck crew.

There were no other ships around them, nowhere one could come from — save the Lagrangian points of the planet ahead of *Mongoose*, and those were a full watch away. They'd be altering course soon to veer away from those, having calculated just how fast the pirate frigate — the likely fastest of the pirate ships — could accelerate and where they must alter their own course to ensure they couldn't be caught.

The plot laid it all out in bright lines.

Where each planet was and would be, where each of the private

414

ships was and was headed — provided they each stuck to the plan, dim, oblong shapes showed how close *Mongoose* could come to each planet and not be caught up by the pirates, the effective range of each ship's guns — further than in *darkspace* and they'd fire true, with no jerking and veering about, only the calculable degradation of power over such and such a distance.

It was all, as Dorsett said, just maths.

Bloody boring.

"I'll be in my cabin, Mister Villar, you have the deck."

"Aye, sir."

Outside her cabin, she caught sight of Isom and Nabb, along with Dockett, and the trio were, once again, huddled in heated discussion. She'd noted that several times the last few days and it worried her because she relied on those three so much — tension amongst them could mean nothing good for *Mongoose*.

The trio broke up before she drew close enough to query them, with Dockett heading down the companionway and Nabb forward. Isom remained at the hatch to her quarters and opened it as she arrived.

"Cook's made a bit of an early supper, if you like, sir," Isom said.

"I would, I think," she answered. Eating would relieve the tedium of their watch standing.

Isom nodded and went to leave, but she stopped him.

"Isom, do you and Nabb have some sort of issue with Mister Dockett?"

"'Issue,' sir?"

"I've noted the three of you in discussion several times — heated discussion, if I'm any judge."

Isom shook his head. "No issue, sir, not at all. We've some things to settle is all."

"That sounds very much like an issue to me."

"Nothing to worry you, sir." Isom stepped out and began to slide the hatch closed. "I'd best check with Cook and let him know you'd like your plate."

SIXTY-THREE

The feints, the dancing about, as Hacking had named it, were done, and *Mongoose* and the other private ships were on to the attack on Erzurum itself.

The planet was mere hours away, with all of the ships streaking toward it — slowing, so as to make orbit.

They'd feinted at the planet itself twice before, but turned aside, in efforts to draw the pirates more off guard. If they thought this, too, was a feint, then they might not commit their full force.

Soon, though, it would be clear that this was no feint, and any ships within range of Erzurum in *darkspace* would be rushing to its defense.

On the plot, the pirate gunboat at Erzurum's L1 point winked out of existence as it transitioned to *darkspace* to make its latest report. *Hind* was disappearing behind the planet's bulk while the frigate they all hoped was ill-manned and damaged came into view. It was possible *Mongoose* would be the first to see if their hopes were in vain, for they were very nearly within range of the orbiting frigate's long guns.

"Begin evasions, Layland," Alexis said.

"Aye, sir."

Mongoose's thrusters fired, edging the ship away from her previous course, then again, changing that.

Alexis clenched her jaw, then forced it to relax.

This was *not* what she and her ship were meant to do. Not this flying into the teeth of the enemy with little in the way of firing back.

She glanced at the images of the other private ships on her plot, those visible to *Mongoose's* optics, at least — the others, coming in on the far side of the planet, were merely icons on the plot.

Each was a bare hull, as hers was. No sails, masts, or suited figures. For all the world appearing dead and lifeless as they hurled stern-first toward the planet.

Every bit of her being balked at that, too. Proper ships put their broadsides to the enemy and attacked. The stern was the most vulnerable — even with the ship's rudder and plane folded flat to provide a bit of extra protection. The conventional drive engines were still exposed and vulnerable and that was where her fusion plant was located.

But stern-first it had to be, in order to slow the ship enough to make orbit around Erzurum. Newton, the right bastard, demanded it.

"Three minutes' time and we're in range of a frigate's guns, sir," Dorsett said.

The number was a bit arbitrary, as they'd been in extreme range for some time. The number was picked for when a strike from those guns might have enough power left behind it — not dispersed by distance and particles of dust — so as to do *Mongoose* actual damage and not merely tickle a few nanometers of thermoplastic from the hull.

Alexis watched the frigate, the image held steady by *Mongoose's* optics, despite the ship now being edged about by her thrusters. With luck, that would throw the guns off enough to miss, as their knowledge of where *Mongoose* was at any given moment was out of date. The light from her latest maneuver wouldn't reach the planet for some time. Until they were closer, the frigate would be firing with a guess and a wish.

She realized that while her jaw was unclenched, her hands were gripping the edge of the plot hard enough to leave her knuckles white.

"I bloody *hate* normal-space," she muttered.

"Amen, sir," Villar said, making her realize she'd voiced her thought aloud.

There was no warning of the attack. Lasers in normal-space were not so visible as they were in *darkspace*, where the light was compressed and made coherent by the ever present dark matter. No, here, the best one got was an instant's flicker, and that only if there were significant amounts of dust or other matter in the way to flare as it was destroyed.

Mongoose's sensors were able to detect the shot as it arrived, but most of the crew would see nothing unless they were struck.

"A full broadside, sir," Dorsett said.

Alexis nodded. She could see the traces of the shot laid out on the plot now as well as he. She pursed her lips.

"Well, that answers the question of how damaged the orbiting frigate was, and how well-manned," Villar muttered.

"Not entirely," Alexis watched the plot intently. "They might have moved surviving guns all to one side, we'll know in a mome —"

New traces appeared on the plot, but fewer than before. The frigate had rolled to present her other side and fired, but there were only half as many as the first.

"Still enough, if they manage to strike us," Alexis said. "How well-manned we'll know in a minute or two, as they reload."

The next broadside came two minutes later, and Villar sighed.

"I suppose one should never count on the enemy's incompetence," he said.

"No," Alexis agreed.

Two minutes was not so short a time to reload the guns, not with these conditions. The first reload, with fresh shot set to hand, and no return fire — the test would come later, as the frigate's crew grew weary of lifting the canisters, checking the guns' barrels, and as *Mongoose* began to fire her own guns in return. Still, it was not so very *long* a time, either, and Alexis had to admit she'd been feeling a bit of hope the pirates manning that ship might be less capable.

"Inform Mister Hacking he may fire at will," Alexis said.

Creasy bent to his console to pass the order along. "Aye, sir."

Hacking was in the stern, commanding the chasers there. With only two guns to reload and his pick of the crew, Alexis expected him to put the pirate crews to shame with his rate of fire. Still, there was only the single pair of guns there and maneuvering *Mongoose* to present her broadside would take time she didn't have, save the twice they'd accounted for in their orbital calculations, and those to be saved for any ships transitioning in or the last few moments.

She clenched the edge of the plot again, feeling helpless. This wasn't the proper way to handle a ship at all. She should be able to read the winds, see if she might eke a bit more speed out of *Mongoose* with a change to the sails, and buy time she might use to bring her broadside to bear.

No, the most she could do here to buy a bit of time was cut into the evasive maneuvering, and that only left her ship more vulnerable to being struck.

Villar edged around the plot to her side.

"It's frustrating, sir, to have so few options."

Alexis shared a glance with him. "Do remind me, Mister Villar, should our travels ever take us to Earth, that I do dearly wish to spit on a particular grave."

THE PRIVATE SHIPS continued to approach Erzurum, taking the occasional strike from either the frigate's or *Hind's* guns as they flew straight into the pirate's teeth. Each passing minute made the delay of the light from their position reaching Erzurum less, refining their position for the defenders and making their gunnery easier.

That worked both ways, though, and it was time they showed the pirates that the oncoming fleet had teeth of its own.

"Ready, Creasy?" Alexis asked.

"Aye, sir."

She watched the plot. Around the planet, *Hind* was on the side facing *Mongoose*, the frigate on the other. Pennywell, with his *Gallion*, and *Oriana*, still under Wakeling, were on the far side of the planet, with *Gallion* not even visible on the plot. She had to rely on a relay from Lawson's *Scorpion*, far enough around to keep the two in sight, to note its location and relay signals.

"Now," she said.

The signal went out, not all at once, for there was the communications delay to consider — nearly a full minute, still, to *Gallion*, the farthest from *Mongoose*. That signal went first, relayed through *Scorpion*, then to *Oriana*, also relayed, and then to each of the others in turn, so that all would receive it at the same time.

As one, or as nearly one as such an independent group of captains could manage, each of the private ships cut its engines. Thrusters fired to rotate them and set their broadsides to face the planet, the exact orientation controlled by ship's computer, rather than their helmsmen as it would be in a proper *darkspace* action. Guns came to bear and then, as nearly one again, fired.

Those defending ships had the same problem with the closing distance as the attacking. Jink and dodge though they might, there was only so far they could do so in a given time. It was merely a matter of filling the possible space with enough shot to ensure a few hits, and the private ships, at least for the moment, had more ships and more guns than the two in orbit around Erzurum.

Mongoose rolled, as well, presenting her other side and firing even before her first lasers reached the planet, then rolled still as her crews rushed to reload the first. Most made it — the advantage of having shot to hand and not having to lay the guns to a target themselves. They merely had to slap new cartridge home and close the breaches, wipe down the breaches fore where the crystalline barrel met the shot's lasing tube, then rush to the other side and reload those guns there as *Mongoose* continued her roll.

It took nearly until the reloading was complete for the results of the first broadside to be visible to her. The images were processed by the ship's computer even before Alexis could fully register them, and *Mongoose* adjusted her roll slightly to account for this new knowledge of the target's position.

The guns fired again and the ship's thrusters lit, bringing her stern around again and firing the engines to continue the deceleration toward Erzurum.

"It's all a bloody dance," Hacking muttered. Parrill had the guns so that he might have a brief rest from his time with the stern chasers, where'd be returning soon.

Alexis caught her lower lip between her teeth, a bit torn between the sterility of it all compared to an action in *darkspace* and satisfaction as the images on the plot showed shot after shot striking home on the *Hind*. Images relayed from the ships on the other side of the planet showed the same.

Clouds of thermoplastic boiled off the ships' hulls, holes, divots, and ravines were dug as shot struck home. It was a somewhat surreal sight, as the damage all appeared to be nearly magical — with the lasers not being visible in normal-space.

There was no way to tell which of the private ships had made the strikes, either, much less a guncrew, so there were no cheers from the gundeck, nor shouts of wagers made and lost over who'd struck true.

She caught Hacking's eye. She wouldn't say so, there was no need to, but she disagreed with him. This wasn't the dance. The dance was in *darkspace* where ships and men dodged and feinted from their own efforts, each responding to the other, not simply executing some preplanned strategy.

Hacking yawned.

"Pardon me, sir," he said. "I believe I'll retreat for a bit of a nap before taking on the guns again."

"Of course," Alexis said.

Hacking left the quarterdeck.

"We did them more than a bit of damage, sir," Dorsett said, hunched over the tactical console.

Villar was studying the images as well.

Mongoose shuddered as one of the shots the pirates fired in return struck home. Images from the hull showed her it was only a bit of damage to the thick, folded-over planes, and nothing that would be a risk to them, but there'd be more. And the damage they'd done to the *Hind* and frigate, she saw, might be more than a bit, but was not nearly enough.

Both ships were still in the fight. A gun or two might have been overset or struck, but the ships were sound and firing back. They did far less damage to the private ships than they'd received, though, for they had to divide their fire between six possible targets.

One similarity a normal-space battle had to one in *darkspace*, and one Alexis wished were not the same, was that the action seemed to speed up as the distance closed.

Now that they were in decent range and slowing to make orbit, the private ships were better able to devote the time to firing their broadsides. It seemed like no time at all before the quarterdeck chimes struck and it was time for the next.

"On my mark," Alexis said.

Creasy hung his fingers over his console.

"Now!"

Again the oncoming ships pirouetted to present their broadsides and fire, then spun to present and fire the next, as their crews rushed to reload.

Closer, with less lightspeed lag in knowing where their targets were, and less distance for the beams to diffuse as they traveled.

Both the *Hind* and frigate were momentarily obscured, first by clouds of thermoplastic boiling off their hulls, then by the next broadside flashing coherent through those clouds.

"Another!" Alexis called, seeing how much of their shot must have struck home.

It would take time for her order to get to the farther ships, and they might already have begun to present their sterns to the planet again, but those closest to her would hear.

"Aye, sir!" Dorsett called, himself caught up in the excitement.

Mongoose rolled, Alexis couldn't tell about the other private ships as her eyes were on *Hind*.

"No more'n a minute, sir," Layland said.

Alexis nodded. That was the time she'd have left to play with if she chose. Perhaps enough for one extra turn and broadside than they had planned now. After that, their engines' thrust would not be enough to put them in orbit around Erzurum — they'd overshoot and have to maneuver more.

It was not so difficult a thing to do, but she wanted her ships — and she was thinking of them all as hers now, plotting what they'd do and trusting their captains, even Wakeling, to follow her lead — to make orbit nearly as one, dropping their boats full of men onto the planet to take and hold what infrastructure they could.

With six ships to fire at an oncoming fleet and that threat to the pirates' homes and livelihood, she hoped her little fleet would have the upper hand for once in this.

Hind's bow came out of the thermoplastic cloud from their last attack, great holes and rents visible in her hull. Still she fired back — sporadically, as her thrusters must have been damaged and she rolled slowly to set her aim. The cloud cleared a bit and *Hind* moved on, revealing her gunports all knocked in and the hull between them as well, like a spacer's grin after a fine brawl.

Alexis was tempted to call for another go, but held off. They had one more roll and broadside scheduled for their approach and that would be closer and better aimed. She'd save the extra for that and possibly finish off *Hind*.

The frigate bore damage as well. Not so much as *Hind*, but enough to show she'd felt the blows.

Alexis enhanced that image, looking closely. Their next attack would put them close enough to reliably target a part of the ship, and she wanted to know where to concentrate their fire.

Some of the frigate's gunports were knocked in as well, but not nearly so many nor so much as *Hind's*. She thought there might be more damage to the hull around the quarterdeck, and if they were able to break through there, then the frigate would be more difficult to manage and possibly without her officers — if the pirates even worried about such things, which they might not.

"*Yes!*" Dorsett called, then, "Sorry, sir! But look at *Hind!*"

Hind was, indeed, a sight.

She was nearly three-quarters out of the thermoplastic cloud, but the cloud itself was lit up and flickering like a lightning storm. Bright flashes within the cloud were echoed by flashes of the lights on the ship's visible hull — not proper signals, only brightening and darkening to no purpose.

"Is it —"

White fire streaked in lines over *Hind's* hull, following some paths only it could explain, then the cloud burst with it as the ship's fusion plant was breached. Cloud and ship both became a miniature sun in orbit around Erzurum, roiling and billowing into a ball of plasma that sent *Mongoose's* optics dark to compensate. Anyone on the planet's surface, looking up, might have been blinded in an instant, but the sight was over in nearly the same.

The ball of roiling fire shrank in on itself and went out, ship and who knew how many crew consumed all in an instant. Bits of the ship, either flung loose as the explosion tore at the ship or somehow not consumed in the conflagration, spun about in their orbit.

"Signal to all ships," Alexis said, "put fire on the frigate now and don't let up. And let our guncrews know there'll be no let up until that frigate's done for."

"Aye, sir," Creasy said, sending the signals.

Their original plan had called for meeting both the *Hind* and frigate in orbit, assuming both those enemies would still be whole when the private ships arrived. They'd fight those while the ships' boats took infrastructure on the planet's surface and used that threat to force the *Hind* and frigate into surrender.

Now, with *Hind* gone, they could pour double the fire onto the frigate — perhaps do for her before they dropped the boats. If they could, then overshooting the planet a bit would not be so bad. They could still drop the boats to attack the surface, unopposed by any ships in orbit, and make their way back.

"Signal to all ships," Alexis said. "Target their satellite constellation whenever the frigate's not in sight."

"Aye, sir."

Mongoose and the ships nearest her had a few minutes while the frigate was on the opposite side of Erzurum. With *Hind* gone, they could turn their attention to other targets, and the pirates' satellites were the first.

There were not so many, perhaps three dozen, but they'd represent a good bit of expense and the pirate colony would rely on them for everything from communications to geolocation. Destroying them would both make it clear that Alexis' ships were prepared to do more damage and hinder the pirates' response to her boats — if all the satellites were destroyed, then the pirates might have no notice at all of the boats' approach.

Alexis felt some of her tension ease.

Gallion and *Oriana* were already pouring fire on the frigate, which was firing back, but less effectively than before. Three, perhaps four, of her guns were silent and two more seemed to be slower than the others.

In ten minutes' time, the ship crossed into *Osprey's* line of fire and then *Mongoose's* a few minutes after that. Unless the frigate changed her orbit, she'd now be facing constant fire from enemies who'd each have some occasional respite while she did not.

"Signal from the *Delight*, sir," Creasy said.

"On the plot, Creasy."

"Aye, sir."

Malcomson's face appeared, a wide grin breaking his beard.

"I tol' ya, lass, an' reit at 'em's best."

His voice was barely audible over the screeching wail of the piper visible behind him. How *Delight's* quarterdeck crew could think with such a thing in their midst, Alexis couldn't fathom.

Alexis answered his grin.

"We're not there, yet," she said.

"The bread's all jam-side up, lass, once we're in orbit."

"Transition!"

Alexis spun to Dorsett at the tactical console. They'd been expecting one or more of the pirate ships to transition to normal-space around Erzurum at any moment, so why was his voice so filled with urgency.

"Multiple transitions — Lunar L5." He tapped his console. "L1, as well. Another at L5."

The navigation plot was showing the new arrivals — three, now four, ships at the L5 point nearest *Mongoose*, two at L1, between the planet and its moon.

"Transition — L4," Dorsett said, as the plot painted that contact, as well, far around on the other side of Erzurum, but visible to the private ships there.

"I shouldn't hae spoke so soon," Malcomson said.

SIXTY-FOUR

The images of the other captains shook and went dark occasionally as their ships were struck, knocking the communications lasers off target. The pirate ships were all still some distance from any of them, but they were coming on hard and firing as they did so.

"We're buggered," Lawson said.

Alexis had to agree.

The plot told the story well enough. The private ships were committed to either orbiting or passing close to Erzurum, nothing could stop that now, and the pirates had waited just long enough to show their own forces there to ensure that they couldn't escape. Even if they scattered, there were only so many ways they could change their course, and each could be caught up, if not by a ship of superior strength, then by two or more.

Mongoose shook, causing all of the images to go dark for a moment until Creasy could lay his lasers on the others again.

Alexis spared a glance to Villar, who was bent over the tactical console with Dorsett, but there was no miracle of an idea coming from there.

"Oot're in," Malcomson said, his voice backed by a ululating wail.

"Yes, orbit or flight," Lawson said. "And would you stop those bloody pipes for a moment, so we might think? I'll mute you, otherwise."

Malcomson snorted, but nodded to the side and the sound of his piper faded a bit.

There was a pause as each captain scanned their own navigation plot, and *Mongoose's* told the story they were all seeing. Colored cones ran off from each private ship's course, showing where, with their current course, speed, and acceleration, they might get to. The image was not encouraging, for nearly all of them could be caught up and kept in engagement by multiple pirates.

An hour or two earlier, that wouldn't have been the case — even a few minutes, for some, as they'd then have had enough speed to outdistance their pursuers by continuing on their courses and slingshot around the planet. Now, though, they'd slowed enough that there were fewer options.

"There's only one place we can come together as a single force now," Lawson said, "and that's still our best option."

Alexis could see the other captains nodding. They might not like it, but it was their best chance.

"We continue on," she said, "join in orbit and make a united defense."

"It'll be a bl ... grand ... stand," Pennywell said with a scowl, his words cut off as his ship was struck and the communications laser jittered.

Alexis suspected it was just as well, for she had no need to hear the "last" she was certain he'd included.

"And we must still drop our boats as planned," Kingston said. "More than defense, it's our hands on their infrastructure that will convince them. They've no satellites left at all now, so —"

He cut off and there was a heart-stopping moment where Alexis watched the image of *Osprey*, expecting it to disappear, as *Osprey* was the smallest of the private ships and most vulnerable.

Then Kingston's image came back, blocky for a moment, then clearing. His eyes were a bit wider than before and he gripped the plot edge, but straightened.

"So they know we'll not hesitate to wipe their ... from the surface if need be," he finished.

Mongoose shuddered with what felt like a full broadside striking home, the off-gassing jets of vaporized thermoplastic from her hull acting like thrusters in their own right. The images of all the captains went blank.

She spared a glance for the helm, but Villar was there with Layland, both doing what they could to jink and spin *Mongoose* out of the line of fire while keeping her on track to make orbit with the others.

The images came back, all save Lawson's.

"We've a laser down," Creasy said, "likely fused by that last." He tapped at his console. "I'll reroute through *Osprey*."

"— decided then?" Pennywell was saying. "Ah, thought we'd lost you for good, Carew."

"Very nearly, I think," Alexis said. Villar had moved from the helm to Dorsett's side at the tactical station, and Dockett was there as well now. The bosun's face was grim as he nodded to something Villar said. "You were saying we're decided?"

The others nodded.

"Let's be about it, then."

THE DECISION MADE, Alexis turned her attention to fighting *Mongoose*.

Three, no four, of the pirates seemed to be concentrating their fire on her. Two gunboats and two of the merchant hulls — though the latter seemed to not be recent acquisitions, as they had more guns than she'd expect of a merchant.

Luckily, at least for *Mongoose*, the second frigate had appeared at

L4, far enough past Erzurum that it was no danger to her at the moment. The frigate in orbit had taken enough damage that she was firing only sporadically, and from fewer than half her guns.

Another broadside from each of us and she'd have gone up like Hind, Alexis thought. *Another broadside, another hour, a single bell more.*

She sighed. There was no use thinking what might be different with any of those things. What mattered was the action at hand.

Mongoose shuddered again.

"Roll and give that bastard two in his teeth," she ordered.

"Aye, sir."

The nearest and most aggressive of the pirates was striking them with nearly every shot, but he'd come from L5 and was nearly behind *Mongoose.* A gunboat trailed him, rolling out of his shadow now and then to fire, then back to the shelter of the other ship.

Mongoose's chasers were scoring, as well, but those lighter, fewer guns were a mere nuisance.

"This will put us off our orbit," Villar said quietly.

Alexis nodded. Nearly every maneuver was putting *Mongoose,* and the other private ships, off their planned orbit and rendezvous, but there was nothing to be done about it. If they bore straight in, they'd be destroyed as they came on — and barely able to fire back, as the pirates were keen about keeping out of the private ships' firing arcs.

Already one of the merchantmen and a gunboat were in orbit around Erzurum, having come from the nearby L1 point and taken up a defensive position in reinforcement of the damaged frigate.

The projection on the navigation plot, constantly updated as each ship maneuvered, showed their coming positions in orbit as more of a scattered handful of ships, rather than the neat, defensive formation they'd agreed upon.

"Coming about," Layland said, "rolling now."

"Fire as you bear," Alexis said.

Creasy passed the order along to Parrill on the gundeck. Hacking was on the bow chasers.

Mongoose was turned nearly ninety-degrees to her course, stern engines off for a moment, rolling to target the trailing pirates. Each gun was locked down to the deck, its firing angle well-known to the ship's computer, which was controlling everything but the loading of fresh shot.

Her port broadside fired, each gun in turn, with minute adjustments made before each by the ship's computer, a rolling barrage like fireworks, where the path of each shot itself was invisible and one could see only the effect.

The pirate merchantman was bows on to *Mongoose* and so close that every shot struck home. Dorsett had laid the crosshairs on the ship's image well, giving the computer a certain target — just to port of the angled bowsprit, at the very edge of the ship's sail locker.

The first shot fused the hatch shut, thermoplastic melting and flowing to seal the port edge. It would take a work crew hours to cut the hatch itself away, along with most of its frame, and install a new one.

Perhaps less, as the next shot arrived and ensured they'd not have to cut anything away.

The remainder of the hatch went, exposing the sail locker to vacuum — a tiny puff of air rushed out.

The third and fourth shot arrived as one, those guns, through some quirk of their aim and the exact distance of the target, convincing *Mongoose* to fire them together.

Furled sails, rolled tight and stored to either side of the locker, evaporated, their fine, metal mesh, infused with gallenium, shot of sparks and arcs of light as it went. What bit of the shots' energy wasn't spent on the sails made it to the inner hatch — thinner than the outer, meant only to contain vacuum, not the power of two ship's guns, it went as well.

Not into vapor, for much of the shots' energy had been spent on the sails, but molten.

The tough thermoplastic of the hull was meant to dissipate energy quickly, spreading it out across the thick, wide hull. The airlock's inner hatch, though, had little enough depth, and what couldn't transfer through its frame quickly enough sent drops and chunks of the hatch flying about. They cooled quickly, but not quickly enough.

Men nearest the hatch, those on the foremost guns, died as bits of molten plastic holed their suits and bodies. The gun captains, standing more to the ship's centerline, caught what remained of the lasers' energy and were cooked in their vacsuits.

The next of *Mongoose's* guns fired, then the next and next, on down the line.

The lasers, with nothing to impede them now, shot down the ship's gundeck turning all in their path to slag or vapor. The thermoplastic of the gundeck's bulkheads was colored black, as most were, the better to absorb any shot that made it within, but there were always bits.

A worn hinge on a cot along the center line, showing brightly. A shot cannister on the racks, shiny from racking into a gun's breach over and over again. A bit of metal on a vacsuit.

Shot splintered — energy reflecting off those bits before they themselves were vaporized.

Some splinters struck men, holing suits and burning flesh. Others struck the guns themselves, worst along the crystalline barrels, which splintered the beams even more.

Mongoose's guns continued to fire, one after another along the port broadside, turning the other ship's gundeck into a foggy, melting charnel house.

Then she rolled, thrusters firing, to bring her starboard broadside to bear.

THE GUNCREWS' cheers echoed over the quarterdeck speakers even as *Mongoose* rolled to present her starboard side.

Alexis' own smile was tight. They'd raked the bastard, bow to stern, and she could see jets of thermoplastic and even bits of guns flung out through the pirate's own gunports. She shut down thoughts of what that gundeck must be like, and how many deaths she'd just caused — there'd be time enough for that when her own ship and crew were safe.

Mongoose began firing again, and the cheers subsided as those guncrews went to work reloading the port broadside. Alexis caressed the edge of the navigation plot, eyes fixed on the target ship.

There was this about a normal-space action, she supposed. In *darkspace*, the ship was steered from the helm, the gunners laid their guns, and the gun captains fired on her order. Here, with the ship deciding the best maneuver, far faster than any of the crew could, it was almost as if *Mongoose* herself was part of the crew — responding to her orders as best she could.

I've a guinea for you if that bastard blows, Alexis thought, though what *Mongoose* might do with it was beyond her. Perhaps a bit of gilt, as a fine guncrew might reward themselves with earrings or new tattoos in port.

The guns fired, thrusters flared.

The pirate captain had ordered a turn — too late, and wrong, as well.

The first broadside had come in along the port edge of the sail locker, traversing the gundeck at a bit of an angle, port to starboard.

His turn was to port — perhaps he'd misread the angles, perhaps it was his normal evasion, perhaps he thought to bring his starboard broadside to bear on *Mongoose* and give her a taste in return. Whatever his reason, the turn reduced the oncoming ship's angle to *Mongoose* to nothing, if only for an instant.

Mongoose's starboard broadside flashed out, gun after gun, thrusters firing in between to correct the angle. The rate of fire, and the thrust was far greater than before, as though the ship recognized there was an instant's opportunity that might not come again. Perhaps she did, for the computer knew to calculate a target's vulnerabilities as well as Alexis did.

The crew stumbled, then again, as those thrusters fired at full power, overcoming the ship's inertial compensators for a moment.

Shot after shot lashed the length of the pirate's gundeck, finding little to impede its path after the first broadside. Little until the aft bulkhead and the engineering spaces beyond.

Unlike the *Hind*, this ship was dead on to *Mongoose*, and there were no clouds of vaporized thermoplastic to hide what happened.

The ship's stern expanded, the hull splitting, and then seemed to be sucked back in to a growing ball of fire. That fire raced forward, faster than the eye could really see, but the watcher's minds filled in the bits that couldn't be comprehended.

In an instant, where before there was a proper ship and, perhaps, a hundred men, a miniature sun blazed for a time. *Mongoose's* gundeck, ports open to vacuum, lit up and men flinched away even as their vacsuits' faceplates darkened against the glare.

SIXTY-FIVE

The guncrews were cheering again, even as they blinked to clear the afterimage from their eyes.

Mongoose came back to her course, stern toward Erzurum and engines firing to slow her for orbit. The time to fire had taken a toll and the plot showed it, *Mongoose* would miss her planned rendezvous in orbit, overshoot the planet by a bit, and have to come back to meet it.

It was worth it, though, to have done away with at least one of the enemy. Two, for a time, at least, as the trailing gunboat had put about angled away from *Mongoose's* path, not wanting to continue pursuit so closely now that her larger consort had been destroyed.

Alexis and Villar hunched over the plot.

"Is there a way to correct, do you think?" Villar asked.

Alexis shook her head. Even with every bit of thrust the conventional drive could manage, they were still going to overshoot the planet. Overshoot, out past the ships coming in from the other side, and be left amidst the pirates coming on from that direction, including the second frigate.

437

"Loop here," Villar asked, "around the moon and then back behind them?"

Alexis frowned. The plot said it might be possible, just barely. But that would put them farther from the planet and the rest of the private ships — alone against whichever of the pirates might choose to attack them. It would also deprive the other ships of *Mongoose's* boats and men in their attack on the surface, and that might make the difference.

"No, we'll have to accept being under fire for a time — the only hope the full force has is if we can take enough of the key bits on Erzurum to force the pirate force to back off. Without that, there's little to bargain with and they'll simply stand off and pound us all to bits."

Villar took a deep breath. "It'll be a heavy pounding, with most of the crew off in the boats and not manning the guns."

Alexis nodded. "Creasy?"

"Aye, sir?"

"My compliments to Mister Dockett, and I'd admire did he speak to the Engineer about a bit more thrust to the drives."

"Aye, sir."

"We'll be the closest target for that frigate for nearly ten minutes," Villar said.

"Have the landing forces ready themselves and the boats. They'll be off shortly."

IN THE END, it was not the second frigate that they were to worry about, but the first.

Mongoose was ahead of nearly all the other private ships, set to flash by the planet, no matter the extra bits Dockett and the engineer had managed to eke from her drives.

The first frigate, the one which had been in orbit all along and been battered to near submission by the private ships, came around in her orbit. Guns fired, taking aim at the nearest, easiest target.

One found an engine nozzle, destroying it and throwing off *Mongoose's* thrust, so that the ship's course began to skew wildly. Another found a weak spot in the folded rudder, perhaps where a pirate gunboat had once done some damage and where the repair was weaker than the rest. The next broke through that spot, exposing the ship's stern, and the rest, whether on target or only near misses, were enough.

Mongoose's quarterdeck went dark.

Alarms screeched through the darkness for a moment before emergency lighting came on, dim and stuttering as the ship shook from hit after hit. The jerking about caused by the skewed thrust stopped, but that was no relief, for its end meant that there was no thrust at all. The darkness and alarms told the story.

"Power's out!" Creasy called. "Engineering's breached."

"A report on the damage, Mister Villar!"

"Aye, sir!"

Villar made to dash off, lifted from the deck, and then grunted as Alexis grasped his arm and dragged him back down. With the ship's power out, there was no artificial gravity and they were reliant on the magnets in their vacsuit boots to stay on the deck.

Villar grunted again, this time pushing off properly and sailing toward the hatch. Layland went there as well, his own controls dead as the rest, to help Villar open the hatch by hand.

Alexis glanced around. They were helpless, blind and helpless for the plot and all the quarterdeck consoles were dark. There was little she could do until she knew the extent of the damage, though. The engineer might restore power in a moment's time if it were only cables cut and not a true SCRAM — a full shutdown of the plant. Or the plant itself might be breached by the next shot and they'd all become part of a miniature sun to echo that of the pirate they'd only recently dispatched.

Minutes dragged on and Alexis followed Villar's progress in her head. Down the companionway, then aft — there were three, no four, hatches before he made the hatch to engineering and the airlock there.

Mongoose shook again as she was struck by fire. Not to the stern again, she thought, given how they all jerked about. The altered thrust must have set the ship spinning and that, at least, would keep her from being targeted there.

The quarterdeck hatch slid open, long before Villar could have made it aft and back, but the sight of him there along with Dockett told her all the story she needed. Dockett must have met him midway with the news.

"SCRAM," he said.

Alexis closed her eyes.

"Get the men to the boats."

MOST OF THE crew was already prepared to go aboard the boats for the assault on Erzurum, it was only a matter of passing the word to the rest.

There was the emergency lighting, of course, which Creasy set to flashing in a way no spacer ever wanted to see, broadcast over suit radios that, thankfully, worked as they were in normal-space, but the word was also passed man to man. Each member of the crew passed the word, making sure those around him heard it, even as they headed for the boats.

Some were tasked with notifying the remoter areas of the ship, in case even the emergency power was out there and the suit radios didn't reach. One to Merriwether and his loblolly boys in the orlop, another to the purser, Dursley, where he looked over the hold, to Isom and the other servants huddled near the magazine, and to those in the magazine itself where shot canisters' capacitors were charged. Others had the chore of moving select supplies from the hold to the boats.

Alexis stood near the hatch to her own boat, grasping arms and ticking off names in her head as her boat crew and others passed — Naval tradition of officers being first-on and first-off a ship's boat told to bugger itself. She couldn't be at every boat, nor search the entire ship herself, but she'd see those assigned here were all aboard.

Nabb came to her side, not in line to board.

"Have you seen Isom?" Alexis asked.

Nabb shook his head.

Alexis cursed under her breath. Isom and the other servants should have been aboard by now. They spent actions in a bit of the hold underneath the magazine. A tight fit, but it was safe — surrounded by the heavy bulkheads of the magazine itself, the engineering spaces aft, and any bits of the retracted keel forward.

But she'd seen not a one of them.

"Damn."

"I'll go down to see about them, sir," Nabb said.

Mongoose shook and the line of waiting spacers braced themselves, then continued filing into the boat.

"No," Alexis said. "You stay with the boat and see everything's stowed away properly. I'll see to Isom and the others."

"Sir, I —"

"See to the boat, Nabb!"

ALEXIS LAUNCHED herself away from the docked boat, letting her feet leave the deck and sailing down the companionway to the lower decks, then aft, through the maze of the hold. Midway through, the ship shook mightily and even the emergency lighting flickered for a moment. There was no way of telling where *Mongoose* was now, nor which of the pirate ships she might be in range of, but someone was clearly still shooting at her.

Another lurch of the ship caused her to impact a huge vat of beer and she eased her feet to the deck, letting her boots latch on. Going would be slower, but at least she wouldn't be flung about so easily.

There were lights and voices ahead, and she turned the lights of her own vacsuit helmet on.

"Who's there?" a voice called.

"*Mongoose,*" she answered and went closer.

Three men — no, not all, Sills and Paskell, who'd been with her aboard *Nightingale,* and Coburn, one of the women hired aboard at Penduli — were struggling to corral a crate floating about between them.

"Stay back, sir," Sills said. "Bugger's small, but has a lot of mass."

Paskell ducked out of the way as the crate knocked against another vat, then the three grasped it and got its momentum stopped.

"More rations for the aft boats," Paskell said.

"Bring it and come with me," Alexis said. "We've not seen Isom, Cook, nor any of the ship's servants at the boats."

"Aye, sir."

The four made their way aft, past the deserted and locked purser's station and the carpenter's, similarly locked up tight, to the aft companionway and then down to *Mongoose's* very bowels.

The magazine was a half level above them, the keel, fully retracted for normal-space, took up nearly all the space forward. Alexis and the others squeezed into the narrow carpenter's walk, a space that ran the length of the hull, barely wide enough for a man to go by edgewise, and meant to access and repair any breach of the hull. The space was still aired, so there was that, but Alexis noted the others kept their faceplates halfway closed — ready to flip closed in an instant if they were exposed to vacuum.

The hatch to the little space the servants went to in action was still closed and Alexis tugged at it, but it refused to open.

The ship shuddered. One of the pirates, at least, had noted that while *Mongoose's* lights might be dead, the ship had launched no boats and had a crew aboard. They weren't taking chances that the ship's plight might be some ruse to escape or attack.

"Come give me a hand," Alexis ordered and the others leapt to, pulling hard on the hatch. Alexis pounded on the hatch and called out, "Isom! Cook! Watford! Are you in there?"

Paskell braced himself and heaved at the hatch. "It's stuck fast, sir, warped in the frame just there."

Alexis looked where he was pointing and her blood chilled. Part of hatch's frame was indeed warped and she could see a bubble where the thermoplastic had melted and reformed. That meant heat, and the source of heat was likely a bolt of shot come through the engineering spaces.

"Isom!" She watched Paskell tug again to no avail. "There are tools in the carpenter's locker, come on!"

Back up the companionway, her fingers trembled as she keyed the locked hatch of the carpenter's workspace, hoping the batteries on such spaces were still working — all the time picturing Isom, who'd been so loyal, a hand to steady and guide her, even though he had no business at all even being aboard a ship in action. If the space had been breached from aft and there was no word from the inhabitants over their suit radios, what did that mean? She couldn't bear the thought.

Paskell and Coburn caught up cutters and flung themselves ahead, Alexis and Sills close behind. They were already at work when Alexis approached.

"Best close your helmet, sir," Sills said, doing so himself, "in case there's vacuum."

Alexis did, her faceplate darkening against the glare of the cutters working their way around the hatch. Sills set the companionway hatches so that they had a bit of an airlock to work with if the space was in vacuum — an open hatch to the companionway, then the hatches up and forward closed.

In a moment the hatch was free and air rushed by. The space beyond was dark. Paskell and Coburn tossed their tools aside and entered, then began passing out bodies. Alexis couldn't tell for certain who was who, but the suits looked intact, their helmets sealed.

Another figure was passed out, this one missing an arm, but the suit looked to have sealed around the wound.

Alexis took each in turn, passing them along to Sills who was nearest the exit. She tried to get a look through the faceplate to see who was who or at the suits tell-tale lights to see if the person inside was alive, but didn't delay. She recognized Cook being handed out next, from his size, and passed him along.

"That's the lot, sir," Paskell said over the radio, he and Coburn exiting. "Bit of shot come all the way through, though what put them all out, I couldn't say."

"Get them to my boat and get aboard yourselves," Alexis said.

"Aye, sir."

They each grasped one or two of the limp forms and started for the hatch.

Mongoose shuddered and spun wildly. Alexis' helmet struck a bulkhead and she saw flashes of light.

"Hurry, sir, we're bloody skeet for them this way!"

She grasped the hatch edges and pulled herself through, Paskell sliding the hatch behind her.

Then she heard something — or thought she did, a soft *chittering* not possible in the vacuum, but —

Bloody hell ...

She glanced back at dark space, her helmet lights playing over shadows as the hatch slid.

I could be rid of the thing ...

She felt a pressure on her chest, like a bundle of limp, warm fur, and then a cold dot on her neck, as though a tiny nose nuzzled her.

"Damn me — belay that!"

Through the gap of the nearly closed hatch and into the tiny dark space. Her helmet lights caught the shape of the little box, vacsuit gloved fingers fumbled with the latches to release the clamps that held it tight to the deck, then she was back and Paskell slid the hatch shut and dogged it.

"Can't believe we nearly forgot about Boots, sir!" Sills said.

"Here," Alexis said, shoving the case into his arms. "Take the vile thing and get it aboard a boat."

SIXTY-SIX

The boats were loaded and all but hers already away when Alexis and the others reached the boarding hatch. She waved the others aboard and slid into the cockpit — there was a seat for her aft, but she wanted to be able to see what was going on around them.

"Get us away, Gutis," she said, sliding into the seat to his right.

"Aye, sir."

There was a muted thump as the boat released from *Mongoose* and pushed away. The boat, at least, had its own power and grav generators, so it was only the spinning of the stars outside the viewscreen that she had to deal with. That soon eased as Gutis brought the boat under control and out of *Mongoose's* uncontrolled tumbling.

The first sight of her ship brought a lump to her throat. The hull was pocked and lumpy from being hit, and the ship itself was dark, as though already dead. She supposed it was — a ship might have a soul, but her crew was the lifeblood and *Mongoose's* was streaming away in their boats.

Gutis backed further away, leaving Alexis to watch *Mongoose* tumble into the distance. She shook away the sadness — most of the crew, save those struck down in the fight, were aboard the boats, and that was the most important thing. The boat's console was tracking *Mongoose*'s path, and that would be as predictable as any other — they wouldn't have to worry about her being blown willy-nilly by *darkspace* winds and broken up on some shoal. Once they'd dealt with the pirates, they'd almost certainly be able to find and recover her — if the plant could be repaired, even to support half its capacity, then *Mongoose* might yet live again.

"Still, I imagine Dansby will be quite cross with me."

"What was that, sir?"

"Don't mind me, Gutis, see to your board."

"Aye, sir."

Gutis' eyes had remained on his board throughout, Alexis noted, turning the boat about and putting it after the others, which were already streaming toward the planet.

A planet which was, she saw, quite closer than she'd expected. The time since *Mongoose*'s fusion plant had shut down seemed like an eternity. She quite expected them to be past the planet, past the pirates coming from L4, and possibly even past that point itself.

Instead, they were very nearly even with Erzurum, only a little ahead of the other private ships, which were in the last bits of making their orbit and dropping their own boats.

"Signal — no, I'll do it. You take us toward the planet — we're still after your original target." Alexis reached for her side of the console and laid communications lasers on the four other boats. "All right, lads, we may not have the ship in orbit, but we've more aboard our boats than expected and we can still make our targets. Stick to the original plan, aye?"

A moment after she received an acknowledgement from the other boats, Nabb slid the cockpit hatch open and came to her side.

"Them you brought back're all settled, sir," he said. "Isom's took a blow to the head, but looks t'be all right soon as he comes to — thought you'd like to know."

"Thank you, Nabb. The others?"

"Cook lost an arm, but the suit sealed right. Snow shot through the leg, but the same. Looks t'be the banging about what put them out — that and air loss. Likely not clamped down or have their face plates shut, thinking they were safe as any down there."

Alexis nodded. At least they were all alive.

"Boots is shook up, but not a hair harmed — that crate Isom found is padded well and sealed."

Alexis grunted. "Thank you, Nabb. We're headed for our original targets on the surface, so will you see the lads are all armed? With so many more aboard, you'll likely have to open the arms locker for it."

"Aye, sir."

That done, Alexis turned her attention to what was happening around Erzurum.

The private ships were either in orbit or nearly so. *Scorpion* and *Osprey*, Lawson and Kingston, had put themselves alongside the battered frigate in orbit and were boarding. Alexis hoped they were right about the ships the pirates had left in orbit and there was not too large a crew aboard — both Lawson and Kingston had let loose their own boats, so their ships were lightly manned. No more still aboard than could fight the guns and maneuver in orbit.

Gallion had taken up position between the planet and L1, the closest of the Lagrangian points, and was engaging the pirates approaching from there — a captured merchant and two gunboats.

One gunboat, as Alexis watched the other peppered with shot from *Gallion's* broadside, went dark and started its own tumble. *Gallion* rolled to fire again and the remaining ships veered off — thrusters and engines firing to send them far wide of the planet, perhaps to join up with their fellows.

Shot continued to come in from those other pirates, though, and some of it close to *Mongoose's* boats, all of which were flinging themselves about to make the targeting more difficult. The little boats could accelerate and decelerate much faster than the massy ships in normal-space, they needed only a few more minutes before they might be close enough to the planet that the ships themselves were more tempting targets for the attackers.

It was minutes they didn't have, as shot streaked through their formation.

One of the boats was struck midway down the hull. The off-gassing thermoplastic set the boat to tumbling and the pilot tried to right it, but the tumble continued. Alexis nearly cried out, wondering who was aboard and who was now dead, as the shot had gone straight into the aft compartment which would be crowded with *Mongoose's* crew.

"'At's Shallcross, sir," Gutis said, eyes never stopping their dance from console to screen and back again. "He's a deft one, him." His own fingers sent their boat in even harder evasive maneuvers, even as his half-heard mutters seemed to be coaching the other. "'At's it, Shallcross, a bit more ... fire a port-aft ... there y'go, lad, there y'go ... y'got her, y'do. Handsomely, lad, handsomely ..."

Indeed Shallcross did seem to. The boat was under control and heading now toward *Scorpion* and the boarding of the orbiting frigate.

"See, sir?" Gutis asked. "Easy as —"

Their boat jerked hard to port and down, so fast and far that Alexis thought she could hear a whine from the inertial compensators and she was actually lifted from her seat, held in place only by her belt.

Shot flashed past where they'd been an instant before, visible only as alerts on the console.

The boat spun end for end and Gutis fired the boat's own guns. Tiny things, useful only for other boats and ground targets, really, and controlled directly from his console, which was why they were even less useful in *darkspace*.

Gutis settled them back on course to Erzurum, which had grown quite large. They were nearly within the orbits of the ships and minutes away from atmosphere.

The pilot patted his console.

"'Er guns might do no more'n tickle 'em, sir, even up close, but I'd not think we're toothless, all entire."

Alexis grinned back. "No, Gutis, I'd have no one think that of us."

"Should be the last sent our way though, sir." He jerked his head aft. "Bigger fish 'tween us and them now." He twisted the boat in space to line up with the planet and studied his board. "Just have to get us where we're to put down now ..." He watched his board, then reached for the throttle. "Just there and —"

The boat shook, their view of the planet spinning away, only to be replaced by stars and then the planet again. Alarms sounded, each trying to outdo the other, and the console was awash with red, flashing and strobing.

"*Where'd you come from, you bloody bugger's fart!*"

The boat spun, shook again, then dove, and Alexis was pushed back into her seat.

A shape flashed past the viewscreen and Alexis had barely time to register another ship's boat before Gutis had theirs in a sharp turn to starboard.

He began a muttered, cursing litany of the red flashing on his console, but Alexis didn't need to hear that the inertial compensators had been all but destroyed — that she was being flung about with every maneuver told her that. Her gorge rose as Gutis spun the boat end for end vertically and went into a diving roll.

"Best get yer harness on, sir," Gutis said. "This'll be rough."

It already was, and she said a silent prayer for the crew in the back, hoping they'd all been strapped into their seats before this started. She struggled with her seat's shoulder harness and managed to click it into place just as they turned sharply to port and went into a corkscrew that had her gorge rising again.

"Helmet back on too," Gutis muttered.

Alexis struggled with that, finally clicking it into place against the stresses of the boat's twists and turns.

She saw that Gutis' vacsuit helmet was still attached to his seat and wondered if she'd be able to stretch far enough — or even raise her arms in some of these gyrations — to help him with it. If the boat was close to being deaired, he'd need that, but was busy with piloting.

"Keep yer helmet on, sir ... can't be worrying about your puke flying about my face." Gutis shot her a quick look. "Full respect, an' all, o'course, sir."

Alexis didn't bother to answer, merely swallowed again, hoping she wouldn't have to experience another episode of that within the limited confines of her vacsuit helmet — once as a midshipman was quite enough — and managed to sort out what the boat's board was telling her.

They were in-atmosphere now, the edges of it, at least, and under attack not by the pirate's ships but by another boat. Likely from a captured merchant ship, held back at Erzurum when its ship was sold off to provide transport on the colony — and now defense against the attackers.

She could see that some of the other boats from the private ships were similarly engaged. Here and there the sky, now blue as they descended farther into atmosphere, showed a dark cloud where a boat, attacker or defender, she couldn't tell, had been blotted from the sky.

The private ships all had boats better armed and armored than the typical merchant, though, so the thought had been they'd carry the day.

They were spinning more than dodging up and down now and the boat shook as it was struck again.

"Grav's barely holdin'," Gutis muttered. His fingers danced over the controls. "Right, then, follow this, y'bastard."

The bottom of whatever had held the boat in the air dropped out and the boat with it. Alexis' throat filled with what seemed to be her entire insides and she clenched her jaw against it.

The boat dropped straight down, but spun to put the cockpit pointing up.

The sky above was blue at the edges, but turning purple and still dark just above, stars barely visible still, until they were blotted out by the shape of the attacking boat.

Gutis's eyes narrowed and his fingers tightened on a trigger.

"Come straight at us but we ain't there," he muttered. "Got this for you, though."

Flashes appeared along the boat above as Gutis fired. The atmosphere between the two boats sparkled as dust vaporized. Great clouds of steam and liquid hull material gushed from the boat above, very nearly like blood, then an explosion rocked its stern.

The boat dropped very nearly like *Mongoose's* had, arcing slightly from its momentum, but mostly falling now.

"Ha!"

Gutis spun the boat again, this time to face the planet, and their fall slowed. He cut his glance from the viewscreen to the console.

"They're done, but we're not much better, sir."

The boat leveled off, moving forward some now, but still dropping quickly. Too quickly for comfort.

"Inertial compensators all but gone and the grav with it — enough to slow us, but we'll not make our destination." He glanced at Alexis. "Near a settlement or no's the best choice I can give you, sir."

"Near, but not too," Alexis said. The decision was sudden, but they'd need transport to get to the men and boats from the other private ships once on the surface. She looked at Gutis, and saw that he was tense now, where he hadn't been while fighting the other boat. His jaw was clenched and his face white, a thin sheen of sweat on his brow despite the still cool air in the cockpit.

Alexis wondered if it was really a choice they had.

"Do me best, sir," Gutis said. He tapped his console and spoke to the men aft in the passenger compartment. "If that last weren't enough t'get y'strapped in, lads, this next'll do for you." He turned to Alexis. "Best you head back, sir. Passenger compartment's safer for what's to come — I can keep her level for a bit while y'make yer way."

Alexis took in his hands, clenched on the controls, knuckles white, and thought of him alone in the cockpit as the surface of Erzurum rushed at them through the viewscreen. She reached across the small space and laid a hand on his forearm.

"I think I'm best off here, Gutis. You've seen us this far — you'll see us the rest of the way."

SIXTY-SEVEN

What choice Gutis had in their landing spot was less than either he or Alexis might prefer. They wound up in a heavily forested area some ten or more kilometers from the nearest settlement.

The engines were all but gone — shot away in the action with the other boat, and Gutis shutdown the fusion plant as soon as they came to a stop to avoid its exploding too. His hands moved rapidly, almost of their own volition, while his eyes held a wide, glazed look.

The pilot turned that look from his now dark control board to the mass of greenery and pile of plowed up dirt outside the viewscreen.

"We're down, sir," he said, back straight and eyes fixed forward.

The trunk of a very large tree, larger than Alexis thought the boat's bow could have sheared through without crumpling as far back as the cockpit, only two meters ahead of them.

"So I see," Alexis answered. She carefully eased her cramped hands from the seat's arms. "I presume we'll not be lifting again."

"No, sir," Gutis said, barely moving anything but his lips. "Rather not lift this boat again, me."

Alexis unbuckled and rose. "Let's see to the lads, then."

She waited a moment, but there was no movement from the pilot. "Gutis?"

She grasped the pilot's arm and he rose with her pull, eyes still forward.

"The tree ..." he said.

"Come on, then," Alexis said, guiding him to the cockpit hatch.

"Big tree ..."

"Wondrously big, Gutis, but we didn't strike it."

"Broke the boat, sir — sorry about that."

"It's quite all right, Gutis, we'll get you another."

THE BOAT'S passenger compartment was dark and smoke-filled, but Nabb and a few others were already up and working on the hatch. Light came in and smoke poured out as it opened and the occupants leapt out to the forest floor.

Outside, the smell of melted hull material was overpowering and mixed with the scent of burning vegetation. Smoke rose from the boat itself and all along a hundred-meter furrow plowed behind it. Snapped and uprooted trees — none nearly so large as the one in front of the boat — were scattered along the path.

Alexis steered Gutis to the edge and two spacers lowered the pilot to others who took him in hand. They settled him off to the side and left Creasy to watch him while Alexis and Nabb examined the boat.

The boat, once viewed from outside, was a wonder of its hull properties for having stayed together. The outside was pocked and scorched with laser fire and streaks of melted material where they'd come too fast through the atmosphere at times.

"There'll be a pint or two comin' his way from the lads, sir," Nabb said, nodding to where Gutis sat.

"And well-earned," Alexis agreed.

That settled, everyone out of the boat, and, after examination, with some assurance that the boat was not going explode at any moment, Alexis retrieved a radio and tried to determine what was happening with the battle above.

What she discovered was not entirely heartening.

Though all of private ships had sustained some damage, it appeared *Mongoose* was the only one which had been taken out of operation. They were in possession of Erzurum's orbital space, with the orbiting frigate taken and its pirate crew captured. The oncoming pirate ships and gunboats had retired to take up orbit around Erzurum's moon, with more arriving from *darkspace* as time went on.

The surface actions were successful, with nearly all of the objectives taken, but there were a much larger number of ship's boats belonging to the pirates on-planet than had been expected. Those boats, one of which had sent Alexis and her crew crashing to the surface, made for an odd sort of standoff.

While the ships in orbit stared off with the pirates around the moon, the two forces in-atmosphere were settling into the same, with neither having the numbers necessary to be sure of dislodging the other with certainty.

Mongoose's boat had the poor luck to come down in an area essentially held by the pirates, with no other forces from the private ships nearby to support them.

This put them in a rather poor position, with their own boat disabled. If they were to call for help from their own forces, that call would likely be heard by the pirates too. Those pirates were closer and it was unlikely any boat from their own ships would be able to make its way to them for rescue.

It appeared they were on their own, at least until the situation changed or they were able to make their way to a place with friendlier skies above them.

Moving was something they'd have to do soon, certainly, for the crash site was easily visible from the air and might soon be investigated by the pirates.

Alexis looked around, trying to recall the brief, harried glimpses she'd had of the surrounding terrain as the boat came down.

Somewhere in, perhaps, that direction was a settlement — they might be able to seize some form of transport there.

"Nabb?" she called.

"Aye, sir?"

"I know spacers aren't fond of it, but I'm afraid we've a bit of a hike ahead of us."

Nabb nodded. "Expected that."

"Find Dockett, will you, and the two of you see to getting the supplies off the boat and divided amongst the crew for carriage — the wounded, also. See who may be able to walk and who must be carried. All of them armed — firearms for any with some skill."

"Aye, sir."

THEY WERE ALMOST ready to start off. The crew was formed into two columns, supplies — as much as they could carry — spread out amongst them and everyone armed. Those too wounded to walk were on hastily cobbled together stretchers carried by men with a lighter load of supplies.

It had taken longer than Alexis was comfortable with and she kept scanning the skies, expecting to see a pirate boat come upon them at any moment. She wanted to be well away and under cover of the forest canopy soon.

She came around the boat's bow and found Nabb, Dockett, and Isom huddled in an apparently heated conference near the boat's hatch. The three looked up at her appearance and stopped talking, Dockett leaving the other two and walking toward the stern while Nabb and Isom came toward her.

Alexis caught Nabb's and Isom's arms as they went to pass her on either side.

"A moment, you two."

She waited until Dockett disappeared around the boat's stern, then tugged the pair into position where she could see their faces. Both were looking down, as though children who knew there was a scolding in the works.

"The two of you've been chivying Dockett about something, and I'll have the what of it. We've enough trouble and enough to do without tensions amongst the crew."

Nabb and Isom shared a look, each nodding his head slightly at the other, then frowning back.

"One of you, out with it now!"

"It's really nothing, sir," Nabb said.

"Not nothing if it has this effect on my bosun," Alexis said. "The man goes nearly apoplectic at the very sight of you two."

"There's a dispute about a debt, sir," Isom said. "Nothing more. I'm sure we'll work it out in time. No need to bother yourself."

"A debt?"

"We're owed from your duel, sir," Nabb said. "Us and your boat crew — most of 'em, least ways."

Alexis' brow furrowed. Stranded on a hostile world would not be where she'd worry too very much about gambling debts, but she knew the crew took these things seriously. They had the oddest notions about right and wrong sometimes, and would take a stand over seemingly insignificant slights.

Still, she'd expected all the betting on that duel would have been settled — at least those aboard any one ship. She supposed the bets that went between ships would have to wait until they were all back on some civilized world — though she really didn't know how Dockett might have arranged that.

No matter that, though, if there was tension over Dockett's book, and possibly more over bets with the other crews, she'd best find out the details and try to smooth things over. Their band had enough troubles without borrowing more.

"He's not refusing to pay, is he?"

Isom shook his head, then sighed. "There's only a bit of disagreement about the terms."

Alexis frowned. "How can there be? I do recall winning, after all."

Nabb scratched at his neck and looked away.

"You *did* bet on me to win, didn't you?"

"Oh, aye, sir! Never else!" Nabb said.

Isom elbowed him. "You tell her the rest."

"Nabb?"

"It's only how the betting fell out, sir," Nabb said after a long pause. "Most of the money from the fleet had Spensley killing you, truth be told, so there were fine odds on you killing him, and that's where most of *Mongoose's* coin went, see?"

Alexis nodded. "So, what? Most of are lads are set to collect a tidy sum, but it's from the other ships and collecting it might have to wait until we're well away from Erzurum and know just how many of the other ships' crew are still alive to collect from. It seems reasonable to wait."

"It's not that, sir," Isom said.

Nabb shook his head.

"Well *what* is it, then?"

"It was Nabb's thought at the first, sir."

"More Creasy's," Nabb said.

Alexis resisted the urge to grasp the two by their collars and shake them.

"*What* thought?"

Nabb took a deep breath. "There were a lot of money on Spensley killing you," he repeated, "and we all betting on you killing him ..." He paused. "Then Creasy says, 'What about her slicing the bugger up and then leaving the bastard alive once he's all cryin' and helpless, such as she's like to do?'" Nabb shrugged. "Dockett had to figure the odds special on that."

"Once Creasy said it, sir, it did seem obvious," Isom said.

"Nearly all the old *Nightingales* put their money there, sir," Nabb added.

Alexis stared at them, mouth hanging open and aghast. "You bet that I'd maim the man and leave him alive?"

"More that you'd see no need of killin' him, sir, once he was all helpless and such."

Isom nodded. "There is a certain trend, sir, once one looks for it."

"I — there is no *trend*, I'm certain."

"That Coalson bloke you had to kill twice," Nabb said, "then that Hannie fellow what run off afire, we're told."

Isom nodded. "Captain Neals, though not physically damaged, certainly had his career ... well, maimed would not be so very harsh a description for a frigate captain to be put in-atmosphere with no hope of commanding a ship again."

Alexis stared from one to the other and saw that they were serious.

"Now, look, you two, this is *not* something I do, no matter Creasy's delusions — and recall, please, it's him who talks nothing but bloody, spectral Dutchmen and 'spirits of the Dark' inhabiting the ship's vermin!" She noted they both winced at that, for they, and the rest of the crew, didn't like it a bit when she named their little mascot a vile creature.

"Coalson," she went on, "was thought dead when I put a broadside into his boat, there was no reason to think he still lived, and I did kill him properly when next we met."

Isom shrugged. "Set him adrift in *darkspace* with just a suit, sir."

Nabb nodded. "Not a proper killing — I mean if one wants to be *sure* of a thing, sir."

Alexis pondered that. She'd had the chance to see Coalson hung, or could have simply put a flechette or laser through the man's eye, but instead she'd cast him adrift in *darkspace* — a fate most spacers considered the worst of ends. She'd wanted him to suffer for what he'd done to her family, after all, but had there been some other motive?

"I had to run from that agent in Hanover and escape. It's not as though I could have killed him and didn't; it's that I simply couldn't."

"I'd imagine being set afire would ... irritate him, sir," Isom said.

"Probably all right now," Nabb allowed, "but it's the spirit of the thing, isn't it?"

"Yes. Creasy was clear there was a sort of — what did he call it? Symbolism?"

Nabb nodded. "That were it."

"I never so much as scratched Captain Neals! And we never fought, either, not like that!"

"Could've left him on Giron for the Hannies to take, sir," Isom said. His face was harder than usual. Isom had his own reasons to hate the former captain of *Hermione*. "Or killed him on the way back. No more than he deserved."

"Regardless," Alexis said, "I never maimed him at all."

Isom shrugged again. "Captain without a ship. Spend his days putting thumb to tablet with an open sky above him and end Admiral of the Yellow if he's lucky, sir?"

"I —" Alexis broke of her next protest. That *was* a horrible fate for a man who'd once commanded a frigate, once one considered it. Aside from the lack of command, Neals would have a port admiral looking over his decisions every moment and the opportunities for profit, something she knew the man had dearly loved about commanding a frigate, were far less.

"This is nonsense," she said at last. "I've killed any number of men — and I can't believe I'm having to somehow defend myself by saying that."

"Oh, aye, sir," Nabb said. "When the heat's on you'll put a man down quicker'n spit. Every lad aboard knows that."

"It's only when you've a moment to think, sir, and the man's no threat any longer," Isom said.

Alexis frowned again. Did she truly hesitate? And was it some sort of failing?

"I shot a pirate dead between the eyes when I was just fifteen," she said, her stomach quivering a bit at the memory and that figure's visits to her dreams.

"And since, sir?" Isom asked.

Alexis opened her mouth to respond, closed it, then frowned. The two were beginning to sound like one of the Sick and Hurt Board's surgeons who thought everyone should talk about anything that bothered them — forever asking questions and insist she think about it.

"It's all right, sir, it really is," Nabb said. "There's some of the lads see it as a kind heart — others think it's a right cold one that'd leave a man scratching at the deck with a sword through his tongue." He shared a glance with Isom. "I think they take the side of what they need in a captain, either way."

This was quickly getting deeper than she cared to ponder at the moment, what with *Mongoose* being surrounded by pirates and reliant on the dubious steadfastness of the other captains.

"I see nothing at all wrong with having granted Captain Spensley a bit of mercy," she said finally. They could settle that at least, and move on. "I settled the matter, and there was no reason to further anger the crew of *Oriana* by killing him when he was clearly out of the fight."

"Nothing wrong at all, sir," Isom said. "Not saying it was."

"Long as Dockett pays," Nabb muttered.

AUTHOR'S NOTE

Thank you for reading *Privateer*, I hope you enjoyed it.

If you did and would like to help support the series, the best thing you can do is leave a review at Amazon, Goodreads, or even your personal blog — reviews help other readers determine if a series is to their liking and authors, especially indy authors, rely on such word of mouth to get our books in front of new readers.

You can also join my email mailing list at www.alexiscarew.com/list. The list receives no more than one or two emails per month, with updates on my next book, as well as recommendations of other authors you might like. You'll also receive some free short works in the Alexis Carew series.

Yes, there will be more books in the Alexis Carew series. By the time you read this, I'll have been hard at work on the next one for several months.

Privateer does end on a bit of a cliff-hanger, and I apologize to readers who don't like that sort of thing. In the past, I've been able to end the main story with the last chapter and then set up the next in the epilogue, which I think has worked well. With *Privateer*, though, the story itself is longer — one of the dangers of following a career like

Alexis'. In order to fit her term in the Barbary into just one book, it would have to be nearly twice as long as any other in the series, so I had to find a reasonable place to break it up.

Regarding the naming of the region of space known as the Barbary, it comes from two sources.

First the ancestry of the settlers there, driven out of Hanover — or at least made unwelcome in the wealthier worlds — traces back to the North African coast which first bore the name Barbary.

Second, it comes the spacers (and earlier sailors) penchant for naming things. Sailors of the 19th century named an area of San Francisco the "Barbary Coast" for its predatory dives, opium dens, and places of general ill-repute, which would target sailors, much like Wheeley's Casino.

"The Barbary Coast is the haunt of the low and the vile of every kind. The petty thief, the house burglar, the tramp, the whoremonger, lewd women, cutthroats, murderers, all are found here. Dance-halls and concert-saloons, where blear-eyed men and faded women drink vile liquor, smoke offensive tobacco, engage in vulgar conduct, sing obscene songs and say and do everything to heap upon themselves more degradation, are numerous. Low gambling houses, thronged with riot-loving rowdies, in all stages of intoxication, are there. Opium dens, where heathen Chinese and God-forsaken men and women are sprawled in miscellaneous confusion, disgustingly drowsy or completely overcome, are there. Licentiousness, debauchery, pollution, loathsome disease, insanity from dissipation, misery, poverty, wealth, profanity, blasphemy, and death, are there. And Hell, yawning to receive the putrid mass, is there also."

- Asbury, in Benjamin Estelle Lloyd's *Lights and Shades of San Francisco* (1876)

It would be little wonder for the spacers of Alexis' universe to carry such a naming tradition forward and so call these worlds.

For those wondering at the sheer, unadulterated madness of "Commodore" Skanes putting the *Hind* onto shoals and then, despite her overwhelmingly superior firepower, surrendering to a handful of gunboats without a shot fired in return ... well, I must point you to Captain William Bainbridge of the USS *Philadelphia*.

In 1803, the *Philadelphia* was sent to the Barbary Coast (the African one, and the original) and, having run aground off Tripoli, Captain Bainbridge jettisoned most everything he could in hopes of lightening his ship — including the ship's guns, despite there being some pesky gunboats about, and sawing off the ship's foremast in a further attempt to lighten it.

Bainbridge then, knowing his ship was lost, surrendered the *Philadelphia,* and he and all his crew were taken captive by the Pasha — but only after seeing to it that *Philadelphia's* stores of gunpowder were wetted and her supplies made useless, as well as drilling holes in the ship's bottom.

He did these things in order not to see the enemy gain from the ship or supplies in her capture, but despite his efforts, the Tripolitanians (yes, as near as I can find, that's correct) were able to refloat her and get her to Tripoli's harbor.

Bainbridge's act was one of trying to deny his ship and supplies to the enemy, we'll have to see if Skane's actions were similarly driven or merely desperation on her part.

There was a further action, which will almost certainly make the basis for some future adventure of Alexis', to destroy *Philadelphia* in Tripoli Harbor, carried out by Lieutenant Stephen Decatur of the *Intrepid* (the captured and renamed Tripolitanian ketch *Mastico*). *Intrepid* engaged in some subterfuge to enter Tripoli Harbor, board *Philadelphia*, and set her afire.

Admiral Lord Nelson, no stranger to daring actions himself, is said to have called that effort "the most bold and daring act of the Age."

Again, thank you so much for reading the series and I hope you're looking forward to the next book as much as I am.

J.A. Sutherland
    September 23, 2017
    The Barbary Coast
    San Francisco, California

ALSO BY J.A. SUTHERLAND

To be notified when new releases are available, follow J.A. Sutherland on Facebook (https://www.facebook.com/alexiscarewbooks), *Twitter (https://twitter.com/JASutherlandBks), or subscribe to the author's newsletter (http://www.alexiscarew.com/list).*

Alexis Carew

Into the Dark

Mutineer

The Little Ships

HMS Nightingale

Privateer

Dark Artifice

Of Dubious Intent

coming early 2018

ABOUT THE AUTHOR

J.A. Sutherland spends his time sailing the Bahamas on a 43′ 1925 John G. Alden sailboat called Little Bit ...

Yeah ... no. In his dreams.

Reality is a townhouse in Orlando with a 90 pound huskie-wolf mix who won't let him take naps.

When not reading or writing, he spends his time on roadtrips around the Southeast US searching for good barbeque.

Mailing List: http://www.alexiscarew.com/list

To contact the author:

www.alexiscarew.com

sutherland@alexiscarew.com